THE TRUTH HURTS

*Also by Nancy Pickard
in Large Print:*

The Blue Corn Murders
The Whole Truth
Ring of Truth

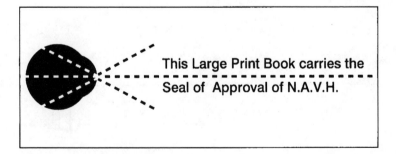

This Large Print Book carries the
Seal of Approval of N.A.V.H.

THE TRUTH HURTS

Nancy Pickard

Thorndike Press • Waterville, Maine

Published in 2002 by arrangement with Atria Books, an imprint of Simon & Schuster, Inc.

Thorndike Press Large Print Basic Series.

The tree indicium is a trademark of Thorndike Press.

The text of this Large Print edition is unabridged. Other aspects of the book may vary from the original edition.

Set in 16 pt. Plantin by Ramona A. Watson.

Printed in the United States on permanent paper.

Library of Congress Cataloging-in-Publication Data

Pickard, Nancy.
    The truth hurts / Nancy Pickard.
        p. cm.
    ISBN 0-7862-4675-8 (lg. print : hc : alk. paper)
    1. Lightfoot, Marie (Fictitious character) — Fiction.
2. Civil rights workers — Fiction.   3. Stalking victims —
Fiction.   4. Crime writing — Fiction.   5. Alabama —
Fiction.   6. Large type books.   I. Title.
PS3566.I274 T78 2002
    813'.54—dc21   2002028907

*This book is dedicated,
with awe and respect, to all of
the known and unknown heroes
of civil rights movements everywhere.*

Author's note: The Miami Book Fair is a real, and wonderful, event, but I have taken the liberty of moving it to the spring.

1

Marie

The nice thing about my kind of fame is that I can still find a grocery store where I can go in my shorts, a sloppy T-shirt, with ratty old plastic thongs on my feet and no makeup on my face, and no one will recognize me. There are still plenty of places in the world — if I seek them out — where nobody's going to brake their carts and squeal in the produce aisle, "Oh, my God, you're Marie Lightfoot! Can I have your autograph?"

That has never happened in this store. Not yet at least. If it ever does, maybe I'll shop by phone. But for now, I'm blissfully anonymous, at least until the Miami Book Fair starts in three weeks. Why did I ever agree to appear there while I'm still in the middle of a book? I'll have to drop everything for a day and don my "author" persona like a witch puts on her "glamour." I'll flick my magic wand and twirl three times and transform myself into a public figure again. Then there will be television interviews and pictures in the newspapers; then there will be crowds and autographs and stacks of my own books to sell, and I'll feel like the grinning bull's-eye in the middle of a promotional target. After that, maybe even a few shoppers in here will recognize me the next time I come in, but probably not. I hope not.

Fame is, as they say, definitely a mixed blessing.

Today I'm just a working writer, standing ninth in line at the Publix supermarket in West Bahia Beach, and feeling happily inconspicuous. This chain has huge stores, scattered all over south Florida. This one is my favorite because it is way out of my neighborhood, making it even less likely that anybody I know, or anybody who might know me, will spot me.

This being south Florida in early April, it's even more crowded in Publix than usual, because not all of the spring breakers have taken their hangovers home yet. Some of them — the girls in bikini tops and cutoff jean bottoms, the boys in baggy swim trunks and shirts they've thrown on just to come indoors — are in line with me, mixed in with the retirees in their tidy shorts outfits and their muumuus. The kids are buying bread, cold cuts, and bottled water; their elders are here for their frozen dinners. Me, I'm here to stock up on fresh fruit, because our long-running drought has dried up my little backyard crop of avocados, oranges, grapefruit, and limes this year.

Sometimes I wonder if maybe I'm the biggest fruit in the bunch.

Here I am, again, alone in a crowd, like some character out of one of those old private-eye novels. Hell, even Travis McGee — from those great John D. MacDonald detective novels — had his best bud, Meyer. Who have I got next to me, really? And I'm a woman, for God's sake! Aren't we supposed to be the relationship sex? Aren't we supposed to be talking on the phone every day to our girlfriends?

I must've missed that lesson.

Where are my husband, my children, my best girlfriend?

I don't see them here in my shopping cart.

When I'm writing — oh, hell, anytime — *this* is what generally passes for a social life for me. Going grocery shopping. Eating alone in a restaurant, writing in a notebook while strangers around me carry on their apparently normal lives. I do have a boy-friend, Franklin. There's that to be said for me, but we've conducted most of our love life in such intense privacy, madly enjoying only each other's company, that a person could be excused for confusing it with an isolation chamber. And by God, I have friends, too. I do. Male friends, female friends. None from my childhood, except for my screenwriter cousin Nathan, whom I adore, but he lives three thousand miles away in L.A. Nathan's my only family, re-ally. I sure don't count my Aunt Julia and Uncle Joe — his parents who raised me — as Mom and Dad. Ugh. No way. It's hard enough for *Nathan* to call them Mom and Dad, and he's their real boy. But I have other friends besides him. I do. One left over from high school. Three people I sort of keep in contact with from college. A lot of business friends and acquaintances. I'm pretty close to my longtime agent and ed-itor. I have an assistant now, Deborah, and she's beginning to feel like a younger sister, for better or worse. Of course, except for her and my boyfriend, Franklin, and a few business friends from around here, all of my other "close" friends are an airplane ride away, but we're still *friends*, it still counts. It does.

These people around me, though, some of them seem to have friends with them right here and now, but that's only because they're kids on spring break.

Take the two boys in line in front of me, for instance.

"Dude," mutters one of them to his lanky, sunburned friend. "Check it out."

I check it out, too, as if I'm actually a part of their conversation: it's the cover of this week's *US* magazine, which features a famous female singer in a photograph that reveals a lot of the chest from which her dulcet tones emerge.

"Oh, man" is his friend's considered judgment.

Being a writer — even a best-selling one — is usually not anywhere near as public as being a movie star, at least not when I'm out in "real life," like this. Not that I don't use what fame I have, every chance I get, to help sell more books. I do. (My specialty is the section in the bookstores called True Crime, the one with all those hot titles — *Dying to Be Loved* — and gory covers.) Then I'm recognized as Marie Lightfoot, and glad of it. But times like this, I just want to pay for my juicy fruits and get back home to work.

The kids in the front of the line are

having trouble coming up with enough change to pay for their stuff. They're digging in their pockets and backpacks and pooling their quarters, dimes, nickels, and pennies on the counter in front of the cashier. She's keeping a hand firmly on the handles of the plastic bag that holds their groceries and she looks suspicious, as if she thinks they might just grab it and run. That would be interesting: I'd get to be an eyewitness to a true crime, but hardly of the sort that I usually cover. My books are long on sensational murders and heinous killers — not on teenagers copping Doritos and bean dip.

"Just charge it, for crissake," one kid says to the other.

That seems to light up the ol' beer-saturated brain cells. Now all his friend has to do is dig through his fanny pack and backpack to find a MasterCard or a Visa he can use.

While I wait, I peruse the rest of the magazine and tabloid racks.

Hm, what have we here?

I'll be damned, Bigfoot's been sighted in Washington State again. Isn't that amazing. And my goodness, it appears that he has fathered twins this time. I'm tempted to pick up the tabloid and open it to find out who the lucky mom might be — Janet Jackson? Hillary Clinton? Rosie O'Donnell? — but what would the people behind me think? Oh, but will you look at that? Elvis is flying UFOs again. He must have trained out there in Nevada when he was doing all those Vegas shows. And here's a little color picture of —

Oh, my God.

"Ma'am? You want to move your cart on up? Ma'am?"

I barely hear the cashier. The world just stopped for me. I can hear the other shoppers only through the deafening roar in my ears. I feel sick. I have to hang on to the handle of my shopping cart. There is a little photograph of *me* in the upper-right-hand corner of the tabloid newspaper, *The Insider.* And not just me, either, but me and my boyfriend. I've been on magazine covers before, that's not the problem. *He's* been on the front pages of newspapers before, *that's* not the problem. My boyfriend and I have even been photographed together, now that we're going public about our relationship, so that's not the problem, either. Everybody knows now that Marie Lightfoot, the true crime writer, is dating Franklin DeWeese, the state attorney of Howard County, Florida. They know I'm a white woman; they know he's a black man. That's not news anymore. What's different, appalling, shocking to me about this particular cover on the newsstands is the headline, printed in a small typeface, but one that is all caps, all black, and all too easy to read: "Best-Selling Author Hides Her Racist Past."

"Ma'am? You going to check your stuff through now?" the cashier asks.

My hand reaches out for the top copy and places it in my shopping cart and I move numbly toward her. "Yes, I'm sorry."

I'm sorry, I'm sorry.

Yes, I hide it, wouldn't anybody?

But it's not my past, it's my parents'. I'm not a racist; I date a black man, for God's sake. It was them, it was my mother and my father. It was them. And I haven't hidden anything from Franklin. He knows. . . .

And now it appears the rest of the world will, too.

"That'll be seventeen dollars and twenty-seven cents, ma'am."

No, Angie — the young checker's name is Angie, according to her name tag, which I stare at as if somebody has just walloped me with a two-by-four — *you have no idea how much this will cost us, and neither do I.*

I hand her my cash, take my change and

my bags with the tabloid newspaper tucked down inside one of them.

"Have a nice day," she says.

I was actually having a pretty nice life until five minutes ago. I was, that is, if you don't count the fallout from my "racist past." I can explain that — I *have* explained it in a book I've only partly written, because I only partly know the truth. It's called *Betrayal*.

BETRAYAL

By Marie Lightfoot

———◆———

CHAPTER ONE

June 11, 1963
Alabama

"We're taking you to a house where there's a room prepared for you. You won't be the first man to stay there."

His name was James.

He was very black, very scared, very angry, very young. Only eighteen. He'd gotten into a car with three white men who said they were there to help him. He hadn't quite believed them, but refusing them had looked more dangerous than going with them. He had just been kicked out — literally in the seat of his pants onto the pavement in front of the Stuart County Jail — and he knew that if he hung around it would be bad for him. It wasn't his town, it was a white town. Worse, he didn't know a soul in the tiny black neighborhood, and even if he did, who was going to risk themselves for him, anyway?

If only he had a buddy, he thought, then maybe he wouldn't have had to get into a car with these white men. He knew he'd feel braver in the company of a black friend. Maybe together they could have walked away, stolen away over fences and across the cotton fields. But everybody else who had been arrested at the voter registration line in Beauchamp three weeks ago was either still back there in that jail hellhole, or they'd already been sprung.

As the Plymouth sped along dark back roads, James was afraid to talk, but he had a million questions in his mind — who are you guys, why are you doing this for me, where are you taking me?

"You won't be the first man to stay there," the driver had said.

James had heard that word, *man* — heard the white man say it — and felt so overwhelmed by it that he nearly missed hearing the rest of what was said. Never, never before in his whole eighteen years had he ever — ever — heard a white man call a black male a man. He was so accustomed to being called boy that to hear this white man call him a man nearly knocked him over with shock. If he never heard it another time in his life, it would still be proof of something he had long disbelieved, evidence that had always eluded him that white people — some white people, maybe only these three out of all the world, for all he knew — could change. For whatever reason, whether they really wanted to, or not, apparently they could change the habit of their minds and their mouths.

His grandmother had always told him so. "You foolin' youself, Grandma," he had always shot back at her.

They made him fold himself in half in the backseat of the Plymouth so he wouldn't be seen, which meant that he didn't know that night that he was being delivered into the heart of whiteness, as he would call it ever after. All he knew was the information that his own senses delivered to him moment by moment — the rank smell of his own body, the feel of rough upholstery under his cheek, the sight of the plastic back of the driver's seat, the bitter taste of his own unwashed mouth, and the oppressive sound of the silence among the four men in the Plymouth, a silence broken only by the hum of the tires on the road below him.

20

After a while, he decided that it wasn't that they were ignoring him by not talking to him, it was more like they were even more scared than he was.

This was a revelation to him, too.

But he could see it clearly — the fear on their white faces, the tense way the driver stared straight ahead at the road, the way the shotgun passenger kept looking around in every direction, and how the man who sat in the backseat with James kept glancing out the back window, as if he was looking for headlights that might suddenly appear on the road. It was only their fear, their obvious fear that kept James from believing he was being driven off to be lynched in the dark woods.

If these three white men were going to do that to him, they wouldn't be scared like this, he figured. They'd be excited, maybe, and drunk, and maybe a little bit scared, but not much, because who was going to stop them and even if they got stopped, what cop was going to interfere? Or even if a cop did that much, like stop the car, make them all get out, that would be the end of it for the driver and his friends, and the cop would just take James back to jail for "protective custody."

Or turn him loose on these white roads in the dark.

No, they were too scared for that possibility, he believed. Wanted to believe. So maybe they really were in the Movement. He'd heard of white people who risked their lives for it — like those Christians who hid Jews in Germany — but he'd never believed it, not really. His other grandma had always warned him to never trust a white person, because when push came to shove, he was the one who was going to get pushed and shoved.

It was miles before somebody finally said something.

"Anybody coming?" the driver asked the white man in back.

"No," answered the one beside James. He removed his gaze from the receding blacktop road long enough to say to James, "We're on a timetable. We have to pass by a certain house in Stebanville within a certain time span so they know we've made it safe that far. Then we've got three other times to meet before we get you to where you're going to be for a while."

James didn't move from his doubled-over position.

"It's probably safe for you to sit up now," the man beside him said.

He unfolded himself slowly. Even then, he listened to them with bent face and lowered eyes, in the subservient posture in which he'd always listened to white people. He wanted to blurt out "Where you takin' me?" but he didn't, he just listened hard. He felt ashamed. He knew he smelled. When the guards at the jail had hung him from the water pipes by his wrists two days ago, he had tried desperately to control himself, but finally his bladder had let loose and he had soiled himself inside his trousers. At least he had managed to hang on to his bowels, but when you didn't get near washing water for three weeks and you lived in a ten-by-ten cell with five other men and an open hole in the ground for a toilet and people getting sick all around you, there wasn't any chance you were going to come out smelling anything but rank. No shave in three weeks, either. He was ashamed to feel so offensive. A small, toughened part of him found humor in thinking that was the true proof of the helpful intent of these men: nobody but do-gooder Movement white people could have stood to ride for hours like this in a closed car with him. It was so cool outside on this June night that they had to keep the windows rolled up all but a crack.

As if he'd read James's mind, the driver suddenly said, "I'm sorry we couldn't stop to let you clean up. You must feel like shit."

"I smell like it," James mumbled.

He saw the man beside him smile in the darkness.

"If you can stand to wait," the driver continued, "there's a place up ahead where it'll be safe to pull in long enough for you to shower and they'll give you clean clothing."

"I can stand it," he made himself say, in spite of his resistance to talking to them, "if you guys can."

They laughed at that, too hard, too loud, from too much tension.

James felt the mood shift in the Plymouth then. There was a thaw, a sense that they were all in this together, whatever "this" was. James was pretty sure that he knew exactly what it was. Black people who persisted in trying to obtain their right to vote — their right to anything — tended to end up in jail, and when they got out they then tended to end up beaten, burned, hung, and dead. Especially young black men labeled "trouble-makers," like him.

They introduced themselves to him. "I'm Marty Wiegan," the man next to him said, and then Wiegan pointed to the driver. "That's Austin Reese." He pointed to the man riding shotgun. "And he's Lackley Goodwin."

He committed a little something about each of them to memory. Marty Wiegan had thin black hair pulled in strands across his scalp. Austin Reese wore aviator glasses. Lackley Goodwin was fat. When he turned around to look out the rear window he saw a parking sticker for Jim Forrest College on the window. They didn't look old enough to have kids in college there. Did one of them work there? That made him nervous all over again, because the school's slogan was "Segregation Now, Segregation Forever." What was somebody who worked for Jim Forrest College doing giving him a ride from jail?

"We have a house for you to go to," the fat man riding shotgun, Lackley Goodwin, told him while continuing to keep an eye on the scenery. "I'm sorry we can't tell you where. In case we get stopped, it's safer if you don't know much. As far as you know, we're just three crazy strangers giving you a ride home from jail."

"My home's not this way," he told the men.

Apparently, they knew that. They didn't bother to answer.

"How was it, in jail this time?" the man beside him, Marty Wiegan, asked in a quiet, respectful tone of voice.

They knew a little something about him, then, if they knew it was a "this time." James turned his face to the window and shook his head, staring out at the trees racing past. He almost didn't answer, because it was such a stupid question. What did they think it was like this time, or any time? Did he have to explain the word *bad* to them? Did he need to establish a whole new standard of horror for these white people?

"Bad," he muttered.

"We only ask," Wiegan said, with an apologetic air, "because we have to document this stuff. I'm sorry to ask you to talk about it, but we have to know, so we can inform the lawyers, so we have specifics to protest, facts to file, you know how it is."

He didn't, didn't know about that end of it, because nobody had ever asked him before now. He only knew about anger and fear, action and reaction. Sometimes

— most of the time — he didn't really believe anything would change. He tended to join marches and voter registration drives out of a burning driving resentment more than anything else, and not because he believed any good might come out of it. In fact, only bad had come out of it for him up to now. Only pain, bruises, broken bones, indignity, disrespect, humiliation, failure, degradation, starvation in jail cells, and the impoverishment of somebody who spent too much time being angry and getting thrown in jail to be able to hold down a job. But it wasn't as if he had any real job prospects in the world anyway. As long ago as when he was thirteen — five long years before this — he had decided that if the choice was between being a tenant farmer, which was tantamount to slavery, or being an "activist," he might as well lay his life down for something more than a few acres of dirt that he'd never own outright.

For the next few miles, in a dry voice, without embellishing anything, James told them how it had been in jail "this time." Marty Wiegan wrote it all down in a spiral-bound notebook and asked him to sign it, which he did, thinking, What the hell, if they don't kill me for this, they'll get me for something else. As he explained things to them, they didn't say a word, not even a murmur at the worst parts. But he thought he saw shame and pain on their faces — he recognized it because he had seen it every day in the mirror — and that was a revelation, too.

They were approaching a town — a mere pause in the road with only four or five houses — and the driver slowed the car, as if he were going to stop at one of them. But the shotgun passenger said urgently, "There's a truck around to the side. I don't know whose it is. Keep going. Don't stop!"

They held their breaths as they passed the small frame house with its lights on and an old green pickup truck parked in the shadow of it. Frightened into silence again, they kept on driving through the night. The truck didn't follow them, but they kept on going anyway.

"Just go on to the Folletinos," the shotgun passenger finally advised in a quiet voice that wasn't meant to carry over into the backseat, where James heard it, too.

It was the only hint he got of his destination.

2

Marie

Somehow I manage to exit the Publix store, find my way to my car, and collapse into the driver's seat without having hysterics.

"I'm not going to cry."

That would be stupid. This was bound to happen someday. Today *The Insider*, tomorrow what? *People*? The Sunday book review of the *New York Times*? I can see it all now — an in-depth analysis of all my books, looking for clues to my past, to my psyche. Well, good luck to them! I've never had much luck following those clues to myself.

"Calm down."

I'm already overreacting; tears would only drown the lily. This is not like me, to panic. I'm *not* going to race back in and purchase every copy of the damned tabloid in order to keep anybody else from seeing it, although God knows, I want to. But I can't buy all of them in south Florida, much less the whole state, or New York City, where my publisher is, or the rest of the world, where my books are sold. And I'm not going to —

I don't know what else I'm not going to do.

Thinking straight, that's apparently one of the things I'm not going to do for a while longer.

What I'm *going* to do is force myself to open the tabloid, *The Insider*, and read what it says about me. "Read it," I command myself. "It's just a stupid tabloid story. It can't hurt you." Oh yeah? The problem here is that I'm really frightened and full of dread of the unknown, and what I really feel like doing is opening my car door and throwing up.

"Read it!"

I pull the newspaper from the grocery bag and prop it against my steering wheel. My hands are shaking. How interesting. Okay, here it is — the article, with a headline that makes me want to ball this paper up and then rip it to pieces.

MARIE LIGHTFOOT HIDES RACIST PAST

"Damn you, damn you, damn you!"
Underneath that, it says, in the tabloid

style of short sentences, unattributed quotes, and lots of exclamation marks,

Marie Lightfoot is famous for ripping the covers off other people's lives in her best-selling books. But in an exclusive Insider *story, we have just learned she is a stranger to the truth when it comes to her own life!*

I'd laugh at the style if it weren't for the substance.

In fact, Lightfoot is not even her real name, sources tell us.

Sources? *What* sources? Who? The "why" is easy enough to guess — at the bottom of each page there's a notice saying "Cash for Tips!" and an 800 number for tattlers. It appears that somebody has betrayed me for $500, or more.

The real name of the popular author of The Little Mermaid *is Marie Folletino. Informed sources tell* The Insider *that she is the only child of well-known segregation- ists from Alabama!*
"They were racists of the very worst sort!" our sources tell The Insider. *"They*

belonged to the KKK, and worse!"

Rumors. Only rumors. Unproved rumors.

And there's more!

I was afraid there might be.

Both of her parents mysteriously disappeared on June 12, 1963!
They have never been heard from since! Foul play is definitely suspected. But Marie has never divulged THIS true crime to her readers, even going so far as to change her name legally from Folletino to Lightfoot.
And now even her handsome boyfriend, a popular and respected Afro-American prosecutor in Florida, knows the terrible truth about his famous lover.
"His family is furious," sources tell The Insider. *"It breaks his children's hearts to know their father is dating a woman from that kind of family!"*

Like most sentences in tabloids, this one is ambiguously close enough to a truth to be un-actionable. I don't think that anybody in Franklin's family knows about my family history, but it is certainly true that his ex-wife is "furious" that he's dating me, and his parents aren't thrilled that I'm from "that kind of family." In their lexicon that means "white." As for "his children's hearts," it's only his six-year-old daughter who dislikes me, not his three-year-old son, but I wouldn't go so far as to say it breaks her heart. At least, I hope not. That would break *my* heart. Did somebody from this rag actually talk to one of the DeWeeses, or did they just make this up, assuming they could link it to some kind of truth?

It hardly matters now. If there's damage, it's been done.

Maybe the worst of it is how they've trivialized my life.

My God, I hope I've never treated any of the people in my books like this. I hope I've never made innocent people feel as I do at this moment. I hope I've treated them sympathetically, allowed them to continue to hold their heads up even after my books came out. There's no sympathy in this article for the child I used to be, no respect for the woman she became.

The Insider *says: this is a woman who writes books about the lies and crimes in other people's lives. Now will she have the decency to face the public with the truth about her own?*

Decency? Why didn't these people have the decency to call me first?

"What is she hiding?" our sources want to know.

Why would anybody care?

We want to know, too! Will you tell your readers the truth NOW, Marie?

Why *should* I? Even if I knew the whole truth, which I don't.

"What a hypocrite! If she can lie for so many years about her own story," said a former fan, "then how can we trust her to tell the truth in her books? If she couldn't even tell the truth to her own boyfriend, when does she ever tell it to anybody?"

Oh, please.

"I'll never buy one of her books again!" said the former fan.

How very convenient that they located

an anonymous fan. I wonder if that might be one of their own editors?

Let us know what YOU think!
E-mail, call, or write to The Insider *today!*

That's it. But now I don't know whether to laugh or cry. It looks so ridiculous, written like that. Surely any halfway intelligent person who reads it will have to wonder if they made it all up. But that won't help with the people who *aren't* halfway intelligent. And it won't stop the story from spreading. It won't stop rumors. It won't stop my name from being linked with the damning word *racist.* It won't stop people from hearing those rumors and believing them and deciding I'm a horrible person and they don't want to read me anymore. And if enough people decide I'm despicable and they stop buying my books, then my publisher won't want to publish me anymore.

"Stop it," I command myself. "Don't get maudlin."

But I can't stop people from seeing this, and I can't stop the story from being almost true. I've written down some of it, the parts I think I know from questions

I've asked of people over the years. I've even given it a title — *Betrayal* — in case I ever gather enough material to finish a book about it. I've got the beginning of it, the part I like, the part that could fool a person into thinking that Michael and Lyda Folletino were decent people.

It's the ending — their ending — that eludes me.

A man named "James" was witness to part of it.

When I met him, "James" was only one on a list of several names that I'd compiled of people who might be able to talk about my parents. By the time I tracked him down he was fifty-two years old, living in the North. He told me that he still wanted to be identified only as "James." He was an attorney by then — in his expensive gray suit, he looked like one — and when I interviewed him, he called himself "a compromised man."

"I used to be principled," he told me. "I once was brave and young and foolish and desperate. I think I liked myself better when I was desperate. Sometimes, I wish I was still afraid to die."

BETRAYAL

By Marie Lightfoot

———➤•◄———

CHAPTER TWO

June 11–12, 1963
Alabama

They sped on, scared, with few words among them.

Miles down the road, the white men told James to duck down again.

Sometime later, when he felt the car slow to a crawl and then begin a winding climb up a gravel road, the one riding shotgun said quietly, "When we stop, open the door on your side as quietly as you can, just enough to get out of the car. There will be a door to a house right beside you. It's unlocked. Run in. That'll be where you stay for a few days until it's safe to take you north. When you get inside, don't turn on a light. Close and lock the door. There will be a bathroom for you. Clothes. Water. Food. Stay in there until someone comes to you in the morning. Oh, and unlock the door in the morning so they can get in."

The one beside him muttered, "Good luck, James."

The Plymouth stopped. Austin Reeves, the driver, said, "Go!"

Without another word, without pausing to thank them or even knowing if he should feel grateful — for who knew how this would end? — James did exactly as they directed him to do.

He found himself inside a bedroom. The only light slipped in around the drawn curtains at the window, and that derived from the moon. But he could see enough to tell it was all as they'd said it would be. There was a bottle of cool milk on a table under the window in the light of the moon, and he gulped it down like food. It was a few moments before he realized he hadn't heard them drive away. He peeked out the window. They were gone, whoever they were. Wherever this was they'd brought him. In the single fast look he allowed himself all he saw was a gravel driveway and a tree, a magnolia, its large, shiny leaves reflecting moonlight. But nothing about what he saw told him where he was. It could be anywhere, or at least that's what he thought until he turned around again. He could make things out better in the darkness now.

No, James decided then, this couldn't be "anywhere." It was too nice, too grand for that. James had never been in a bedroom so nice. He'd never lived in a house with indoor plumbing, much less one with a bedroom with its own private toilet and bathtub and shower. For a dangerous instant, James wanted to laugh out loud, because he didn't know if he could figure out how to make all the fancy white knobs work right in the bathroom.

When he ran water in the tub — figuring it out at the same time that he realized it didn't take a genius to use inside plumbing — he nearly fainted when water pipes rattled and rumbled in telltale betrayal of his presence there. But the people who owned this house must know he was there, they must be on his side, he figured, and he relaxed enough to sink down into the first real tub bath of his eighteen years.

After that, he slept as if he had no worries but an empty stomach.

In the morning, he found food in the room, supplies that he hadn't seen in the dark the night before when he'd been so hungry he thought his stomach would keep him awake all night. Now he saw that in a corner there was a large tray of food covered by a dark cloth. There had been crackers there all along, salami, milk that was warm now, though he drank it anyway. There was bread and cheese that had gone dark orange from sitting out too long, but he ate that, too. There was even a cake — an entire chocolate two-layer cake with chocolate icing — and a basket of cold fried chicken and another one of biscuits that were still soft inside even if their crusts had gone rock hard. It was the best meal he'd ever eaten outside of his grandma's Sunday dinner, and the only reason her meals took first place over this one was that he had sat around her table in safety and contentment. Here, he ate alone with his worry about what was going to happen to him next. This was operating like a modern-day underground railroad, he understood that much by this point. So he supposed they'd come for him and move him along to another safe place and then another until he could catch a train or a bus or hitch a ride up north.

It wasn't safe for him down home any-more, not since this last arrest.

Not that it had ever been "safe," really. But James had no desire whatsoever to live anyplace but in the South. He'd heard about northern winters and hard factory work that sounded less like opportunity than it did like slow tedious death. But he did want to remain alive long enough to land someplace where he might have a chance to make his own decisions about his own life. He didn't know if that was possible for a black man anywhere in the world. But he knew for sure that possibility was gone for him in Alabama now and probably in any of the neighboring states. He'd been in jail too often; he was too well known by law enforcement and by white supremacists groups, which were not always two different things. He was thought of as a troublemaker now, an agitator. He knew what happened more often than not to young Negro men who got themselves into this fix. Their own people got too scared or resentful to take them in — a lot of Negroes hated the protests and the voter registration efforts, because it rocked a boat that was already overweighted with fear and trouble. So there was probably no place for him to go and be safe around here, no place his own people would welcome him. And now, wherever he showed up, he'd be a marked man — the first to be noticed, the one to be beaten, jailed again, rendered ineffectual through sustained, vicious persecution by the people with the power.

There's no such thing as home anymore, James thought, and he felt as if he'd drown in the wave of anger and loneliness, of pure sorrow, that swept over him then. His "home" at the moment was this room out of a fantasy. He could be lost in space, for all he knew.

Then he heard the sounds of other people in the house, a murmur of many voices — a woman's laugh — a rattle of pans so close it made him jump off the bed, because it startled and frightened him. He spent the day listening closely, getting an impression of a family living on the other side of the wall. There was a man, a woman, at least one child, a baby. Those three were white people, he judged. There were two others who sounded like black women, just on the other side, and he guessed one was a cook, the other a housecleaner. He could hear them clearly, talking housework, a little gossip about people he'd never heard of except one time when he thought one of them mentioned "Mr.

42

Lackley." That would be Lackley Goodwin, James thought, one of the three men who'd delivered him here. He never heard his own name, or any mention of the room he waited in.

No one visited him that day, though he sat nervously with the door unlocked.

But after dark, there was a soft movement at the door to his room. He watched the door slowly open, saw a tray with plates of food inched onto the floor and got only a glimpse of a pretty, soft black face. She was young, and she couldn't see him, because he was standing behind the door looking at her in a mirror above a dressing table.

"What's your name?" he asked.

She jumped, then whispered, "Rachel."

"Thank you, Rachel."

A hesitation, then, "That's all right."

She left the food for him, quietly closing the door behind her. James felt desolate when she closed the door. He wanted to cry out, Wait! Loneliness besieged him again. He missed her, without even knowing her. But he didn't feel so bad that he couldn't eat what she'd left for him. He wondered why she couldn't come in and then he realized she might have been scared. Grateful for the hot

43

food and cold milk, if resentful about being treated like he was dangerous or invisible, James wolfed it down.

Nothing happened until four hours later.

There was yelling.

That was the first hint that something was wrong in the other part of the house. They weren't screams like there was someone in terror or pain. But they were sudden, loud, urgent, a man's voice shouting, "Lyda! Lyda!" Then silence. Then a muffled sound of feet running on stairs, of doors slamming. Briefly, James heard water running in the kitchen on the other side of the wall where earlier that day he had heard voices that sounded like black women.

Then, so abruptly that it made him bolt off the bed and stand at rigid attention, the outside and only door to his room banged open, thrust back against the inside wall. A white woman ran in and said, in what he would always think of later as a breathless shout, even though it may have been merely a whisper: "You have to get out of here. People are coming for you. Be ready. I'm sorry. God be with you."

He had a fleeting impression of beauty, of a ghostly presence, a small blond woman dressed in white. Strangely, later, he thought he remembered bare feet, pale, thin, tiny bare feet. Was she beautiful? He wasn't sure. Was she as delicate in appearance as she was small in stature? He couldn't have said, though he thought she was. What about her voice, was it light, soprano, alto, hoarse? A whispered shout was the only way he knew to describe what he remembered hearing that night. As quick as anything, she was gone again, leaving the door standing wide open behind her.

Shocked, frightened, James crossed to the window to peek out from behind the curtain, not daring to risk standing revealed in the open doorway. It was night again, not yet twenty-four hours since he'd arrived on the previous evening. The magnolia leaves looked black, the moon was one night thinner. He would never see this house or its grounds, never know exactly where he had been, or who had hidden him there, except that later that night his next deliverers — two different white people this time, one man and one woman — would slip and mention names.

"The Folletinos. Michael. Lyda."

He would never be able to remember the whole context in which those names were set down. He only knew they were the identities of the people in whose bedroom he had spent the most luxurious night and day of his life up to then, the people who had provided him with clean clothes that fit and with good nourishing food and milk and white sheets and a pillow with an envelope of lacy white cloth.

"Where are your old clothes?" whispered the white woman who came with the white man in the car that crawled up the gravel drive to pick him up and take him away again. Not daring to speak, he jerked his thumb back over his shoulder.

"Get them," she mouthed at him.

Thank God for the big blue towels that were damp and dirty from his repeated washings and dryings of his own soiled self. Only by placing them between his body and his old clothes could he stand to pick up his jail clothes again. Even in the rush, the air of emergency, he had the thought: I hope these towels cover the smell.

They made him lie down in the backseat, like before, only this time he had the whole seat to himself and could stretch out more.

Nobody spoke, nobody explained anything, though at one point in the front passenger's seat the woman began to cry. He was sure those were the soft sounds he heard. The man said nothing. Soon, the soft sounds of a woman crying stopped. It was then that she said a sentence that had the words *the Folletinos* in it, the sentence that informed James those were the people who owned the house. It also told him — he could not later explain why — that the white people in the front seat were angry, bitter, and sad about the owners of the house.

That was all he knew and all he would ever know for many years about those strange, somber, terrifying forty-eight hours in his life. He landed — two days later and many days ahead of schedule — at his sister's ex-brother-in-law's apartment in Cincinnati.

"How'd you get here?" they all wanted to know.

He had no urge to tell them. For one thing, he had no desire to give white people any credit, and he still wasn't sure they deserved it, because he didn't yet know how his new life would turn out. He felt a deep, burning resentment over the fact that a few — goddamned precious few, he suspected — white people might have been heroes in his life; he hated that, didn't want it to be true, wanted to have survived entirely on his own, or solely with the assistance of Negroes like himself. Beyond that, he felt deep inside himself that betrayal was in the air permeating everyplace he stepped, but that he, himself, would never contribute to it. He vowed to always remember everything he could, but he would keep those memories to himself until he began to meet a few others like himself. Once, one of them — another black man — said the name Folletino, and James perked up his ears.

"Who're they?" he asked, cautiously.

"Racists," the other guy informed him. "Dead ones."

"But —" James started to say, then didn't. It was an unusual name, but it must be different people. It didn't make any sense if it was the same people who had hidden him and warned him to get out. Fed him. He wondered what had happened that night to those people. Maybe someday, if the world ever changed enough, if it was ever safe to go home again, he'd try to look them up, find them, ask them, maybe even say thanks. By that time in his life, James had already learned that heroes and villains came in all colors, and that he didn't need any white people to betray him; like anybody else, he could betray himself well enough.

3

Marie

This isn't actually my car, it's a rental, because mine's in the shop. But the cell phone's all mine. I pick it up and punch in a number for my cousin, in Los Angeles. I'd better warn Nathan about this article, so he can let his parents know. I feel better, just thinking of calling him.

Before I can even say hello, he says, "Hey, Marie."

"Damn," I reply. "Sometimes I hate caller I.D. I can't call and surprise you anymore."

"Yeah, and it's a lot harder to make dirty phone calls."

As we both laugh, I imagine Nate seated in his office in his gorgeous cottage in the Hollywood Hills. He's three years younger and much more glamorous than I am. He's got F. Scott Fitzgerald's golden, chiseled looks with the kind of light blue eyes that romance novels call "startling," and he dresses to match. He's athletic and slim and only slightly taller than I am, and I'm only five two. Even in these days of cancer warnings, he keeps his tan up, looking nothing like a grubby novelist, and not much like most other screenwriters I know, either. People stare at him wherever he goes, and it's amazing to be around him because of that. There's more than a touch of the dandy to my cousin, but he's so unusual and pretty to look at, you just have to forgive him for that. Besides, there's a horrible reason that he works so hard to keep up appearances. Nathan Montgomery is probably the most successful failed screenwriter in Los Angeles. He gets lucrative options on almost every screenplay he writes, but not a one of them has ever made it all the way through the pipeline to production. Not one. It's enough to break a writer's heart. I don't know how he keeps going. I couldn't do it. I think, What if I wrote book after book and they all got bought by publishers, but they never made it into print? No, it's too damned hard. I couldn't bear it. Like me, my cousin makes lots of money; unlike me, he has never had the satisfaction that comes from other people enjoying the finished creation.

"How you doin', Nathan? Do you have time to talk to me?"

"Of course, always, t'sup?"

"How do you know something's up?"

"I can hear it in your voice. You sound like you're thinking, I've got to be polite and find out how Nathan is, but I hope he tells me quick, 'cause I've got stuff on my mind."

"Ah, I'm too easy."

"So, t'sup?"

When I finish telling him about the tabloid story, he only laughs at me. "Marie, it was almost forty years ago! And it was them, not you. Nobody's going to hold you responsible for what your parents did! Hell, you can't even be accused of having come under their influence, since they made pretty damned sure they wouldn't be around to shape your life in any way. I don't mean to sound unsympathetic, but I don't see why you're so upset about this."

"Nathan!"

"I'm sorry, I don't. So you haven't told the world all this. That's your right, Marie. And now all you have to do is explain that it was too painful to talk about — I mean, your own parents disappeared, for God's sake. You were just a baby! And worse luck, you landed with Julie and Joe, who are nobody's candidates for parents of the century. Marie, people will understand why you chose to keep quiet about this. They'll probably even admire you for not turning your private tragedy into publicity for your career. I mean, who is ever so discreet anymore? You'll probably make the Ten Most Admired List, just for keeping your mouth shut for all these years. People will be grateful that they didn't have to watch you angst all over their televisions. Nobody's going to think less of you because of this, Marie. And if Franklin does, or his family does, then maybe you ought to think less of them."

"Hey. I'm supposed to be the big sister who lectures you."

"Yeah, well, you're hysterical. Somebody's got to be in charge."

"It's not just what people will think of me, Nathan."

"Then what is it?"

"It's what people will think of them."

"Who?"

"Mom and Dad. Michael and Lyda."

I never know what to call them, how to refer to them. My parents.

"Marie, I hate to break it to you, but they deserve it."

I don't say anything. I'm thinking about

53

what I do for a living. I write about mysteries. Murders. Disappearances. Terrible crimes. Tragedies that happen to perfectly innocent people who don't seem to deserve their fates. I go to a lot of trouble to explain why these things happen. Who did them. Why they did them. Why victims become victims and killers become killers. I explain where and when and every detail of how so that people can understand as much as it is humanly possible to understand how such awful things can occur. Maybe I can't just write off my parents, because I want to understand them. Maybe I want to understand them, because I want to forgive them. But how can I, ever?

"You can deal with this, Marie. What the hell, it's only publicity."

"And any publicity —"

"Is good publicity. Yeah, baby."

"Love you."

"Too."

Of course, we're too cute to bear when we get like this, and we probably ought to stop using that infantile farewell from our childhoods. But we cling, there's no way around it, even a continent apart, Nathan and I still cling to each other. I hope he hasn't just said all that to make me feel better; I hope he's got the right bead on things, but I don't know why I'd think he would, since he never has before.

Speaking of preparing somebody for embarrassment, I punch in the number of the Howard County state attorney's office and leave a message on his voice mail: "Franklin, look up the Web site for that tabloid newspaper that's called *The Insider.* There's a story about me that you'd better read, and the sooner the better. It mentions you. I'll talk to you later. I'm really sorry about this."

It's still early, only 10:30 a.m. My assistant is due at eleven. I feel an inner cringe, thinking of having to show this article to Deborah Dancer. While it's true that my boyfriend knows everything about my family that I know, I've never felt an obligation to divulge it all to Deb. I think she kind of idolizes me, and I think I've kind of enjoyed it. What is she going to think now, of working for a boss who's been labeled racist, and who didn't even prepare her for the possibility of this embarrassment?

Having been lectured by a loving but astringent cousin, I drive home feeling as if I've been patted on one cheek and slapped upside the other. Which is pretty much how I felt years ago when I interviewed

55

people who knew my parents. Few of them could seem to make up their minds whether they loved the Folletinos or hated them, including "James." It was he who originally clued me in to the historical enormity of June 12, 1963, the night my parents "left."

"First I was in jail," he told me, "and then I was on the run, so I didn't even know that it was a hell of a week in the South."

BETRAYAL

By Marie Lightfoot

⊰⊶●⊷⊱

CHAPTER THREE

For six straight days leading up to the cataclysmic events of June 12, 1963, mind-boggling news seeped out of the South. It moved, as fast as television could beam it, around a mesmerized and appalled world. And that was even *before* the seventh day, when apparently nobody took the good Lord's admonition to give it a rest.

That stretch of seven days started, maybe symbolically, with seven black people being terrifyingly forced from a Trailways bus and then jailed in Winona, Mississippi. Ironically, they were fresh from a nonviolence leadership-training course. Just as the world was already worrying about their fates, a courageous Movement leader traveled to Winona to try to free them, and he promptly vanished into a cell there, too. All that week, no word of their fates leaked out of that black hole.

Then police attacked people praying in a voter registration line in Danville, Virginia. With fire hoses and billy clubs, local cops sent forty citizens to the hospital, for the "crime" of wanting to vote.

Then came U.S. Deputy Attorney General Nicholas Katzenbach, boldly proclaiming the federal government's intention to integrate the University of Alabama. All hell broke loose. Governor George Wallace vowed to block the schoolhouse doors.

Tensions were running high, as the saying goes. It was hard to imagine how they could run any higher. But then came the night of June 12, 1963, when everything good and bad seemed to climax all at once. President John F. Kennedy gave a surprise speech on national television, the most important speech on "the Negroes" since Lincoln's Gettysburg address. Kennedy branded civil rights a moral issue, lifting it higher than the political arena for the first time. Enraged by the speech, a bigot in Mississippi hopped into his car and raced through the dark streets to assassinate the black civil rights leader Medgar Evers in his driveway. Evers's wife and children were in their living room, having just watched the president's speech, when they heard the gunshots that killed their husband and father.

On that same night, and mostly unnoted by the rest of the world because there was so much other bigger news to cover, there were violent reactions to the speech and the assassination in towns and cities all over the South, including in little Sebastion, Alabama, northwest of Birmingham.

In Sebastion, a local cell of civil rights workers was broken up that night, and the young white couple who betrayed them disappeared forever.

"We called ourselves Hostel," Eulalie Fisher reminisces from her grand Victorian home on the main street of Sebastion, decades later when it's safe to admit such things. She's eighty years old now, a grand dame of the South, and still a beauty with her white hair arranged softly in a chignon and her slender, graceful body wrapped in a silk robe. Smoke rises from the cigarette in the long silver holder she weaves through the fingers of her right hand. She takes only small, infrequent puffs, but uses the holder as a wand to wave, point, underline, and otherwise punctuate her remarks. Her accent is refined and yet deeply southern, like grits soaked with the finest New England maple syrup. ("I was sent away to finishing school," she says, the explanation for many a cultured inflection among the older women of the South.) "It was meant to be a pun, a play on words, if you will. *Hostel,* because we provided safe houses for black people on the run. And *hostile,* which was how we felt about segregation."

Michael Folletino started it, she claims, shortly after he moved to Sebastion from L.A. with his new bride, the former Lyda Montgomery. In secret, he "felt out" the residents of the town, discreetly determining which side they were on, segregation or integration, and winnowing from the sympathizers those, like Eulalie and her husband, Clayton, who might have some courage to go along with their private convictions. He was in the perfect position to do so, having accepted a position as a professor at an all-white college and as the husband of a local girl, the socially prominent daughter of dyed-in-the-cotton Old South whites.

"Of course, Lyda went right along, but then she loved him madly, and she'd always been a rebel.

"Our little band, Hostel, operated like a

modern-day underground railway. We provided safe haven to people, mostly black people, in danger. We arranged transportation for them to safer places. And all the while, we continued the pretense of being bigots, to keep our activities a secret. We couldn't afford to be open in our opposition to segregation, not if we wanted to continue to help people who were in the direst need. If we had behaved like anything but hypocrites, we'd have been watched constantly, and harassed. Our homes would no longer have been safe places for anyone to hide. We couldn't have come and gone unobserved in our cars. And so we acted the roles we'd been playing all of our lives anyway — traditionalists, with a sentimental soft spot for 'good' Negroes, a sense of our own superiority as white folks and rich ones, and a hatred for the integration that challenged all of that."

For two years, Hostel operated like that, Eulalie claims, successfully ferrying the wounded and the frightened, the threatened and the vulnerable, to relative safety. Some refugees stayed a night or two at Eulalie and Clayton's big house; a number hid in the parson's chamber attached to the back of Michael and Lyda's beautiful home.

"A parson's chamber was a bedroom that was built onto the back of a house," Eulalie explains, stabbing at the air with her cigarette in its holder, as if she is pointing to an actual location. "The door was left unlocked, so that itinerant preachers would have a place to spend the night. Michael and Lyda had the only parson's chamber in town, and it was perfect for our purposes."

She pauses, turns, and lifts her face, as if to gaze into a mirror, while the smoke from her cigarette trails away from her. "I think that Michael and Lyda may have picked that house for that reason, alone. After they disappeared, her brother sold it, and it was never again used for such a noble purpose. But then, none of our houses ever was again." She pauses for an even longer moment, lifts her chin a little higher as she seems to gaze into the invisible looking glass. "And none of us was, either."

4

Marie

I walk into my home with the tabloid in my hand, only to be met in the kitchen by my assistant, Deborah, with a computer printout in her hands. But that's not what I notice about her first. What fills my line of vision is the distress on her face. *She knows,* is my first thought, and I feel ashamed, because I've let her down. *She'll feel betrayed by me, because I didn't confide in her. When she inquired about my family, I brushed her off, saying that I really didn't want to talk about them.*

"Hi," I say, feeling my face grow warm. "You've seen it?"

Deb — only a year out of journalism school, tall and skinny and teetering over me on her platform sandals, dressed in one of her outrageous sundresses, with her platinum hair frizzed out like a 1960s radical — Deborah, funny, naive, and as smart as her near-perfect score on the SATs — starts to

63

cry as she approaches me.

"It's so *mean*, Marie! How could anybody *do* this to you?"

I feel ashamed all over again, only this time it's because I realize that I've underestimated her. She's not going to blame me for keeping my secrets. Of course she isn't. That wouldn't be like her at all. She's going to feel bad for me before she even thinks of herself. I should have given her the same benefit of the doubt that she's now so generously giving me.

"How did you find out about it, Deb?"

"From this E-mail," she says, handing it over to me. "It's so *mean!*"

I look at the piece of paper, expecting to see a printout copy of the tabloid article, but there's more than that. When I see what *else* is written there, accompanying the article, it causes my breath to hitch and gives a greater and more ominous significance to her words.

Dear Marie,

How do you like my little surprise, Marie? How should I spend my five hundred dollars? I know! Why, I believe I'll spend it on additional surprises for you, Marie.

Paulie Barnes

My God. It's the tattletale, the "unnamed source" who sold my life to the tabloid. But I've never heard of a Paulie Barnes. Who is he? Where's he coming from? And why is he picking on *me?*

There's a P.S.:

Don't waste time trying to trace my E-mail address. It's encrypted. If I could choose an uncoded one, it would be executioners@capefear.com. How do you like that one?

My insides do an unpleasant dance when I read that. This is a spooky coincidence, because I was thinking of John D. Mac-Donald just this morning in the checkout line at Publix. One of his most famous novels, and the scariest book I ever read, was *The Executioners.* When Hollywood made two movies from it, they changed the title to *Cape Fear.*

Anyone who has followed my career and read interviews with me would know that whenever I'm asked to name my favorite books, I always mention that one, and how deliciously it frightened me the first time I read it many years ago. Does this "Paulie Barnes" know that?

"Who is he?" Deb is asking me. "Who's

this Paulie Barnes, Marie?"

"I don't know."

To his P.S. he has added:

Like Max Cady, I'll be around, Marie.
Count on me. Your own parents abandoned you, but I will never leave you.

If I felt a chill before now, I feel downright flash-frozen now.

"And who's Max Cady?" Deb wants to
know, dabbing at her tears of outrage and
sympathy on my behalf. She obviously
hasn't read that book, or she'd know instantly. Out of all the fictional villains in
the world's literature, Max Cady isn't one
you'd ever forget. Or, at least, I never have.

I glance up at her, trying to keep my own
voice steady.

"He was the bad guy in a suspense novel,
Deb."

"Weird" is all she says.

I don't tell her that he was a true psy-
chotic, probably one of the purest ever
portrayed in fiction. He was out for revenge against an entire family, because of
what he perceived that the father of that
family had done to him. He could not be
stopped by the cops, or by any other con-
ventional means. He just kept coming at

66

them, like a missile with a malevolent consciousness, aimed in one direction only, from which he could not be deflected except by his death, or theirs.

I smile reassuringly at Deb, or at least I hope it's reassuring.

There's no reason for her to have to worry about this.

"There are a lot of nuts in the world, and this is just one more of them. Let's sit down, Deb, and I'll tell you the truth behind the tabloid story. Forget about this Paulie Barnes, he's just some nasty ol' tattletale who used me to make a few bucks. Screw 'im."

She laughs a little at my show of nonchalant bravado, and I'm relieved to hear it. If she understood the meaning of his literary references, she probably wouldn't find me so amusing, but thank goodness she doesn't, at least not yet. It strikes me that this dear young woman is more or less a part of my small "family" now. As Nathan is. And Franklin and his children. And the scattered few I count as real friends. Is somebody — this Paulie Barnes — really after me and, by innocent association, them?

I try to shake it off as Deb and I sit down

at my kitchen table so I can tell my story to her, the one that's overdue for her to hear. No doubt I'm taking this strange E-mail contact too seriously, and only because I was already shaken up by the tabloid story.

And maybe that's how he planned it, is the unwelcome thought that pops next into my mind. The problem with being a writer is that sometimes I have too much imagination for my own good; the problem with being a true crime writer is that my imagination can work overtime when it hops onto violent tracks. This may be one of those times. *But maybe he planned to throw me off balance with the tabloid revelation, forcing me to deal with the public fallout from that, while he moved in closer for his own purpose. Whatever that may be. Max Cady.* The Executioners. Cape Fear.

I can't bring myself to think about those implications now, or what they suggest about some malign stranger's "purpose" in my life. It's probably all nonsense anyway. He's probably just some trickster, shooting his meager wad by hawking my story to a tabloid. And that's probably going to be the last of it, and all we'll ever hear from him.

It's a lot of "probablies."

"I was born in 1963," I begin, and then

slap my forehead to demonstrate what a moron I am. "Wait a minute! We don't have time for this! I've got to proof my galleys, and you've got to get my publicity material mailed off to the Miami Book Fair. And you know what? You don't have to hear this all at once from me right now, anyway. I've written it down. I'll give that to you and you can take it home and read it, if you want to."

"Okay," she says, and then blushes. "Franklin called."

I'll bet he did. "Thanks, I'll call him right now."

After rooting through my files to locate my unfinished book, *Betrayal,* and handing it over to Deborah, I leave her working in my living room. That leaves me free to quietly shut myself in my office to make the call. Let her think I want to talk intimately, romantically to my boyfriend. I may be doing that — I certainly hope so — but I'll also be talking privately to my prosecutor. I want some advice about what to do — if anything — about this Paulie Barnes, who has disturbed my life like a tornado dropping down from a cloudless sky.

But once I've told him everything, my prosecutor's best advice turns out to be, "Let's take the kids and go to the Keys for the weekend, Marie. I've got a friend with a condo on Key Largo that I can rent if it's empty, I think I can manage to leave work a little early, we can scoop up the kids from their schools, and all drive down together."

"That's a fabulous idea, Franklin." I am, in fact, overjoyed at the idea of a weekend trip, a minivacation, and an escape from the fallout from the tabloid article. At the same time, I'm a little unnerved by the prospect of a weekend with his children, though I don't say so. If we do this, it will be our first time for such intense togetherness. "But I have to . . . I want to . . . pick up my car from the shop tomorrow, and it won't be ready until late afternoon. Why don't you take the kids and I'll meet you down there?"

"Deal. Nobody will be able to find us. We can talk." There's a pause and then he sounds as if he has moved his mouth closer to the phone. "We just won't be able to do much else."

"With the kids there, you mean?" I laugh a little. "How do parents ever manage to have sex after the kids are born?"

"I'll show you," he whispers into the mouthpiece, sending sexual electricity shooting through me, and pushing an involuntary little moan out of my mouth.

Neither of us speaks. The silence is erotic. I'm really sorry to have to bring our conversation back around to a less sexy topic. A little huskily, I say, "What about the tabloid story, Franklin?"

"What about it?" he asks, sounding a little hoarse, himself.

"Aren't you upset?"

"After I got over my initial reaction, no." He has backed away from the mouthpiece of his telephone and is sounding businesslike again. "I don't think it's worth getting upset over. Hell, you've had reviews that said worse things about you than that did, Marie. And I've got political opponents who say things about me that make tabloids look like church newsletters."

I have to smile, albeit wryly. It's true, what he says.

"Well, then what about this Barnes person, Franklin?"

"In the first place, that's probably not his real name —"

"Oh, right." I feel like smacking my forehead again. "Duh."

Franklin chuckles. "In the second place, he hasn't done anything illegal. And in the third place, fuck him."

This time I'm the one who bursts out laughing, not only from the tension-relieving surprise of hearing Franklin say that, but also because he and I so obviously think just alike.

Take that, *Paulie Barnes, whoever you are!*

While I'm at the phone I check for messages, wondering if there is a reaction from anyone else yet. I think *The Insider* only went on sale today, but I know the mainstream media check the "tabs" for leads on stories. Ever since the *National Enquirer* broke the news about one of the Clinton sex scandals, and they turned out to be dead-on with their reporting, nobody has dared to ignore or disdain the tabloids to quite the same degree as before.

Sure enough, there's a message waiting for me from the publicist assigned to me at Hudson House, my longtime hardcover and paperback publisher.

"Hi, Marie!" Over the phone, Connie Dellum sounds even younger than she is; her voice has a high, lilting cheerleader quality that normally I find endearing, although maybe I wouldn't if she weren't also as efficient as she is young. But this morning that trilling voice sounds wildly inappropriate, though that's not her fault. On my voice mail, Connie enthuses: "I don't know what's going on all of a sudden, but I just got into the office and there are messages from *Time* magazine and Fox News, wanting to interview you! This is so great! Do you want me to have them call you? Or should I get their numbers and tell them that you'll call them?"

"Great," I say, unhappily.

Oh, Connie, if you only knew, which you will soon enough. You're going to have a hell of a publicity challenge facing you now. I suspect the head of publicity will step in and take over, after consultations with the president, publisher, my editor, and my agent. Publicists get used to handling anything — canceled airline flights on book tours, bad reviews, drunk authors, and signings where nobody shows up. Like a jack-in-the-box, they pop right back up. But this may finally test their resilience. How are they going to put a good "spin" on an author labeled "racist"?

If *Time* and Fox are on my trail, can *Newsweek* and CNN be far behind? There's no hot scandal consuming the news right now, so I'll make a tasty little bit of filler for them. I can just imagine myself as an item in sneering columns of celebrity news. But maybe not just yet, not if they can't find me to get a denial, or a "no comment." While I feel a bit calmer since talking to Franklin, I don't feel sufficiently sanguine to talk to any journalists, not even to tell my side of the story. But then, what is my side of it, and what is the story? All I can say is, "I was a baby. I never knew my parents. And I don't know much about them."

Quickly, I place a call to Connie to tell her why I'm suddenly so "hot" — if she still doesn't know — and to ask her to see if she can find out the real name of the "source."

When I return to my living room, I find my assistant curled up on the couch, reading the chapters I've written about my parents. So much for getting any real work done today, I guess. But I pass on by without saying anything, and just head on into the kitchen to fix us some lunch. Let her read. As fast as Deb reads, and as short as that partial manuscript is, it won't take her long to finish.

And after all, it's not as if she holds the whole story in her hands.

I don't know if anybody does.

BETRAYAL

By Marie Lightfoot

⇒•⇐

CHAPTER FOUR

June 12, 1963
Sebastion, Alabama

Eulalie and Clayton Fisher had invited the upper social stratum of Sebastion over for a supper in their backyard that night, the evening of Monday, June 12, 1963. The news had been so alarming all week long that people felt they surely deserved one night off to take a breath, to chat comfortably at the Fishers with folks they'd known their whole lives long.

Eulalie planned a casual, elegant picnic of fried chicken, boiled shrimp and crawdads, Alabama bayou jambalaya, sweet potato pie, cold rice salad, sliced garden-grown tomatoes, corn on the cob, pecan pie, gallons of sweet iced tea, and sufficient mint juleps to drown a mule. Hostel members and segregationists alike were invited, as usual, on the assumption that the one group didn't even know of the existence of the other one.

Shortly before the party, the news got out around town that the president was fixin' to give a big televised speech on civil rights that same night. John F. Kennedy and his brother Robert were no icons in the white community of rigidly segregated Sebastion; liberal idols to be toppled, was more like it.

"This is goin' to be painful," Eulalie observed to Clayton as they dressed in their rooms upstairs before the party. "Even worse than it usually is. I am truly dreading it. We're going to have to turn on that big TV so everybody can watch the speech, and then we're going to have to listen to those bigots hoot and holler at our president."

"We have to do it, Eulalie," Clayton reminded her.

"Well, I think I *know* that," she snapped back at him.

He was dressing in baby blue and white seersucker; she was slipping on a soft white dress. They were in their early forties then, he the president of a local bank, she the obvious next in line to be the social matriarch of Sebastion when her generation's turn came 'round. They had no children. Clayton was a deceptively mild man, practiced at foreclosing on small farmers with a personal sympathy that belied his impersonal task; she was deceptively intimidating, accustomed to getting her way without coating her "requests" with sugar as other women did. Some people found him mealy-mouthed; many people thought her bossy. Nobody said that to their faces.

Just as they regularly did, Eulalie and Clayton were going to stage, on this evening, a little show of hospitality for the local bigots, people they had grown up with, played under the eyes of nannies and mammies with, gone to school with, "come out" into society with, joined the country clubs with, done business with, and all with false smiles to fool the fools who thought them friends. They felt they had to do it, just so the segregationists couldn't suspect how far the Fishers and a few others like them — the Goodwins, the Reeses, the Wiegans, and the Folletinos — had traveled from being one of them. And just so they wouldn't suspect that those same white families associated with some of the black people in Sebastion — people like Rachel and her fiancé, Hubert, who both worked for the Folletinos — in ways that went beyond employer/employee into something perilously close to friendship. While it was true that, if asked for either Rachel's or Hubert's last names, neither Eulalie nor Clayton could have provided them, at least they would have felt bad about it. There was still a gap, but it was perhaps the narrowest that Sebastion had seen since its founding.

"If we don't fake it, we'll destroy Hostel," Clayton reminded her, apparently oblivious to her earlier warning shot. "If people start lookin' at us suspiciously, we won't be able to hide anybody anymore, and then what good would we be to anybody, Eulalie?"

"Well, I'd like to know why you suddenly think you need to lecture me about this, Clayton Fisher! Lord in heaven, I think I know we aren't doing this for our own amusement! If it were up to me, I'd tell them all to their faces what I think of them, but then we'd have to shut down Hostel."

Her husband patted the soft June air in a conciliatory way.

"Yes, yes, Eulalie, settle down now."

She hated being told to "settle down," as any woman would have.

"Do you think I'm a horse, Clayton? Are you going to tell me to giddyup and go, now?"

He did privately think that his wife needed to be "reined in" now and then, but he'd sooner kick himself in his own side with spurs than to tell her so. Instead, he did what he was best at — putting a benign interpretation to almost anything. Clayton made a show of shooting his cuffs and looking at his watch. "You're right, Eulalie, we'd both better giddyup and go! That doorbell's going to start ringing any minute now."

They both, and quite realistically, feared getting shot up or burned out, if the secret of Hostel escaped into the community at large. Social standing wouldn't help them then. Money wouldn't save them. Their home, Clayton's ancestral mansion built before the Civil War, could go up in flames. Even the bank might go down. But if the worst ever did happen, if their "friends" and neighbors found out they were traitors to the precious status quo, the Fishers knew it would be much worse for the black folks in town, because everything always was.

Clayton and Eulalie descended to greet the fifty or so guests they were expecting for supper. It seemed like a coincidence at first when their backyard filled with only Hostel members and townspeople who didn't claim an allegiance to either side but only went about their business hoping to be undisturbed by history. People had been invited for six o'clock cocktails, followed by a seven o'clock picnic, but by six-forty-five there wasn't a known Klan member in sight, nor any known white council members, either. Although the absence of those people relieved a bit of tension, it did seem odd, to say the least.

"Where *are* they?" Eulalie whispered to Clayton.

He shrugged imperceptibly, and sipped his mint julep.

"Why aren't they here yet?" she insisted.

"I don't know, dear. Why don't you go call them and find out?"

"I'm not going to call my invited guests to ask why they aren't here!"

"Well, then, I suppose we'll just have to wonder."

The hosts weren't the only ones who were beginning to wonder. "Where *is* everybody?" Marty Wiegan's wife asked Clayton. By "everybody," he knew exactly what she meant: the majority, the people on the other side, the ones who weren't supposed to know.

He smiled his gracious smile and joked, sotto voce, "Maybe my wife forgot to mail their invitations, accidentally on purpose."

"I did no such thing," Eulalie remonstrated, coming up behind them. "And where are Michael and Lyda, I'd like to know? At least if *they* weren't coming, you'd think they'd let me know before now!" She clapped her hands to get the attention of her guests. "Hello, hello! Clayton has an announcement, ya'll!"

"I do?" he asked, turning toward her.

She gave him a little shove. "Of course you do. Tell them to start eating!"

"Start eating, folks!" he called out with good humor.

Slowly the eighteen people who were there began to form a line and then to fill their plates from the abundance that Eulalie's own "colored help" had put out. But the conversation was desultory, as if none of them could keep a topic going. What had looked like coincidence was beginning to look unnervingly like a plan.

Was Eulalie's party being deliberately snubbed?

Heads kept turning toward the house whenever one of the help pushed through a doorway with more food or plates. When the garden gate clicked loudly shut, several voices stopped in midconversation and people turned to stare to see who was coming, but it was only Lackley Goodwin, who had stepped into the front yard to have a smoke with Austin Reese. The two men looked startled when they saw how many faces — expectant, apprehensive faces — were turned their way.

"It's just us, folks!" Austin called out, with a wave.

But once everyone had turned back to their plates and uneasy chatter, he and Lackley moved over to Clayton, who was standing with Marty Wiegan. Austin said quietly, "Why aren't Michael and Lyda here? Have they called? You know we delivered a package to them last night."

Clayton patted the air in his habitual way, to silence such dangerous talk.

"I'm sure they have their reasons, Austin," he said. "The baby may have colic."

"You're taking a lot for granted, Clay," Marty Wiegan said. It was sharply put, but then he was northern-born. Nervously, he patted the long dark strands combed across the top of his head. "Have you called them to find out?"

"No, Eulalie wouldn't let me." Clayton smiled at a passing guest and said to her, "You need to refill that drink, darlin'!"

"Clayton Fisher, you'd get me drunk!" she trilled back at him.

He smiled, turning the warmth of it onto his male friends and fellow Hostel members. "But that needn't stop anybody else from callin' who might desire to do so."

Marty Wiegan turned at once to go into the house to call the Folletinos.

"I wonder if one of us ought to just go over there and see," Lackley Goodwin worried out loud. "Austin, why don't you come up with a sudden need to make sure you turned off your garden hose before you left home?"

"I wouldn't do that," their host said quickly. He looked around and then lowered his voice so only they could hear him. "If there's trouble, we can't be associated with it, you know that, Lackley."

They all knew that. It was their agreement: they stood together, but they fell alone. It was the only way to protect one another and the purpose of Hostel. But none of them had ever "fallen," not yet. Was it happening to Michael and Lyda, even as the rest of them stood in the Fishers' backyard pretending to be having an ordinary party?

Austin stabbed at the bridge of his eyeglasses. "We can't just —"

"Yes," Clayton corrected him, and suddenly the bank president was standing there in the place of the genial host. "We can."

By the time that Eulalie ordered Clayton to shepherd everyone into the television room to watch the speech, some of the "neutrals" were starting to come up with excuses to go home. They may have been ignorant about the existence of Hostel, but they were exquisitely attuned to social nuance. For so very many of Sebastion's most respected couples to boycott this party could only mean that Eulalie's social ship was sinking. The "neutrals" had no intention of going down with it.

"*Such* a lovely party," they assured her. "'Bye-bye, Eulalie."

"Should we send *every*body home?" Clayton whispered to his wife as they stood in their open front doorway staring at the departing backs of four guests.

"Not on your life," she hissed back. "Nothing is wrong."

"My dear, something is —"

"We will act as if nothing is wrong, Clayton. Turn up the sound so everybody can hear it. Make sure everyone has a drink who wants one."

He shook his head — an unusual display of disagreement — and obeyed her.

5

Marie

By the time I have lunch ready, Deb has read it all.

She bounces into the kitchen looking pretty bug-eyed.

"Wow, Marie. That's an amazing story!"

"Are you hungry? Sit."

She obeys. "I have a million questions for you."

I put a plate in front of her and a platter of sliced cheese and fruit, with crackers between us, and then I sit down across from her. "Okay. Shoot."

"Are you sure you don't mind? It won't bother you to —"

"Nope. Ask."

"Well, one thing I wondered as I read it is, are they really sure your mother was involved the same way your father was? I mean, if she was always a rebel, the way Mrs. Fisher describes her, then why would she fall in with the segregationists?"

"My parents may not have done it for a 'cause.' "

"What for then?"

"I don't know. For money, maybe."

"Oh." Deb looks shocked at the idea of that, and I don't blame her. It *is* shocking to think of selling out people — especially ones engaged in a risky and righteous struggle — for a mere material reward. I'd almost rather they had done it because they believed in something, even something reprehensible.

"I come from a long line of traitors, Deb," I tell her gently.

"What do you mean?"

"My grandparents on my father's side were Hollywood screenwriters, like Nathan, only they were Communists who gave up their friends' names to the House Un-American Activities Committee."

"The McCarthy committee?"

"Yes. In the fifties."

She looks nearly as shocked as when I suggested that my parents might have done it for the money.

"Like father, like son," I say, lightly. "It makes a kind of sense."

When she doesn't seem to know how to go on tactfully from there, I help her along a bit. "What are your other questions?"

"Well, I have another one about your mother."

"Okay."

"It doesn't make sense to me that she did this terrible thing, and that she also warned James and helped him escape. Does that compute to you?"

"No, now that you mention it, but maybe that wasn't her."

"What wasn't?"

"The woman in white who ran in to warn James."

"He said it was —"

"No, he said he thought he met my mother."

"But have you seen pictures of her?"

"A few. And they do look like the person he described to me," I admit. "Short, blond —"

"Beautiful?"

"Yes, she was very pretty."

Deb puts a square of cheese between two crackers and smiles at me. "Like mother, like daughter."

I smile back a little grimly. "God, I hope not."

"Oh, I'm sorry, I only meant —"

"I know. Thank you. That was ungracious of me. But that's only a couple of questions, Deb. You've still got 999,998 to go."

She laughs a little, looking embarrassed.

"Deb, it's okay, really. This is helpful to me."

"It is? It doesn't, like, make you feel bad?"

"Not at all," I lie. "What else?"

"I guess . . ." She spreads out her hands in a helpless gesture. "I guess it could all be summed up by just a few questions — what happened next, what happened to them, and where's the rest of the book so I can finish reading it?"

"That's all there is."

"That's all? You haven't written the rest of it yet?"

"No, that's all of the story there is. I don't know any more."

This is not entirely true. There is a little more that I've written down, but I'm not going to show it to her. I'm probably not going to show it to anybody. It's too personal, there's too much about me in it. Plus, some of it is so . . . sentimental . . . that it's even hard for me to believe.

"You *don't?*" Deb exclaims, eyes wide. "What the tabloid said is *true?*"

"I'm afraid so, if you mean — is it true that my parents were never seen again. If they were, whoever saw them has never said so. If you just want the basic facts about it, I can tell you in three sentences. That same night, June twelfth, I was left in Sebastion for my aunt and uncle to raise. My parents were apparently dropped off somewhere at a crossroads just out of town, by a friend who didn't know what they were up to. And that's the last that anybody has ever heard of them, as far as I know."

"Marie! That's awful! How old were you?"

"About seven months." I smile at her. "But I'm bigger now."

She looks across at me with so much sympathy and concern in her eyes that I have to avert my eyes; I look down at the slice of orange dangling from my fork. "What do *you* think happened to them, Marie?"

I take my time raising the fork to my mouth, eating the slice of orange, swallowing, dabbing at my mouth with a napkin. Then I finally look back at her. "Some say they were murdered by members of Hostel, out of revenge for the betrayal, but I don't think I believe that. For one thing, the members of Hostel were otherwise occupied that night, to say the least. And for another, it would just be so antithetical to the very nature of people in the civil rights movement, or so it seems to me." I take a breath. "Of course, I don't actually know what every single one of those members of Hostel — the white ones — did after they were released from police headquarters. And I don't know if there were any black members who escaped the net. So I can't swear that's wrong. But it just doesn't feel right to me, for whatever that's worth."

"What else could have happened?" she asks me quietly.

"Maybe they were killed by somebody in law enforcement to keep it from coming out that there was any campaign against integration. Or maybe they just ran away, Deborah."

She looks horrified. "And *left* you? A baby?"

I shrug. "They betrayed lots of people, not just me. If they escaped somewhere, I would have been an encumbrance, I would have slowed them down and made them more easily identifiable." I laugh a little. "Hell, they could be living under a witness protection program. Maybe they're your next-door neighbors. Maybe they're mine."

"So, you think they're still alive somewhere?"

I look up, startled. "Oh, no. I don't. I think they're dead."

Her eyes start to fill with tears on my behalf, and I can't have that.

"How about some iced tea," I suggest, getting up from the table, "and a bowl of frozen custard with sliced peaches?"

Like me, Deborah can almost always be distracted by food.

What I have, that I'm not going to show her, isn't even written up in proper true crime book fashion yet. It's still in the form in which I heard it from the black people I interviewed who used to work for my parents. One of them was Rachel Anderson. Another was her fiancé, Hubert Templeton. Both of them were important members of Hostel. I also talked to an old woman who used to cook for my mother and a part-time housecleaner who was there that night, but both of them were already too old to remember much, or perhaps they didn't want to. Rachel's memory was a little better — she confirmed most of the story that James told me, the parts she had reason to know, like bringing him food, and feeling a little scared of him.

But it was Hubert who claimed to recall almost everything.

While Deb is dealing with journalists who have seen the tabloid story and who have my home phone — fobbing them off for now, but promising that I'll call them — I pull out the remaining pages in their original rough form, and privately read them through again.

BETRAYAL

By Marie Lightfoot

⫸●⫷

CHAPTER FIVE

"Rachel told me your daddy got a telephone call kinda early that night," Hubert Templeton says. "She said he said hello and then he just listened. When he hung up, he started hollerin' for your mother. They was all dressed to go to some party at Miss Eulalie and Mister Clayton's house that night, but they changed their minds about all that. They went into a room to talk private, and when they come out, your mama was pale as a ghost, Rachel told me. Your mama grabbed up Rachel and said, we got to get the baby dressed, and your daddy, he called me on the phone to ask me to get over there quick as possible in my car. So that's what I did."

I ask him, "What did my father tell you?"

"He said it was better if I didn't know."

"He didn't give you any explanation?"

Hubert shakes his head, no. "You got to

understand, we was used to jumpin' into action without no explanation. That's how Hostel was. Quick action, your daddy allus said, quick response. Move, he allus said, before anybody knows you're gone. Somebody would give us a name and a location and we'd go hurryin' off to pick that person up. Take 'em to a safe place like your mama and daddy's house. So when he said, come on over, I just did what he said, and I didn't think nothing about it, not until I saw this time was different."

"My heart is breaking."
Michael Folletino supposedly said that to his wife when he took the baby from her arms. There were three people, not counting Lyda, who were there to hear him say it, although only one of them remembers it like that and the other two kind of doubt it. But whether he actually said those words, or not, apparently they all saw the truth of it in his face. They say he looked shattered. He appeared to be a man who was desperately going through the motions of trying to save himself and everyone he loved, but who had already lost all hope that he could manage to do that. The witnesses — one maid, one

cook, one yardman, all black — saw and heard how Lyda, herself, refused to give in to that despair until Michael and the baby were out of her sight, driving away in their car. Then, supposedly, Lyda leaned her face against the back of the front door and wept hard and deep.

"It has all gone wrong," she is alleged to have said.

One of the witnesses claims that Lyda also said "my baby," and another witness thinks she said "we can't escape from this."

But memory is short and time is long, so who knows if that is true?

When Hubert drove up, Michael and the baby went off with him.

"We took you to a black motel and rented a room and left you in it."

Hubert, former Hostel member, former employee and friend of my parents, isn't glad to meet me, and he's even less happy to tell me what he remembers of the night my parents vanished. Apparently, he used to love them, but no more.

He explains that it was a "black" motel catering only to Negroes and that my father was extraordinarily lucky it even existed on that road between Sebastion and

Birmingham. Most black families, when they traveled, stayed in homes of kinfolk, he tells me, or they slept in their vehicles for lack of any hotel that would accept them along their routes. But there was a tiny sprinkling of black-owned lodgings and the highway between my hometown and the "big city" had one of them.

"Rundown, nasty place," Hubert describes it. "Where nobody'd think to look for a white child. I rented the room with the cash your daddy gave to me. One buck fifty for the night, pay in advance at the front desk, and I asked for a crib, like he told me to. I remember the old man, the owner, he said, you not gonna let that baby cry, is you? I assured him that you were already asleep, that you slept as sound as money all through the nights. I think you were, in fact, asleep in the backseat where you daddy had laid you down on blankets your mamma gave him. I expect you were lulled to sleep in the car on the ride to the motel. I don't remember you even letting out so much as a squeak. And you hardly stirred when I carried you inside — your daddy stayed hidden down low so nobody'd see him and wonder. I took you in and waited for the owner to bring up the crib. When he did, I didn't let him see you, kept your face and your little hands hidden deep in your blankets. He didn't care. He wasn't a grandma who'd want a peek at you. He didn't even bother to make up the crib for me, as I remember. But that was good. I just closed the door in his face and made up your crib and laid you in it and even then I don't think you let out a peep."

Hubert then walked out of the room, closing the door without locking it, and then he got back in the car with Michael.

"But your daddy, he couldn't bear it, to drive off like that without seeing you were safe in the room. He felt like a coward, I expect, huddling down like that, asking me to take you in. So real quick, he got out and ran into the room where you were sleeping. I imagine he just looked down at you, because he would have been afraid to wake you up with a hug or a kiss. It was important for nobody to find you yet. Later, later, we were counting on your crying to bring people around to look in on you. Eventually, somebody was going to complain about the baby crying. Or the maid was going to find you."

The two men left a bottle of milk in the crib with the baby.

"Your mama, she wrote out a card where she spelled out your name and little things about you like what you would eat and what you wouldn't eat, and how whoever found you should take you to your aunt and uncle and show them the card, which said to give them a good reward.

"It scares me now," Hubert admits, "to think of doing that, of trusting strangers to do right with a baby. Couldn't ask no-body who actually knew your folks to go get you, for fear of getting them in awful trouble by association. We had to leave you to the proverbial kindness of strangers. Lord, I don't know if I could do such a thing today. The things that could have happened to you, it chills my blood to consider them.

"But I guess we did right. Nobody harmed you, or took you for their own, or tried to sell you, or gave you away to bad people. They just did exactly what your mama's card asked them to do. Your aunt and uncle gave a twenty-dollar reward."

His smile is sardonic.

"I suspect your mama and daddy thought you was worth a little more than that. They'd have been angry at your aunt and uncle for being so cheap."

Then he leans toward me. "Listen here to me. Maybe you wish your mama had left a letter for you. Maybe you think they should both have written to you, for you to read later about what happened and how they loved you. But you've got to understand there wasn't time, for one thing, and that people didn't do that kind of thing then, you know, like today practically every grandparent leaves a video for their grandkids to hear about their lives. Everybody's got memoirs and albums and such. But your folks were too young and too busy for that, and I kind of wonder if they couldn't leave any written words for you because they knew they couldn't tell the truth, not all of it anyway. Anyway, they turned — whatever they said — they took a chance of getting their friends in trouble and most of us had already lived through near all the trouble that we or our families could stand."

"When your father came back to the car he looked sad and grim as death, but he wasn't crying and he didn't say a word to me. I didn't talk either, as I recall. What was there to say by that time? We drove back fast to pick up your mother, and when she got in the car, she insisted on me staying up front with your daddy.

Lyda, your mama, she got in back and sat there rigid as stone, staring out the car windows. I'll never forget. I thought she looked held together by nothin' but sheer will. I think for a little while she was mad at your daddy, mad at him for being the child of Communists, mad at him for not protecting her and you, mad because he couldn't keep their fate from coming down on them like it did.

"The three of us, we rode silent out of Sebastion.

"I was past being scared, I guess.

"Eventually, I don't recall where, I sensed your mama move. I turned my head to look at her and I saw her place her right hand on your daddy's right shoulder. She scooched up to the edge of the backseat until she could lay her head against the back of his driver's seat, with her hand pressed down on his shoulder. Your daddy, he tilted his head back, as if he wanted to lay it against her head, but they couldn't quite reach. But they drove like that for a long way, with nobody talkin'.

"They let me out at a safe house. Safe for me, not for them, I thought. I shook hands with both of them. Your mother, she said, 'Thank you, Hubert,' and your daddy told me to watch my rear end, and then I stepped out of the car and watched them drive away.

"I never saw either of them again."

He grimaces, looks me in the eye. In my ears, his rendition has sounded like the memories of a conflicted man who can't quite make up his mind whether my parents betrayed him, or not. One minute, in the telling, he's portraying Michael as a loving father; the next minute, he acts as if I'm pulling memories out of him that are even more bitter than they sound on the surface. But what he says now is unambiguous. "Later, after I heard what they done, I was glad of it. I been glad never to see them again."

"But you must have asked, didn't you? Didn't you ask my father what was going on? I mean, you left his baby in a motel, you hurried back to get my mother. You must have wanted to know —"

"Yeah, I did, but like I said, he told me I was better off not knowin'."

"What did you *think* was happening?"

"Well, I figured some ol' cracker white boys had found out your mama and daddy was helpin' Negroes and they was out to kill 'em for it. It seemed like a logical explanation to me. And if that was the case, your daddy was right — it was surely better for me, the less I knew."

"What if that *wasn't* the case?"

He shakes his head again. "That's why I get so confused when I tell about it. I get mixed up between telling it how it felt to me at the time, and telling it like it really was."

"But how do you *know?*"

Hubert looks at me as if I'm the backward child of those parents. "Because they was on the crackers' side, that's how. That's what Mister Clayton found out. We all know that now."

Lyda looked as shocked as any of them when the car came back up the driveway less than twenty minutes after leaving for the motel. Nobody had expected it to go that quickly.

Michael left the engine running, with Hubert sitting inside the car.

From behind curtains, they all watched him run back up to get her. Hubert's fiancée, Rachel, kept an eye on him, still in the car, as well.

"I haven't had time to pack anything," Lyda protested, when he said, "Come on."

He put an arm around her and pulled her out of their house without giving her any chance to grab a sweater or even her purse. "It won't matter," the witnesses heard him say. "We have to go now. Leave everything —" They say that he looked back over her shoulder in the direction of the three dark people standing in the deepest shadows of the front hall. His eyes seemed to say to them, *We're sorry. You'll be safe. Don't worry.*

The three of them knew that was true. He was sorry. Look what he was losing. And they themselves were most likely in no danger. And they wouldn't worry. They were good at not worrying about things they couldn't control, especially when it came to white people. They didn't, any of them, assume their employers would get out of this all right; they just knew to their bones that this no longer involved them.

They say that Lyda didn't look back.

How could she have, one of the witnesses had thought, sympathetically, at the time. If Mrs. Folletino looked back she would surely turn into the salt of tears.

As for the child . . .

They had, themselves, lost children — at least one child each — to poverty and its attendant, stalking weaknesses, illnesses, and deaths. Their own hearts had already been broken and scarred over. They couldn't feel for the child without aching for their own lost babies, and so they didn't. To a person, they chose to believe she would survive, and they were right.

I did.

Almost forty years later, Eulalie Fisher recalls it.

"I should have been paying attention to his speech, I suppose, but all I could think of was: where are they? Why didn't they come to my party? Every single person I invited had R.S.V.P.'d yes to me. So either they were lying then, or something had happened since then. I sat there in my living room with the Wiegans, the Goodwins, and the Reeses, and all I could think of was, how come not a single one of those bigoted bastards and their mean ol' wives has crossed my threshold tonight? I remember somebody suggested that maybe they were making some kind of a 'statement.' But a statement of what? What were they trying to get across to us by being so rude to me like that? Did they know about Hostel? Or did they finally figure out we thought different from them? Were they drawing a line in the dirt?"

The only people left to watch the big

speech were the Hostel members.

They were also the only ones who had fully realized that something dangerous might be up. "The more we sat around there by ourselves," Eulalie recalls, "the more nervous we got. Then the speech came on — the one where Kennedy said he was going to fully commit the federal government to the cause of civil rights, because it was the moral thing to do. I know there are people who still say he had a lot of nerve talking about morality, but nobody ever said Kennedy didn't *know* the difference between right and wrong. Anyway, you'd have thought we'd of cheered, being all by ourselves like that, in good company, so to speak, with nobody to have to pretend in front of. But we didn't. The truth is, we were scared as the dickens. That fat Lackley kept walkin' to my living room windows, pulling back my drapes, and peeking outside until I finally had to tell him to sit down. I don't remember a single sound of traffic. The whole town seemed to have gone silent on us.

Eulalie sent her extra party help on home to their black part of town. And then just a few minutes later, she even told the live-in help to leave.

"Go to your daughter's," she instructed her maid.

"Stay with your mama," she advised their gardener/driver.

"Eulalie," Clayton commented upon overhearing her, "don't you think they can decide for themselves where they want to spend the night?"

She started to snap at him but suddenly realized the truth of what he was implying — that she was treating a grown woman and man as if they were children or slaves — and Eulalie Fisher flushed with embarrassment. She leaned forward so that Clayton caught her in his arms and gently embraced her.

"So much of the worst of us is purely habit," she murmured.

"That's the truth, my darling," he said. "We're all unconscious creatures, even the best of us, and even at the best of times."

"I'm frightened, Clayton."

"Don't be, Eulalie. We'll be all right."

"Oh, Clay!" She pulled away from him in exasperation. "Even you can't possibly find a silver lining in this!"

He smiled tenderly at her. "But my dear, we haven't even seen a cloud yet."

"No cloud! What do you call the absence of thirty-two guests at my party?"

"Good riddance?"

"Oh, Clay, you're impossible!"

Even in her indignation and anxiety, Eulalie had to laugh at his joke. That's what he could always do for her, make her laugh when she didn't want to. It annoyed her no end, but she needed it, and she knew that she did, especially tonight. With a grimace of exasperation, she took his hand and pulled him back into the living room to be with their guests.

When the speech was over — and just shortly before Medgar Evers got ambushed in Philadelphia, Mississippi — the remaining six guests started nervously gathering their belongings. One by one, and fairly quickly, they moved up to Eulalie to give her a peck on the cheek and to Clayton, who kissed the ladies good night and shook their husbands' hands. To one another they said ambiguously, though the meaning was clear to all of them, "Y'all call us if you need anything tonight, y'hear?"

"And that's when it happened," Eulalie remembers, with a shudder.

The first sign of trouble was the sound of the doorbell, which Clayton went to answer by himself. His guests were still in the living room, finishing their good nights to his wife. He returned to them with two suited FBI agents at his back. Twenty additional agents and local police officers came around each side of the great old house, all of them carrying weapons, and some of those guns were drawn.

"As if it wasn't Miss Eulalie's house!" Eulalie, herself, remarks indignantly, many years later. "As if I had submachine guns stashed in my potato salad and Bolsheviks under my bed!"

That was bad enough, but it was going to get a lot worse.

The eight members of Hostel — Goodwins, Wiegans, Reeves, and Fishers — were walked — not driven — down to the Sebastion jail that night.

It was a deliberate public spectacle that drew vicious attention: hollering, name-calling, tomatoes and rocks thrown, horns honking, even a few hotheads flinging themselves at the detainees and getting in a few punches at the men before the agents or cops slowly . . . so slowly . . . pulled them off.

"That parade they made of us, that was the point," Eulalie recalls from the safety of her boudoir forty years later. "They had put out the word before we even set foot downtown. They wanted to show us off so everybody in town would know who their enemies were." She takes a puff, more like a sip, from her cigarette and delicately releases the smoke into the pretty room. "Nothing was ever the same in Sebastion after that, which is maybe the way it should have been, all along."

They were paraded to the jail, fearing for their lives with every step.

But nobody in the dinner party was arrested that night, and not ever.

Frightened to death, yes, and threatened with prosecution, jail time, and worse, but not a single one arrested. They were all released after an hour of hassling, and they were even driven back to their homes.

"We couldn't figure it out," Eulalie admits. "Until later that night."

That's when they found out where the actual arrests were taking place — across town where black members of Hostel lived and where they, too, had gathered together to watch the Speech. Their cheering had broken out just about the time that another phalanx of FBI and local cops burst in — less politely, by far.

Every black member of Hostel who could be found that night was arrested and jailed. Within the month they were tried and convicted by an all-white jury of any charge that could be trumped up against them. By and large, the black men served prison terms ranging from three to six years. The women were either acquitted or served token sentences and then allowed to return home — except they had no homes.

On that night of June 12, 1963, all of their houses were burned down.

"As much as anything," Eulalie says, "what destroyed us was what Sebastion looked like the next morning. Tuesday, June thirteenth. Not a one of the white people was in jail or charged with a single thing. We'd been singled out, yes. But not actually harmed beyond the damage to our reputations, which were hypocritical at best, anyway. But in the black end of town, there was pure devastation. I think they — the black folks — looked at the difference and they gave up on us that night. I really do. After that, they weren't interested in our help. They'd still take our money donations, but they wouldn't look us in the eye. They'd use any lawyer we hired for them, but they never said thank you, and why should they? The FBI and the cops told them that we had bought our safety by handing them over. It wasn't true! We knew we hadn't done that, but we knew who did do it. There were only two other white people who knew the identities of everybody in Hostel, the only two white Hostel members who didn't quite manage to make it to my party that night.

"Michael and Lyda. Our founders. Our traitors. That's who betrayed all of us, their white friends. We got over it, more or less. But they downright ruined the lives of a lot of black families that terrible night. An FBI agent Clayton knew even told him so a few weeks later. The agent told us it was Michael Folletino who handed over the list to the local police. Clayton asked him, *Why?* Why did Michael do that to us? And the FBI agent said, Michael never was your friend, Clayton. Michael Folletino worked for us."

6

Marie

So there it is, the rest of the story, all that I know except for a little bit having to do with my parents and how they met. But who knows what any of it means? They seemed, in this telling, to be acting like a couple who feared for their lives. If they were planning to disappear, they don't seem to have prepared for that possibility ahead of time.

I toss the pages aside, the way I'd like to toss Michael and Lyda Folletino aside, for good, and just then my phone rings. Without waiting for Deb to get it, I pick it up and say hello.

It's Connie, my young publicist.

"That was fast," I praise her.

"I have a friend there. The name you want, the source for that terrible story, is Paul Barnes. Need me to spell it?"

"No." I'm silent for a second, absorbing this useless confirmation of the name on the E-mail that was sent to me today. "Where'd they send the check?"

"They didn't pay for it, Marie. He didn't charge the tabloid for it, he said he was doing it for free."

Damn. "So he can't be found that way," I muse aloud. "Connie, do you know how the tip came in?"

"E-mail, they said. Supposedly, they tried to reach you to get your reaction. Did they?"

"Not that I'm aware of." When she wants to talk about other interviews, I make an excuse and hang up, telling her I can't talk right now.

Well, at least now I know one small thing that Paulie Barnes doesn't know that I know. He lied when he said he would spend his five-hundred-dollar reward on surprises for me. *Big deal.* That is worth exactly what he got paid — nothing.

"I'm going home now," Deb announces, sticking her head in to tell me. "Are you okay?"

"Yes, if this day ever ends," I grouse, and then I wave her out the door, but she surprises me with a quick, warm hug before she leaves.

Is it still Thursday? How can that be? What a day this has been! I'm exhausted.

The publicity campaign to counter the tabloid story is well under way here and in New York. Tomorrow, Deborah will continue to field phone calls and E-mails with a careful response we all worked out together. In New York they're figuring out ways to capitalize on the publicity. As for me, I haven't forgotten the strange little E-mail from the person claiming to have been the source of all this trouble and bother.

Even so, when I check my E-mail one last time before going to bed, I am taken unpleasantly by surprise to open one from anns@frame.org and find that it holds another message from "Paulie Barnes." Once again, the other address, executioners@capefear.com, is typed in the body of the text, instead of in the actual E-mail address line.

This guy seems to have a talent for jumping out of the bushes.

Is this more than one person who's sending these, or is it one person with multiple E-mail addresses?

For a moment I just stare at this second one, feeling snakebit, and debating whether or not even to open it and see what he says this time. His first little message felt nearly salacious, the way he kept repeating my first name, as if he got some kind of perverse pleasure out of the mere act of typing it. It gave me a nasty feeling, as if I'd touched something vile, even though there wasn't a single "dirty" word in it, nothing overtly sexual.

"Hell," I say, and double click on it to open it:

Dear Marie,

I wonder what you're doing tonight.

Are you rereading today's publicity about you?

You can thank me for any extra book sales that generates for you. Although I must say, I have in mind another way for you to express your gratitude.

But that can wait a little while.

Why don't I tell you what *I'm* doing tonight, right now, at this moment. I'm seated in front of a computer in a public library — can't say which one, can't say where — and I'm writing this E-mail to send to you. We are now officially in Step Two, Marie. Perhaps you didn't recognize Step One for what it was when it arrived today? Wait until you see Step Three. I feel sure you will recognize it for what it is, quite easily.

But I was setting a scene, wasn't I?

To my right, there is a huge cinnamon bun dripping with white icing. Can you smell it, can you taste it? We're not supposed to bring food in here, but who's to stop me? To my left, I have one of your books turned over so I can see your photograph on the back cover. Very nice! There you are in full color, close enough for me to touch, as I am doing . . . now. When I run the tips of my fingers over your pretty face, over your throat, your shoulders, your breasts, the glossy paper feels as smooth as your skin must surely be.

Now don't get me wrong, Marie.

Don't misinterpret these words.

Yes, I find you attractive. And, yes, I certainly feel a certain sexual charge from moving you around like my own queen on my own chessboard, to suit my own ends. But be assured I'm no serial killer, no stalker. I am neither of those banal manifestations of evil. That would be tedious, and I'd so hate to bore you. I confess, you never bore me. Quite the opposite, I find you — and my mysterious connection to you — deeply fascinating. I feel sure that you will become intrigued, too, both by me and by what you are about to learn about yourself through me.

But I digress. Where was I?

Ah, yes, I was admiring your photograph and touching it.

Look at you! What a lovely smile you have, and natural blond hair — apparently — and you're a little thing, aren't you? I happen to know exactly how old you are and I must say you don't look it. You could pass for late twenties, easily. But for as small as you are in physical stature, you have a great big presence in the world, don't you? I wouldn't be interested if you didn't. The ordinary bores me. That — keeping me from being bored — seems to be a developing theme tonight, doesn't it?

I expect you are reading this in your office.

You have an office in your home, don't you? It's at the southwest corner opposite the guest bedroom, on the other side of the west wall in your living room. During the day it's bright and sunny, open and airy, just like your public face.

But what about me, you're wondering by now?

Who is this stranger who has so suddenly and dramatically dropped into your life, this man who knows your secrets and who is writing to you so intimately out of the blue?

I will be happy to tell you more about myself.

But that can wait.

Since this is only one of the messages I will be sending to you — and you to me — there is no hurry. At least, not yet. So, relax. Don't worry about me. It's late. Go on to bed. Drift sweetly into "easeful sleep" as the poet says. (How do I know you will be reading this tonight instead of in the morning? Because you always do check your E-mail right before you go to bed, don't you?) Tonight, a third communication will slip into your E-mailbox, like a burglar slipping through your sliding glass doors while you are asleep in your bedroom on the second floor of your home.

Sweet dreams, Marie.

"Paulie Barnes" it's "signed" at the bottom, just as before.

Anybody could guess that I check my E-mails last thing at night. Don't most people with Internet access do that?

"I'm not going to let you scare me."

Without hesitation, I take the steps that are required to instruct my E-mail server to reject any messages from "anns" or "ftoasdr."

What an ass this man is! Trying to make me think he has seen, or even been inside of, my home! So he knows the layout of it, so he knows it's "bright and sunny," so what? My house has been pictured in *Architectural Digest*, and bits and pieces of it have appeared behind me when I've been interviewed here. Plus, any plumber or carpenter with access to the private cul-de-sac on which I live could have scouted out my property. It isn't difficult to look in windows that are almost always open.

As I know well, it's easy to write or talk as if one knows more about something than one really does. I do that all the time in my books. I can take two palm trees, a dirt yard, and a sunny day and turn them into three pages of atmosphere if I need to. Apparently, this jerk can, too. His supposed familiarity with my home is not enough to convince me he's any kind of authentic threat to me. He's just a pervert getting his kicks, probably one of the tiny minority of my readers who ought to be chained down.

"I'm cutting you off, right now."

You'll have no more E-mail access to me, Paulie Barnes.

Unless he uses other addresses, a tiny voice warns me. I override it by thinking, *And since I'm going to delete your message — right now — there will be no response from me to you, either.*

"So he knows my parents disappeared, so what?"

I'm talking to myself, convincing myself, as I climb the stairs.

Out of sheer pique and perversity, I've left my downstairs drapes open. From the stairs, when I look down, I can see through the glass that wraps nearly around my house, out to the glittering lights along the Intracoastal Waterway. Boats are moving along it even now, so late in the evening, as they always move, twenty-four hours a day. But none of them will dock at my shore-line, because it's a nearly sheer cliff with no docking access for any size boat.

"Anybody who lived in Sebastion at the time knows that much."

When I reach the top, I turn around and run back downstairs again.

"I'll just double-check the door locks and the windows."

And the alarm system. And call the guard at our security gate to ask him to be a little extra alert tonight. And pull the drapes closed, after all. And then maybe I'll take some pots and pans upstairs with me and hide them just inside my door so that if a burglar happened to wander in, he'd make an awful clatter and wake me up. I keep a gun in my bedside table — because I write about some truly awful men — and I'll just check it to make sure it's loaded.

And then I won't give this guy a second thought.

Should I call Franklin and tell him about this?

No, I'd wake him up. He's got court in the morning.

And anyway, I don't want to start taking it too seriously.

He may have rumbled a day of my life, but he's not going to spoil my sleep, or anybody else's. I'll take a shower. I'll sleep like a baby. And tomorrow afternoon, I'll drive to the Keys to be with Franklin and the children. In the Keys there will be no publicity, no interviews, no E-mails, no surprises from tabloids, and no Paulie Barnes.

7

Marie

It's Friday morning. I suffered no night-mares. The sun rose again in the east. My store-bought grapefruit tasted almost as good for breakfast as those I pluck off my own tree in wetter seasons. And now Deborah Dancer and I are companionably at work out back on my patio. Before she came to work full-time for me, Deb was a feature writer for our local newspaper. Although she liked that well enough, she says they didn't stock their refrigerator nearly as well as I do. Or let her work barefoot.

Deb's seated at the patio table going through the mail she didn't have time to get to yesterday. I'm stretched out on a chaise, deep into editing the galleys for my next book. (It's *Anything to Be To-gether*, a shocking story about a minister who was sent to death row for murdering his wife.)

All of that is interrupted by the telephone, which Deb answers.

When she puts it back down, she says, "That was Tony at the gate. FedEx is coming in with a package."

It's not even five minutes before we hear the doorbell.

When Deb comes back onto the patio, she's opening something.

I wouldn't even have noticed her return, except that she drops something onto the bricks, where it lands with a soft thud, and she exclaims, "Oh, my gosh, Marie, this is so weird!"

I look up to find her staring at me with a strange expression on her face. There's a FedEx envelope in her left hand and a paperback book lying at her feet. From here, I can't see what it is. For a strange, suspended moment, time seems to float between us like a bubble that's about to be violently broken.

In this odd little bubble of time, while I wait to find out what's so "weird" that it would make her drop a book, I see all sorts of emotions playing across her young face. One of them is the mundane, but unhappy realization that I hate to be interrupted when I'm writing or editing. "Please don't interrupt me unless a hurricane is bearing down," I warned her when she first came to work for me, "or your hair is on fire."

"What if yours is?" she impishly asked me then.

"Let it burn."

Already, after only a few months on the job, Deb knows that if a class five hurricane were on its way, I'd probably say, "You go. I've got to finish this sentence."

Normally, I might fix her with a baleful glare.

Normally, her expression might say, Oh, shit.

But in this pause, I feel no annoyance, just tension.

My number two black lead pencil is poised in my right hand at the galley's edge; the forefinger of my left hand touches the page, pointing to the spot where I stopped working. Out of my peripheral vision, I see boats moving on the Intracoastal Waterway a hundred yards away and down a cliff from us. I can hear traffic on the Bahia Boulevard Bridge, feel sweat under my T-shirt, taste and smell the orange juice I drank for breakfast. I don't want to be aware of these things; I don't *want* to know what the matter is. I want to be lost in my work-trance, oblivious to everything except the printed pages on my lap.

I lay my pencil down on the galleys.

In slow motion, Deb bends over and picks up the book.

Then she holds it face out to me, and I see that it is a copy of *The Executioners* by John D. MacDonald.

First, my stomach lurches and my skin gets gooseflesh.

But then I am suddenly disgusted and furious.

"Give that to me!"

She walks it rapidly over to me and releases it into my hands, as if she's glad to be rid of it. I grab it from her, and make an angry show of slamming it down into the wicker wastebasket to my side.

"There's a letter that came with it —"

"Give it to me, too."

She fishes it out of the FedEx package and hands it over.

I make another production out of crumpling it up and tossing it in the basket to go with the damned book, no offense to John D.

"Aren't you even going to read it, Marie?"

"No, I am not."

She looks like a spooked kid who wants somebody older to reassure her that this is nothing to worry about, so I say, "It just pisses me off, that's all. But don't you even give it a second thought, okay? If I know some of my fans, this guy is locked up in prison with too much time and not enough rehab."

Deb laughs at that, as I hoped she would.

"Believe me," I continue, "these guys are all bow and no arrow."

She sits down again but doesn't look entirely convinced. "Okay."

"Hey, it's all grist for the writer's mill," I suggest, smiling at her. "It just gives us a little more insight into the minds of criminals and perverts." I cock my head at her. "Such a lovely place to be. Are you sure you want to stay there with me?"

"Yes!" She sits up straighter, as if trying to demonstrate her resolve. "If I didn't, I might never get to see Franklin again."

I laugh, while she blushes. "That *would* be a terrible fate."

"Did I tell you," Deb blurts, "that one of my roommates — Tawna? — is pissed off because he's dating you? She says why should white women get all of their best men? I told her, I don't know about that, but I don't think you can help who you fall in love with, you know?"

I nod, without exactly committing to that opinion.

When Deb blushes even deeper, I look

out toward the Intracoastal, pretending not to notice that her complexion has turned rosy. She has a massive crush on Franklin, but it would mortify her to know that we're aware of it. How can we not be, since the poor kid stumbles all over her feet and her words whenever he's here? God knows, I understand her feelings. I'm pretty crazy about the man myself. Whether or not I'm in love with him is another question, and one that I'm not prepared to answer yet; whether or not I have any choice in that matter is still another conundrum that I don't want to have to solve at this moment. So I give her a moment to collect herself, before I look at her again.

Her non sequitur has nicely broken that other tension.

"Deb, would you go in the house and check my E-mails again? Print out anything new that has come in. I'm expecting something from my agent."

That's a lie, intended only to get her off the patio so that I can fish the damned letter out of the wastebasket.

When she's gone, I read:

Dear Marie,
What is the point of my contact with you?

Why have I gone to the trouble of planting a news story to get your attention, then followed that up with a second and third message to make sure you understand how well I know you, and then had the gift of a book delivered to you?

It is so that you will take seriously my book proposal.

You're tempted to laugh, aren't you? You think you've heard it all before, don't you? No doubt many people come up to you with book ideas. But I'll wager that no one has ever approached you with this one.

Marie, you are a true crime writer. I love to read about true crime. So you and I are going to combine forces, only this time you *are going to be the victim in your next book.*

I am going to kill you, Marie.

You are going to write the book about it.

Isn't that brilliant? Wouldn't any editor jump at the chance to publish a book like that? Just think — the famous writer describes her own demise, right up to the very moment before it happens! Imagine the suspense, Marie. Imagine the television coverage, and the exciting, suspenseful movies that will be made from our story. What a "hook," as they say in Hollywood! Just think of the diabolical inevitability of the ending. And don't worry about that — I'll write the epilogue.

It will be a blockbuster best-seller, I'm sure you agree.

But we have work to do before that time.

So let's get down to business.

Here are your initial instructions, Marie:

1. *Fire your assistant immediately.*
2. *Contact no law enforcement.*
3. *Write our first chapter and E-mail it to me by 2 p.m. today. It must contain a full description of these past two days. Build suspense for our readers! Share your initial disbelief, your embarrassment or anger, your growing horror and dread, Marie.*

Are you thinking, This is absurd? Are you thinking, This can't be for real, and whoever he is, he doesn't mean it, he can't do it? It is for real, Marie, and I do mean it. Not only that, but I can do it.

But why should you do it?

I'll tell you why. Pay very close attention now, Marie.

If you disobey, first I will hurt Deborah Dancer, your girl with the ridiculous clothes and the hair that looks as if she stuck her finger in an electrical outlet.

Do I have your full attention now?

Good, because you need to know that after I hurt her, I will turn my attention to your boyfriend and his children.

And speaking of him, by "law enforcement" I don't mean him.

Do tell him everything. You have my permission to do that.

Then, we won't have to force him to leave you. He will abandon you in order to save himself and his family.

Then you and I will be on our own, writing partners to The End.

It gives a whole new meaning to those two words, doesn't it?

Start now, Marie. Fire Deborah. Write the first chapter and E-mail it to me by 2 p.m. today in the addressed reply block I have thoughtfully provided for you.

Yours truly,
Paulie Barnes

"Marie, you *did* read it!"

She returns to the patio, catching me with the unfolded letter on my lap. "No message from your agent, sorry," she says, and then, after a moment, tentatively, "what does it say?"

I hold up a finger, bidding her wait a sec while I pick up my cell phone and ring Franklin's office.

"Is he there?" I ask his secretary, Arvida Waid.

"Still in court, Marie," she says.

"Ask him to call me, will you please, Arvida?"

"Sure thing. I could page him — ?"

Not while he's inside a courtroom trying a case. "No, just have him call as soon as he can. Tell him — tell him I heard from our friend Paulie Barnes again."

"Barnes?"

"Yes. Thanks, Arvida."

After I turn the phone off, I glance up at Deb again.

"Is everything okay?" she wants to know.

I still don't answer her. I can't; my mind is busy demanding its own answer of me. *You have to decide now, Marie. In this moment. Will you err on the side of caution or cynicism? If you err on the side of caution, no one can possibly get hurt and the worst that can happen is that you will look and feel like a fool for believing him. If you err on the side of cynicism, it is possible, however unlikely, that someone may suffer for it. You can't ask Deb to make this decision; that wouldn't be fair.*

She is standing in front of me, looking quizzical and a little worried now.

"Marie? What's wrong? You're scaring me."

The sundress she has on today is bright yellow with a print of purple seahorses. As accessories, she has chosen bulbous yellow earrings and a matching necklace and bracelet. Franklin thinks she's cute; he says it makes him smile just to see her.

Decide, Marie. It's up to you. What's it going to be?

"I'm sorry, Deb. I don't want to say this. I'd give anything not to have to say this. But it appears that I have to, because you have a right to know. This idiot" — I wave my right hand dismissively over the letter — "says in here that if I don't do what he wants me to do he will hurt . . ."

I swallow, feel myself frowning.

Deb looks horrified. "He'll hurt you?"

"No. I'm so sorry. I hate this." My mouth snaps shut, because it doesn't want to utter the next words I have to say. I swat away a fly that buzzes near the lip of a glass of lemonade I have sitting beside me. But finally I have to say it. I have to tell her. It wouldn't be right not to warn her. "He says he'll hurt you."

Deb blinks, opens her own mouth, but for once nothing impulsive comes out. Finally, she squeaks, *"Me?"*

I propel myself from the chaise, take hold of her right wrist, and pull her over to sit with me at the patio table. I look into her shocked blue eyes and try to sound a lot more calm than I feel inside. "That's what he threatens, but I don't believe it for a minute. It's the craziest thing! You'll never believe what this nut wants. He claims he's going to force me to write a book with him!"

"*What?* A book? What kind of book?"

"A true crime book. Don't even worry about that part of it, it's nothing. It's not important. This is all nothing, I'm sure of it. If it were just me he threatened, I'd throw the damned thing away again. But it's not just me, it's you. He says that I have to fire you —"

"*What?* No!"

"Of course I won't," I assure her quickly. "But, Deb, the problem is that we don't know for absolutely sure that this guy can't do what he says. He knows my E-mail address, he knows where I live, he knows just enough to make us careful. I think the thing for us to do is to fake it for a while. Apparently, he wants everyone out of the way, starting with you. So we may need to make it look as if you're packing up and getting out of here. You may need to stay away for a few days."

"I *won't*," she proclaims angrily, stubbornly, though there's fear in her eyes.

"Yes, you will," I inform her in a tone that tells her I will brook no further argument. "Just to be on the safe side. There is plenty of work you can do from home, and I'll keep paying you no matter what."

"I don't care about that!"

"Well, your roommates will when the rent comes due. Besides, Deb, just think how embarrassing it would be for me to have to tell your parents that I let you get killed. They'd be so annoyed at me."

"Yeah." She laughs nervously. "They're picky like that."

"Give me time to find this guy, Deb. Let me make sure that he is already locked away somewhere and that he won't be getting out anytime soon."

"You really think he's a convict?"

"I don't know. I suspect so. That probably makes the most sense, because who else has time to cook up stupid threats like this? And even convicts can arrange for packages to get delivered. Anyway, I'll find out. Or, what's the point of dating a prosecutor?" I squeeze her wrist, to take the edge off what I must say next. "Listen, I don't want to frighten you unnecessarily, but I've got to tell you that he sounds nasty. And smart, if you can judge intelligence by the way somebody writes." I smile, mocking myself, which makes her smile back at me instinctively. "His threat is pretty clear. I'm to follow his instructions perfectly, or he'll hurt you in order to prove to me that he means this. He doesn't say what he would do, just that he'd hurt you. The thing that bothers me, the thing that convinces me that we have to take this seriously for a while, is that he knows anything about you at all, Deb. He knows your name. That you work for me."

What I don't tell her is that in the letter he referred to her as "your girl with the ridiculous clothes and the hair that looks as if she stuck her finger in an electrical outlet." He knows that much about us. About her. And that's way too much, to my way of thinking. If it's an empty threat, it's a frightening one. It has definitely got my attention with its convincing details, with its promise to harm Deborah, Franklin, the children.

"Come on," I urge Deborah, taking her hand and tugging her up out of the chair. "We're getting you out of here."

"*Now?*"

"I'm afraid so. We're not messing around with this nut. He may even be watching the house." She flinches and then stares around with wide eyes. I could bite my own tongue. I hope that she won't think to ask, How can he be watching us if he's in prison? Trying to reassure her, I put an arm around her in big-sister fashion. "It's probably all a bluff. But if he's watching to see what I'll do, let's make a show of looking upset —"

"That's easy," Deb whispers.

"— and of following his directions."

"I don't want to!"

"I don't, either. But for the time being, if he says jump, we'll hold our noses and do it." I keep her moving, urging her off the patio, into my home. I am not about to take chances with her life. I'd much rather take the chance of looking like an idiot. "I'm sorry, but I think you're going to have to tell your friends and your family that I've fired you."

"No!" It's a wail. "*Why?* I'll feel humiliated! And they'll hate you!"

"But he may check up on it, Deb, and it will be better if everyone around you thinks it's true."

I usher her around my living room, picking up her belongings, stacking them in her arms, hanging her purse over her shoulder and then prodding her toward my front door. I'm in a hurry to get her out of here, because I don't want her involved in this at all.

Once outside, with Deb standing with her arms loaded and her eyes brimming with tears, I touch her face. "I'm so sorry about this. I hope I'm just overreacting. Tell you what — when it's all over, and we know there's no danger, I'll personally apologize to everybody you had to tell you were fired, okay? Deb, I really don't think you have a thing to worry about so long as you stay away from me."

In a frantic, tearful whisper, she pleads, "But how will I know what's going on?"

"I'll figure out a way to let you know."

She nods, looking miserable. Then, obediently, she turns and starts to walk off toward her little white VW bug that's parked on the street. But then she turns around and runs back to me.

"This is *crazy!* Isn't it, Marie?"

"Yes, it is. But maybe he's crazy, too."

"What kind of book?" she asks, looking stubborn again. "What does he want you to write a book about anyway?"

I was hoping she'd forget that.

I let out a breath. *Dammit.* "He says he's . . . oh, this is so stupid! He claims that I'm going to write a book about . . ."

"What? *What?*"

I say it in a rush. "About my own murder."

"Oh, my God!" Even with her arms full of stuff, she manages to clutch at me. Gently, I back away before things start falling out of her arms.

"Yeah, but it's nonsense. He claims he's going to murder me and I'm going to write about it. But that's not going to happen, Deb. It is *not* going to happen. In the first place, this is not real. He can't do it. And even if he could, we'll find him first. But you can see why I say he's nasty, and why I don't want to mess around about this. You need to go. I'll be all right. Truly, I will. But I will worry myself to death if you don't leave right now."

She looks disconsolate, young, and vulnerable as she walks away a second time. But this time she gets into her little white VW Beetle and drives away.

"Damn you," I whisper to a stranger named Paulie Barnes.

8

Marie

There was one more page to his last communiqué, an autobiography of sorts, though it is impossible to know if any of it is true. I pull it out of the pocket of my shorts, where I stuffed it, and stand on my front stoop and read it over again.

I'll tell you about myself.

Since part of what follows is fiction, it seems appropriate to speak of myself in the third person.

Paulie Barnes (what I'm calling myself) loves to read about true crime, the deaths and rapes and burglaries that really happen. None of that made-up stuff for him, no mystery novels, no fictional detectives, or make-believe cops. Give him the truth any day over fantasy; he is tough enough to take it. Give him real blood and guts. Make him feel as if he is actually there on the scene with the victims, the killers, the cops.

He loves it. Pour it on.

Until recently, his favorite true crime author was Ann Rule. His favorite book of hers was **The Stranger Beside Me.** *You remember that one, of course. It was the incredibly bizarre true story about how she was writing a book about a serial killer when she discovered he was a friend of hers. His name was Ted Bundy.*

(Don't you love the chills that story gives you, Marie?)

Stranger than fiction, that's how Paulie likes it.

Now, however, his favorite true crime author is: you, Marie.

And then he wrote:

How's that for a bang-up start? I'm good, aren't I? I should be, I've studied your books enough to pick up your style of writing. It's a little sensational for my taste — you can see that I possess a more elevated style — but I have seen for myself that it is fun to write your way, and it certainly is a thrill to read, I'll be the first to admit that.

Why, I can hardly put it down!

One thing that is true, however, is that my new favorite book is going to be the one we will write together, Marie. I even have a working title for us. We'll call it Last Words, *with a subtitle,* Best-selling Author Marie Lightfoot Tells the Horrifying, Tragic Story of Her Own Murder, Right Up to the Moment of Her Death.

Please do believe me when I promise you that ours will not be one of those omnipresent serial killer books. Yawn. Aren't you sick to death of serial killers? Couldn't you just line them all up and shoot them? That's an amusing thought, a mass murder of serial killers.

No, I am not one of them.

Rest assured, I am something different. I am something new.

And you alone will have the privilege of discovering me.

I stick it back down in my pocket.

How could my life turn upside down so quickly? Yesterday morning I was standing in a grocery store line enjoying being anonymous, and now some anonymous creep has disturbed my peace of mind, my work, my employee. He has even managed to dredge up my past — the last thing I want to happen. But not the worst thing. *This* might be one of the worst things that could happen, this awful feeling of being invaded by an insidious, invisible virus. I feel as if I've been "hacked," like a computer.

Is this what victims of stalkers feel like?

It's ninety degrees, but I am frozen to my front stoop.

When Deb's Volkswagen disappeared from my view, it looked filthy brown instead of white, but that was merely proof of her good citizenship. We're in a prolonged drought in south Florida. It's so bad that we'd almost rather hear that dreaded word *hurricane* than endure much more of this. God, what we wouldn't give for a decent tropical storm. Winds of forty, even sixty miles an hour would be fine; a little four-foot storm surge, we can live with that. Just give us rain! Here in Bahia Beach — our city of 100,000 souls in between Fort Lauderdale and Pompano — water restrictions are tight enough to squeeze tears from a shark. Our street addresses dictate the days we may dampen our seared yards, and even then we're limited to such odd hours that only the most dedicated lawn jockeys still do it. Washing cars and boats is completely verboten, except at commercial outfits that are exempted so they won't go out of business.

As my cousin Nathan would say, it's drier than a witch's wit.

I glance around at my neighbor's sad brown yards, putting an anxious expression on my face. If somebody is watching, let him think I'm frightened. I was a little scared, I'll admit that. But now, what I am increasingly feeling is — pissed. If this jerk is watching me, then let him get a damned good look at his prey.

Let him think I'm doing exactly as he says to do.

"Like hell." That instantaneous, rebellious thought is followed in my mind by another one, a cliché right out of a pulp western. "You son of a bitch, I'll get you for this." That sentiment makes me want to laugh at myself, but I restrain the impulse to show any amusement to anybody who's watching me.

My righteous indignation gets me moving again.

As I finally turn around and head back inside, I feel an urge to close all of my sliding glass doors, pull down my windows, shut my drapes, and flip the thermostat to "cool." My hand is reaching for the switch when I suddenly stop myself. Is it really the heat that's bothering me? Or am I still more scared than I want to admit? Is it cooler I want to feel, or safer?

"Which is it?" I demand of myself.

The inner answer, disturbing and surprising me, is *safer.*

With some effort, I resist the strong impulse to lock myself in. In a symbolic sense, it's too late anyway. He has already penetrated my space. A shiver — a premonition? — raises gooseflesh on my arms. I rub them vigorously, angrily, to make them go away.

This time I do what I should have done earlier: protect the "evidence" from my own fingerprints. After I fix myself a glass of iced tea, I fetch a roll of plastic wrap and a plastic grocery bag from my kitchen and carry them out to my patio. There I carefully spread the plastic sheeting over the front of the letter, smoothing it out some more as I do so, and then turn it over and cover the back, too. Now I can handle it without destroying any remaining fingerprints, not that I expect there to be any on it. Surely he has been more careful than that. But even the smartest felons make stupid mistakes, so maybe I can be more careful than he from now on. Next, I slip the FedEx envelope and the book into the grocery bag without touching them.

On my way into my office, I open the bag and give the envelope a good look for the first time. On the FedEx routing sheet, there's a name, address, and phone number for the "sender," but I'm guessing that's all as phony as his E-mail addresses. But there's a credit card number under "method of payment," and so maybe we can trace him that way.

Back in my office, and seated in my swivel chair behind my desk, I study this new E-mail more closely. The glass of iced tea is sweating at my elbow. I pick it up to sip, concentrating for a long moment on the cool wet feel of it in my hand, the scent of mint, the tang of the lime juice I squeezed over the ice. I take a long drink, prolonging this last moment of relative peace. Finally, I set down the drink and pick up the printout. It captures my total attention, as if it held a gun to my head, which in a maddening way, it does.

I'm supposed to write a chapter and e-mail it to him by two?

I look at my watch: it's already almost noon.

There's not much time, *if* I'm going to do this.

I hate it that everything's moving so fast,

that he is giving me so little time to stop and think before I have to act, or not act. Hamlet had more time than this! No doubt Paulie Barnes wants it that way, because it makes it more likely that I'll do what he wants.

"But you *will* stop," I instruct myself. "And you *will* think hard about it first, even if it means writing like a madwoman after that."

Okay, then. How paranoid do I want to be about this?

Should I hesitate to use my house phones, for fear he has somehow managed to tap them? Tapping's not hard to do or hide, so it's better to be safe than sorry, I believe, until I can get my house "swept." As for my cell phone and portable phones, I never think of them as being "secure," anyway, even on normal days. What if he has some kind of high-tech listening device directed toward my home? Well, if that's the case, he overheard Deb and me this morning, and so he already knows that I only pretended to fire her, so that damage would already be done.

I tell myself: let's assume that worrying about a distant listening device is *too* paranoid, but that worrying about the security of my telephones is not. Therefore, I will take the chance of saying what I want to on my own property, but I will refrain from using the telephone to talk about this problem.

This is ridiculous! my ego protests.

Never mind, walk through this process anyway, I tell it.

Okay, next . . . what about E-mail and my computer? How secure?

Can I use E-mail to contact anybody I want to?

I think so. I have firewalls to deflect hackers from trying to steal data. I never download anything unless it's from somebody I know and trust, and even then, I'm careful, so I don't believe that any Trojan horse has trotted into my computer to dump a nasty load of spy ware. I'm hooked up to the Internet through my local cable system, which makes me less vulnerable to attack or infiltration than I would be if I had a dial-up system. I know that there are viruses and "worms" capable of squirming into a computer — any computer — and taking control of it, even down to recording every single keystroke and reporting them back to the "master." A hacker could even steal one of my books in progress that way, although why would anybody want to? But overall — thanks to my computer consultants — I believe I am as protected as I can be from all but the most brilliant and determined of hackers. Which might be your average sixteen-year-old, but never mind.

All right then. Phones, no. Computer, yes.

That means I can e-mail for advice from experts who are not officially in "law enforcement," and I will.

But am I really going to do any of the rest of it, just because he says so?

Yes, I am, because of what he threatens in the letter.

If you disobey, first I will hurt Deborah Dancer, your girl with the ridiculous clothes and the hair that looks as if she stuck her finger in an electrical outlet.

Do I have your full attention now?

"Yes, you nasty son of a bitch, you do."

Good, because you need to know that after I hurt her, I will turn my attention to your boyfriend and his children.

When I read that the first time, outside on the patio, my heart nearly stopped. Hurt Franklin? His children? Even now, reading those words again, my palms go damp and my mouth goes dry.

. . . And speaking of him, by "law enforcement" I don't mean him. Do tell him everything. You have my permission to do that. Then, we won't have to force him to leave you. He will abandon you in order to save himself and his family.

Then you and I will be on our own, writing partners to The End.

It gives a whole new meaning to those two words, doesn't it?

"I'll give you a whole new meaning," I mutter, hoping bravado trumps fear.

It's clear that I have to play along, at least for a little while longer.

But I don't have to do it alone.

That would be a mistake.

I will forward these messages — right now — to two people who are not officially "law enforcement." One is a private investigator I employ now and then. The other is a freelance criminologist. I'll let those experts tell me if they think we should take this guy seriously.

Until I hear back from my experts, and just to continue on the safe side, I'll follow "Paulie's" directions to the letter.

I sit down with my computer. I raise my hands until they hover over the keyboard. Now or never. My fingers make the first keystrokes as I begin to write the strangest chapter of — quite literally — my life.

9

Marie

Just before I finish chapter 1, I hear the chirp
that alerts me to new E-mail. Immediately, I
divert into that program to see if any help
has arrived — a private eye on her white
horse, or a criminologist on hers.

Yes! Here's one from my private investigator, Erin McDermit.

In person, Erin doesn't look like anybody's stereotype of a female private eye.
It's true that she's athletic — nearly six
feet tall in the black running shoes she always wears with her trademark black
pantsuits (even in the subtropics) — but
she's a thin woman, a blonde with a cover
girl complexion who doesn't look as if
she could possibly be as strong as her
résumé hints she is. It lists her years as a
police officer, several black belts in a
martial art, exceptional firearms prowess,
and degrees in law and accounting. I

originally hired Erin because she struck me as being as smart as the computer jocks who staff her office for corporate investigative work and as tough as most of the ex-cops she hires to do her dirty work, now that she can afford to remain above the fray and just administrate. I don't know if she's honest, if all of her methods are legal, or ethical. When it comes to PIs, I'm a don't-ask, don't-tell kinda gal. I do know her firm is one of the best in south Florida, in a highly competitive, sometimes even lethal business. If she has ever overcharged me, it would take an accountant who's smarter than I am to prove it, and even then, I'd probably still feel she gave me my money's worth.

It's an air of latent violence in Erin, a feeling she inspires that here is a woman who would do literally anything to accomplish her ends, that makes me wonder about her. To be frank, it's also why I keep hiring her.

I've rarely seen Erin McDermit in the flesh; we conduct most of our business electronically. But I believe I could spot her anywhere, even from a long city block away, because of her height, her long stride, and that Johnny Cash outfit, not to mention the old-fashioned pageboy, and the way she sticks her hands deep into the pockets of her suit jackets, as if she's got guns in both of them. There's a definite Wyatt Earp flavor to Erin. The few times I have been around her, I've always been struck by how when she sits down she habitually turns her face to the person who's doing the talking, but she turns her legs toward the nearest exit. Now there's a telling detail I'll put in a book if I ever need to include a description of her.

Not surprisingly, when she talks, it's blunt.

As I peruse her E-mail, it's what she says, not how she says it, that takes me aback.

"What an asshole!" her E-mail begins.

Hey, it's probably just some harmless idiot getting his rocks off, but let me see if I can trace anything from the E-mail. Do you want me to assign somebody to watch your house 24/7? No charge. My pleasure. You've given me lots of business doing all those background checks for your books.

I'll get back to you asap on the E-mails.

In the meantime, personally, if it were

me, what the hell, just to be on the safe side, I'd do exactly what the little shit head says.

Cheers, Erin

Well, *shit*, to quote Erin. She was supposed to tell me it's all baloney, not offer a twenty-four-hour watch on my house as if this might all be legit! Damn!

Maybe there will be better news in the next E-mail, from Dr. Aileen Rasmussen. As I start reading, I can picture Aileen vividly, too — seventyish, letting her hair go gray, carrying thirty pounds more than are good for her five feet four inches and looking deceptively motherly. She's a "mother," all right, but not in that glorified sense of the word.

The good Dr. Rasmussen's E-mail is equally succinct, but unlike Erin's it makes the blood pound in my head from annoyance.

Marie. Male. Control freak. Intelligent. Organized. Determined.

She has a phony, staccato way of communicating that makes me want to scream, "Subject, verb, object! Aileen! Try it sometime!"

Her E-mail continues:

Cold-blooded enough to display a sick sense of humor. Sexually focused on you. Angry at you for some reason. A grievance? What did you do to him? Combination of all that worries me. Don't you have any idea who he is? My advice? Take him seriously. Be very careful in regard to the children. See me. Soon as poss. When?

Aileen

Right, like I haven't thought about being careful with the children. Do I have *moron* tattooed on my forehead? Thanks so much for that useful tip, Aileen. And, don't I "have any idea who he is?" Well, gee, if I did, I might have mentioned that in my E-mail to you, don't you think so? "What did you do to him?" Oh, yeah, thanks, Aileen, blame the victim.

Damn, again. *Victim?* That would be me.

I take the repeated, calming deep breaths I often have to take before replying to Aileen Rasmussen. Just to be on the safe side, so I won't say anything overly snide to her, I write back to Erin McDermit first, telling the private investigator, "Yes, thanks, I'd like you to source the E-mails and to stake that watchdog outside my house. Wait until Monday to do it, since I'm going to be gone until then anyway." (If I were Aileen, I'd probably insult Erin McDermit by advising her to make sure her operative stays invisible, as if a pro needs to be instructed like a student in Private Investigation 101. One of these days, I'm really going to let Aileen Rasmussen have it between her smug eyes. If I ever find somebody better. Please, God.) "You're awfully kind to offer to do it for free, Erin, but I've got to turn that down. This is a bigger job than I deserve to get for free. I also want you to put a watchdog, your very best, on my assistant, Deborah Dancer. . . ." I give her Deb's vitals. "You'll have to be the one to tell Deb we're doing this, since I don't dare contact her directly right now." Then I write, "In fact, I'd like you to relay messages between us," but I immediately delete it. Maybe this computer is secure — Erin's own experts did that for me — but what if it isn't? I'll take that chance for myself, but not for Deb. If Erin says to do what he wants, and what he wants is to separate me from Deborah, then I'll stay completely away —

unless and until I find an absolutely fool-proof way to get around him.

I finish by saying, "Ain't this a hell of a way to spend your time & my money?

"Thanks.

"Marie."

My heavily self-censored E-mail to Aileen Rasmussen reads like this:

We're taking the kids away with us this weekend. Should be safe. "Paulie Barnes" says he won't hurt anybody as long as I follow his instructions, so that's what I am doing. I think we'll be all right for a while, don't you? I do want to see you when I get back. Is Monday okay? Send me a time that works for you, and I'll show up then. Thanks, Aileen.

Marie

There. Why do I keep going back to this woman for my research into criminal psychology if she aggravates me so much? Okay, she's good, but wouldn't *half*-good do almost as well? Or maybe I just like being repeatedly poked with a stick.

While I'm still pissed off from the effort of writing politely to Aileen, I return to the task of putting the finishing touches on the first "chapter" of my "assignment." By the time I finish and come out of the writer's trance, I find that the ice has melted in my glass of tea. The sun is almost directly overhead, and I am sweating in my open house. I see through my screen door that a seagull is swaggering on top of my patio table, leaving me souvenirs as he scavenges for crumbs.

It's one o'clock and Franklin hasn't called me back yet.

"Isn't he out of court?" I ask his secretary when I call again.

"Oh, that devil." Arvida laughs. "I heard he slipped out as soon as the gavel came down. I guess he knew if he came back here I'd hand him more work to do. Y'all are going to the Keys today, right?"

Great. And who else knows?

I tell her yeah, and she tells me to have fun.

There's no answer, next, on Franklin's cell phone, but then if he is already in the car with Diana and Arthur, he won't pick it up. His ex-wife forbids him to use a phone when he's driving them.

I'm sure they're fine. I'm sure of it.

But I'd like to see for myself. There's just enough time left for me to eat lunch, pack for my trip to the Keys, and hit

Send. When I do, I feel a welling up of helpless rage in me.

"How *dare* you, Paulie Barnes."

Forget "how dare he." Who *is* he?

Years ago when my first book came out and I got my first obscene letter, I took it to a cop. "Hang on to this stuff, Marie," he said, "so you'll have evidence if you need it."

"I don't want to hang on to it," I protested. "I want to burn it."

"I know. Listen, most of these guys, they're creeps who don't have the balls to do what they say, but there's always the stray psychopath you have to watch out for."

Thinking of that advice now, I pull out that file of nasty mail and put it in a canvas briefcase. To that, I add paperback copies of each of my books so we can review who's in them. Maybe there's a disgruntled relative in there or, more likely, a killer who hates the way I portrayed him. Next, I stick in three file folders packed with information about murder cases I have considered but rejected as book ideas. I haven't looked inside a couple of them for so long that they give off that old-file smell of dust and mold. It is not beyond the realm of strange possibility that some egotistical murderer in there feels unfairly "left out" of my true crime hit parade.

"Egotistical murderer," I grumble. "Now there's a redundancy if I ever heard one." Finally, I slide into the brief-case the "evidence" I've wrapped in plastic. In my mind, I keep wrapping the word *evidence* in quotation marks because I'm not even positive that any crime has been committed against me. I know it's a federal offense to make threats through the mail, I don't know about E-mail or package delivery services, and I don't want to take the time to look that up, not when I've got my own personal prose-cutor to ask.

Once all that's done, I start tossing clothing and toiletries into an overnight bag. I won't need much in the Keys — clean underwear, shorts, T-shirts, a swim-suit, sunscreen and deodorant, and that's about it. At the last minute, I fold in a pearly, silky bathrobe that's pretty but modest. With the children there to see us, Franklin and I won't be able to run around naked anymore.

"Great." In a spasm of self-pity, I grumble some more. "I was already ner-vous enough about spending a whole weekend with them, and now I have to worry about this, too."

The Howard County prosecutor and I have been carryin' on for more than a year, but we only went public a little while ago. Very public, as it turned out, complete with articles in glossy magazines and tabloids, although why they're so interested in either of us escapes me. *People* magazine called us "the glamorous best-selling writer and her handsome true crime chaser." Puhleeze. Yuck. The phone calls I got after that one! I got teased by people I hadn't heard from since high school. "Marie! Where'd you get *him?*" They did everything but squeal oo la la. That was all right. The worst part was that unbeknownst to us at the time, a couple of publications snapped photos that included the children. I can still recall the unpleasant jolt I felt when I opened a magazine and saw that! We would never have approved of it if they'd had the decency to ask first — which is why they didn't ask first, of course.

Bringing Arthur and Diana into our relationship is proving to be a slow, delicate process, even without invasive photos appearing all over the world. Franklin's little boy likes me, judging from the way he flings himself at me whenever he sees me, yelling, "M're! M're!" But Diana is holding back, suspicious and resentful of this woman who is not her mom. Whatever limited natural charm I may have, it sure isn't doing the trick with her; I'm at a loss for ideas about how to win her over, or even if it's right to try. Maybe we made a mistake in bringing the kids into the middle of our romance. Maybe it was too soon, at least for Diana. On the other hand, it's possible there will never be a good time for her.

Sometimes I worry — what if we all get attached to one another — the kids and I — and then Franklin and I break up? I'm already besotted with Arthur. The thought of never seeing that cutie pie again — never mind his father — makes me tear up. As for Diana, all I can really ever do is be myself and let her be however she needs to be toward me. One of us has to be the adult, I guess, and since she's six years old, that pretty much leaves it to me. Damn.

"Time," Franklin advises me. "Patience."

I thought I had plenty of time, but now I wonder. . . .

"No!" I give the overnight bag a fierce zipping up. "You *won't* hurt us."

My Mercedes is in the shop. Without

Deb here to give me a ride, I'll have to call a taxi. My plan is: I'll pick up my car and drive on down to the Keys from there. And then Franklin will know what to do. He'll eat this guy like guacamole with chips. We'll find this bastard and we'll add 140 years onto whatever sentence he is already serving.

10

Marie

"You know, Marie," says the owner of the foreign car shop as he hands over my keys, "the Germans actually do make Mercedes that are younger than you are."

"No!" I exclaim, feigning disbelief. "Really, Ernie?"

Joking with Ernesto Perez outside his garage makes me feel better; gazing into his well-worn face, I feel safer. The day turns almost normal again. The anxiety about "Paulie Barnes" recedes. It's almost certainly a hoax, I decide again — a prank, much ado about nada.

Here, just off noisy 1-95 near the Bahia airport, the air smells like burnt oil, as it always does. I feel a hot breeze lift the hair at the back of my neck, and I need sunglasses merely to look at my blinding white car. Ernie's shop qualifies for a drought exemption, which is a good thing, as it would kill this man to turn a dirty car back over to its owner. For just a moment, standing in the sunshine shooting the bull with Ernie, I let myself relax into a seductive illusion, one that Florida weaves better than any other state. It's the fantasy that here, if nowhere else in the world, the sun always shines, and none of us have anything to worry about except how to find the shortest way to the nearest beach.

I'm so glad to get my car back; she's been gone three days.

In a wild impulse born of a passion for a white Mercedes 280SL that I saw in front of the Plaza Hotel in New York City, I located a car just like it — a vintage two-door sports coupe with both a hard and soft convertible top. A few months ago, I traded in a sensible sedan to get it. The other price I pay for it is the amusing crap I take from this man who is old enough to be my father and who treats my automotive baby like a pampered grandchild.

"Most people," Ernie says now, warming to his theme, "most people, they drive cars that were born after they were. Not that this isn't a beautiful car, Marie. I certainly agree with you there. I think it's the prettiest car that comes in here, except for those old Jaguars, but they're crap, they're only good for using as caskets or planters."

I have to laugh. I've known a few owners of those.

With every passing second, my worries about "Paulie Barnes" feel increasingly surreal. Out here in the real world, the only attack I have to fear is from salt air and pollution on my precious paint job.

Ernie continues, "And not that I don't like ordering parts for you —"

"I guess not, Ernesto," I shoot back, "since your markups on my replacement parts probably paid for that fancy new sign you've got out front."

"Not quite," he says happily, running a finger over his right eyebrow, "but close. What I like best is when we have to order parts to be specially tooled for you because Mercedes doesn't make them anymore. Then there's overseas shipping, always a pretty penny, franc, or sou, and we have to add a little bit of a surcharge for handling all that repressive paperwork —"

"Oh, that *is* hard on you, Ernesto."

"But listen, Marie, I got a bone to pick with you."

"You do? I swear I haven't neglected an oil change."

"You'd better not." Like a magician with a rabbit, he pulls a glossy magazine out from behind his back and then stubs his right forefinger at it. Thank God it's not the tabloid. "This is you, isn't it?"

I make a show of leaning over to peer at the photographs he means.

"Sure looks like me."

"How come you never told me this was you?"

"What do you mean I never told you?" I tease him. "You know my name. It's attached to my bills and I pay them. Who else could I be?"

"But you never told me you're a famous author!"

"Oh, right, like I want you to know that, Ernesto. Now you'll probably charge me even more for spare parts."

He rubs his chin, looking judicious. "I don't think it would be possible for us to charge you any more than we already do."

"Oh, well, that's a relief," I joke.

Ernie laughs with all the pleasure of a man who knows he makes a nice net profit, but then he waves the magazine at me again. "It says here you write those true crime books. How can you stand to write about that awful stuff?"

"You mean, what's a nice girl like me doing writing about serial killers?"

"Yeah, why do you do that?"

I smile at him. "I have to, to be able to afford you, Ernesto."

"Right," he snorts. He points to the magazine pictures again. "This is your boyfriend, huh?"

I tense, feeling that maybe we have just arrived at the real point of this conversation. "Yep."

"People ever give you problems about that, Marie?"

"You mean because Franklin's black and I'm not?"

"No," he says, scornfully, "I mean because he's a lawyer. Of course, because he's black! People ever say things to you, either of you?"

"Not really," I tell him, cautiously. "Why? Are you going to?"

He gives me a disgusted look. "I got a black son-in-law."

"You do?"

That earns me a second disgusted look. "What do you think I am, a bigot, or something? Hell, I got no prejudices, I'll even work on British cars! Marie, I got two grandchildren with the prettiest skin you ever saw. They look like they were made of butterscotch. I could just eat them up. Wanna see a picture?" At my encouraging nod, Ernie drops the magazine to the ground at his feet and digs into his back pocket for his wallet, from where he flashes a small photograph of adorable children.

"Oh, Ernie!" I gush.

He beams for a second, but then he says, as he puts his wallet back in his pocket, "I just worry sometimes, is everybody going to be nice to them? That doesn't make me a bigot, does it?"

"Not in my book, Ernesto. But, listen, is everybody always nice to you?"

He thinks about that, then laughs. "Hell no."

"Anyway, the world's changing."

"You think?"

As proof, I point at my own picture on the ground. "Looks that way."

"Bet you get some nasty mail though."

I feel a painful inner flinch, as if he has applied a tiny electrical shock to my heart. In the second afterward, I feel sick. I have to swallow bile before asking, "Why do you say that, Ernesto?"

His mouth arcs down again, only this time with no humor in it. "World may be changing, but there are still plenty of jerks in it. Those jerks see pictures like that of you and him they might think it's their job to pull the world back to uglier times when they liked things better. Aw, listen to me, a philosopher with a lug wrench. I don't know anything about that, but I'll tell you what I do know, Marie." He waves a hand over my car without touching it. "Pretty soon you won't even be able to claim this as an antique car. It'll be so completely overhauled, not even the doors will be original equipment."

"Then I'll sell it as new."

The joke is older than the car, but he chuckles at it anyway.

Ernie gallantly opens the driver's door of my little convertible and bows low to me as I drop in behind the wheel. Because of the drought, I haven't raised either top in weeks. Rain is rare as an empty beach; sometimes I'm afraid that rain has become extinct in Florida, like fifty-eight kinds of tree snail already are. Still, I have to admit that, like a teenager, I love driving with the top down. I even got my hair chopped short so it can ruffle in the hot wind without whipping into my eyes.

"Happy trails to you, Marie," Ernie sings, his usual farewell, "until we meet again."

"Which probably won't be long," I sigh, for his amusement.

"I'm counting on it."

We grin at each other and then I flip him a wave as I pull away.

"The hell with you, Paulie Barnes," I declare as I turn my coupe south toward the Keys. I feel better now. I reach over and adjust the visor on the passenger's side to block the sun that's now on my right side. "I'm on vacation and you're not invited. Crawl back under whatever rock you call home."

Oh, my car runs so nice. The steering wheel, covered in tan leather, feels so good and familiar under my fingers.

"Bless you, Ernesto, and all of your grandchildren's children."

Half of Florida must be going to the Keys this weekend, judging from the traffic on the highways. I jockey for a place in the seemingly endless line of vehicles heading south. Franklin, Diana, and Arthur expect me to arrive at our rental condo on Key Largo by four-thirty for an early dinner. From only brief experience, I already know that the nervous systems of children are wired for regular feedings. Delay that and you pay a stiff price in whining. Since their father will be the only adult with them until I arrive, he'll be the one to suffer if I'm late. Out of sympathy for him and for their stomachs, I choose the straightest — if not the prettiest — shot into the archipelago known as the Florida Keys.

The one I'm headed for is Key Largo, an island at the top of the scorpion's tail that ends at Key West. Once on the Keys, which are a series of islands connected by the spectacular Overseas Highway, there are only two roads going north if you need to escape a hurricane, or get to the mainland in a hurry. There's no hurricane or even a tropical storm in the forecast, unless I count the symbolic "storm" that Paulie Barnes thinks he's brewing in our lives. In these circumstances, I can't say that I'm crazy about the idea of going where it can be difficult to leave, but I know that if all else fails, we can always rent a boat and sail away.

That would mean leaving my car, though. I'd be *really* pissed about that.

Traffic is bumper to bumper, a huge clot of rush hour and weekend travelers going nowhere fast. Too late, I realize I made a mistake by leaving my car top down. At this speed there's no breeze, the heat's ferocious, and it's no pleasure to idle behind semitrailers and be deafened by motorcycles streaking between lanes. I feel as if I'm eating exhaust as well as inhaling it. What was I thinking? I wasn't, apparently. "This is your fault, too," I grumble to the pseud-onymous Paulie Barnes. "You distract me and make me do crazy things." I reach over to the glove box and fish around until I find an old but edible mint to pop in my mouth and a floppy-brimmed hat to plop on my head to shade my face and the back of my neck.

Most sane people would hate these con-ditions, but as a true Florida fanatic, I am no more than slightly annoyed by the state's drawbacks, by its tourists, its flying cockroaches, its traffic. I'd be willing to put up with much worse than that for the priv-ilege of living in this state where I'm never more than a few hours away from sun-shine, or a few miles from the water.

But even I have to admit it doesn't look so beautiful here and now.

Around Homestead, the smoking rem-nants of brush fires have turned the air acrid and the scenery bleak. Everywhere I look, dead, blackened trees pierce a smoky sky. Only last week, a fifty-mile stretch of both of the roads into the Keys was closed off and on for three days by fires that burned out of control until they sizzled themselves into the Florida Bay.

While I'm idling behind stalled traffic, I try again to raise Franklin by cell phone.

Surely they've had time to reach Key Largo by now.

All I get is his recorded voice, so they're either still in the car going somewhere, or maybe they're out swimming.

"They're fine," I tell myself.

But it makes me want to be with him. Right now.

What could feel safer than being in the company of the Howard County state attorney? Franklin will know what to do next, and he'll do it. How should *I* know what to do about a psycho pen pal? I'm just a writer, even if I do know a bit more about crimes and solving them than most writers do. But still, I'm only a writer. Franklin's the one who will know how to handle this situation: God knows, he's in charge of practically everything else involving criminal activity in Howard County. Personally, I can't even imagine bearing so much responsibility for so many people, and yet he carries it off with panache, if not always with pleasure.

Feeling a strong need to hear his voice, I try his cell number again and again, like a teenager with a crush, but I just keep getting the recorded message.

I don't leave one of my own, except to say, "I'm on my way."

What else can I say, to a recording machine that he might play out loud for anyone to overhear? *"Hi, honey. We're being stalked by a psycho maniac killer who has threatened your children if I don't do what he says. See you soon. Bye. Love, Me."*

Yeah, right. What I want to say to his recording is, "Dammit, where are you guys? Aren't you there yet?"

I will not worry about them, I try to convince myself.

But the rush hour traffic is giving me way too much time to imagine terrible things happening to Franklin and his kids. Plus, I get spooked when strange men in other cars throw appraising glances at me, and then feel foolish when they drive on by. Not only do I have too much time to think, I obviously have way too much imagination. I use it to picture how very silly I'm going to feel when I have to call Deb's friends and family to say, "I thought we were in danger. I panicked. It was nothing." I also have too much time to wonder if Ernie was right; maybe there is a racial motive to the E-mails in my suitcase. There hasn't been a single hint of that in the messages. But, still, maybe that recent spurt of publicity has triggered this nutcase to write to me —

"Enough already!"

I feel confident that no one around me will pay the slightest attention to a woman yelling at herself and slamming her steering wheel with the palm of her hand. If they notice me at all, they'll think it's road rage, and avoid me.

I'm sick of worrying the problem to death in my mind.

"I need music. A talk show. Something to distract me. Anything."

I glance down at the old-fashioned dashboard that Ernie's guys have delicately reconfigured to accommodate more modern appurtenances, though it horrified the antique car purists among them. Nevertheless, I got my way and now I have a CD player, a push-button radio, a tape deck.

I push On, expecting to get National Public Radio.

A man's voice, deep and somber, reverberates out of the speaker closest to me.

"Cape Fear," the voice says. "By John D. MacDonald."

If the traffic weren't already at a dead halt, I'd be slamming on my brakes at the shock of hearing those words coming out of nowhere.

"What?"

That's no radio program and it's no "coincidence," either.

Wildly, with my heart beating overtime, I punch buttons, searching for Eject. The radio/tape/CD system in this car operates so that if there's a cassette in the slot, that's what comes on when you push On. If there's a CD in it, that's what you hear. Otherwise, you get the radio. So this has got to be a tape or a CD that somebody has placed in my car, and they've pushed it all the way in so that when I punched On, it would instantly begin to play.

Damn him, he has jumped out of the bushes again!

Sure enough, a tape slides out of the slot.

This time, though, even with my adrenaline racing, I remember: fingerprints. Before I grab it, I get a tissue out of my purse and use that to protect the surface of the cassette.

I hold up the tape to try to read its label in the glaring sunshine.

In my haste, I fumble and nearly drop it.

"Damn it, damn it, damn it!"

Just then, the traffic begins to move again, and I have to look away from the tape in order to keep up with the other cars. Finally, by maneuvering my steering wheel with one hand and the tape with the other, I'm able to read the label on it.

What I see there gives me such stomach-dropping chills that I might as well be riding a roller coaster instead of a highway: *Cape Fear*, by John D. MacDonald, the label says. It's tape one, side one, of a recording of the mystery novel originally known as *The Executioners*.

My heart jolts as it did when I read the E-mail that mentioned Franklin's children, even harder than it did when Ernie asked me if I get any weird mail.

Against my will, I jump to the obvious and horrible conclusion.

"You've been in my car. You rotten son of a bitch, you've been in my car. When did you *do* it? *How* did you do this?"

My car was at Ernie's shop for three days.

There was plenty of time.

11

Marie

For several miles, it's all I can do just to breathe.

When my heart rate returns to relative normal, I am angry all over again.

"Move!" I scream at the cars ahead of me. And then an infuriating thought occurs to me: *He'll want me to write this all down for him. My reactions to finding the tape. How I feel driving into Key Largo. How I tell Franklin about this, how he responds to this news.*

I start creating paragraphs in my head as I go, not because I want to, but as an attempt to regain some objectivity. I'll never be able to think clearly if I can't detach myself from the fear and loathing that I'm feeling now.

How will I write it, if I have to, if he forces me to?

"Here's how, you repellent little voyeur," I whisper.

By the time I pull into Key Largo, I have several whole scenes written in my head, most of it made up out of whole cloth, scenes that purposefully portray me as frightened, vulnerable, and obedient. I'll pretend to give him what he wants. I'll make him think exactly what he wants to think.

I feel especially, perversely proud of chapter 2, which reads like a true crime potboiler, if I do say so myself. . . .

When Marie finally reached the outskirts of Key Largo, it was only 4:20 p.m. It's a damn good thing it's daytime, she thought, since she was feeling thoroughly spooked. If she'd had to arrive at night, she'd be even more scared than she already was.

The farther south she'd traveled since discovering the terrifying cassette in her tape deck, the more the Keys began to feel like an all-too appropriate destination for all of them — for her, for Franklin and his children. Here, atop this fragile string of fossilized coral that was strung like a necklace between the Atlantic Ocean and the Gulf of Mexico, Marie felt "endangered," herself, just like the Keys, the only coral reefs in America. They were one of a kind. Just like her, like Franklin, Deborah, the children, like any human being. The Keys were in perpetual danger of destruction; its creatures were in danger of extinction. Just like her.

After the tape, it was a whole lot easier to believe the worst was possible.

It took Marie fifteen frustrating, frightening minutes to follow Franklin's written directions and the map he'd drawn for her. It led her to a barely perceptible driveway that turned straight off Highway 1 onto a single-lane road that wound through a stand of thick, beautiful forest. There, in the woods, the sunshine disappeared and the day turned instantly cooler.

Marie almost wished she hadn't turned in here, because it was too dark all of a sudden, too shadowy. She caught a whiff of something rotting — old leaves, perhaps, left to decay on the floor of the forest. It was totally silent back in here, save for the purr of her car's engine. Highway 1 could have been miles away, instead of mere yards behind her.

She drove in deeper, feeling increasingly isolated and uneasy.

But then, back farther among the tall, arching trees, she found a remarkable condominium complex — a series of interlocking redwood buildings set so elegantly among the foliage that no unit was completely visible from the road. It was private and quiet back in here, which might have delighted her some *other time, but not now! On this weekend, she'd have preferred a hotel room in a crowded tourist trap where there might be witnesses to anything that happened and to any stranger who lurked by their room.*

Even when she spotted Franklin's black Acura, it wasn't enough to reassure her.

She had to know they were all right, and she had to know it now.

Marie parked hurriedly in the empty slot beside the Acura.

Without even stopping to grab her luggage, she rushed out of her car, desperate to see them, to find them, to touch them, to make sure they were all right. Breathlessly, nearly sobbing in her urgency, she raced up the steps leading to the unit.

Its front door was wide open, as if somebody had just gone in, or out.

Oh, my God, she thought, please, please —
"Franklin? Arthur? Diana?"

"Marie!" Franklin smiles a welcome at me. At the same time, he gives his daughter a thwak on the top of her head, but so gently that it barely moves her beaded braids. "See? I told you she'd get here on time."

"Ow, Dad, that hurt!"

"I barely touched you."

183

"It still hurt! Don't hit my braids, okay?"

Over six-year-old Diana's head, out of her line of vision, her father makes a face at me. "Okay. I'm sorry. I won't."

There they are, looking surprised at my sudden entrance, but also looking alive, healthy, perfectly normal, right down to the resentment on Diana's pretty little face.

"Traffic bad?" Franklin asks me.

I can only nod, yes.

"M're! M're!"

"Hi, Arthur!" I manage to get out only the two words before Franklin's three-year-old son leaps into my arms, knocking out what little breath I have left in my chest. I am still no more than a couple of feet into the living room, and now I stagger back under his weight, and he and I both laugh. Arthur grabs both sides of my face with his chubby hands and plants a sloppy kiss on my mouth. I hang on to him for dear life, hugging his hot, sweaty, smelly little body until he squirms to get down. Down on the floor, Arthur grins up at me, and shouts, "Hi, M're!" into my face, as if I were still miles away.

Looking into his sweet face, I realize I would do anything to protect him.

"We were just leaving you a note so you could find us, Marie."

I look up at Franklin then. With a relaxed smile on his handsome face, and dressed in red shorts, a yellow T-shirt, and huaraches, he hardly resembles a tough prosecutor. He just looks like a daddy and boyfriend.

"I found you," I say, inadequately, knowing it must sound stupid.

We met each other over the expanse of his desk when I interviewed him for a book I was writing about a murder case he prosecuted. Franklin DeWeese was only two weeks divorced at that time, and at first I fought the attraction for that reason alone. I didn't want to be anybody's rebound romance. We were also both concerned about possible conflicts of interest until I finished writing about his case. But the attraction between us was too seductive to resist. At the beginning, I thought it was all for fun; but here we are, and my heart is swelling at the mere sight of his son's beaming face.

Franklin cocks his head at me, as if to ask, Something wrong?

"Hi, kids," I say. "Did you get my message, Franklin?"

"Are you kidding?" He looks wryly down at his daughter. "I have been firmly instructed to leave the phone unplugged and my work at home." But then, as he looks back up at me, his expression changes, because he has apparently sensed something in my tone of voice, in my face. "Why?"

I smile, because I don't know what else to do, and because I can't blurt it all out in front of his children. "I heard from our friend again."

His expression hardens instantly. "Is everything all right?"

"What friend?" Diana wants to know.

"Somebody you don't know, honey," I tell her. And to her father, I just say, "Yes, I think so."

"What did he say this time?"

I glance meaningfully at the kids. "I'll tell you later."

Arthur holds up an insistent hand for me to grasp, and I take it. I'm not at all sure which of the two of us needs it more.

I once described Franklin DeWeese in a book I wrote in which he was a feature player: Forty years old at the time, five foot eleven inches tall, approximately 170 well-toned pounds. As state attorney for Howard County, he is the chief prosecutor for the twenty-first judicial district. He is a Democrat who beguiles conservative Republicans by being fiercely pro–death penalty, a perverse position for a black man, in my opinion, but never mind. We argue about it, rarely conceding any points to each other. He runs a main office and five satellite offices with a staff of assistant prosecutors, paralegals, secretaries, and other administrative personnel, numbering between 400 to 450 persons at any given time. He is in charge of prosecuting or defending all suits or civil or criminal motions on behalf of Florida in the county where we both live. That means, all felonies, misdemeanors, criminal traffic and juvenile cases as well as some civil cases. From arrest through arraignment, discovery, depositions, motion recovery, pretrial hearings, and the appellate process, my very own Franklin — Diana and Arthur's daddy — supervises it all, including special requests for the empanelment of grand juries.

What a guy? I sure think so.

Plus, he was the oldest and beloved son, a football star in high school, attended good colleges, was editor of his law review, married and divorced, had two children.

His résumé, in my book, reads like the perfect prosecutor.

Franklin's not perfect, not even close, but he'll do for now.

Being a state attorney will never make

this man wealthy, not as my work does for me. Franklin has to get reelected every four years just to keep his job. And while it may lead him to higher office someday, or become a stepping-stone to private practice, I believe he stays with it because he still likes to feel like somebody's hero. The electorate's. A victim's. A suffering family's. His assistants', who idolize him. As for me, the brutal truth is, I don't even particularly like prosecutors as a breed, finding most of them too dogmatic and punitive for my taste. Show me a law student with black-and-white opinions and I'll show you a future DA. And yet here is one of them, looking tall and handsome, stalwart and honorable, just like a hero.

"What's the matter, Marie?"

"Not a thing," I lie, and hide my face by smiling down at Arthur.

From several careful yards away, Diana asks sullenly, "Can we eat now, Dad?"

At that moment I look from one to the other of them — daughter, son, father — all of them as deliciously, naturally brown as caramelized sugar on top of a crème brûlée — and I silently vow not to wreak havoc in their lives. In that, if in very little else, their mother and I are surely in perfect accord.

Since I don't know what else to do at the moment, I squeeze Arthur's hand, grin at the unsmiling face of his sister, and say, "Yeah, Dad, what are you waiting for? I'm starved, let's eat!"

Arthur, who adores my car, begs to ride to dinner in it.

"You can't," Diana tells him. "Mom says convertibles are dangerous."

"Please!"

"Sure," his father says. "Diana, you can ride with me."

"I get to go with *Dad*," she says, turning defeat into triumph.

Since the Mercedes only holds two people, we do drive both cars. Franklin and Diana lead the way in their black Acura, while Arthur and I happily follow behind, singing "Polly Wolly Doodle" at the top of our lungs. I taught him that, along with "Oh, What a Beautiful Morning," which we never ever sing any later than noon.

The road back to the highway doesn't seem so shadowy now.

12

Marie

After dinner at a family-style seafood restaurant we go back to the condo to watch a video of *The Lion King*, while munching popcorn that I concoct from supplies they've brought with them. Dinner didn't satisfy our appetites. Any of them. Behind the couch, the grown-ups intertwine their fingers every secret chance they get; Franklin rubs his middle finger into my palm suggestively, over and over, until I think I'm going to have to jump his bones right there in front of the kids.

I sublimate by eating too much popcorn. There isn't a moment when the kids aren't underfoot, not a second when the adults can talk. I can't even ask Franklin to take a walk with me. The children are far too young to leave unattended, especially in a strange condo, particularly one that's only a short walk away from deep water.

Every time we have two minutes alone for a whispered conversation, one of the kids bounds in to interrupt us. Diana, especially, clings to her father, demanding his attention whenever he turns toward me.

Finally, Arthur's head is nodding and his sister is quietly curled up on her father's lap, humming along with the songs. Out of sheer desperation, I run upstairs and grab the E-mails and my "assignment" out of my luggage.

If I can't tell him about it, maybe he can read it.

Back on the couch, I pass to Franklin the E-mails from last night and today.

"Read these, please."

Diana stirs. "What's that, Daddy?"

"Legal stuff," I tell her.

"Daddy! You said you wouldn't work this weekend!"

"I won't." He smiles down at his daughter, gently twists a beaded braid around his fingers. "But I've seen this movie a million times. Just let me read this, okay? And then I'll put it down."

"Okay," she says, but grumpily.

I observe Franklin as he begins to read, watch his face as a crease appears between his eyes, see the corners of his mouth drop down. He stares over at me, looking alarmed. I point at it to keep him reading. "When did you get these?" he asks me, sharply enough this time to make his daughter demand, "Dad! Stop reading that!"

"Diana," he says, "watch the movie."

"Last night," I tell him, quietly, and then I hand over to him the second E-mail and my finished "assignment." "And this morning. And here's what I wrote in response to it."

Without taking her gaze from the TV screen, Diana wants to know, "Is that a legal case for Marie, Dad?"

"Sort of, Pumpkin."

"Do you have to do it?" When he doesn't answer her, she presses, "Do you, Dad?"

"Do I what, Pumpkin?"

"Do you have to do this legal case for Marie?"

"It's not like that, Diana."

"What is it like?"

"It's like —" Franklin looks at me over her head, and the expression in his eyes speaks silent volumes of shared shock and anger. Behind the couch, his hand squeezes mine so hard I wince. I feel an enormous relief to have finally told him, to be able to share the responsibility with him, even though I would give anything if he weren't involved in such a horrible, threatening way. But what Franklin says to his daughter in the mildest of tones is, "It's like, as soon as I finish reading this, it will be time for us to feed popcorn to the fishes."

"But, Dad, it's night! They're sleeping."

"Nobody sleeps through popcorn, not even fishes."

Even Arthur hears that and, struggling to come awake, asks, "Are we really going to feed the fishes? I want to feed the fishes!"

Franklin pops a fat kernel into his son's mouth and then one into his daughter's mouth, and that takes care of any more questions for a while, except for one Diana asks her father when he takes her hand to lead her outside.

"Does Marie have to come?"

Soon, we're all four seated side by side on a wooden dock, our bare feet dangling down. The darkness, the caressing air, the gentle murmur of water lapping against the pilings — and the stern warnings from their father not to make any noise and wake the other condo residents — have all worked magic on the children. Even Arthur is really quiet now, squealing only a little bit whenever fish break the surface of the water to nibble the popcorn we toss in.

I look over their heads into their father's eyes.

His preoccupied expression tells me that his prosecutor's brain is already working on our problem, but there's also a kind of peacefulness in his face, as there is on the children's and which I feel on mine, too. Right now, there's no arguing, no resentment, no apparent danger; there's only the four of us, peaceful and quiet.

Without a word, Franklin points up at the sky.

I look, and see a full moon just emerging from behind clouds; it's spectacularly orange and huge, and my breath catches at the sight of it.

"What?" Diana wants to know, hearing me.

Franklin taps his daughter's shoulder and, still without saying anything, points up for her to see, too.

"Wow! Is that the moon, Daddy?"

Her father strokes her back. "Sure is."

"Where? Where?" her brother demands.

"Up in the sky, you Dumbo!"

"You're the Dumbo, Dumbo, Dumbo!" Arthur chants, making a funny face and an even funnier voice that makes us all, even his sister, laugh. But when Arthur finally sees the moon, his jaw drops and his eyes widen. "That's not the moon, that's the sun!"

"No, it's really the moon," I assure him.

"Awesome," Diana breathes.

I feel Arthur's little body stiffen beside me. "What's that?"

"What's what, Arthur?" his dad asks, still looking up.

"I hear a whale, Daddy!"

We all become very still again, trying to hear what he means.

"I don't hear anything," I admit.

"I do!" Diana exclaims. "Listen, Daddy, it's over there!"

Franklin and I turn our heads to the north-northwest, toward the Florida Bay and the Gulf of Mexico. And then we hear it, too, the engine of a boat, coming closer. In the incredibly still night, it sounds unnaturally loud now. I feel my heart begin to pound uncomfortably fast. Franklin swings his feet back up on the dock and, without even using his hands, shoots to his feet so that he can stare into the distance.

"What's the matter, Daddy? Is it a whale, like Arthur said?"

"No, honey, it's a boat."

Between us, the children relax. It's just a

boat. A boat is no big deal to them. They're children of south Florida, as accustomed to seeing boats as other children are to seeing cars and trucks.

The sound seems to be coming straight at us.

In the northern sky, a thunderstorm is moving into the Miami area north and east of us. The storm's too far away for us to hear thunder, but we can see lightning illuminating clouds in a spectacular light show that sets the children to oohing and aahing. Their father remains standing, continuing to keep a lookout over the water, listening to the approaching motor.

As the boat nears us, I stand up, too.

"Let's go in, Franklin."

Both children object with loud no's.

"Shh!" Their father puts out a hand toward them to quiet them, and then to me, as if to say, Not yet. Wait.

"Franklin, I really think we need to go in."

And still he stands there, staring into the distance, listening.

"Come on, kids." I hold down my hands to them, wanting to grab them and run to safety with them. Wild images race through my mind: bombs thrown, explosions, shots fired, bodies falling, children crying, blood flowing. Arthur obediently places one of his small hands into mine, but Diana looks up at her father and sees that he isn't going anywhere. She mulishly refuses my hand. "Come on, Diana!"

She folds her little arms across her chest, hiding her hands.

"Franklin, please!"

And then, just a moment before I detect it, Franklin hears the boat engine turn away from our direction. I see the change, in a relaxation of his shoulders. Only then do I actually hear the shift of sound.

"They've turned north," he observes.

We form a tableau for a moment, all four of us quite still, even the children, waiting to be sure that what he said is true.

"Yes," I agree, but I continue to help Arthur get to his bare feet anyway.

"Why are your hands all shaky, M're?"

"The better to tickle you with." I make good on the fib. When he squeals as loud as a piglet at play, his sister hisses at Arthur and me, "Shh! Dad said to be quiet!"

Meanwhile, the sound of the boat engine vanishes into the distance. It wasn't anything to do with us. I feel as relieved as if a hurricane had veered off course and passed us by. But now I also have to admit something to myself: after this, I won't be able to pretend, not even to myself, that I'm not frightened.

"Why is Marie afraid of boats, Daddy?"

"She's not, Pumpkin." Franklin reaches down a hand to Diana, and she lets him pull her up to her feet. "It's just time for all of us to go to bed, that's all." With his free hand, he briefly spans the back of my neck, touching me reassuringly.

Franklin carries his tired boy and Diana hangs on to his waistband, sleepily trailing behind. Having refused my offer of a hand to hold, she now clings closer and closer to her daddy's legs, until he reaches around and scoots her forward so that he can guide her back home without tripping on her, or making her stumble.

I trail behind, carrying the empty popcorn bowl, eating the old maids, and feeling plenty sorry for myself.

As we walk back "home," I admire the picture they form together. I feel terrible for bringing a snake into their precious lives. And I'm determined not to be a jerk about Diana's rejection of me. The child is naturally and admirably loyal to her mother, and she's scared of losing her daddy to a woman she hardly knows and doesn't even like. God knows I don't blame her — I lost my daddy, too — but it still hurts a little, every time she does it.

Whenever Franklin brings the children and me together, he gives Diana a little private talking-to beforehand, coaching her to give me a chance, asking her — telling her — to be polite, at least. It hasn't worked yet, although I shudder to think how much more rude the child might be if he didn't do that much. I have asked Franklin not to apologize for his daughter's behavior and not to punish her for disliking me. "Patience," I throw back at him, when he's embarrassed or worried about his daughter's bad manners. "Time."

"Why do you think Arthur has accepted me so quickly?" I asked Franklin one time. He grinned a little shamefacedly and admitted, "Arthur's a guy. He likes pretty women and cool cars."

I had to laugh at that. "Like father, like son?"

"And," Franklin had added, "Arthur's got an easygoing nature. Diana's more high-strung. She gets mad and then she wants to get even, just like her mother."

Like her mother, my eye.

The child's a born prosecutor.

Like father, like daughter, too.

★ ★ ★

When Franklin hoists the kids to his shoulders to carry them upstairs to bed, he mouths at me, "I'll be back."

After half an hour goes by, I realize that I'm not hearing any more noise from upstairs. I climb up to investigate and find them all asleep together in a pile on the master bed. The book that Franklin was reading to them — *Goodnight Moon* — lays open in his relaxed right hand.

I tiptoe out of the room, feeling oddly reassured.

If he can fall asleep like that, maybe the situation's not so scary after all.

13

Marie

I take a shower and wash my hair. With the taste of spearmint toothpaste in my mouth, and with my hair still wet and fragrant from a balsam shampoo I found in the bathroom, I crawl into one of the twin beds in the room assigned to me. But after a few minutes of staring like an insomniac at the ceiling, while listening to the crash of surf on rocks, I get out of bed again and turn on my computer, connecting the modem to a phone plug in the wall. Within seconds I have an E-mail connection.

Surprise.

There it is: another E-mail from him.

Dear Marie,

I don't have to ask what you're doing, do I?

You're in Key Largo with Franklin, Diana, and Arthur.

Reading that, I literally gasp. He *knows*.

They're sweet children, aren't they, even if the little girl can't adjust to your presence in their lives. Don't worry, she'll probably come around. If she lives long enough to do it. But then, that's in your control. Her safety, I mean. Of more immediate concern to *you* is whether or not *you'll* live long enough for it to make any difference.

That doesn't concern me.

I have read the assignment you sent to me.

Bravo! Good for you for following my instructions by dismissing your assistant. That was fast, appropriate, work. I also like the honest way in which you depict your terror. And hers. I can tell you're very realistic, far more so than Ms. Dancer is, apparently, but then you have the advantage of more maturity and a more difficult life from which to draw strength to face hard choices directly. You don't hide from the truth or from what is difficult, do you, Marie? That's excellent. You will need that courage as we work together.

Not that your writing in this draft is perfect; it's sloppy in places.

I understand you had to hurry, however, so I'll make allowances for first-draft mistakes. Don't worry about your professional reputation. You may be assured that I'll edit and rewrite everything later — afterward — when I have the luxury of time that you no longer have. But, really, apart from those quibbles, and for the purposes of a first draft, your work is remarkably adequate. You're a consummate professional, aren't you? Quite the little pro.

But our relationship is not all-business, Marie.

Not at all. It's personal, too.

For heaven's sake, what could possibly be any more intimate than the relationship between a murder victim and the one who kills her? So why do you say nothing directly to me? No greeting? No fond message for your writing partner? No comments, no questions?

We can't have that! No, that won't do.

So, don't be shy. Talk to me, Marie!

In addition, here's your next official assignment, due by noon tomorrow.

Chapter 2: How was your drive down to the Keys? Did anything unusual happen to you? If so, write about it. Also, write an account of telling your lover about me. Where were you when you told Franklin? What was his reaction when you informed him that his children are at risk from me? Don't leave them out! I'll be displeased if you leave them out. Let us get to know them, Marie! Don't waste *too* many pages on them, but do tell us enough to give our readers a chill at the thought of any harm befalling little Diana or Arthur. You might mention their soft skin, their wide and innocent eyes, their touching trust in their father. Of course, that's just a suggestion. You know how to do it better than I. You're so good at putting halos over victims, so adept at making them seem all-good and the killers seem all-bad. We want *our* potential victims to appear sympathetic to our readers, too, just as you've done in your other books. And don't hesitate to make me seem as villainous as possible! What a terrible person I must be, to even think of hurting a single hair of their adorable heads, yes?

Blah, blah, blah, you know how to do it, you've done it often enough.

Finish this second assignment, dear, and submit it to me at the new E-mail address above. You didn't think I'd keep using the same one, did you? There are a million different places to send E-mail these days, my darling, and even more ways to do it anonymously, so don't even try to predict where your next E-mail is coming from. It could be Alaska, it might be Bucharest, it could be the E-mail café on Bahia Boulevard, or even your neighborhood library, the little one on S. E. Twenty-first Street.

I would taunt you to "catch me if you can," but you can't. I won't waste our time — your very limited time — with such childishness. It will be so much better for you if you simply relax and do as you're told. Some things get easier with practice, Marie.

Are we having fun yet?

I am, how about you?

No? Well, perhaps you'll have fun with the little surprises I have arranged for you this weekend, Marie. You may have already enjoyed one in your car. Don't worry, they're nonlethal. For now. You have followed my instructions thus far, so there is no reason for me to harm Deborah or any of the DeWeeses. Or you. But I believe you will find my little surprises convincing, anyway.

I can't wait to hear what you think of them.

Yours truly,
Paulie Barnes

"Hi, Marie."

I nearly jump out of my skin at the sound of a man's voice, whispering near my face, and the whisper of a man's cologne filling the air around me. I whirl around, expecting I don't know what, but what I find there is Franklin, bending down to read the E-mail over my shoulder.

"I didn't mean to startle you."

"Jesus! You scared me to death!" I fling my arms around his neck and hang on to him, pressing my head against his. He puts his arms around me, pulls me down off the chair and onto my knees so that we're kneeling nose to nose, pelvis to pelvis.

"I'm sorry," he whispers between kisses.

He tastes deliciously, mysteriously like strawberries.

When we pull apart enough to speak, he says, "I can't believe I fell asleep. *Goodnight, Moon* does that to me every time. Are you all right?"

"Oh, sure. No problem."

He laughs a little, quietly. "You're saying

that was a dumb question?"

"Prosecutors," I remind him, "never ask questions to which they don't already know the answers."

"That's only in court."

I rub my forehead against his, like a cat. "I wanted to scream at you when you wouldn't leave the dock."

"I figured. But I didn't want us to panic."

"Yeah, well, we could all have been calm and dead."

He puts one hand on the back of my head and pushes my face toward his and kisses me again, and this time it's long enough and hard enough to make me forget I was ever annoyed at him for any reason whatsoever. Oh, I do adore the taste of strawberries. When we part this time, I sigh. "Are you trying to suck the tension right out of me?"

"Is it working?"

I see deep concern in his eyes, which are a lovely light brown. He can communicate all sorts of things to juries with those eyes, and he's certainly expressing some of them to me now.

"I'll say. I'm a deflated balloon. But we really need to talk, Franklin."

"I know." He tugs at a lock of my hair,

points silently toward the first floor, and starts to pull me to my feet along with him. "Let's go downstairs so we don't wake the kids. I'm sorry about Dia—"

I place my fingers over his mouth. "Shh. It's okay."

"No, it's not, but I don't know what else to do about it. I just don't know what her mother filled her head with before this weekend."

I feel a little sick at the thought. "What do you think she said about me?"

He shakes his head, either because he doesn't know, or because he doesn't want to tell me. "Probably nothing worse than what she says about me."

What Truly DeWeese says is that their father abandoned them in order to have an affair with me. No part of that sentence is true. He initiated the divorce, but only after three years of failed marital counseling, and even then only with Truly's consent, and he didn't even *meet* me until after it was final. But they are both lawyers, and so the money and custody battles were meaner than they might have been between normal people. I try to remember that this can't possibly be the only story in the world with only one side to it. Truly's got her side, too, and maybe it's more understandable than her ex-husband makes it sound when he complains so bitterly to me.

"I'll be down in a minute," I tell him.

After he leaves my bedroom, I grab my canvas briefcase.

Thank God. Now he'll take over.

I leave the computer on, but switch off the room lights, so the entire second floor is dark except for the "night-light" of my screen. Then I make my way down the carpeted steps in the dark, holding on to the briefcase with one hand, feeling my way down the wall with the tips of my fingers with the other, testing my way with my toes before committing my feet to the descent. From the steps, I can see out through the windows that wrap around the living room — out to the water gleaming darkly under that amazing moon. There's one wide band of light, like a spotlight on the water, waiting for someone to walk on it.

When I step onto the first floor carpet, he is there in the dark, startling me again, making me cry, "Oh!" on a soft, involuntary breath. Franklin takes my briefcase, lays it on a nearby chair. Then he takes my hand, now free, and tugs at me to follow him.

"I think you enjoy scaring me," I accuse him in a whisper.

He doesn't defend himself but, instead, leads me silently into an empty bedroom on the first floor.

I see a queen-size bed, made up, empty, waiting.

Without speaking, as if we are one body with one mind, we turn down the quilt, the blanket, the sheet. With eager fingers we undress each other, letting our clothes fall into a pile on the floor. My palms slide around his waist to his back as his hands cup my hips. His skin is smooth and cool to my touch, his lips are warm.

He lays me down on my back on the bed.

"The children?" I whisper as he lowers himself toward me.

"They won't wake up until morning."

"Such good children," I murmur, reaching for him.

Afterward, Franklin pulls me close so that we are pressed together again, skin to skin, heart to heart.

"Don't you dare go back to sleep," I warn him.

"Not a chance," he says, managing to

sound relaxed, amused, and determined all at once. "Let's put on some coffee. And I'm hungry as hell, are you?"

"God, yes."

"Then we'll figure out what to do about the son of a bitch."

"Ah. I do love the sound of the word *we*."

I reach for one of his hands. "Listen. I'm incredibly sorry to bring this down on your family. I can't even begin to tell you how sorry I am."

"It's not your fault, Marie."

"Thanks. In spite of everything, I have to tell you that I'm really glad that I'm not alone tonight."

Franklin strokes the side of my face.

"You're not alone."

"Not even in the shower?"

"*Especially* not in the shower."

14

Marie

Some time later, I'm propped against the kitchen counter, dressed in the same clothes I shed a little while earlier in the bedroom. Franklin has slipped back into his shorts and a T-shirt. We're barefoot and slightly damp. I watch as he measures grounds into an automatic drip coffeemaker that the condo management has supplied, and I can almost smell the finished brew. We've already started on cheese and crackers. This is a pretty nice place, I realize with a feeling of some surprise as I come awake to my surroundings at last. There's nothing like a little hot sex followed by a hot shower to relax a girl.

"Do you take the threats seriously, Franklin?"

"Are you kidding?" He gives me an incredulous look. "You and my kids have been threatened — of course, I take it seriously." Then he feigns a tone of nonchalance. "Somebody wants to kill you, Marie? He wants to hurt my kids? No shit, what's for dinner?"

The pretense vanishes and I see in his eyes how he really feels.

"I'm taking it seriously, too," I tell him, "partly because Erin McDermit and Aileen Rasmussen seem to think I should."

"You talked to them already?" His tone is sharp.

"Well, yeah." His tone scares me, and I get defensive. "Was that a mistake? Do you think I shouldn't have done that? I couldn't get hold of you, and Aileen's freelance and Erin hasn't been a cop for years now, so they're not officially law enforcement anymore, and so I thought it would be okay —"

"Hey, it's okay." He pats the air to calm me down. "You had to talk to somebody. I'm just sorry it couldn't be me. You did the right thing, a smart thing."

"Really?" I calm down a little. "You think so? I don't want to make a mistake and risk —"

"Do you have any ideas who this guy could be?"

"Maybe." I give him all of my theories about demented fans and killers I've

213

known. Then I run and fetch my canvas briefcase.

"What have you got?" he asks, coming closer.

I start pulling things out, one by one. "You've seen the E-mails and what I wrote in response to them."

He grabs for the items in plastic. "What's all this?"

"That's something he sent me today. I don't know if you noticed or not, but each of his E-mails has the phrase executioners@capefear.com. John D. MacDonald wrote a book that's had both of those titles —"

"I've read it. Scary book, especially for lawyers. All about how some things have to be solved outside the law."

"Yeah. Let's hope that's not the case this time. Remember the movies they made of it, with Robert Mitchum and Robert De Niro? Well, this Paulie Barnes sent me that copy of the book today. And then — get this, I haven't even told you this, Franklin — he left a book-on-tape in my car for me to find today, and just guess which book it is."

When his jaw drops, I add, "Hell of a coincidence, don't you think?"

"Coincidence?" he says, sarcastically. "Sure."

Now he looks a lot more worried, and that worries me. "You picked your car up from Ernie's?" he asks me, and when I nod, he says, "We'll check with him, to see who had access. Where's the cassette?"

"In my glove box, wrapped in a Kleenex."

"Good. What else have you got there?"

"Well, here's a folder with all of the obscene and threatening mail I have received over the years."

Franklin sees how thick it is, and gives me a look of amazement. Then he lifts the cover and starts to read the first letter inside. After only a moment or two of perusal, he flips the folder shut again. It must be some mark of distinction that my fan mail has managed to disgust even a hardened prosecutor.

"You look like you just stepped in slime," I observe.

"This is awful stuff, Marie. With fans like these —"

"With fans like these, I may have enemies. But my gut feeling is that Paulie Barnes is not in that file of perverts."

Franklin, who is now rooting through the refrigerator, looks up in surprise. "Really? Why not?"

"Wrong style for any of them. If you ever get the dubious pleasure of reading through that whole file, you won't find many of my pen pals who can even connect two consecutive thoughts, much less construct whole letters that make sense. This guy seems pretty well educated to me, don't you think so? He uses correct grammar, he moves logically from one paragraph to another, he even builds up a kind of suspense, the way a novelist might, like in the way he'll sometimes use single-sentence paragraphs."

Franklin pulls out the cheese, mustard, and pickles. "I thought that was considered a literary cheap thrill."

"It can be, but you'll note he used it effectively." I give a shiver. "Made my skin crawl a few times. Hey, if you're going to make bologna sandwiches, I want mayo on mine, please."

He reaches back in for it, while suggesting, "So if it's not a fan, it could be one of the killers you've written about?"

"I guess they could want revenge on me for slandering them."

"Do you slander them?"

"Honey." I fake a thick southern accent. "I'd never say anything about a murderer that his own mother wouldn't say for money."

Franklin laughs at that, having known plenty of murderers and their mothers, himself. As he sets himself to constructing sandwiches, I add, a bit indignantly, "No, I don't slander them! But they may think I do. It's the truth they can't stand to hear about themselves."

"So . . . six books, how many murderers?"

"Eight, counting codefendants, but three of them are already dead."

"Review their names for me — the living ones."

"There was Anderson McDermott, who killed college girls. Nadine and Rowena Perkins, the twins who killed their boyfriends. And your guy — A. Z. Roner, who killed nurses."

"Roner's on death row. Where are the rest of them?"

"All still behind bars, as far as I know."

His voice and glance are sharp as he hands me my sandwich. "You haven't checked?"

"I haven't checked? Franklin, most of this only happened since this morning! I had to get Deb to safety first, then write his fucking assignment, then pick up my car and drive down here, then —"

He takes a big bite of his. "You're right."

"— and spend the evening with the kids and —"

"I said I'm sorry," he claims, with his mouth full.

"No, you didn't." I set down my food, and take a breath. "Okay. Time-out. I'm sorry, too. It's been a long day. But I don't need you acting like I'm some first-year paralegal who hasn't done her job right."

Wisely, he says nothing this time but instead pulls two coffee cups down from a cabinet, holding them out for me to point to the one I want. I choose a mug with an alligator on it, leaving him with a pink flamingo.

"Eat your sandwich," he says, "while I make a phone call."

I pick it up again, though I'm not very hungry anymore.

By the time I've forced down every bite, Franklin is off the phone, having spoken to someone working the night shift in the mysterious bowels of the Florida penal system.

"They're all still inside," he says, confirming what I already know from hearing his end of the conversation.

"One of them could be writing me from inside, for kicks," I theorize out loud, but then I punch my own hole in that. "But they've all been in prison for longer than I've employed — or even known —

Deborah. I don't think they could know about her, much less know that we were coming down here. How in the hell did he know that?"

"Somebody on the outside could be telling him things."

"I guess. That seems kind of far-fetched to me."

Franklin laughs a little. "And the rest of this *isn't?*"

"No. I don't think it *is* far-fetched, Franklin. I mean, look at what you and I do for a living. If we're going to hang out in swamps, don't we take a chance of stepping on snakes?"

"Well, then, I don't think the idea of an accomplice is so far-fetched, either," he argues back at me. "The E-mails did say executioners, after all. Plural."

"Damn. It did, didn't it? Oh, great, that's just what I want, a whole gang of them. Although he sure sounds like a lone wolf to me."

"Those five murderers you wrote about, Marie, the ones who are still in prison? How'd you get along with them at the time?"

"Like gangbusters," I say, with a wry smile. "They thought I was their best friend at the time. I think it's very rare for people

219

like them to get to spill their guts to somebody who's just listening, not judging, and who doesn't have an agenda like prosecuting them or defending them."

"Writing a book about them is not an agenda?"

"Yeah, but they get to thinking it's their agenda, that finally they're going to get to tell the world everything they've always wanted to say."

"What about the ones who never admit they did the crime?"

"Oh, they're especially 'cooperative,' because they think they can manipulate me into writing the story their way, to get them off. I guess they hope the governor will read it and say, 'Oh my God, that poor fellow, I've got to commute his sentence.' "

"They talked easily to you?"

"After a while, they almost all do."

Franklin fills my cup with coffee. "How'd they feel about you when your books came out?"

I make a face that has nothing to do with the bad coffee. "Just about like you think they'd feel."

"Betrayed?"

"Oh, yeah. Somehow it never seems to occur to these guys and gals that I am actually going to tell some serious truths about them. Like that they're narcissistic, sadistic, egomaniacs, etcetera."

"Any of them fall in love with you?" he asks, bluntly.

I grimace. "I suspect one or two may have. I mean, think about it, Franklin. It's not because of my great beauty or natural charm, believe me. These are guys who haven't seen a woman in ages, and here I come, all big eyes and tell-me-more."

"Works for me." His smile is thin. "That could be what this is all about, Marie."

"Ah, sweet mystery of love," I say, disgusted at the idea of it.

"If one of them is e-mailing you from prison, I think we can find that out pretty quickly."

I tense up. "What's this 'we' business, white man?"

"I'm saying, I'll find out."

"No, you won't."

"Why the hell not?"

I point upstairs, to where his children are asleep.

"You think I'm not thinking about them? Of course, I am. They — and you — are first on my mind in all of this. But, Marie, checking out this kind of stuff comes as natural to me as breathing. It's what I do. He'll never know I'm the one who's checking up on him."

"If he thinks there's law enforcement of any kind —"

"He won't know that, hell, he won't know anybody's doing anything. How would he know, Marie? He may be good — though I doubt it — but he can't possibly know who's checking out criminal databases." He puts his coffee cup down on top of the folder of "fan mail." "I'll get an investigation started on *these* assholes, too."

"No! I don't want you involved, Franklin!" Maybe it's just because I'm so tired by now, and maybe I'm overreacting, but I feel suddenly panicky, as if the whole situation is slipping out of control. "He wants you out of the picture, Franklin, and I do, too!"

He looks completely taken aback by my attitude.

But not half as much as I am.

"Oh God, Franklin." I feel miserable and confused. "All the way down here, I looked forward to turning this whole mess over to you, I really did. But now I realize there's just no way I can justify doing that, not when your involvement might jeopardize your children."

"You told me you were glad you aren't alone."

"I was. I am! But Franklin, the whole point of threatening Deb was to get her out of the way and that's the whole point of threatening your family! To get you out of the picture. He wants me alone. If we don't do what he tells us to, something terrible may happen. Maybe it won't, but we don't know that. I can't promise it won't. You can't, either!"

"Well, forget it, Marie. I'm not leaving you alone. The key here is making him *think* I will. All we have to do is make it *appear* that we're doing what he wants us to do."

That pulls me up short. "What?"

"That's how you handled it with Deb, right? You only appeared to fire her, but you didn't really do it."

"So what?"

"Marie, use your head. We can do that, too."

"Use your own damn head! Your children are in danger!"

"Goddammit, Marie, I am not putting them in danger, will you please understand that? I would not do that, all right? I am not a moron and I am not an irresponsible father. Or, maybe you think I am?"

"No. Of course, I don't. Of course, you're not. I just think you may be underestimating —"

"No. I'm not. You're *over*estimating him."

But you weren't there, in my car when that tape came on. You didn't feel what I did when I heard those words.

"I am involved," he says, cutting off each word in emphasis, "and these are not decisions you can make for me, Marie."

"All right!" I throw up my hands in frustration. If I have to capitulate to this I will, but I feel discouraged and deeply unhappy giving in. "But I'm telling you, Franklin, you'd better damn well stay invisible."

We both glance upstairs again.

"You don't have to tell me." He reaches for me and pulls me into an embrace that starts out stiff and awkward for both of us. But after a rigid moment, I let myself melt into his body, and allow my head to rest heavily against his chest. He's too tall for me, really, I've often thought; we'd make a better-looking couple if he were shorter or I were taller, but that's not how we are, and somehow we fit all right, anyway. With all our differences of skin and height and weight and opinions, even with all of that, we fit pretty comfortably most of the time.

"Tomorrow I'm bringing in a couple of detectives," he murmurs.

I jerk violently out of his arms and back away from him.

"No, Franklin, please don't do that!"

"I'm a prosecutor, Marie! A sworn agent of law enforcement. It's what I do and I'm going to do it. These guys, they always say, Don't tell the cops, but you have to, you need the kind of help that only cops can give you."

"These *guys?* We don't know anything about him, Franklin! This isn't a kidnapping, it's not a hostage situation, he's not one of *these guys!* He may not be like anybody you've ever run across before. He said he's new, he said he's something different, and what if he is? You don't know what you're doing. None of us does, yet. Please, just take the kids and go home tomorrow and let this play out a little more until I get a better sense of who he is and what he wants. He won't hurt me, not yet, not if he's telling the truth about doing an entire book with me."

"Marie, I have to do what I believe will protect all of us."

"Even if it kills us?" At a loss for any more words, all I can do is whirl on my heel and leave him standing there. I half-expect Franklin to say something conciliatory, to put out his hand, to try to stop me from running away from him when I'm angry. But no strong hand reaches out for me, no loving voice says, "Marie . . ."

In the unhappy silence, I run upstairs to my bedroom on the second floor.

Again, I undress and get into bed. This time, instead of falling asleep I lie there, listening to him slowly climb the stairs, use a bathroom as he gets ready for bed, turn the water on and off, flush the toilet, put the seat and lid back down. I close my eyes, feeling very alone again, and tears sting them. But then I sense, more than hear, him entering my room. Childishly, I keep my eyes shut and pretend to be asleep.

I smell toothpaste, then feel a soft kiss on my temple.

I begin to cry, and then to sob, and Franklin takes me into his arms and holds me while I try to stifle any noises that might awaken his children.

"I'm sorry," I blubber. "I don't know what's the matter with me."

"Yeah, I can't imagine," he says, with gentle sarcasm. "Somebody wants to kill you, they've completely disrupted your life and your work, they've threatened people dear to you whom you can't possibly defend, and you can't imagine why you're so upset." I hear a smile in his voice in the dark. "This is a natural reaction, baby — a

226

little *delayed,* maybe, but perfectly natural."

"Franklin, I was so scared when I heard that tape," I confess in a tearful whisper. "And I'm so tired right now I don't even know if I can sleep, and I'm so scared of doing something wrong that will hurt you and the kids."

"We'll be fine, we'll all be fine, believe me."

I turn my mouth toward his and our embrace begins to turn into something else . . . until we hear a little voice call out from another bedroom.

"Daddy? Daddy!"

Franklin groans softly. "I'm sorry."

"It's okay. Go."

He gently disengages, and I slump back down onto the pillow. The last thing I'm aware of before I fall asleep is the warmth of his hands on my shoulders.

I am asleep in my bedroom, my cat and small dog are sleeping near my feet. My mother and father are also asleep in their bedroom at the opposite and far end of this stark all-white ultramodern undecorated house in which we all live. Long corridors separate me from them, them from me. I bolt up in bed, shocked awake by something terrible.

Below, in our basement, a deadly creature

227

has entered. It is "only" a dog, but it is a hound from hell. It is Cerberus, ferocious, devouring, and its growling bark awakens me.

It is standing under a small square grate in my bedroom floor. I can see its deep brown color, its terrible snarling face full of hunger and hate.

I race screaming from my bedroom, running through corridors. "Daddy! Daddy!" I am trying with all my heart to scream for him. "Daddy! Daddy!" But no matter how hard I try my scream is weak. He'll never hear me. He'll never come running to save me, to kill the dog for me. I can't call him and I can't find him in the house! The corridors all stop at walls or sharp turns that don't lead to my parents' room.

In the single bed in the condo, my eyelids fly open like windows pushed up violently.

I am screaming, "Daddy! Daddy!" inside my mouth, though my lips are sealed shut, as if I am paralyzed.

My God.

Did I wake Franklin, or the children?

No, the screams didn't get out of my mouth.

I get up and make my way into the bathroom where I bend over the sink to splash water onto my face.

My God, I'm frightened.

My heart is pounding.

I return to bed, too dazed to think clearly.

What did the dream mean? Am I in danger right now, this minute? Did we bolt all the doors to this place? Yes. Yes!

Nothing can get in, nobody can get in to get us.

I remember everything about the dream.

I was not a child in it, I was me, now, an adult screaming for her daddy. The sound and the appearance of the hound were horrifying, and yet even in the dream I knew that I was in no immediate danger from it. It couldn't have gotten to me through the grate, there was no other way in. And even as my dream self — in a gauzy, flowing white gown — ran screaming down the blind corridors, she knew that if she awakened her father, and even if he raced to her rescue as she knew he would, there was little he could do that she couldn't also do. And she would only be placing him in danger, possibly even a danger greater than her own. What if he felt he must go down into the basement and attempt to kill the beast for her? What if he called for emergency backup and then all of those people were put in danger, too?

All because she couldn't — wouldn't — didn't — face it, herself.

She wasn't a child anymore.

I'm not a child anymore.

If I go looking for "Daddy" — for somebody, anybody, to save me — they won't be able to save me any better than I might save myself and I might destroy them by asking.

In my half-sleep, half-awaking state, I'm dazed and confused.

Destroy Daddy? How can I destroy a man who's already dead? My father is dead, I've always known that, deep in my gut and my heart, even if I have no facts to support it. I cannot wake my father from the dead. He cannot save me this time.

"This time?" I whisper to myself. What do I mean by "this time"?

When my heartbeat finally subsides to normal and my body unclenches, I remember that the last thing I heard before I fell asleep was one of Franklin's children calling, "Daddy, Daddy."

Ah. *That's* why I dreamed what I did, I assure myself.

There's no deep meaning to it. Not at all.

I merely heard that and my unconscious picked it up and put it into my dream in the strange way of such things. And

230

anyway, why would I be dreaming about my own mother and father now, after all these years?

A new thought comes to me: *What a bitter irony this is . . .*

My anonymous "murderer" cynically predicted that Franklin will abandon me in order to save himself and his children. Instead, I can't get him to leave no matter how hard I argue in favor of it!

But by the time I finally fall asleep, I have devised a perfect strategy to force Franklin to remove himself and his children to safety and to leave me to my own fate.

He may hate me for it.

"But I have to do it," I tell myself as sleep finally wins again.

And tomorrow — today — I will do it. I will. I have to.

Paulie Barnes isn't the only one who can plot surprises.

15

Marie

I awaken to an earthquake. At least that's what I believe is happening as my body bounces helplessly in the bed. But earthquakes don't squeal, I think then, with the one-sixteenth of my brain that is awake, they rumble. And they don't smell like syrup. This one squeals. And smells like maple syrup. I open my eyes to discover that the quake is only one small boy, jumping from the floor to my bed, bouncing up and down, jumping down to the floor again, and then repeating the whole process.

I shoot up in bed and grab hold of him.

"Wake up, wake up, M're! We're going swimming in the ocean and we're going to see Big Bird and we're going swimming in the swimming pool and Daddy's fixing pancakes right NOW! Come on, come on!"

"You run on down, sweetie. I'll be right behind you."

He races away, hooting, "Pancakes!" all the way down the stairs. I can hardly believe Franklin is already up and cooking, but I suppose that parents don't really have much choice in the matter. Go to bed at 1 a.m. and your kids still get you up at 7 a.m., isn't that how it works?

Well, if Franklin can get up this early, I suppose I can, too.

In a flash, I'm out of bed, brushing my teeth, running fingers through my hair to comb it, pulling on fresh shorts and a T-shirt and running downstairs after Arthur.

If I hurry fast enough, maybe I'll forget the bad dream entirely.

"What's this I hear about Big Bird?" I inquire as I enter the kitchen.

All three DeWeeses look up, with varying degrees of welcome.

"There's a nature center on Marathon Key where college students are counting hawks as they fly over Florida." Franklin looks as tired as I feel, but he manages a good morning smile for me anyway. *If there is any lingering upset between you and me,* the smile says, *we don't need to inflict it on the kids.* "There was a flyer for it in our door this morning, and Diana found out all about it." His smile turns wry and apologetic, as if to say, I'm sure that's just what you want to do, go count hawks.

"Cool," I say, reassuringly. "I love bird-watching."

I smile at Diana, who crooks up the edges of her mouth as if she's been told to be nice to me.

"I promised the kids we'd take them to the beach to swim," her daddy adds. "Then lunch. Then we'll go see the hawks, how about that? Diana really wants to see the hawks."

"Me, too!" Arthur protests. "I want to see Big Bird, too!"

"They're big *birds,*" his sister informs him with all the exaggerated patience of a superior six-year-old. "Not Big Bird."

Arthur sticks out his tongue, pinches her, giggles, and runs away.

"OW," Diana yells, and the chase is on, turning into a game of tag around the furniture and up and down the stairs, while their father serenely continues to turn bacon and stir pancake batter. Over the happy din of the children's play, he says, "How'd you sleep?"

"Okay, except I had a strange dream about my parents."

He gives me a look, part curiosity, part wariness. I've told Franklin as much about my parents as I know, which is enough to make him almost as leery of mentioning them as I am.

"Why do you suppose you dreamed about them?" he asks me.

I shrug it off. "Indigestion. Listen, about the birds — I have to work this morning, but I'd love to spot hawks later."

"Work!" His voice fills with mock horror. "I promised Diana and Arthur that I wouldn't work all weekend, so are we going to have to extract the same promise from you?"

I stare at him to let him see that I can't quite believe he said that. "I have a second chapter to write for our friend Paulie Barnes, remember?"

Looking reluctant, as if he doesn't want to give in to any of it this morning, he nods. "Right, okay, but only if we can come back and pick you up to take you to lunch with us."

This seems a rather cavalier reaction, considering how seriously he was taking things last night. And now he's only thinking about whether I go to lunch with them?

"How'd *you* sleep?" I ask in return, as I see that Franklin actually looks *more* tired than I feel. There are bags under his eyes, and his whole face seems to droop a bit.

Maybe he tossed and turned all night and so he isn't tracking well this morning.

But he turns on the television with the remote control, and so my question is drowned out by the sound of cable news.

After breakfast and dishwashing, I walk them out to their car, carrying the children's life jackets for them. Before Diana steps up into the backseat, I slip something into her hands, and then move away before she can see that it's a little beaded bracelet that will look pretty with her swimming suit. On the other side of the car, I give Arthur — in the name of sibling equality — a plastic toy to bob upon the waves. Franklin belts the kids into their car seats, closes the car doors, then takes me by an elbow and walks me around to the rear of the car where the children can't hear what we say. "How do you feel about staying here by yourself this morning?"

Ignoring that, I counter, "I thought you were at least going to *pretend* to leave today."

He looks annoyingly sure of himself, as if the pancakes have made him invulnerable. Usually, I find Franklin's self-confidence attractive, but it worries me today. "He said in his E-mail that he expects me to abandon you, but he never said you had to make us leave here. Right?"

"I guess, but —"

"So we're staying."

I nod, but only because it wouldn't do to stand out here in the parking lot and scream at him in front of the children. But while I appear to be acquiescing, what I'm really thinking is, *You're forcing me to take extreme measures.*

Diana has twisted around and is staring at us through the rear window.

"Have fun," I mouth at her, and get a tiny but real-looking smile in reply.

Tiny is better than nothing. Tiny is progress.

When Diana waves good-bye to me the bracelet slides down her arm.

I wave them off, and then go back inside to do what I must do. I feel encouraged by that little smile and that wave, even if they were crassly bought. If Diana DeWeese can smile at Marie Lightfoot, then all good things are possible. Right now, however, I have to write a chapter that I don't want to write. But first, I must make a phone call I *really* don't want to have to make.

Before I start to write, with bated breath I check my E-mail.

Thank God, there are no new messages from Paulie Barnes, but strangely, there is one to me from Franklin. How sweet, is my first thought. It must be a love note. Why else would he send me an E-mail when I'm right here in the same condo?

When I open it, I see why.

Now I understand why he looked so tired this morning, why he avoided my question about how he'd slept, and why he seemed so sure of himself when we were outside by his car.

His E-mail to me is a copy of a message he has sent to Paulie Barnes.

"Franklin, no!" I cry aloud, as if he's there to hear me.

Caught between feelings of fury and dread, I read what he has done:

"I hope you don't object to the fact that I'm writing to you," it begins. "Let me make it clear that Marie has no idea I'm doing this."

She certainly does not, I think when I see those words. Franklin's E-mail goes on:

I think you must agree that this letter from me in no way violates your rules. Marie has told me everything, but only because you encouraged her to do that. In every way, she has done as you asked. You told her not to notify law enforcement, and she has not done that. You told her to fire her assistant, and she did. In your most recent E-mail, you encouraged her to write to you in a personal way, which I'm sure she will do.

You have not forbidden me to do the same.

Man to man, prosecutor to criminal, let's talk about this.

Oh, Franklin! He should have written it and then sat on it until this morning. The light might then have dawned on him in more ways than one. When the sun came up, he surely would have hit Delete. But now — we're all going to be stuck in this new situation he has created by letting his testosterone get the better of him.

You seem to think I will leave her, because I'm afraid for my own skin and kin, as it were. You have badly misjudged me. I will *never* leave her to deal with you by herself. Never. I will take whatever steps I need to take to protect my children, but I will not abandon Marie in the process.

You also seem to think that I will not

only disappear into thin air, but that I will tie my own hands so that I cannot identify you, locate you, arrest you, prosecute you, and see you punished as you are virtually begging to be. Exactly whom do you think you're dealing with here? A first-year assistant prosecutor? A law student? A boy?

Allow me to familiarize you — or possibly reacquaint you — with the laws you have already broken, keeping in mind that you have not yet done anything that cannot be bargained down. You haven't killed anybody. You haven't harmed anyone yet. It is still possible for you to step back from the edge *now.* It is still possible for *you* to disappear from Marie's life before you make things any worse for yourself than they already are, and let me make it clear to you that they are on the verge of becoming very, very bad — for *you.*

For example, I strongly advise you to look up on the Web: Florida State Criminal Statute 836.10. You may access that information by entering "Florida statutes" in your search engine. Pay particular attention to the mandatory sentencing requirements as they may apply to you.

You may contact me directly at . . .

And there, Franklin offered his own E-mail address, circumventing me entirely. He signed it with the full weight of his authority, "Franklin DeWeese, Esq., State Attorney, Howard County, Florida."

Shit! I've got a choice right now. I can hang my head in my hands and moan. Or, I can stomp around the condo and curse like a sailor.

For the next few minutes, before I force myself to sit back down and write my "chapter," I turn the air bluer than the water in the bay.

16

Marie

"Red-shouldered hawk at two o'clock. Here, ma'am, you can look through my binoculars. See him? He's just a speck on the close end of that little white cloud. Can you spot him?"

"No, not yet. Oh, there he is! Yes!"

At the Bird Watch Nature Center on Marathon Key south of Key Largo, a handsome young bearded biologist says to me, "Your children can mark it on our board if they'd like to."

"She's not our mother," Diana corrects him.

Apparently, the bracelet didn't buy much.

"Oh." His smile is gentle; his tone of voice is tactfully neutral in response to this awkward information she has given him. "Do you want to mark down that we just saw a red-shouldered hawk?"

"Sure." Diana shrugs, but she looks thrilled when he hands her a black Magic Marker. "Where do I mark it?"

"Right here." He points to a series of hash marks beside the name of the hawk. It is only one of several raptors, including kestrels, snail kites, and ospreys, listed vertically on a white erasable board. Some of the species have several slash marks beside their name, some show none. It is the tally for the day's count of migrating hawks flying over the Keys on this migration route. Like the biologists who spend their days counting birds, Franklin and the children and I are standing on a balcony of a two-story wooden building, looking up and to the northeast, scanning the sky in that direction, from which most of the birds fly in. It is quite handy to have an activity to distract us, since neither Franklin nor I are fit to talk to each other at the moment. While Franklin helps Arthur try to look through a telescope and I search the sky for other birds, Diana asks the biologist, "Why do you count birds?"

"Lots of reasons. This bird, here" — he points to a name, SNAIL KITE, on the board — "is endangered. Do you know what that means? It means that there aren't very many of them anymore. We try to help keep track of just how many there really are, so we'll know how well they're doing. That's one of the reasons we do it. We also like to find out about their migration patterns, which means we want to know where they travel every year and how far and how long it takes them to get there."

"Like when we came down here from Miami?"

He laughs, though not at her. "Yes, like that. What's your family's last name?"

"DeWeese."

"Well, if I were counting DeWeeses" — even Diana smiles at that — "and I spotted your car through my binoculars, I'd count, one two three four DeWeeses —"

"No, there were just three of us in the car."

"Three DeWeeses and then I'd know there were at least three of you still remaining in the world."

"There's also our mom at home!" She's really getting into this business of counting DeWeeses. I'm tempted to observe that if her father continues to behave recklessly, there may be fewer DeWeeses to count. And, possibly, one less Lightfoot, too. "And we have cousins! Oh! And aunts and uncles and I've got a grandma and two grandpas!"

"Well, good, then the DeWeese species must be doing very well."

At the sound of Diana's giggle, her father turns around to smile at her — avoiding aiming any of that smile at me — and to ask the young man, "You band birds, too, don't you?"

"Yes, we do, sir, just across the highway at a kind of duck blind we've set up for that purpose. We lure the hawks down, capture them, band them, and then release them again."

"We'd like to see that, too," Franklin tells him.

But the young biologist frowns a little and nods discreetly toward the children. "They're a little young. You have to be completely quiet over there. It's not really for children." When Diana's face falls, he adds gently, "I don't think you'd like it anyway."

But Arthur, who overheard all of that, now gives a full-throated roar: "We'll be quiet!"

The biologist grins at me. "I rest my case."

That seems to settle it, but as we drive away from the hawk-spotting station, Franklin won't give it up. Why does this not surprise me? Stubborn is his middle name. When he spots a sign saying

BANDING STATION, he turns off the main road and starts down a one-lane gravel road in that direction.

"He said it's not for kids," I remind him, straining to sound cordial for the sake of the little ears in the backseat.

"Maybe not for his kids, but mine will be quiet, won't you, guys?"

"Yes!" come deafening shouts from the backseat.

I remember the scientist's doubtful expression and his polite words. "He said they probably won't like it —"

"Yes, we will!" Diana protests, her voice rising into a whine. "Dad, we will. Won't we, Arthur?"

"Yeah!"

They're not my kids, and Franklin's in no mood to do anything I ask him to at this moment, so I stop fighting it. But I am left with an uneasy feeling about this side trip.

"And, anyway, I want to see it," Franklin insists.

"And whatever *you* want . . ." I mutter, leaving the rest unsaid.

The two adults in the front seat are steaming, and not because of the humidity. When Franklin and the kids returned from swimming, I pulled him aside into the kitchen just long enough to hiss, "I found your E-mail! What the *hell* do you think you're doing?"

"Taking over," he informed me, coolly. "It's my job."

"My life is not your 'job'!"

"My children's lives are!"

"That doesn't give you the right to unilaterally —"

That's as far as we got before those same children interrupted us.

We don't have to drive far down the gravel road to find what we're looking for. Franklin pulls the car off onto a shoulder and parks it there. We both help the children out of their car seats and then take their hands to cross the road, with Arthur holding on to me and Diana grasping her dad's hand, of course. "Okay, kiddos." Franklin's tone holds warning. "We're going to all go together and we're going to keep very very quiet. If you can go all the way in and come all the way back out without saying a single word out loud, there is frozen yogurt in your future. Shh, Arthur!"

This seems an impossible challenge to me, but off we go.

Barbed wire fences rim the fields on either side of us. Dust rises at our feet. The air smells and tastes like drought — the flavor of roasted earth, dead grass, and overgrown weeds. Franklin and I both carry bottles of water from which the kids and we sip frequently.

The kids are so excited that they start down the path on their tiptoes before settling into an eager trot. Franklin and I follow, stiffly careful not to touch each other.

I'd like to touch him, all right — I'd like to slug him.

When we finally spot the duck blind, he runs to catch up with his kids and grabs them. When they start to squeal, he puts a finger to his lips, and points out the blind to them. Our little troop marches on. It feels hot enough to *bake* a bird. But Arthur and Diana are being impressively good about not making any noise except for the natural crackle of stones and twigs under their sandaled feet.

After a few yards, their father stops us again.

Again he silently points, only this time it's toward some little cages that have been set under the shade of some scrub bushes.

Diana lets out a delighted squeal, which she immediately shushes by clapping her own hands over her mouth. Her eyes grow wide as she stares up guiltily at her dad.

But he only holds out a hand, which she takes, and then he leads her right up to the cages so she can get a good look at what is inside of them. It turns out to be doves and rabbits. Arthur is nearly beside himself with joy at the sight of the sweet creatures. He races right up to them and immediately wants to stick a finger into every cage to pet them.

I hurry after, to gently discourage him from doing that.

"Why are these animals here?" I whisper to Franklin. "Isn't it only hawks they capture? What do they need with doves and bunnies?"

At that moment, a fluttering sound breaks through the heavy air.

We all turn to see what caused it.

We see, in a clearing to our left, that there's something leaping into the air.

"What's that, Daddy?"

"Shh. I don't know, Pumpkin."

Whatever it is, it falls back to earth, but then jumps high again.

It could be a bird bobbing around, except there is something unnatural-looking about it. It takes me a long moment to grasp that it *is* a bird, and that the bird is bait for the hawks. A live dove has been strapped into a leather harness that is cleverly attached to straps that run back to the duck blind. Inside the blind, somebody is working the straps, making the dove leap up and down like a marionette.

A bird of prey with a large wingspan circles above the clearing.

Fascinated, appalled, I stare as it circles, lower and lower, and then dives like a fighter pilot for the imprisoned dove.

Diana catches on to what is about to happen.

"He's going to kill the little bird!" she screams. "He's going to kill it!"

Her little brother, who giggled at the "dancing" dove, now screams in reaction to his sister's terror.

"Daddy! Daddy!" Diana screams. "Save the little bird!"

The hawk, alerted by their cries, swoops out of the clearing just inches above the dove's head and flies away.

The dove, in its harness, settles back to earth.

Within seconds, two annoyed-looking scientists emerge from the duck blind and trot over to us. Our trek to see hawks has turned into a disaster. The children are hysterical, even though the dove is safe. One of the scientists, a young man in a T-shirt and khaki shorts, speaks sharply to Franklin and me over the noise of the children's sobbing. "Did someone give you people permission to be here?"

The other scientist, a young woman, crouches down to try to comfort the children, who are pressed, crying, into their father's legs. "We wouldn't let the hawk hurt the dove," she tells them. "We always pull the dove to safety." Then she, too, looks up accusingly at the grown-ups. "We take very good care of our lures. We feed them well, give them plenty of water, and we never let them stay out there in the sun very long at all. It's not as bad as it looks to children. But they don't understand that, and that's why we don't encourage children to come here."

"We didn't know," I say, spreading my hands in helpless apology. "We're so sorry."

But Franklin, busy dealing with his distraught children, looks less than contrite. "If that's true," he says, "then why do you distribute those advertising flyers encouraging people to bring their children over here? It said this is one of the best attractions in the Keys. It said children love it, and we shouldn't miss it."

"We don't put out flyers," the young woman claims.

"Yes, you do," Franklin insists, and I realize that he's taking out on her some of what he feels toward me at the moment. "There was one in our door this morning."

"No, sir, we don't," the young male biologist chimes in. "We wouldn't do that. We don't want visitors over here, not unless they're invited. It's not really a tourist attraction."

"Then where'd the damned flyers come from?"

"Franklin!" I caution. He is acting like a prosecutor interrogating suspects. The young scientists are being kind to the children, but they look as if they aren't about to take any shit from him.

And then it hits me, the same thought that strikes Franklin at that precise moment, too.

Just like that, we both know where the flyer came from.

Paulie Barnes. *He's here! Paulie Barnes is here on the island.*

Franklin stares down at his children, whose innocence has been lost a little bit, and then he looks over at me. Finally, he admits to the biologists, "This was my mistake. I don't know what to say. I apologize." When he glances at me, I realize that at least a little bit of that is aimed at me, too.

They look exasperated but willing to accept it.

I am not, yet.

Back at the car, I feel raw and furious as I whisper to Franklin, "I wanted you to take them *home*. I *asked* you not to stay. But no, you knew better, didn't you? You know what's best for everybody, don't you? Writing that E-mail without asking me first was a terrible thing to do. And this was a terrible thing for the children. Now, will you please take them home?"

"And leave you here by yourself? Are you nuts?"

"I'll go home, too!"

"No, I won't be forced into doing what *he* wants me to do. And we don't have to leave, none of us do. It was all for show, Marie, a power play, it doesn't mean anything."

"It means something to them!" I point to his children.

When he only tightens his jaw, I have to let it go.

Diana is staring at us through her tears, but now there's a sly little smile on her face. This argument of ours pleases her.

If this cruel episode didn't convince Franklin to remove them far away from me, then nothing I can say will do it.

But it doesn't matter anymore. I've already won this war.

He just doesn't know it yet.

17

Marie

The children, clutching the comfort of their "blankies" and stuffed toys, fall asleep in their car seats in the back of the Acura.

"It's times like this I hate car seats," their father says to me in a low voice that seems to hold a note of appeasement.

I'm willing to give it a try, too.

"Because you'd like to bring them up here?"

He nods, looking both exhausted and ready to kill someone. At least that's no longer me. When I see there's also sadness in the lines of his face, my heart finally aches for him. Yes, he's been acting like a frantic father instead of a cool-thinking prosecutor, but who can blame him for that?

"He's here, Franklin," I whisper, and feel an inner shiver.

"We don't know that," he whispers back,

but there's no contention in his tone now.

"Well, then, how'd the flyer get here?" I ask him, trying to keep my own tone neutral and nonargumentative. "May I see it?"

With one hand on the wheel, Franklin reaches under his seat, pulls out a piece of paper, and hands it over to me. I see that it is a single, letter-size sheet of shiny paper folded lengthwise into thirds, produced in glossy full color, with several attractive photos of hawks. The headline and copy advertise the "Bird Watch Nature Center" as a local magnet for families with children.

"It looks genuine to me."

He glances at me. "It would have fooled you?"

"I'm sure it would," I reassure him. "You found it stuck in the door?"

"Diana did. Actually, slipped under it, I think. As soon as she saw the pictures of the birds and I told her what it was, she was after me to bring her here."

"I understand. Let's figure out what to do about this."

"I already know what I'm going to do," he says, and I feel the wall going up between us again. "I'm going to call the local police, and tell them to look for this guy. In case you're right, and he is here."

"But what are they going to look for, Franklin?" I'm still trying hard to keep my voice and my temper down. "A man alone in a car? A man with extra copies of these flyers? For all we know, this is the only one in existence. In fact, it probably is. There's nothing for cops to go on, Franklin, no evidence of any crime, no probable cause to stop anybody. Is there? You're the prosecutor," I challenge him. "You tell me."

He doesn't say anything for about a tenth of a mile, and then he concedes, "All right. You're right about that. But we're both assuming this flyer is his work, and we don't know that for sure. We have to check it out, we shouldn't assume. So one thing I could do, I could try to find out if any of our neighbors got these flyers, too. I can ask around to see if anybody saw who put this under our door."

"That's a good idea." I feel relieved by his words, because he's right — we are jumping to conclusions. Who knows? Maybe there's an advertising campaign that the young biologists know nothing about, flyers put out by their funding agency, or something like that. "We could do that. That won't break any of his rules. Franklin, first, he put the tape in my car.

Now the hawks, if it was really he who sent us there. Those would be the surprises he alluded to. But how could he be sure that I'd turn on the radio in my car? And if he's the one who did the flyer, how could he be sure that we'd visit Bird Watch, much less that we'd take the trouble to go to the banding station?"

"Most people probably do turn on their radios, so that wasn't hard. As for the bird-watching, he couldn't have known we'd take his lure."

"So to speak. So then, I don't get it."

Franklin shifts around in his seat, as if a sudden burst of energy has shot through him and he can't contain it. "Maybe it's just a game, Marie. This may be pure game to him. He'll sprinkle these surprises around and scare us if he can. When it works, he scores. When it doesn't, he still hasn't lost anything, because he's kept us nervous and on edge. Well, I'll tell you something. If he wants to play games, I'll play a game with this bastard. And then we'll see who walks out of the Coliseum alive."

You're losing control again, I think as I stare at him. The prosecutor, who is famous for his cool, is only human, like any other loving father, and he's losing it. *And that means that I'd better hang tightly on to mine.*

One of us needs to stay in the condo while the children nap in their beds upstairs, so I stay behind while Franklin begins his investigation. I'm hoping the activity will leech out some of the hard, stubborn determination that seems to be growing in him again and which I fear may become dangerous to us all. I sympathize with his need to protect and defend, but I'm scared that if he charges into this situation like a prosecutor in a trial, we may end up with a worse disaster on our hands than just crying children, upsetting as that is. At this moment, if anybody asked me, I'd be tempted to say that Franklin is the greater present danger to us.

When he sets out on his task, I feel relieved to see him go.

"No, I don't remember getting any flyer like that" is the response Franklin hears from everyone who opens a door to him within the condominium development. Nor does he spot other flyers sticking out from under any doors. But then he gets lucky with the condo manager, albeit not as lucky as she'd like him to get.

"Oh, I put that in your door," the woman tells him.

She leans a shoulder against the sill of her own open doorway and crosses her arms under her chest, a gesture that lifts and accentuates her ample cleavage, as he later, vividly, reports to me.

He keeps his gaze fixed on her leathery face.

"Just like the E-mail asked me to do," she adds.

"E-mail?"

"Yeah, the one we got from your travel agent."

The prosecutor is well accustomed to hiding surprise in front of judges and juries, and he calls on that experience now. "I didn't use an agent to book this weekend."

"You didn't? Well, that's weird." She shifts her position, managing to move a bit closer to him in the process. "You want to come in? Come on in. I think I've put a printout of that letter in my files." While Franklin waits just inside her unit, which smells of fried fish, she upends a wastebasket beside a couch, finally emerging in triumph with a copy of the E-mail. "Here it is — see?" She sticks the paper — and herself — right up to his face. "There's your name, Franklin DeWeese, right? Care of the manager. That's me, Margie Conover. Well, you can read it for yourself," she says, though she doesn't back off very far to give him a chance to do that.

The first thing Franklin notices is a return address that looks as meaningless as the ones I got: razen15@pal.com. Below that, the body of the E-mail says: "Please print out the attached advertising flyer and slip it under the door of Mr. Franklin DeWeese, who will be renting a unit from you this weekend. This is material he requested. Thanks." It's clear to Franklin that "Paulie Barnes" wins either way with this trick — if we receive this flyer but don't fall for it, he's still unnerved us; if we take his bait, then all the better.

"Did you go?" she wants to know.

"To the hawk station? Yeah, we did."

"So how was it?"

"Interesting place, but not appropriate for children."

"I saw your kids, they're so cute. If you need a baby-sitter, you could bring them over here and I could watch them for a little while."

There is no way in hell that he's going to turn his children over to a stranger — any stranger — and especially not on this trip.

Franklin thanks the woman without encouraging any of her suggestions — not the offer of baby-sitting, or the more covert suggestions, either.

When he returns to our unit, the first words out of his mouth are, "He didn't deliver that flyer in person. I don't think he's here, Marie. I don't think he was ever here."

"Franklin, there's a message for you to call Truly."

Push has finally come to shove.

His ex-wife's name isn't really Truly, it's Trudy, but it has become a standing joke with him to call her Truly, because she is still so proprietary toward her ex-husband, acting as if only she can ever be "Truly DeWeese." It's a bad pun, but it amuses him, and I have picked up the bad habit of calling her that, too.

"What does she want?"

"She wants you to call her right away, please."

"Was she decent to you?"

"She was fine."

"Dammit. I was hoping she could last a weekend without needing to check up on us."

"It's okay, Franklin, they're babies, she's

their mother, it's natural."

He makes a noise that sounds like a cross between a growl and a snort. But he crosses to a phone sitting on a kitchen counter and punches in the numbers required to reach Trudy via his telephone credit card.

My heart begins to pound too hard for comfort.

"It's me, Trudy. What's up?" The question seems to imply there had better be a good reason, a crisis at the very least, for his ex-wife to interrupt his weekend with his girlfriend and his children. He gets the kids on weekends and part-time on holidays, and he guards that time like a lion. Plus, he only rarely takes any time away from his office — which is the real reason he agreed to such unequal custody. So he has looked upon this weekend as something deserved, rare, special — and all his.

As he listens, Franklin slowly turns around until he is looking at me.

His gaze becomes a stare that turns ugly.

I just stand there, absorbing the blow from his eyes.

I called his ex-wife this morning. I told her what was going on. I encouraged Trudy to command Franklin to return their children to her at once.

When the terse, tense conversation ends,

Franklin puts down the receiver with a slow precision that suggests fury.

"You told her?"

"I told her."

"How could you do that to me, Marie?"

"I can do what I have to do."

"Now I have no choice, but that's why you did it, right? Now I have to take them home. If I don't, she's threatening to come down here to get them herself. Dammit, Marie!"

"Dammit, yourself. I want them safely out of here."

He is furious with me. But even though I feel like the world's biggest traitor, I'm sure it was the right thing to do.

"Franklin —"

He turns on his heel and strides away from me.

"I'm going to get the kids ready to go," he snaps.

I bite back tears and stay behind.

My anonymous "murderer" says he wants Franklin to abandon me. One way or another, he is about to get his way. I hate that part of this. But what else could I do? Franklin's E-mail to Paulie Barnes was, I believe, a terrible misjudgment, and it frightens me. The children's distress at the hawk banding station was painful to behold, and worse for them to experience. Even if no physical harm has come to them, the children will be better off away from here, away from me.

Certainly their mother shares that opinion.

Before they leave, Franklin speaks to me in the kind of tone of voice a person uses when they care about you, but they're so mad they could kill you. "You're not staying here by yourself." He doesn't phrase it as a question. "You're following us home."

"Of course. I don't want to be here alone."

"What about when you get home?"

"I'll make arrangements."

"For protection?"

"Yes. I'll be fine, Franklin."

"Find a way to let me know that for sure."

"Of course." I want to embrace him, but I don't. "I'm so sorry."

"This is not your fault." There is a slight crack of smile. "At least, the general situation is not your fault." Even that slight thaw freezes up again. "You realize you've fixed it so I can't come around, don't you? We'll be very lucky if she doesn't go back to court to try to get my visitation rights to depend on whether or not I try to see you. She'll portray you as a dangerous person for her children to be around and claim that the court can't trust me not to have them around you."

"You're the lawyer," I tell him, alarmed. "Make it not be like that."

He laughs, though he's clearly not amused. "Make the world not be like this, you mean."

"Yeah. Look, this will end. Life will go back to normal. She'll lighten up."

"I don't know why you'd say that, Marie. Where's your evidence? She never has before."

It hits me that this could be true: even when this strange episode is safely concluded — as it has to be! — Truly may well consider me to be a continuing threat to her children's safety, just by virtue of what I do for a living. I'm not even sure I disagree with her. She already has that opinion of their father's chosen branch of the law. At this moment, I may actually be saying good-bye to these three people in a more lasting way than I can bear to consider. For a moment, my chest fills with grief for many losses in my life. I don't want there to be more, not these three more losses, not of this good man standing in front of me looking so upset. Why, I haven't even had a chance to win his daughter over yet. I know I can. Just give me a chance, universe, just give me another chance.

"Give me the stuff you brought down," he demands.

The evidence in my briefcase, he means, and the cassette tape in my glove box. When he sees me hesitate, he explodes. "Goddammit, Marie, I'm the only person in law enforcement that he's allowing you to see. If you don't let me check that stuff out, who will? If nothing else, you need me to keep a clean chain of evidence. If you give it to your private investigator, it's going to get contaminated, and then it's going to be worthless if we ever need it at trial."

Although I think that's an undeserved slur on Erin McDermit, I know he's right, basically. Hating the fact that he has to be involved even so indirectly as this, I go get what he wants and give it to him so he can have them checked for fingerprints: the FedEx envelope, the letter, the book, the cassette tape.

"I'll forward copies of the E-mails to you," I promise him.

"I've got copies of your books, you don't have to give me those."

"You've read all my books?"

I knew he'd read the one he was in and the ones I've written since then, but I never knew he'd also read the ones that came before that.

Franklin gives me a disgusted look. "You must have a very low opinion of me sometimes, Marie. Of course I've read all your books. You follow my trials, don't you? What kind of man would I be if I didn't show as much interest in your work as you do in mine? As a matter of fact, I was a big fan even before I met you. But I'd have read them anyway. I care about *you*, Marie, everything about you, what you write, what you do, what you think, how you feel. I don't think you have a clue how much power you have to hurt me."

I feel stunned by this little speech, and frozen with sudden happiness and also shame. When I don't say anything — I'm feeling so paralyzed with surprise by what he said — he turns away from me as if I've rebuffed him. By the time I move to catch him, to say, "Wait, Franklin, I feel the same way about you," it's too late. The kids are calling to him from their bedroom, demanding his attention, and he's rushing away from me, hurrying to get them and to take them home.

When they drive off, Arthur waves. Diana turns her face away.

And I haven't even remembered to ask Franklin what he plans to do if Paulie Barnes answers his E-mail.

I go back inside the condo, feeling shell-shocked by love and fear.

I lock up everything. Doors. Windows. Emotions.

Right now, I can either worry about love or I can worry about our lives. It seems to me that I'd better worry about the one, or we may never get another chance to pursue the other.

18

Marie

There are no more E-mails from my tormentor, at least not yet. Is this good news, or is it ominous? Why isn't he yelling at me about Franklin's E-mail to him? Is it possible that Franklin was right? Did he scare Paulie Barnes away already? For that, I would gladly eat crow.

Before I pack to go home, I have one more thing to do.

To get anything done, though, I have to push Franklin out of my mind.

I force myself to think of Paulie Barnes's terms: no law enforcement.

But he didn't say anything about private hired protection. After the incidents of the cassette tape and the hawks, I am now determined to set up something more for myself, beyond the simple watch at my gate that Erin promised to give me tomorrow. This is beginning to cost a small fortune. Even so, if Franklin and Truly will let me, I'll gladly pay for guards for their children, too. But if I want closer guarding for myself, whom should I ask? How much protection do I need? A professional? One of Erin's boys or girls?

I guess that makes sense, but . . .

I saw that movie with Meg Ryan and Russell Crowe, the one set in Ecuador where she hires him as a pro to get her kidnapped husband back. Too bad I can't hire Russell Crowe.

I have another idea about whom to hire, but it makes me nervous.

There's a guy, an ex-con, who is grateful to me. He has let it be known that he'd do anything for me, but he hasn't been pushy about it. He's a scary guy, but he has a kind of tact — or maybe *taciturnity* is the better word to describe it. He has kept a distance, contacting me only through proper channels like his lawyer and never surprising me or attempting to get near me. I never intended to take him up on the offer of any help I'd ever need, but desperate times . . .

"Do it," I tell myself.

And so I place a call to his lawyer in Bahia Beach.

★ ★ ★

"Marie!" Defense lawyer Tammi Golding and I became good friends when my last book threw us together in dramatic circumstances. I picture her at her desk where she picked up my call: trim, dark-haired, about my age, short like me, smart as a criminal attorney needs to be to become as successful as Tammi is, and twice as fierce. "Funny you'd call. I was just thinking about you. I've got a new client to defend, a case that might interest you for a book."

"It's always good to know my spies are looking out for my interests, Tammi. Especially if I get stuck for ideas. You never know, I might run out of murderers one day."

"I wish we all could."

"You'd be out of a job."

"You know what?" she asks, with a smile in her voice. That voice has a rasping, sandpaper quality to it that is oddly compelling to juries. "For the sake of humanity, I think I could handle it. What are you doing calling me? Aren't you supposed to be in the Keys with my sworn enemy, the prosecutor?"

"How do you know that? Does the whole world know?"

She laughs. "I don't know about the

271

whole world, but the whole courthouse probably does. Don't you know that you and the prosecutor are hot gossip?"

I groan.

"So why are you calling me? Did you kill him and you need a defense attorney?"

I'm tempted to tell her how close I came to doing that earlier.

"Not yet. Tammi, do you remember how Steve Orbach said he'd do anything for me?"

"Yeah. He means it, too."

Steven Orbach is a twenty-eight-year-old man who murdered his mother when he was thirteen, a fate she richly deserved, and for which he served several years as a juvenile. Shortly after his release he was arrested for a second murder — one he didn't do — and sentenced to death for it. His case consumed a lot of my last book, the one during which I got to know Tammi, because she was his attorney. When he was sprung from death row, Steve thanked me — and sued nearly everybody else. One day, when Tammi gets finished proving how badly they harmed him, Steve may be a rich man. Until then, he works day labor.

"Does he need a job?" I ask her.

"Not really. He's doing construction, making fairly good money, and he seems content with that, or at least, as content as Stevie ever seems about anything."

"Oh." I can't quite get the words out to ask her.

I used to refer to him as Stevie, too — until I met him on death row.

"And he'd drop it in a minute if you asked him to, Marie. So would I." Tammi insists that I saved *her* life, too, during that episode, and while that's probably closer to the truth than any heroics I did for Steven, I've warned her that if she mentions it too often I'll be forced to take it all back. "What do you need him for?"

"I've been getting some nasty E-mails. It happens now and then," I add, with a shrug in my voice so she won't worry. "You know how it is, the nature of what I write attracts cockroaches. Usually, I just toss stuff like that or I delete it if it's E-mail, and then I try to forget it. But this latest batch is more nasty and personal than usual and I just think it might be a good idea to get somebody to watch over me for a while."

"A bodyguard?" She sounds incredulous.

"Well, yes."

"Damn, Marie, it must be bad for you to even think of this. What's Franklin doing about it?"

"Everything he can."

273

"He'd better, or I'll sue his ass."

I laugh. "Aren't you already suing him? So, Tammi, I need a bodyguard, but I want one who could pass for a gardener, or a driver, a houseboy, a personal trainer, like that."

This time, she's the one who laughs. "Oh, my God, Marie, he's going to love this. This will be his wet-dream job."

"Well, that's the part that worries me a little, Tammi. Tell me that Steve's gratitude toward me isn't some kind of weird sexual obsession."

"He's gay, Marie."

"*What?* Steve Orbach's *gay?*" Relief washes over me. "God, that's wonderful."

Tammi laughs at my reaction. "I'm glad you're so happy for him."

"But wait a minute, Tammi, he had sex with the girl he was accused of murdering."

"Yeah, well, he was just out of jail and hoping he was straight."

"But he' s not."

"Trust me. He's really not. He just honestly thinks you're the bee's knees and that he owes his life to you. He's a very serious kind of guy, Marie. Be glad you've got him on your side. You wouldn't want him as an enemy. I can tell you that, just from dealing with him on these civil suits. The guy's implacable. He does not quit when he thinks he's right and he wants something. Do you want his phone number?"

"Yes, but I want you to call him first, do you mind? So I don't just spring this on him out of the blue —"

"And so you have a layer of protection between you and him —"

"You're so smart. Tell him this would be a twenty-four/seven job, Tammi. He'll sleep at my house, he'll go where I go. If that sounds more like prison than opportunity to him, he should turn me down. Or maybe he's got a boyfriend he won't want to leave?"

"I'll find out. How long do you think you'll need him?"

"I don't know. I hope it'll be over soon. I'll pay him well."

"Like he'd let you?"

"You tell him there's no job if I can't pay him."

"I'll tell him you're even more implacable than he is when you want something and you think you're right. Marie, he's going to ask me why you want him, particularly him, for this job."

"Well, to be frank, because he claims to be so devoted to me. And because he has lived through several rings of hell and now he isn't afraid of anything except confinement. And because he's one of the scariest dudes I've ever met, and he's in incredibly impressive physical condition. And because he has spent his whole life with evil people, starting with his mother, and so maybe he'll have a sixth sense about them, so he'll know if one of them gets near me."

"You've convinced me. Now get off the phone so I can call him."

"Thanks, Tammi."

"Should I have him call you down there?"

"No, I'm going home as soon as I pack."

"Good idea. I just heard that the fires have started up again around Homestead. You'd better get out of there while you still can. Should Stevie meet you at your house?"

"No. Tell him I'll call him just before I get there. Call me back right away if he says no, okay?"

"He's not going to say no. You take care of yourself, please."

"That's what I want Steve to do for me."

The traffic is backed up from tourists like me who want to beat the fires before the roads are closed. It gives me too much time to think about endangered species again. The Florida Keys boast the only coral reefs in the entire continental United States, because reefs are more likely to form on the eastern sides of continents where the ocean currents are warmer. For centuries, treasure hunters have dived these reefs, looking for gold and other loot from sunken ships, and now tourists dive to stare at fish. Coral is a living creature, but the reefs that compose the Keys are all dead and fossilized. Out to the east the reefs are still alive, however, though they are in constant danger from people who might love them to death. Living coral is so delicate; a touch of a finger, a brush of a swim fin, a tear from a boat propeller, can kill it.

I feel horribly like coral, myself. A vicious "treasure hunter" has already demonstrated that he can dive into my life with impunity; he can damage and plunder it. Already, he has touched with his destructive anonymous fingers . . . my assistant . . . my lover . . . the children . . . and my own sense of security and self-confidence in my world.

"Why am I some kind of 'treasure' to you?"

This time, I've put up the soft top on my car. I feel safer this way.

The truth is, at this point I don't necessarily look on "no news" from Paulie Barnes as good news. I fear that Franklin crossed an invisible line and that one way or another we will pay for it. How and when and specifically to whom the damage will be done — that's what worries me and leaves me waiting for that shoe to drop.

I feel a touch of despair, a feeling almost of doom, as melodramatic as that sounds even to me. Dammit. I much prefer anger. Maybe it's just that I am traveling alone in my little car. Seen from high above, I'd be only a speck along this highway. I think of celebrities who've been killed by crazy "fans," and although I don't put myself in their category, I wonder . . . one day, will reprints of my book covers say "Tragically and ironically slain by the very sort of killer she wrote about so well . . ."

I feel so damned vulnerable, and yet . . .

"You are just one man," I tell my enemy. "I am a team."

But morbid thoughts continue to obsess me as I cross back to the mainland. *Right over there, in the Florida Bay, that's where game warden Guy Bradley was shot years ago by men who were hunting the long breeding feathers of the great white egret. He was trying to protect a flock of the wading birds and the poachers killed him. Killed him for the feathers. Bradley Key is named after him. And up there in the Everglades, that's where the U.S. Army hanged Chief Chekika, to punish the Seminoles for attacking white settlers. Chekika Recreational Area is named after* him.

So what might they name after me, I wonder in bitter and cynical amusement. Well, if tradition holds, that will depend on where I get killed. Will it be in the future Marie Lightfoot Sawgrass Swamp? Or maybe among the Marie Lightfoot Sand Dunes? The feather hunters pursued the egrets, herons, and spoonbills nearly to extinction, because on the nineteenth-century millinery market, their feathers were literally worth more than gold. The Native Americans were also murdered for economic reasons. *But I'm not worth anything dead to anybody.* He'll never see a penny of any of the royalties from any book he may publish about my death; he has nothing to gain except, what? Pleasure? Some unknown revenge? A fame that he can't even claim in public?

"Motive, what's your motive?"

Well, damn, why not just *ask* him?

It's a startling thought.

Despite his recent admonishment, I still

haven't addressed him directly in my "assignments." I just couldn't bring myself to do it this morning, so maybe I crossed a line, too. I have carefully written and submitted only what he said he wanted for the chapters. But why not try to get him into a conversation? That's what a hostage negotiator would do. And I am definitely feeling like a hostage to one man's desires.

The air is smoky. I see a line of fire on the western horizon, but the road home is still open. Maybe that's a good omen. Or maybe we'd all have been wiser and safer to linger in the Keys. If a fire up here could keep us in, it might also have been able to keep him out.

When I'm twenty minutes from home, I call Steve Orbach.

"Do you want the job, Steve?"

"Yes." His whole life up to this point and his personality seem summarized by the way he says that single word. His bass voice, seeming to come from deep in his chest, gives him the sound of someone much older than he really is; his direct, succinct, aggressive style of speech is the way a soldier's might be.

"Okay, I'm heading home right now. I'll tell you how to get there. When you arrive, you'll see a guarded gate. I will call ahead right now to tell them to expect you. Wait there for me and I'll lead you to my house."

"Should I bring anything?"

"Yes, whatever you need to move in for a while."

"I'll pack a bag."

"Good."

"You know I don't carry a gun?"

Which isn't the same thing as saying he doesn't have one. "No, I didn't know that, but I wasn't even thinking of guns."

"Just so you know."

"Okay. Thank you, Steve."

"Don't thank me," he says so firmly it sounds almost like a threat.

One of the stray facts I happen to know from my book research is that the amygdala is said to be the organ both of fear and of memory in the human body. Fear is, as you may imagine, a big thing in true crime books, so it has behooved me to learn a lot about it. In one book I wrote about a killer who stole his victims' pineal glands, I had cause to study the brain extensively, and I was fascinated by what I found out about the amygdala, which is a tiny, fleshy, almond-shaped organ deep in the skull. Scientists have discovered that in traumatized war veterans and abused children, the amygdala actually shrinks from its original size, thereby consigning episodes in their lives to oblivion. They forget about it, in other words. Or to put it in a way that is perhaps more subtly accurate, they can't remember. This could be viewed, I suppose, as nature's mercy, though it can pose a problem for both psychiatrists and prosecutors who want to dig out those memories.

What this means is that when adults who were abused as children claim they can't remember entire years of their youth, apparently they are telling the truth. As their amygdala shrunk, it acted, symbolically at least, like a tiny fist squeezing fear-soaked memories out of their brain.

I feel as if my own amygdala is working overtime right now, pumping out fear, and I wonder how good my own memory will be of the events of this weekend? Could this be one reason why eyewitnesses do such a lousy job of remembering the traumatic events they see?

Upon arriving at the private cul-de-sac where I live, I spot Steve's old clunker parked by the guard gate. The sight of him doesn't make me feel much calmer, at least not yet. He's not a man whose presence necessarily induces serenity. But that's okay. I feel pretty sure that just having him around will eventually help to get my heart rate back down to something closer to normal. It's just that, first, I'll have to get used to *him*.

The guard waves me through. Steve follows close behind me.

When I see my house, I press my garage door opener.

I roll down my window and wave Steve around me. He pulls into the empty, second slot in my garage. I glide in beside him. When we're both out of our cars, he walks ahead of me toward the door that leads into my kitchen, saying quietly, in his tough, bass voice, "I'll go in first, Ms. Lightfoot."

He's already in the house when I hear a woman scream.

19

Marie

I rush inside my house — and discover Steve standing in the kitchen with his back to me. My assistant, Deborah, is standing in the living room, facing him and looking as if she's going to faint on the spot.

"Deborah!"

"Surprise," she says in a weak voice when she sees me. Her knees give way and she sinks onto my living room couch. "Oh, my God, Marie. I thought it was *him*. I thought it was Paulie *Barnes,* come to kill you, and he was going to get me first! I was just coming out of your office and all of a sudden there was this huge man walking in the door and I didn't realize it was Steve — Hi, Steve — and I think I'm going to faint —"

"Don't you dare pass out." I hurry around Steve to get to her. "I'm sorry we frightened you, but what the *hell* are you doing here? You're not supposed to be here!"

"I know, I know." She looks up at me, trembly, near tears, and quite obviously scared of my reaction, now that she's over her initial terror of Steve. She's literally wringing her hands, not the first time I've ever seen that cliché come to life. The mothers of murder victims do that, too. "I know I'm not supposed to be here."

I set down my luggage that I've brought in with me.

"Then why are you?" I demand while Steve moves around me and then on toward the rest of my house. I sense that he's going to scout it out, make sure we're all alone, just the three of us.

"I had to check on something," Deb tells me miserably. "Oh, Marie, I think I've done something terrible."

"Yeah, we have to get you out of here —"

"No, not that. Oh, God, Marie. I'm the reason that awful man knows so much about you. I think it's all my fault."

"*What?* How can that be, Deb?"

She starts to cry for real, just stands there in front of me shaking and crying. Of course, I give her a hug and pat her back until she can get her tears under control enough to speak again.

"I'm so sorry! I'm so sorry!"

"Forget that, sweetie, just tell me what you think you've done."

She gulps. "Have you looked at your Web site lately?"

It's not a question I expected. "My Web site? Well, no, that's why I have you, so I don't have to deal with things like that." I smile at her. "Why? Is there some reason I should have looked at it?"

"You'd better come see, Marie."

But just as she turns around to lead me into the back of the house, Steve is descending the stairs from my bedroom and startles her again. Deborah flinches, and lets out a tiny scream.

"It's just me," he says, calmly.

"Oh, God, Steve, I'm really sorry I screamed at you."

He actually smiles, which I don't think I've ever seen him do before. Although it doesn't exactly transform his aged, hard face into that of a young man again, it does reach his eyes. Steve Orbach may be less than thirty years old, but he has spent about half of that in prisons of one kind or another. He is heavily muscled, and tonight he's wearing loose jeans with a white T-shirt that shows off his physique, and running shoes. He wears his hair in a very short buzz cut, adding to the general impression of toughness inside and out. Steve has the kind of tight skin and facial bones that give his skull the look of sculpture. He's not good-looking, his eyes are too close together for that and his nose is too large, but he's not bad-looking, either.

"Hi, Ms. Dancer," he says, with a warmth that doesn't really surprise me.

He is, if anything, even more devoted to Deborah than he is to me, because it was her initiative that resulted in his freedom. When we met him, we tried to get him to call us by our first names, but he wouldn't do it and apparently isn't about to start doing it now.

"I'm sorry I scared you," he says to her. "I didn't know you were here."

"Where's your car?" I ask her. "It wasn't outside."

"I had a friend drop me off," she says miserably, "so nobody'd know I was here."

"I'd say *that* worked," I remark, dryly.

Steve looks over her head, at me. "Everything's clear upstairs, Ms. Lightfoot. Where do you want me to put my stuff?"

"You can camp in here, or you can have the guest room on this floor."

"I'll take this couch. More central."

"Good. I need to talk to Deb right now, Steve. Then you."

"I'll be outside," he says. "Checking things out."

I follow Deb into my office and then over to my desk, where she has pulled my author Web site onto the computer screen. Until Deb came to work for me, I used a portion of my publisher's Web site as my own. One of Deb's first jobs for me was to scout out a Web site designer to create an independent site, a place where my readers could reach me directly. After she and I both approved the design, I turned the whole shebang over to Deb. If it needs renovating, she does it. When fan mail, questions, or requests come in, she handles them. It isn't possible for us to individualize every answer, although between Deb and me, we do a fair job of trying. I believe that people who care enough to write to me deserve an answer, but that's only in an ideal world. In the real one, I just don't have time. With Deb to help me, they can count on getting one. Before her arrival, I was way too deeply absorbed in research and writing to pay much attention to fan mail.

Deb always selects a few letters to read to me each day, winnowing out mean ones that will only make me feel bad, like ones that criticize my writing in ways I can't fix. If there's criticism I need to hear, she reads that to me; if there are particularly sweet letters, she reads those, too. We both enjoy those, I think, and I have the impression that the nasty ones hurt her almost more than they bother me. Deb takes a proprietary interest in me now, and resents my critics and foes. I know she takes it all very personally, because she's so young.

So now I'm looking at my own Home Page and it's looking exactly as I thought I remember it, except —

"Oh," I say, with a bit of understatement.

Deb says, sounding miserable, "I added that a month ago."

"That" is a small picture of Deb, herself, at the far left-hand bottom of the page, where it says, "Ask Deb!" When I click on the photo, it opens up into a page that says "Do you have a question for Marie? Would you like to set up an appearance, a speech, or an autographing session? Do you have books you'd like her to sign for you? Whatever your questions, just ask me, Deborah Dancer! I'm Marie's research and administrative assistant, and I'll be delighted to answer your queries. Please contact me here, by E-mail." There's also our fax number and the post office box I use for fan mail.

I like it, I think it's a good idea, but immediately, I also see the problem.

The same photo from the Home Page is here, too, but it's not just her face, it's all of her, frizzy hair and all, and she's wearing that damned horsy sundress.

"He saw this picture," I say.

"Yes," she whispers. "And that's not all. I think I've figured out who he is —"

"What?" I stare at her, incredulous. "You have?"

She waves her hands in front of her, to deny what I'm thinking. "No, not like that! No, I mean, I figured out who he is in the sense of which of the fans who's been writing to me. I don't know his real name, or anything like that, but I'm sure I know which one he is." Deb reaches toward the printer and picks up the pages lying on top of it. "I just know this is him. Look how he tricked me!"

There are about forty-two E-mails, which sounds like a lot, but isn't when we're speaking of eager fans, or of E-mail, for that matter. It's not unusual for a fan to "e" many times in a short burst of goodwill and enthusiasm. I'd probably do the same thing if I got an E-mail back from my favorite writer, or even from her assistant. It's fun to feel so close to fame. But as for responding, I would be happy for Deb to handle all of it for me, leaving my brain and hands free to keep writing the books that inspire those letters.

And now, reading through the forty-two, some of them no more than two or three lines long, in the way that E-mails often are, I wish I had seen these before she did. Maybe a more experienced eye would have caught the way in which he lured her into telling him more about me — and about herself — than she should ever have revealed to a stranger.

"I love Marie's books," he starts out, effusive as a teenage girl. *"It must be so fascinating to work for her! If you don't mind my asking, how does a person get a great job like yours?"* That was his first question, leading her into conversation with him. Over the time the correspondence continued, it appears that he pulled a lot of things out of her. Deb hands me a stack of her replies that she dutifully saved and filed. To that first question, she told him about her educational background, about her first job as a feature writer, and how she originally came to me part-time. He wrote back, *"So, what sorts of things do you*

do for her — besides answer pests like me, of course!!"

"You're not a pest at all!" she wrote back. "Marie's readers are the best people in the world, and it's wonderful to get to 'meet' some of you this way. Well, what I do for her is — everything but write her books! Just kidding. But I do help her a little with her research (I love that!), proof-reading (don't love that! (:>), I run this Web site, run personal errands, do secretarial stuff, and generally try to make myself indispensable to Marie! She's a great boss and I'm learning so much from her."

"You mean you even do her grocery shopping, too, like that?" he asked then.

He made himself sound young, impressionable, ingenuous, and Deb answered in a tone to match his.

"Sometimes, I do! Like today, I helped Marie take her car into the shop for repair. She's got the coolest car —"

"You're kidding?! My mom drives one almost just like that! Hers is a couple of years older than that, and it's blue instead of white, but still, that's so cool to think she drives almost the same kind of car that Ms. Lightfoot does! Where do you guys go to get it worked on?? My mom says it's impossible to find a good mechanic these days, especially for cars like that."

292

All those exclamation points, all those question marks . . . how could he possibly not be sincere?

"I thought he was about fourteen," Deb says. "I thought he was just this sweet, lonely bookworm kid and maybe I could encourage him to become a writer."

She trails off, looking down at the carpet, as if she feels like a piece of dirt lodged in it.

In the space of a few E-mails back and forth they became — or Deb thought they did — E-mail pals. The business about my car repairs is only one of several such small, intimate details of our lives that she trustingly spilled to "Ryan," as he signed himself each time. The most recent was yesterday. My gut clenches when I see it: "Marie's actually taking time off this weekend! Can you believe it? She's going to Key Largo with the state attorney of Howard County and his children. He is soooo handsome, and so nice, too. They're good friends. (:>) Ryan, one of the things you need to know about being a professional writer is that they just work all the time. Really. Forget weekends and holidays. And they hardly ever get vacations. Marie and I work constantly and I love it, but I think you might want to consider that full-time writing is, well, full-time!"

She was indulging in a bit of bragging there, on both of us.

"I'm so sorry, Marie. I'm such an idiot."

"No, you're not, Deb. You're young, that's all, and you didn't realize what was happening here. I don't think there's any way you could have known what he was up to, and to tell you the truth, I might not have realized it, either."

"Really? You wouldn't?"

"Maybe not. The difference is" — I say this gently, not wanting to hurt her, but knowing it probably needs to be said — "I probably wouldn't have gotten quite so involved in writing back to him, and I probably wouldn't have told him so much about us."

"Oh," she says, looking stricken.

I squeeze her arm, try to smile. "But live and learn, right? And Deb, I can't tell you how grateful I am to you for figuring this out and for being honest about it. This may make a huge difference in finding this guy."

"You wouldn't even *have* to find him if I'd —"

"We don't know that. I suspect he would have found another way."

"Are you just saying that to make me feel better?"

"No, I mean it. If he's as determined as he seems to be, he'd have found a way."

"So maybe you don't hate me?"

"Oh, Deb, of course I don't! You have just solved many mysteries, all in one fell swoop. But I'm still concerned about your being here. I was supposed to have fired you, and you're supposed to be gone."

"I know, but I had to —"

"I understand, but now we've got to get you out of here and I have to think up some good excuse to tell him why you were here. At least, if he checks up on you by calling your friends or your family, they'll verify that I fired you —"

There's a look on her face that fills me with new dismay.

"Oh, no, Deb. Tell me you did what I asked you to do. You told them I fired you, right?"

"Yes —" And then it comes out in a burst of truthfulness. "But I couldn't stand to leave it like that! So I told them why —"

"Oh, Deb!"

"But I said they couldn't let anybody know, they had to keep it a complete secret and pretend they didn't know. . . ."

I fan the E-mails in my hands. He's horribly clever. It will be child's play for him to get the truth out of Deb's sweet mother or her young roommates. I can just imagine him calling any one of them and saying something like, *"Hello. My name is Joe Blow and I'm the managing editor for the* Palm Beach Post. *We're looking for a new feature writer and somebody gave me Deborah Dancer's name. Is she available for employment at this time?"*

Deborah hasn't even created the illusion that I fired her.

And to burst it completely, she came to work today.

He'll know. He already knows, I'm sure of it.

When we open my E-mail to see if anything new has arrived, we both see that it's true: he knows.

Dear Marie,

You and your friends don't follow directions very well, do you?

I warned you. First your assistant, then the children.

And while I'm at it, may I inquire — whose bright idea was it for the prosecutor to write directly to me? He claims it was his. If that is the case, the best that can be said for you, my darling, is that if he won't exert the self-discipline required to await my instructions, and if you won't or cannot discipline him, then I will do it for both of you.

Let me ask you something, my dear.

How long has it been since you have read John D. MacDonald's novel *The Executioners*? If it has been a long time, I recommend that you review it. You're in for such a treat. I do believe he sets the standard for building unbearable suspense in his fictional victims and in his readers. His villain, as you may or may not know, is a very bad man by the name of Max Cady who reacts badly — to say the least — when his enemies defy him.

So let's ask ourselves, Marie: what would Max Cady do?

"Oh, my God, Marie!" Deborah is terrified by this E-mail, and I don't blame her. I have to get her out of here and I have to get her to safety. I only hope that my poor young assistant has never ever read *The Executioners*. Maybe she doesn't know what "Max Cady" would do. But I've read it, and I know.

"Steve!" I call out, having heard him return to the house. "Would you come in here? I need you."

And then I make the most difficult phone call of all of them I've made this day: to Franklin, to warn him to arrange immediate protection for himself and his children.

While I have been gone, my private investigator, Erin McDermit, has fulfilled her promise of doing a "sweep" of my home and telephones. Notes attached to them declare them to be free of "bugs," so I feel fairly secure about calling people.

"Can you get cops to watch Trudy's house and the kids?" I ask Franklin when I have reached him at home and explain the situation. The fact that he helped to bring this latest emergency on us does little to mitigate my sense of sorrow and guilt. "Or do you want me to hire somebody? I could get Erin herself to do it —"

"Neither," he says. "I'm going to send them out of town, if Truly will let them go."

"I'm so sorry, Franklin."

"Me, too. What about your safety?"

"I'm taking care of it," I assure him.

There's a pregnant silence, full of many things not said, and then we hang up.

His idea for his children has given me an idea for Deb, and so after I hang up, I tell her, "I want you to make a list of everything you would pack for a trip to Southern California. Steve? When she finishes her list, I want you to take her to the airport. Wait there and I will arrange for a personal guard to meet you with a suitcase for Deb. Deb? The guard will accompany you to L.A. I'm going to call my cousin Nathan and ask him to put you up for a couple of days. If this hasn't blown over by then, we'll find another, even safer place for you to stay for a while."

Her only response is "Oh, God."

Steve's is more practical. "What about you?"

"He's not after me right now. I'll be okay."

"I'll come right back here," Steve says, "as soon as I know she's safely on the plane."

Neither of those events can come too soon for me.

20

Marie

Within the hour, Erin McDermit herself is knocking on Deborah's apartment door and handing the roommates a list of the items Deb wants them to pack for her. A phone call from Deb to them has taken care of their questions about this urgent request — "I have to go to Boston to do some research for Marie. I have to get right to the airport, so she's sending another assistant over to get my stuff."

I've hired Erin to stick to Deb until it's no longer necessary.

The "boss" costs about twice what her other operatives do, but I want the best for Deb, and Franklin's not going to need Erin for the children. I would have "given" Steve Orbach to either of them, but he wouldn't have done the job for Franklin, and it didn't seem wise to send him off to L.A. with Deb. She's too young; he's too weird. Things might happen that she's too naive to prevent. I'm not too naive. And that's why Steve stays with me where he can watch my back — and I can keep an eye on him.

Deb and Erin will be staying with my cousin Nathan in L.A.

When I called him to ask if he could take them in, I said, "I want to make this sound stupid and funny, so you won't worry."

"Fuck that. Just tell me."

"It's going to sound so melodramatic."

"Marie, will you just fucking say it?"

"Somebody has threatened to kill me."

Utter silence. Then, "You're kidding."

"I wish. Somebody — a man, apparently — has been threatening me."

"Since when?" he asks, sounding angry, as if I've been holding out on him. "What's today? Is it still Saturday? I just talked to you Thursday, and you didn't say —"

"It hadn't started yet. I got the first E-mail right after that."

"Okay," he says then, sounding mollified. "So what did it say?"

"He says if I don't do what he tells me to do, he'll hurt Deborah, and then he'll hurt Franklin and his children."

"Shit. What does he want?"

"Oh, it's the creepiest, strangest thing, Nate! He wants me to write a book with him —"

"A *book?* What kind of book?"

"A true crime book about . . . about my own murder."

There was an appalled silence. And then, my cousin said with the driest of wit, "Damn, why didn't I think of that? I could probably have sold *that* script."

It made me laugh, as he intended it to, and then I felt better.

"Send them to me," Nathan said, lightly. "Your tired fliers, your huddled assistants yearning to breathe free. I lift my lamp beside the western shore. Plus, I'll haul out the clean sheets."

While I wait for Steve to return from taking Deb to the Bahia Beach Airport, I turn on a lot of lights and think about my dream of the monster in the basement.

Until that dream, I had not admitted to myself how frightened I am to be alone with so much responsibility for myself and for other people. The truth is, I've always been alone. I've always been frightened, too, although I've managed to avoid accepting any of the burden of other people's lives. I like to think the fact that I have persevered in spite of great fear means that I am brave. I *choose* to think it means I'm brave, even if the rest of that equation suggests that I've been timid, or even cowardly in relationships. Never married, never cohabited, no children —

Paulie Barnes predicted I would learn things about myself.

Damn him, he's right.

The first thing Steve says when I let him back in is, "They got off fine."

"Good. Thank you."

"Ms. Lightfoot, you want to explain all this to me now?"

"Yes, come on in and let's sit down. What did Deb tell you on the way to the airport?"

"She told me about the E-mails, about what this asshole threatened, about how she thinks it's her fault this happened."

I shake my head to deny that. "He would have found me anyway."

"That's what I told her."

I stare at him for a minute, thinking, *And considering your experiences, you ought to know.* His blunt, aggressive way of expressing himself may have convinced Deb in a way I never could have done. It's after midnight now. Steve is sitting on the edge of my living room couch with his knees apart, his elbows resting on them, his hands clasped between his legs, and he's bending his torso attentively toward me. I have to admit that he looks the epitome of sui generis "bodyguard" — all muscle, focus, and grim intent. There's no lightness in this man that I've ever seen, no sign of humor, good or otherwise. There's just this immaculate courtesy and an aura of weightiness, of some kind of meaningful substance. Or maybe I'm only imagining that. Maybe the "substance" is nothing but the self-important air that some ex-cons assume, the ones who do the intimidating rather than being the ones who get intimidated. The bullies instead of the victims.

He's no victim, not anymore.

Whatever Steve Orbach really is, and whoever he is now on the way to becoming in this new freedom, there is something both reassuring and discomfiting about having him sitting in my living room staring across at me like this.

I tell him every detail he hasn't already heard.

He listens without interrupting, and then at the end of it, he asks, "So what do you want from me?"

"I want you to be my eyes, Steve. I don't

need for you to watch *me*. I need you to keep an eye on everybody around me."

"What am I looking for?"

"You may know that better than I do. I think you're looking for people who are paying attention to me with maybe some kind of edge to it, an" — I search for the right word, but can only come up with an insipid one that doesn't even begin to express what I mean — "unpleasantness —"

"You mean like Ted Bundy was unpleasant?"

I have to laugh. He has caught on, all right. When he doesn't smile back, much less laugh, I can't tell if he actually made a wry joke. "Right."

"A predatory look? A devious one?"

"I guess." Steve may be an ex-con, but his grammar, his elocution, and his vocabulary are as immaculate as his clothes and his manners. I remember that when I first met him, while he was still on death row, I was extremely impressed by the discipline it must have taken for him to maintain his body, much less his intellect and his emotions. Now, months later, it seems that he's in even better shape.

"A man?" he asks me.

"I think so, don't you?"

He nods. "And you think that if he's

around, I'll recognize him because I have known his type in prison?"

I'm startled by the dead-on aim of his perception. "Does that offend you?"

"No. I will also look for faces that appear more than once. Repetitive appearances."

"Good. Yes."

"But you know, Ms. Lightfoot, there's no guarantee I can spot this person."

"I know that, Steve."

"Do you expect an attack of some kind?"

"I don't know what to expect. I don't think that will happen right now, not as long as he keeps me writing his damned book for him. If he does attack, or tries to snatch me, I don't think he'd try it in public, do you?"

"Bundy picked up his victims in parking lots, on beaches, in broad daylight sometimes."

"But he did it when there was nobody else with them, unless it was another young woman, and then he would lure her into going, too. You'll always be with me."

"Won't he object to that?"

"We'll find out. He may already know about you. If he does, he isn't objecting."

"I think I can tell you why. He's not going to mind my being around, because he's not going to make his move for a while. You still have to do the research and write the book, right? But when he thinks the time is right, his first move will be to try to separate you from me somehow, or just get rid of me."

"Steven, are you sure —"

"He won't get rid of me."

"Maybe I'm asking too much —"

"That's bullshit. You can't do this all by yourself, Ms. Lightfoot. You may have hired that private investigator and that criminologist, but they aren't here to protect you. I agree that I'm uniquely suited to help you, and I can, and I want to. Besides, you can never ask too much of me, Ms. Lightfoot, not for the rest of your life."

"I don't know about that, Steve."

"That's because you've never been in prison. I *do* know." He shifts his weight on the couch. Almost every time he makes a sudden movement my heart jumps a little and I start to flinch away from him. I've got to stop that. Surely, eventually, I'll get over that instinctive reaction to this strong, rather mysterious, and intimidating person. "When you say I'll always be with you, how literally do you mean that?"

"Pretty literally. What do you suggest?"

"I think you need a pocket of relative safety while you work on the book, and I'll provide that just by being here. I should accompany you wherever you go, so I can check out the crowds. And you need me here for a couple of other reasons, too. One, to check out this neighborhood to see if anybody's been watching or asking questions. And also just to make you feel better."

He surprises me with that last one, but of course in my mind, it's the main reason to have him here at all.

"Steve, I have to say — you're absolutely right that I need you here to make me feel safer and less alone. But I've also got to tell you that you may be the nicest and most considerate guy in the world, and it will still drive me crazy to have you around all the time. I'm a writer. I require solitude. I go nuts without huge doses of it. It makes me feel a little crazy just to think of having somebody in my house day and night for an indefinite period of time."

He pauses only an instant, before pronouncing, "Tough shit."

I'm startled, but I agree with him. *He's here. You need him. Don't like it? Get over it, Marie.*

21

Marie

By Sunday morning, I know that Erin's people are working on my E-mail traces, but they haven't told me anything about it yet. It's too soon. I understand this kind of thing can take a while. With no helpful information coming in, and just when I'm hoping to get a little of my own work done, the morning E-mail reveals new twists to the developing theme:

Dear Marie,
   While you're waiting to see what happens next, is the suspense killing you? Gee, I hope not. Killing you is my job.
   I've changed my mind about something. No, not about punishing you for breaking my rules, but about bringing in law enforcement. I know I told you not to do it, but I've decided that's a bad

idea, storywise. I was thinking too conventionally, don't you agree? Too much like a screenwriter following all the conventions of a hostage movie, and not enough like the original creator that I am.

I've decided that it won't be good for our book if there aren't any cops chasing me and if nobody is trying to protect you. A two-person book might be boring, even though you and I are the two people. Even so, I believe that we need to enlarge our cast of characters, add some action — the more desperate, the better. Let's up the ante. Let's put more people at risk. Let's make things more complicated and challenging not only for you, but also for me. If I am pitted only against you, that's not much of a fight, dear. Too one-sided, with me holding all the cards. I don't believe our readers would like it if you appear to be as powerless as, in fact, you are. They will quickly lose interest if you seem too much the "victim" too soon. Their full realization of how completely I control you and these events must only dawn on them and on you gradually. Let them — and you — fool yourselves into believing you have hope. Let them believe for a little while longer that you might still have a chance to survive, to identify me, and to catch me before I kill you.

Now, in order for us to ratchet up the suspense in that way, I'll need to loosen your reins. I am going to allow you the illusion of freedom, Marie. As of this moment, I give you permission to call in law enforcement agencies of your choice. Maybe, because you're famous and you know a lot of cops, you can persuade them to give you more help than you'd receive if you were just any Jane Doe.

Oh, and speaking of that . . . don't worry about whether or not I'll leave your body so mutilated that not even your own mother could identify it. Not that she could, being already quite deceased, herself. You'll be easily identifiable; they won't need dental records, fingerprints, or DNA to name you. One look at your face and they'll know. Your face may be *all* that's recognizable as Marie Lightfoot, but that's all they'll need.

I wonder who will face the poignant task of identifying you. Don't you wonder about that, too? It's not as if you have relatives who care about you. Well, you do have one, your cousin Nathan. But would you really want poor Nate to have to do it? He's a poet, a sensitive soul. Poor Nathan might be traumatized for the rest of his life. On the other hand, it would give him such delicious material from which to grow his poems and screenplays. Maybe he'd finally see one made into a movie. That would be a great benefaction, Marie, for you to bequeath your cousin through your death — the writing success that eludes him while you live.

But if Nathan doesn't I.D. you, who will?

Your boyfriend could, I suppose. I like that idea, probably more than you do. Imagine the drama of the moment, when the coroner pulls back the covering from your face. See DeWeese's grief! Watch how he chokes back his tears! Imagine his conflicted feelings — how sorry he is that you are dead, but how relieved he is that now his children are safe from me.

Or, possibly, one or two of the police officers who know you will be called to the scene, to identify you. That depends where it happens, I suppose. Frankly, Marie, I don't know whether a bodily

312

identification by next of kin will be required in the particular county in which I plan to kill you. But who cares about that? I couldn't care less, and you will not be in any position to mind.

Sitting here, staring at my computer screen, reading all of that, I can barely even take in the news that he has granted me "permission" to call upon law enforcement. It's three other things that rivet me: He mentioned my cousin Nathan. He mentioned my mother. He didn't mention Deborah.

"Steve!"

He comes running, and then reads over my shoulder.

"He must know she stayed at Nathan's apartment last night!" I say, feeling panicky and sick to my stomach again. "Why else would he even *mention* Nathan? And why didn't he name Deborah as somebody who might identify my body? Is he saying she'll be dead before then?"

My bodyguard says the only rational thing he can say to me at this point.

"Call the cops, Ms. Lightfoot."

Within the hour we are on our way, driving in my car to downtown Bahia

Beach to meet up with Paul Flanck and Robyn Anschutz, who are two of the best cops and investigators I know. My pet criminologist, Aileen Rasmussen, is going to meet us, too.

"Not at the station, Marie," Robyn objected when I reached her home and asked her where she wants us to meet. She and Paul are both off duty today, she told me, which means they're doing me an even bigger favor by agreeing to meet me now. "If we show our faces there, we'll get put to work."

"I'm afraid this will be work, too, Robyn."

"That's okay. At least we don't have to wear suits, and we can meet you in a bar or someplace where nobody's going to bother us. You know how it is when you're out with Paul and me, Marie." I hear a teasing smile in her voice. "All those autograph seekers. We can hardly eat in public anymore, after you put us in your book." Her tone changes. "Do you know Easy Pete's, on the river?"

"Perfect."

So here we are, three of us, seated like tourists at a table under an umbrella at Easy Pete's on the New River. On both banks, opposite and on either side of us, long rows of cruisers, sailboats, and house-boats are picturesquely tied up. Some are live-aboards; some are rentals; all pay the city a fee to dock here. Steve and I arrived first. When the two cops walked toward me, Steve moved out of the way before I could even attempt to introduce them. To say the least, he's not fond of cops. Now, Steve's perched on a stool at the bar behind us, where he can keep a better watch on the customers who come and go.

"Who's your muscle?" Paul asks me.

I grin at Robyn. "Your partner sounds just like a TV detective."

"I know." She rolls her eyes. "It's so embarrassing."

"Which TV detective?" Paul wants to know.

"William Conrad," his partner says, before I can even open my mouth. "Remember him, Paul? Fat. Old. You sure remind me of him."

"I think you're more the Bruce Willis type, myself," I tell him.

"See?" he tells her, and then looks back at me. "Or, possibly a younger Mel Gibson."

"Definitely," I assure him while his partner snorts with derisive laughter. "That's Stevie Orbach, Paul."

Their eyes flash almost immediate recognition, and some hostility.

"No shit," Paul says. "So that's sue-the-bastards Orbach, huh." There are police officers on Steve's long list of people to sue for his wrongful imprisonment and death sentence. "I guess I can't blame him, but I don't have to like him, either. He did kill his own mother, for crissake. And it was a cop who finally got him off. One of the very cops he's suing, I might add. What the hell is he doing with you, Marie?"

"I hired him to be my bodyguard."

Robyn nods thoughtfully. "Now *that's* probably not a bad idea."

I decide this isn't the time to remind them of the facts of Steve's childhood with the monster he called "Mom," or that the cop who got him off was also the cop who put him *in* prison for a murder he didn't do. Instead, I just say, "It's good to see you guys. Thanks for coming down here to meet me."

"Aw shucks," says Paul.

"We're just hoping you'll put us in another book," Robyn says.

Across the table from me, Robyn and Paul look pretty much the same as when they starred in a book of mine, *The Little Mer-*

maid, a story that disturbed and changed all of us. But the disturbing and the changing were all inside of us. Externally, I'm still the same short blond nosy woman I was back then, nosier if possible. Also, blonder. Robyn's still married to her Cuban expatriate and still wears her blond hair backcombed high enough to give her a couple of imaginary inches on her police partner, Paul. And Paul's still the single, all-man, half-redneck kind of guy he's always been. "You're not exactly white trash," I once heard Robyn taunt him. "More like beige trash." "Dammit!" was his quick retort. "My daddy *told* me that college degree was gonna ruin me!"

"You sure you don't want a real drink?" Paul asks me now, nodding at my coffee cup. Although he's offering, neither of them is drinking alcohol, either. It's iced tea all the way for Robyn and a diet root beer for Paul.

"I'm sure. I feel as if I need to keep my wits about me, the few I have left after the last couple of days."

As always, Robyn gets to the point. "What's up, Marie?"

I hand the E-mails to Paul and then give them a chance to read and to trade with each other. Halfway through, Paul looks up, points to the first E-mail, and says, "He told you not to contact us."

"He changed his mind." I point out a later E-mail. "Apparently he's not worried about you anymore."

"I'm insulted," Paul says.

"Crushed," Robyn agrees, without even looking up from her reading. "What about the FBI?"

"He says he doesn't care who I bring in to this. He seems to like the idea of a chase."

"Good." Robyn casts a glance at her partner beside her. "He's arrogant, Paul, just like you. That'll help us catch him." To me, she says, "What else you got?"

I tell them all the rest of it, every damned thing that has happened.

"Marie," Paul says, when I've finished my recital, "you've kept the other evidence, right? The cassette tape, the advertising flyer?"

I give him a look of mock disbelief. "Who do you think you're dealing with here? Those aren't romance novels I write, you know."

Robyn half turns in her seat to chastise him. "Did she keep the evidence? No, she flushed it. Of course she kept the evidence, you numbskull!"

"Just asking." He grins, showing his palms in conciliation.

Robyn and I smile briefly at each other, acknowledging that she has taken this good old boy and trained him pretty well. But both cops look as if they had to severely restrain their facial expressions when Franklin DeWeese's name cropped up.

"I saw that article about you in *People* magazine," Robyn says as she dumps more sugar into her iced tea. There's more than a hint of laughter in her eyes. "How long's *that* been going on?"

"I think they've been publishing for several decades now," I reply, with a straight face.

"Yeah, right, that's what I meant." Robyn waggles her eyebrows. "Of course, I hate to pry."

This time, it's her partner who snorts.

"I do!" she protests, all injured innocence. "You know I can hardly stand to interrogate suspects, Paul! I'm sooo conscientious of their First Amendment right to privacy."

I grin at them. "So do I have a right to privacy here, or am I going to have to indulge your prurient curiosity?"

"It is *not* prurient." Robyn grins, but then quickly sobers up. "I'm sorry, Marie. Ordinarily, what you do with our state attorney would be none of my business, but he's involved, so I guess it is. And his kids are involved, too. So one thing we'll have to do is look to see if there's any connection between DeWeese and this nut who's after you. Like, it could be that he's really wanting to hurt the prosecutor, but he's covering his tracks by making it look as if he's coming at you."

Paul and I stare at her, and then he says, "Much as I hate to say it, that may have been a brilliant deduction, Partner."

"I never once thought of that," I admit.

Modestly, she shrugs. "If it's the prosecutor he's after, he might even think he will hurt DeWeese more by aiming at you."

"No, Robyn, nothing could hurt him as much as threatening his kids."

"Yeah," she has to agree. "Are they the cutest little bugs you ever saw, or what?"

"He could be hiding his real reasons for doing this," Paul interrupts. "Maybe it's about writing a book, maybe it's not."

"I hadn't thought of that, either," I admit. "I haven't had *time* to think, or to get perspective! I guess I've been assuming that he wants to be famous, and that I'm his means of doing that. You know" — I produce a small grin for them — "apparently, there's something to be said for bringing in the experts. So what *else* can you do for me that I can't do on my own?"

"Check out the cassette tape, and how it got into your car," Paul says, "check everything for prints, the usual —"

"We won't find any prints," Robyn predicts.

Her partner turns to her. "Well, aren't you Little Mary Sunshine."

"Marie wants to know the truth, Paul."

"I do," I agree. "Even when I don't like it."

"We'll run his MO through our databases," Paul promises me, "to see if anything similar turns up —"

"Something similar to this? An MO?" I have to laugh at the idea of a "modus operandi" at work here. My laughter comes out sounding pretty cynical. "Yeah, you're sure going to find a whole lot of cases like this one, Paul. He's probably a serial killer who only murders true crime writers like me. You'll find bloody manuscripts scattered all over the country." I feel my control slipping, but I can't stop it. "Quick, call Ann Rule! Better warn her to watch out! And I'll give you Joe McGinnis's phone number, and you'd better call Linda Wolfe. They're all true crime writers, why I can give you a long list. You'd better let them know that a serial killer of true crime writers is on the loose." I put my head in my hands. "Oh, God, I'm sorry."

They're tolerant.

"Sorry," I repeat. "I got a little carried away there."

"Sarcasm beats panic," Robyn observes sagely.

"Yeah, well, I've had some of that, too. When I heard that tape, I thought I was going to run straight off the road. But I'm trying very hard not to panic and to remember that supposedly he isn't going to hurt anybody as long as I follow his instructions."

"Which brings us to your assistant —" Robyn says.

"And the DeWeese kids," Paul adds. "Look, don't worry about your assistant, Marie. She's a long way away, and you've got her covered about as well as anybody can. And as far as the kids are concerned, that's out of your hands, too. DeWeese is a big boy —"

"I'll say he is," Robyn interjects, waggling her eyebrows.

Paul gives her a disgusted glance. "As I was saying, if anybody has the means to protect his family, DeWeese does."

"But Paul, now this guy has something to prove!"

"Like what?"

"Like what's in those E-mails! He threatened certain things — general things — if I
didn't follow his rules. Deb broke one of
them. Franklin offended him. Now he'll
have to show me that he means business,
or he won't have any leverage over me."

"Or," Paul says, "this may be the end of
him."

"You think he won't do anything, and
it'll all be over?"

"Sure, it's possible."

"Probable," Robyn corrects.

"I don't agree," says another voice, and
we all look up to find a motherly-looking
woman staring prissily down at us, as if we
had spilled our milk. "I agree with Marie
that he has to do something now, and I feel
convinced that he will do it." Her glance
stops at me. "That is the bad news, Marie.
I'm afraid I don't have any good news.
Move over, please, so I can order a cup of
coffee." As she sits down, she sticks out a
hand for either one of the cops to shake,
and announces, "Dr. Aileen Rasmussen.
Who're you?"

22

Marie

With a draft beer at one hand and a basket of fried clams at the other, seventy-three-year-old Aileen lectures us as if these two cops seated across from her have never handled a homicide case before, and as if I've never written about them. "It's easier to do a profile when there's a crime scene —"

"We're kinda glad there isn't one in this case," Paul cracks.

Aileen ignores that, pops a clam into her mouth, and gazes coolly at me while she chews and swallows. "When I'm analyzing homicides, I generally start with the closest circle of people around the victim and then work outward. You're not dead, Marie —"

"Yet," I murmur, and Robyn kicks me lightly under the table.

"But you're still the place we should start, first by looking at the people closest to you and then working out in ever-widening circles from there. You probably think it's some crazy stranger who's doing this, but I would say that he has a closer connection to you than that."

"Like somebody I've written about?"

Instead of directly answering me, she takes us all in with a glance. "Have the three of you discussed *The Executioners* yet?"

Paul, Robyn, and I exchange glances, trying not to look dumb.

"No." I speak for all of us. "Should we have?"

"I would think that might seem obvious."

The cops across the table are behaving suspiciously well in the face of her superior attitude.

When neither speaks up, I ask, "Why, Aileen?"

"Marie, just look at his emphasis on it!"

"But that's just a —" Paul begins.

"Clue," she pronounces, leaning forward and saying it as if to a small child. Paul sucks in his cheeks as if he's holding tightly on to words in his mouth, but I notice a gleam of mischief in his eyes. Oblivious as always to the effect she produces on people around her, Aileen sails on to say, "I believe it holds some kind of key for us, so I went and bought a copy of the book and I've been reading it. I also picked up videos of both of the movies that were made from it, and I've watched both of them. I don't suppose you have?"

Three heads shake, but I feel compelled to defend us.

"Aileen, give us a break! Paul and Robyn only just heard about all this a couple of hours ago, and I haven't exactly had time to watch movies."

I don't see that it's necessary to mention *The Lion King*.

It's Robyn who cuts to the chase, of course. "So what have you figured out?"

"*Surely* you've read the book?" Aileen counters. "*Some* time?"

This time, three heads nod. The late John D. MacDonald is still one of Florida's favorite writers, so it's never remarkable to find three out of three Floridians who've read him.

"But I don't remember much except that somebody was chasing somebody," Robyn confesses. "I think there was a family that was frightened, wasn't there?"

"Yes. In the story, there is a terrible man named Max Cady who is clearly a sociopath. He's the villain. When the story opens, he has been released from prison, where he served time for brutally raping a girl. The hero of the book is a witness against him. Cady wants revenge. So he launches a campaign of terror against the hero's family, which includes the man, his wife, three children, and a dog — What? Why are you all looking at one another like that?"

"It's your theory, Robyn!" I say.

"What theory?" the criminologist asks impatiently.

"That the real target is Franklin, not me."

"It fits the story," Paul says. "Somebody that DeWeese has put away wants revenge now, and so he's persecuting DeWeese's family —"

"Which," Robyn eagerly breaks in, "sort of includes you, Marie."

I turn to Aileen. "What do you think about *that?*"

But the damn woman ignores us again. "One of Cady's first acts against them is to kill their dog. It was an Irish setter, I believe. Do you have a dog, Marie?"

"No!" I feel shocked and chilled at the thought of this. I'd completely forgotten that part of the book. "Neither does Deborah. And Franklin's children don't either."

A small frown appears on the criminologist's forehead. God forbid she should be wrong. "Well, the dog itself may not be an exact parallel, then. But I think what's important is that the man who is after you may commit some kind of act that is a kind of equivalent to that, by which I mean he may do something vicious and hurtful to show he can, but he won't kill anybody yet. He seems to move by increments, drawing you in, just as in the book."

"Okay, but what about Robyn's theory?" I insist. "Could it be Franklin he's really after?"

Paul interrupts. "Wait a minute. *Yet?* What did you mean by 'yet,' Doctor?"

Aileen looks over at him. "I read Marie's correspondent as being capable of murder, although" — the frown deepens — "there's something finicky about the way he writes to you, Marie, in his use of language, for instance, and his vocabulary. There's no cursing, no dirty language. He's actually quite a different kind of person than the villain in MacDonald's novel. That man was coarse and brutal. This one strikes me as rather old-fashioned. It's possible that he's an older man. Alternatively, he may be a young man who's stuck in a time warp — reads the classics, hates contemporary culture, that kind of thing. He's a snob. Definitely, a snob. He feels himself to be superior to the run-of-the-mill person." She glances back at me. "And superior to you, Marie. I think that on the one hand he wants to feed off your fame, but on the other hand, he resents your great success, probably feels you don't deserve it compared to a man of his vast intelligence and talent." Her inflection is ironic. "I think our man is well educated. I think he is neat in his personal habits. Very clean, very presentable. Maybe not compulsively hygienic, but a bit on the fastidious side. You might find him wearing a dark suit with a crisp white shirt and a tie and well-shined, possibly expensive shoes. If not that, then at least dressed quite neatly. Certainly, history is replete with murderers who could have fit that description, but my point here is that men like that don't necessarily want to get their own hands dirty. They arrange for clean 'accidents' to happen, or even for other people — minions, if you will — to do their killing for them." She smiles. Her first. "That's an excellent description of some battlefield generals, actually."

"That fits the incidents so far," Robyn

points out. "The E-mails, the tape in Marie's car, the advertising flyer and the birds. It all has a kind of clean and distant feeling about it, now that you mention it."

"Are you saying," Paul asks Aileen, "there could be more than one person involved?"

"I'm saying that I see an ambiguity in his letters, as if he's a man who is capable of murder, but who might not enjoy the mess of it or the feelings he would have afterward. I've never run across killer communications quite like these before. I must confess I feel a little baffled by them."

My jaw drops. Aileen, confessing weakness?

"The one thing I know for sure is that he's dangerous, Marie. Very dangerous. I suppose —" Her expression clears, as if she's just figured something out. "I know what it is. I feel as if it's not your death he's after, or not *just* your death, it's something else."

"Robyn's theory —"

"No, not Franklin's death, either."

"*What* then?"

"I don't know. But I feel there's something else he wants from you. I think that your murder, or even Franklin's, may not be the point of all this, no matter how much he claims it is."

"He wants the book that comes out of this," Paul reminds her.

"Maybe he does, or maybe that's just a ruse to keep her too busy and distracted to be able to think straight."

"It has certainly done that," I grumble.

"So what *does* he want?" Paul says.

The criminologist produces from her purse a copy of *The Executioners* and slaps it down on the table. "The answer is in here, I feel sure. The obvious one would be revenge."

"Marie?" Robyn prods me. "Who's that pissed at you?"

My answer is to hand her a copy I have prepared of a list of the killers I have known, interviewed, written about, and rejected, as well as the names of their kin.

"My, my," she says, perusing it. "A regular hall of fame of murderers. You do keep the most interesting company, Marie."

"Apparently," I say, sweetly. "I'm here with you guys, aren't I?"

Paul laughs, then points to the page. "Anybody on this list fit the description you just heard?"

I turn the paper back around so I can go down the list again, and as I do, I try to picture everybody on it. "No, I'm sorry, not really."

The criminologist places a hand over the paper, covering it, and I look up at her. "We should start closer to home, Marie. Remember, I said that in an investigation we start with the 'victim' and the circle of people closest to her. Lovers. Friends. Tell us about your family, Marie."

"Family?"

"Yes." She's sarcastic in the face of my foggy response. "You've heard the term before? Mother, father, children?"

I stare off into the distance; the riverbanks disappear; an indistinct green landscape appears to my mind's eye. Reluctantly, I say, "All right. I'll tell you what I know about them," and then I do. For the pitifully few minutes that it takes to tell, I have to endure the surprise and sympathy in the cops' eyes. Even Aileen looks nonplussed. I feel increasingly exposed, coerced to reveal private and painful things I never willingly tell anybody, and I hate "Paulie Barnes" for forcing it out of me.

"I don't see what any of that has to do with it," I tell them. "I wish I knew what he really wants from me."

The cops exchange glances, looking a little embarrassed. We know what he wants, those looks seem to say. Regardless of what your fancy-schmancy criminologist thinks. He wants *you*, Marie.

Paul makes a stab at lightening the atmosphere. "I've heard of people who would kill to get published, but this is ridiculous."

We all laugh, but it's a hollow sound.

"Marie," Robyn suddenly blurts. "Who inherits?"

"I beg your pardon?"

"From you, if you die. Who gets it?"

"Oh, my cousin, Nathan Montgomery. He's like a brother to me. He'll get everything I inherited from my parents after my aunt and uncle had them declared officially dead, and he'll get at least some of my royalties. The rest of it goes to other friends and some charities. But Nathan gets the bulk of mine, and vice versa, unless one of us gets married, or has kids." I see where she's heading with this, and say, simply, "Oh, please. No way."

"How should I talk to Paulie Barnes?" I ask my experts, finally.

"I don't think it matters," Aileen says, astonishing me.

"Don't I have to worry about offending him?"

"Not if it's really something else he's after."

"But we don't know that —"

"I'll tell you what I think," Paul says, dismissing the criminologist with a glance. "Since the bastard's already sitting there at a computer, tell him he should go to the Web and pull up the site for the state prison up at Starke. Tell him he can see a video of a cell on death row up there, a full one-hundred-and-eighty-degree video scan of the cell. Might be a good thing for him to think about. And while he's thinking, you could suggest that he look up Florida State Criminal Statute 836.10."

"That's the same one Franklin talked about. What is it?"

"Oh, yeah." Robyn smiles wickedly, and runs her tongue over her upper lip, as if she's licking off something tasty.

" 'Written threats to kill or do bodily injury,' " Paul recites. "Which he's already guilty of. It's a second-degree felony punishable by up to fifteen years in prison. If he's an habitual offender, he can get up to thirty years, with no possibility of parole for ten years. But if he's a three-time offender or a violent career criminal, it's a mandatory minimum of thirty years."

"And this is without even touching you," Robyn points out.

"I don't approve of mandatory minimums," I murmur, on principle.

"He won't, either," Robyn says, sarcastically.

"He might like to know about our sexual predator laws, too," Paul says then, in the false, chirpy tone of voice of a game show host. "How about 00-179, Robyn, you think he'd like that one?"

"Oh, yes, Paul! Why, that's certainly one of *my* favorites."

Paul explains, "It provides in certain cases for consecutive sentences for murder and sexual battery, instead of concurrent sentences."

"What kind of certain cases?" I ask.

He looks suddenly less willing to explain things to me. "Well —"

Robyn gets it over with. "In cases where there's more than one incidence of murder and sexual battery, Marie."

"Oh. Like, if he attacked Deborah and then later, me?"

"Yes," she says. "Like that."

"Well," I say, taking a deep breath. "These things are good to know, I guess."

"*He* needs to know them, Marie," Paul says, turning serious. "He's got to know that if he wants us to take him seriously, we'll do that, all right, as seriously as life in prison or, worst case, the death penalty."

I turn to Aileen. I don't like her, but she has earned my respect as a professional. "What do you think?"

"I told you. Say anything you want to him."

Across the table, Robyn is shaking her head.

"You never said what you think of Robyn's idea that this guy is really after Franklin," I push Aileen.

"That's ridiculous," she pronounces, including all of us in one haughty glance. "His interest in you could not possibly be more obvious. His goal was to drive Franklin away from you, so that he could have you all to himself, although for what exact purpose we do not yet know."

"I think we do," Paul says, flatly.

Since none of us wants to talk about those crimes against me that might earn Paulie Barnes the electric chair, we pay up and leave. Aileen leaves first, in an officious bustle of noise and movement suggesting how busy and important she is and how many other things she has to do today.

"What a charmer," Robyn comments, after she's gone.

Paul says, "You be careful, Marie." He casts a glance at my bodyguard, whom we've all nearly forgotten about and who is getting off his stool at the bar. "Of everybody. Call if you need us, or if anything changes. Otherwise, we'll be in touch." Robyn gives me a quick, comforting hug. I've never been hugged by a cop before, and I grunt in surprise when I feel a gun under her clothing, at her right hip.

"It's your day off," I say. "Why — ?"

"You can never be too careful, that's my motto." She gives me a quick, stern smile. "Make it yours, Marie."

Steve and I walk into my home to find an urgent message for me to contact Franklin's ex-wife. When I call her, the first words out of her mouth are, "Is this supposed to make everything all right? Are you trying to buy their affection? How dare you do this without consulting me first? I'm their *mother.* Franklin says you didn't even ask him. What are you *thinking?*"

"What?" I ask, rendered nearly speechless by her barrage.

"*What?*" she screams at me. "You ask *what?* You send my children a *dog,* and you ask why I'm calling you?"

My heart stops one beat after the word *dog,* and my mouth goes so dry I can barely ask her, "What kind of dog?"

"What do you mean what kind of dog!

337

You picked it out, you ought to know! Do you have any idea how large an Irish setter gets?"

Irish setter. Max Cady killed their Irish setter.

"You can't just give children a dog," Truly rants at me, "without checking with their parents first. What am I supposed to do now? Did you think of that? I don't *want* a dog. If I had wanted them to have a dog, I would have gone out and got one myself, do you understand that? And now, do I keep a dog I don't want, or do I get to be the bad guy in my children's eyes and make them give up the puppy? Have you ever told children they can't have a puppy they think they get to keep? I could just kill you for doing this —"

"Trudy." Finally, I've found speech. "Trudy, I didn't send the dog."

Her voice is deadly. "It came with your *name* on a ribbon around its neck, Marie."

When she says that, I feel as if a chain has tightened around my own neck. And as if that were not enough of a shock, Steve hands me something he has printed out from my computer: a new E-mail from Paulie Barnes.

"Trudy, I have to go," I tell her while I stare at the E-mail. "Tell Franklin I said

338

that Paulie Barnes sent the dog. He'll understand. Tell him to trace it." *As if he needs instruction from me.* "I'm sorry, but I don't know anything about the dog. You and he will have to decide what to do about it. I just know that I need to stay away from you."

"Who the hell is Paulie Barnes?"

"The man who is threatening us, Trudy."

"Perfect." She slams her phone down. With my ears ringing, I stare at the printout in my hands.

Dear Marie,

Life is just one surprise after another, isn't it?

You do understand now, don't you, Marie? So long as you cooperate in every way with my instructions, I will harm no one but you, and even that will not be for a little while. I don't waste time or actions, Marie. I do only that which is necessary to convince you and to advance the plot of our book.

Now let's not waste any more time.

Or do you want the dog to die?

I will give you a second chance to spare your intimates from pain.

Do what I am about to tell you and I

339

will leave them — including the dog — alone.

Marie, in your typical book about a true crime, you devote several chapters to the background of the victim — her family history, her education, her romances, hobbies, jobs, friends, and so forth. Naturally, our readers will want to know all of that about our victim, too.

You, that is.

I'm going to do you a favor, Marie. Before you die, you are going to know yourself better than most people do. I'm now ordering you to research *yourself*. You are to employ the very same talents of deduction, pursuit, intuition, and perception that have made you so good at dissecting other people's lives. If I were a betting man I'd put down money on a sure thing — that you have already done some of this work of your own autobiography. I'd wager you have notes, possibly even actual chapters; in other words, I'm betting you have material that you can send to me now without any extra effort at all. Do it.

But there are no doubt still things you don't know about yourself.

To the worthwhile end of finding

them out, I am providing the following:

An airline ticket to Birmingham, Alabama.

There is an "attachment," and there are five more sentences in the body of the E-mail. When I read them, my heart and breath seem to stop, and I can't move, can't speak, except to whisper to Steve, "Did you read this?"

"Yes."

"I can't think. I can't even read straight. Tell me what I have to do."

It's all very simple: I am instructed to fly to Birmingham, Alabama, in the morning. Once I arrive, I am to rent a car and drive to Sebastion, where I am to find a place to stay. In Sebastion, I am to start researching and writing about the beginnings of my own life.

But there is one more thing — those five sentences that stopped my heart:

I'll help you begin your research, my dear.

Attached to this E-mail you will find the raw facts of certain events that happened many years ago. I want you to rewrite this in your own style and then submit this new chapter to me before you leave tomorrow. (And don't forget to add that personal, chatty little note I keep expecting but have not yet received from you.)

I believe you'll find the enclosed fascinating, since it is an account of the murder of your parents.

BETRAYAL

By Marie Lightfoot

CHAPTER SIX

Their car was forcibly halted that night at the intersection of Four Roads Crossing. One road led south to Birmingham, one led northwest to Memphis, a third went to Atlanta, and the last one pointed north to Nashville. Four pickup trucks cut off each angle of escape. The last one pulled up behind them so quickly it seemed to materialize out of nowhere.

There was nothing they could do, there was no way out, not even if Michael turned their car toward the surrounding fields, because deep ditches lined the shoulders of the crossroads.

Lyda had been right when she predicted, "We can't escape from this."

Within moments, they were removed from their automobile. They were escorted at gunpoint to the truck immediately behind them. A parade of four pickup trucks then proceeded west until it came to a turnoff into private property.

A passenger in one of the trucks drove their car away.

He drove almost nonstop until he reached Oregon, where a relative of his owned a small backwoods plot of land. The two of them removed the tires from the Folletinos' car and put it up on blocks, a common fate for many vehicles in that area. The relative was a sometime mechanic, so it was not unusual to see assorted battered cars around his dilapidated house. They remembered to remove the Alabama license plate and replace it with an old one from Oregon. To complete the battered look they took sledgehammers to the car and beat in its glass, its chrome, and its doors. When they finished, it looked as if it had been in a multicar pileup or had rolled down a mountain into a rocky ravine.

Later, when people asked why he kept such an old wreck around, the Oregon relative said, "Wasn't nothin' wrong with the radiator and I've used some other bits and pieces from it." The truth was, he kept it as a trophy. It gave him a kick, a good laugh, to look at it rusting away over the years and to know they'd been smart enough to pull off a big one. It was a hell of a joke.

Originally, they fought about it, though.

"Why you gotta leave it here?" the Alabama visitor demanded of his kin. "Why don't you just drive it down a ravine and leave it there?"

"'Cause I'd be *in* it, asshole."

"You'd get *out* of it first, dumbshit."

"It ain't a good idea."

"Well, let's burn it."

"Hell, no, a cop'd ask about a burned car."

"They're not going to ask about it if we beat it to death?"

"Why should they?"

It went on for some time like that.

Their debate ended with a sledgehammer in each man's hands.

When the parade of trucks turned in at the private road, they drove for a while in single file until they reached another turnoff. That one led them into a thicket where anything could happen and nobody would see it, or hear it. They didn't take long to do what they had to do.

Possibly to torture Michael, they shot Lyda first.

They did it quick, almost the moment

after they pulled her from the car, removing her just far enough away to make sure no blood spattered on them or their vehicles.

Before they shot her, they put gunny-sacks on Michael's and Lyda's heads and shoulders, so that the fatal mess would be contained within the sacks. They used a pistol to shoot Lyda once through her head, then twice again as she lay on the ground.

Then they did it to Michael, with no wasted effort.

One moment he was still standing, the next moment he lay on top of his wife's body on the ground. Both of them had gone silently to their fates. Perhaps what held their tongues was the shock they felt upon recognizing their killers. After their deaths, their blood drained from their bodies invisibly, merging together, into the dirt beneath them. With a couple of shovelfuls of earth piled on top of it, no sign would show by morning.

There was an argument about what to do next with the corpses, much like the two relatives fought over the fate of the car in Oregon. This time, the grammar was better, but the decision was not.

"We'll bury them."

"And have some coyote dig them up?"

"By that time it won't matter."

"By that time? What time is that, exactly? You're saying you can predict when a coyote might smell the rot and feel an inclination to dig? When will that be, do you suppose? One week from now? One year?"

"Shut up, both of you. I say burn them."

"Oh, brilliant. And we're supposed to think that no one will notice the smoke lingering in the morning?"

"It will look like a campfire."

"Not to anyone looking for missing people."

In the end they had what seemed at the time to be a stroke of genius, though later it would cause them a lifetime of worry they hadn't counted on. In northern Alabama there were caverns of magnificent depth and breadth and inaccessibility — literal holes in the ground where not even the most dedicated and courageous spelunker went — narrow crevices where things could be tucked in tight. They were not cold enough to preserve corpses for very much longer than earth burial would do, but they were chilly enough and deep enough to mitigate the stench.

At the time, the cavern they chose was on private land owned by a sympathizer. It seemed utterly safe. What they couldn't anticipate was that in years to come there would be an environmentalist president of the United States who would annex tens of millions of acres of land for preservation, including five acres that included that very cavern. Nor could they have foreseen the burst in popularity of spelunking, starting in the 1990s, or the technical advancements in the equipment that would allow cavers to go where none had ever dared go before.

From the moment the first caver got permission to go down, the conspirators who killed the Folletinos never took another easy breath — until one of them went down into the cavern — using that newfangled equipment — and at considerable risk, found the bones.

And hid them deeper.

23

Marie

"Birmingham."

Hardly able to believe I'm doing this, I push my driver's license toward the airline ticket agent. I have purchased a companion ticket for Steve, at full price for both of us. He will have to put up with a tough security check to get on the airplane, because he fits some of the terrorist profile — tough-looking man, single though not traveling alone, buying a one-way ticket at the last moment. He'll just have to tolerate it. There's no way I'm going alone. Paulie Barnes said nothing about taking a friend. But he didn't say I *couldn't* take one, either, and if ever in my life I needed one, it's now. Steve Orbach is not the one I'd choose in other circumstances, but he's the only "friend" I've got with me right now. As we go through the security checkpoint and then wait for our plane, he never leaves my side.

Before we board, I use an airport phone to call Franklin's office and leave a recorded message for him: "I'm going out of town. I'm fine. Don't worry about me. I'm sorry about the dog, and I hope everybody's okay. I'll let you know when I'm back."

On the flight to Birmingham, I skim *The Executioners*, highlighting plot points with a yellow marker. It starts with an idyllic family scene — a lawyer, his pretty wife, their nubile teenage daughter, their two young sons — all enjoying a day at a lake. But the lawyer's worried. A man he once helped convict for the vicious rape and beating of a girl who was the age his own daughter is now, is free and threatening them. As the plot progresses and the family grows more frightened of their stalker, Max Cady terrorizes them in agonizing increments. He poisons their beloved dog. Insinuates that he will rape their daughter. Shoots and wounds their youngest boy. As MacDonald vividly describes him, Cady is by today's standards of villain a cliché, but he didn't seem so back in 1957 when the novel was first published. He's a brute, "simian," with a low brow, dark hair, a powerful and stocky man who smokes "well-chewed" cigars.

As I close the book and stare out the plane window, I am suddenly struck by the uncanny coincidence of that fictional family by the lake and the four of us by the ocean. Paulie Barnes couldn't have planned that, but oh, how the coincidence of it plays sweetly into his hands, because it gives me a fierce case of the quivering shivers.

I suddenly miss Franklin very much.

"What's wrong?" Steve asks me, alert to my moods.

"This." I hand him the book to read. "Too close for comfort."

Maybe he'll see something in it that I haven't been able to. My reading only shows me what it always has: a psycho on a mission of revenge against a lawyer, taking out his fury on the lawyer's family, pursuing them far past the boundaries of their ordinary scruples into a raw, terrifying territory in which the only way to stop him is to become just like him: brutal, homicidal, criminal.

This holds no clues for me, however, or none that I can detect.

I said as much in my first and only (so far) personal E-mail to him, the one that accompanied the chapters I have written about my own family, and my rewrite of his account of the murders.

Dear Paulie Barnes,

What do you want me to say? That you've shocked me? Of course you have, especially with that last message of yours. That I'm scared of you? Of course I am, who wouldn't be? That I feel furiously angry at you, but that I also feel helpless to stop you? Of course I do. Do you want to know if I am doing everything I can think of to stop this craziness of yours? You bet, even if you're not a "betting man." Do I sometimes think this whole business has no reality, that I'm dreaming it, that I will wake up and it will all dissolve in the sunshine? Yes, I do think that, about every five minutes or so. Do I wonder why in the world you're doing this, and to me? (Sarcasm is a temptation here, but I'll try to avoid it.) Yes, I do wonder. What is it you want from this personal little note, hm? Shall we chat about Florida's penal code, the one that can sentence you to prison for most of your life? That's what my cop friends would like to talk to you about. Me, I don't want to talk to you at all. But since you insist, what's your opinion of the nuclear nonproliferation treaty?

I added, "Your turn to talk now," and signed it, "Yours truly, You know who."

Okay, so I couldn't entirely avoid sarcasm. We'll see what it gets me.

"When did he write this book?" Steve asks me, and I see he's already up to page twenty. I take it back from him, turn to the copyright date at the front, and point to it so he can see. "I thought so," he tells me. "It seems kind of old-fashioned."

I'll admit it's "dated" now, and reads melodramatically; it's not subtle, no sir. It might not scare readers today the way it did me when I first read it twenty years ago. Steve may not be impressed with it at all. But all I can say is that I hope I'll be alive someday to reread my own books. I hope I get the chance to live long enough to find them quaintly "dated," too.

Every time I fly into Birmingham International Airport, what I notice as far as I can see is green, green, everywhere green. There are so many trees that the streets and neighborhoods below us look as if they were inserted with great difficulty into a thick forest that might overgrow them at any moment. From the air, Birmingham looks like one of those jigsaw puzzles with a thousand pieces, every one of them green. The downtown skyline has a distinctive touch: four modest skyscrapers all in a row, like building blocks. There are other tall buildings, of course, but that quartet announces "Birmingham" to me.

This largest city in Alabama is set in a leafy valley framed by gentle, forested mountains that are the lower trailing edge of the Appalachians. It's beautiful, although people who aren't from here don't necessarily like to hear that praise. In their view, Birmingham's not supposed to be — is not allowed to be — lovely. Neither is Alabama, although it is arguably the most geographically interesting state in the Union, with everything from bayous to mountains, marshes to canyons, beaches to rolling farmland. By the reckoning of people who've never been here, Alabama's supposed to be as unappealing as illiteracy, poverty, and racism. As for the infamous city of Birmingham, it is supposed to be polluted because of its past incarnation as a mining and steel manufacturing center, and ugly, because of its former reputation as the most segregated city in America.

But the steel mills are long gone. And it

was always true that not everybody in Birmingham, black or white, was proud of that segregationist title, even way back then. If they had been, Birmingham never could have changed, and change it has, more than many cities, although maybe that's because it had a longer way to come.

"It's green," Steve says, sounding surprised, leaning over me to see out the little window. We were lucky and got seats together. I offered him the seat by the window, knowing how cramped he'd be in the middle, but he insisted on placing his body between me and everybody else. "Hell of a difference from the drought back home."

This is his first airplane ride, he claims, and it has been interesting to watch him react to all the things I take for granted — the metal detectors, wands, and "patdowns," the seat belts, the flight attendants, the takeoff, the clouds, the view down below, the peanuts and free drinks, even the magazines and the barf bags in the backs of the seats.

"Have you ever been outside of Florida?"

He shakes his head no, and settles back in his seat again.

"I've been here on book tours," I tell

him. "But I never tell people that I was born near here."

"Why not?"

"So they won't ask about my family. Southerners always ask about family."

Who were your people? It's the archetypal southern question.

The story in my briefcase doesn't answer that for me. Nor does it identify the people who killed them. The way it's written, the conspirators could have been anyone from either side of the racial divide or the civil rights movement. Those were the days when segregationists called what they did "the civil rights movement," too. Black or white. Integrationists or segregationists. Who were they? Who were the unnamed men who killed them? I can't divine that truth from the account that Paulie Barnes sent to me.

"You believe this?" Steve asked me, skeptically, after he read it.

Yes. Just as I've always known in my heart that they're gone — dead — I do believe enough of this account to accept it as basically true. Of course, I can't prove it, and maybe I never will be able to prove or disprove it. But I don't think Paulie Barnes just made it up to torture me, as much as he seems to enjoy doing that in other ways.

Was he one of the people at the cross-roads?

If he wasn't, how does he know so much about it?

Am I dealing with one of the men who killed my parents?

If so, why does he want to kill their daughter, too?

As we deplane, I feel the uncomfortable mixture of dread and excitement that I always feel when I return to where I was born.

Alabama. Birmingham. Sebastion.

Though I try to avoid them, they fascinate me.

When I meet people from here — when they're traveling outside their state and they tell me where they're from — sometimes I think they look like a flinch waiting to happen. They look as if they're afraid I'm going to despise them once I know where they're from. I recognize it, that inner wariness, because that's the same way I feel when people ask me about my family. In the case of residents of Birmingham, especially ones who lived here in the bad old days, I can see it in their eyes, that dread of what the rest of us will think of them when we know where they live.

There's such an unspoken, painful history in that look they get on their faces, because they've seen terrible and glorious things, maybe even taken part in them: freedom rides and beatings, voter registration drives and lynchings, burnings, torture, fire hoses and dogs set onto children, the NAACP and the SNLC, the Ku Klux Klan and the White Citizens Council, hatred, terror, violence, and four innocent little black girls murdered in a church bombing in 1963, the same year my parents died. But they've also witnessed — or, themselves, shown — the love and the extraordinary courage that inspired the very best of them.

The late naturalist Loren Eisley used to point out that we think we're the pinnacle of evolution, but the truth is that evolution has never stopped. New creatures, he liked to say, are still coming out of the swamp. Evolution stepped forward in Birmingham, Alabama, in the 1960s and 1970s, and a new and better kind of American began to crawl up on the shores, out of that terrible, bloody swamp of prejudice. Maybe it's a city that is destined always to be the nation's "forge," where raw materials are burned into steel and people are, too. In Birmingham, it was courage, not cowardice, that tilted the scales in the civil rights war back then. Like every other city in the country, they're still fighting local skirmishes and there's still a ways to go before reaching justice, but I think it's a city that has won the right to be recognized for both its natural and its hard-earned beauty. To insist on seeing it as ugly is tantamount, in my mind, to insulting the very people — the black people, the children, a few white people — whose blood ran in its streets. Their sacrifice had a magnificent and awesome beauty, and that was Birmingham, too.

If my parents had to die, I wish I could claim it for that good cause.

We have no trouble hiring a car. I splurge and rent a Lexus. If these turn out to be my last days, I'll be damned if I'll spend them in a cheap car. When we step outside the airport to take the shuttle to where we can pick up the vehicle, we discover that it is a beautiful day in Birmingham.

With Steve driving, I direct him out of the airport to I-65 north. We'll miss most of the city, and we'll drive through a bit of the Black Belt — which refers to the color of the soil, and not to the race of the inhabitants. Then we'll head on up toward cavern, lake, and mountain country. I don't need a map.

Sebastion sits on flat land with farms all around, but the foothills of the Appalachian Mountains loom within an easy bicycle ride from the town square. It's a square that used to be charming and bustling. But unlike some other Alabama towns that have thrived on tourism since the bad old days, Sebastion's population has declined from its high of 10,000 people around the time I was born, to half that now. When I recite those facts to Steve, to fill the silence in the car, he asks me, "When's the last time you were here?"

"In Alabama?"

"In Sebastion."

"Five years ago."

"Why'd you come?"

"I was making a stab at finding out."

"About your parents?"

"Yes."

"So what did you find out?"

He hasn't read my chapters yet. "I found out that most people don't like to talk about it." As the Lexus rolls along the interstate, I stare unseeing out my window. "But I didn't press very hard, not like I usually do with a book about other people.

When I poked, and people drew back, I pulled back, too."

"Are you going to do that this time?"

I glance over at him. "Not if my life depends on it, no."

The Old Southern Inn is the only lodging left in town, we discover, but fortunately, like the Lexus, it's fashioned for the luxury trade. I'm all for luxury right now; give me feather beds, champagne, and pâté de fois gras if I never sleep anywhere else, or eat another meal outside of Alabama. And if I do, I'll make up for it by feeling guilty later.

We've arrived at a vast two-story Colonial home painted an immaculate white, with a matching, classic, white picket fence. A wide cement walk leads up to a front center door. Narrow strips of leaded glass frame the door on either side. There's a colonnaded front porch and a second-floor balcony, both running the length of the house and then wrapping around it. Grand old oak trees shade the front yard, and we can see others towering over the house in back.

Similar impressive old homes line the street, but few match this one for its superb state of repair. Just to the east there's a rambling Victorian monster complete with turrets and five different shades of blue paint. It looks like a retirement home for Victorian ghosts. To the other side, there's a smaller bed-and-breakfast, The Gingerbread Cottage, with a paint job cute enough to make your teeth ache.

"If you were staying there," Steve mutters, nodding toward the gingerbread architecture, "I'd have to go someplace else."

"There are limits," I agree. "But this looks nice."

As he pulls into and parks in a gravel parking lot on the east side of the Inn, I read to him from the brochure. "It says here we're getting twelve-foot ceilings, heart pine floors, nine fireplaces, two parlors, a library, a formal dining room, a piano lounge, a private suite with its own bathroom and porch or balcony, full breakfast, coffee anytime, cable TV/VCR, telephone, fax, and Internet access."

"Just like my old cell at Starke," he says.

I stare over at him. "You made a joke."

Deadpan, he says, "Yeah, well, don't expect it to happen twice."

As we stroll up the front walk, I spot the reason why these grounds look so nice: Hubert Templeton, the once-young black man who helped my father deliver me to a motel, is just coming around one side of the house with clipping shears in his hands. For a moment I'm caught in an emotional time warp. Mr. Templeton's black hair looks thinner and more gray than it was when I saw him last, and he's carrying more weight on his large frame. And yet he's quite a bit younger than my father would have been by now. I'm struck hard by the idea that my father would look older than that if it were he who was walking around the corner of the house toward me.

"What's the matter?" Steve asks, because I've stopped walking and am just standing and staring. "Who's the old guy?"

Old guy. Hubert Templeton isn't all that old, probably only just past sixty, but I suppose even that looks old to somebody in his twenties, like Steve. Plus, even from this distance it's plain that the signs of a hard life are on him, aging him faster than he ought to. Feeling a sudden urge to make contact with him again, I step off the walk, onto the grass, and start to call out his name. But I don't even get it out before he turns back around and disappears behind the house again.

"He saw me," I murmur to Steve, and then tell him who it was. "I know he saw me."

Have I changed that much, too? Or did he realize he was looking at the traitor's daughter and decide he didn't want to talk to me again? As abruptly as he moved to get out of my line of vision, I'm sure it was the latter.

In the foyer, we wait at a beautiful, tiered, walnut reception desk for somebody to receive us. There's an old-fashioned ledger lying open on the desk, with a fountain pen near it. Incongruously, amid the genteel elegance, there's a small, square glass ashtray tucked nearly out of sight under a little ledge of the desk. The bottom of the ashtray is dewy, as if it has been recently washed out, but not completely dried. I look around me. Every wall is papered in busy floral prints; all the furniture looks antique; the "heart pine" floors gleam from a recent polish. Even though there's air-conditioning, the house is a little warm and stuffy; the wooden paddles of overhead fans stir the air. Over a scent of lemon wax, I detect a lingering aroma of bacon, from the "breakfast" part of "B&B." Classical music drifts down to us from upstairs.

I pick up and ring a brass bell that's sitting on the desk.

Within seconds, a tall, bony, middle-aged woman comes hurrying through a doorway, wiping her palms on her black jeans. She's wearing a man's dress shirt over them, its tail hanging out, its sleeves rolled up, as if she might have been washing dishes when she heard our summons. She brings with her a noticeable waft of cigarette smoke, which explains the ashtray. When she speaks to us, I smell a strong breath mint.

"Oh, hi," she says in a voice so soft I can barely hear it. The whole South seems encompassed in those two syllables, which rise and fall and rise again in an accent as thick as the leaves on the crepe myrtles lining the street outside. "I'm so sorry! I hope y'all haven't been waiting long? Welcome to the Old Southern Inn. Will y'all be checkin' in with us today?"

"I hope so."

"Well, that's wonderful. We're so glad you're here." Her smile is tentative and her glance only fleetingly meets my eyes. As she scurries behind the counter and turns a page in the ledger, she glances up at my companion. "Y'all must be the Sullivans? Mr. and Mrs. Sullivan, come all the way from Dallas?"

"No, we don't have reservations."

"That's all right, we have plenty of room." She picks up a pen and poises it over her ledger. "May I ask your name?"

"Marie Lightfoot."

Is it my imagination, or does this woman freeze for just an instant at the sound of my name? If so, the moment passes so quickly I think it probably never happened, and she gives me another of her swift glances, like a shy woodland creature. She looks to be in her forties, a big-boned plain woman with a lot of flyaway reddish hair going to gray.

And then I change my mind. "No, I'll tell you what. I know this is going to sound a little strange, but that's only my professional name. Let's use my real name. Marie Folletino."

This time, when I see her freeze, I know it's not my imagination.

Her hand seems stuck to the fountain pen it holds. Since she's not looking up, not saying anything, since her mouth seems frozen shut, I force myself to keep talking. "I was born here in Sebastion. Have you lived here all of your life? Maybe you knew my parents, Michael and Lyda Folletino?"

Still not looking at us, she says, "That name's familiar. I believe my father may have known them, you could ask him, if you like."

"What's his name?" And then I realize she hasn't told us hers. "I'm sorry. I didn't catch your name, either."

"My name's Maureen Goodwin, but I go by Mo."

"Goodwin? Is your father Lackley?"

She looks surprised, if not exactly pleased. "You know my dad?"

"My parents did. I met him a few years ago. Was that Hubert Templeton we saw outside just now?"

"Most likely. He does yard work all over town."

"My parents knew him, too."

"It's a small world." Her accent is soft and lush, and it glides from one sentence to the next so sweetly that one could almost fail to notice how abruptly she changes the subject. "Oh! You know what? There is a message for you, Ms. — Follentino. I told her I didn't have a reservation under that name, but they said you might be checking in."

She seems not to know which of my names to use. Don't feel bad, I want to tell her, it confuses me, too.

"A message? Nobody knows I'm here."

That's probably not quite true: Paulie

367

Barnes probably knows.

She smiles a little. "If they knew you were coming to Sebastion, this is the only place you could be."

"Oh, right." She hands me a pink slip with no name, but only a telephone number on it. When I see the Los Angeles area code, my heart beats faster. *Deborah!*

24

Marie

"Will you excuse us for a minute?" I say to her, already turning to leave. "I need to return this call."

She puts her right hand on a telephone on her reception desk, and lifts it to hand it to me, but I shake my head as I pull my own cell phone out of my purse. "No, thanks. I'll use mine. Steve, come with me."

He follows me back out onto the veranda, where I lead him into a far corner, even as I'm dialing the number.

"Erin? It's Marie. I got your call. How's —"

"She's fine," my private investigator tells me, sounding her usual clipped, efficient self, and I begin to breathe again.

Erin McDermit has an exceptionally low-pitched voice for a woman, and it's not by accident of birth or from smoking either.

She told me once that she purposely culti-
vated that husky tone so that strangers
wouldn't be able to tell if it was a man or a
woman who was calling them, or coming up
suddenly behind them with a gun.

"We're comfortable," she tells me now,
in that remarkable voice that always gives
me the rather unnerving sensation of talking to a sexy man. "I think we're safe. Your
cousin told us we can have the place while
he's gone."

"Nate's not there? Where'd he go?"

"I don't know. He acted like it was a big
secret."

"I thought it was your job to get secrets
out of people."

"You want me to find out?"

"No!" I hasten to halt the bloodhound.
"He's probably got a new girlfriend."
Which is none of my business until he
chooses to tell me about her. Just because
Nathan agreed to hide my assistant, that
doesn't give me carte blanche to invade all
of his privacy. "Why'd you call, Erin?"

"My people have been working on the
E-mails."

"And?" My heartbeat picks up again, but
this time in hope.

"Bad news. Your Paulie Barnes knows
how to hide in plain sight, Marie. He not

only used a remailer, he used a cypher-punk remailer, and then chain remailed it. On top of that, he's giving you encrypted reply blocks."

"Are you speaking a language that is known to the United Nations, Erin?"

"You want I should translate?"

"Please."

"Okay, but you don't really want details, do you?"

"God, no. Just start talking, and when my eyes glaze, stop."

"I can't see you. How will I know?"

There's humor in her voice.

"It will be accompanied by snoring."

"You just don't know what's interesting." She means it, too. "Here's the deal: there are depths of anonymity on the Web, and he is using some of the deepest ones. One of the first levels is, if you want to send somebody an anonymous message, you can subscribe to a kind of service that's called a remailer. You e-mail them your message. They hide it behind an anonymous return address and remail it to your recipient.

"The second level is to send it through chain remailers, which are just what they sound like, a chain of remailers who each add another layer of anonymity, with new anonymous return addresses. You could do that into infinity, creating such a maze that nobody could ever track back through it to find you. Remailers operate all over the world, Marie, so your messages from Paulie Barnes could have started anywhere and then gone through remailers in Finland, Japan, Nigeria, Australia, you name it, everywhere but Alpha Seven, and I expect that's next.

"But that's not the end of it. Your guy has taken it to still another level, which is exactly what I would do. He's using cypherpunk remailers and not only that, but cypherpunk chain remailers —"

"Cyberpunk? Like, binary codes and tongue studs?"

"No, *cypher*, as in wartime codes. As in *cipher*, with an *i*. As in zero, unseen, invisible. Cypherpunk."

"Shyte. As in *shit* with an *i*. What do they do?"

"First he sends them an encrypted message, which he probably knows how to do because when he subscribes, they tell him how. Your E-mail address is encrypted in that message."

"Great," I say, with a sigh.

"The cypherpunk service decodes the message and then sends it on to you with an anonymous return address."

"What's the point of that?"

"The point is to keep anybody who finds him from being able to monitor where he is sending E-mails."

"So we can't find him from either end?"

"That's right."

"And he complicates it even further by using a chain of cypherpunk remailers?"

"Yes."

"Good grief, Erin."

"Your eyes glazing yet?"

"No, I'm riveted by this. But why can't we find him by tracing him through the E-mails that I send back to him, Erin?"

"Because he has closed that door, too, the clever bastard. Remember I used the term 'encrypted reply block'?"

"No, but what is it?"

"It's like those self-addressed, stamped envelopes that you use in publishing, only you might say it's written in invisible ink. The way it works is, he provides you with a preaddressed, but empty, E-mail. You write your reply inside of it and send it off to him. It is routed back through all those same layers of remailers before it reaches him."

"Are you saying you can't find him through the E-mails?"

"Bottom line, that's what I'm saying."

"Can anybody find him that way?"

"Sure. All you'd need are a million court orders, a phalanx of international lawyers, the help of the FBI, and the cooperation of governments on several continents."

"My God, Erin! This is unbelievable!"

"No, Marie, this is the twenty-first century."

"Isn't there any other way to trace them?"

"You mean, like, follow the money?"

"Yeah, like."

"No. These services take one-time credit card payments through secured servers. The amounts would show up on his credit card bills under some kind of innocuous designation. They never bill twice. They keep no logs. They never sell their membership lists to third parties. Hell, most of them don't even keep a membership list, Marie." She sounds annoyed. This computer age is making her job both easier and harder. "You sign on, you pay, you log on each time, but they keep no record of you. Marie, these services are almost nonprofit. A lot of these guys ain't in it for the money. What they're in love with is privacy, secrecy, and conspiracy. They hate laws, regulations, and governments. They're libertarians, is what they are, or anarchists."

"And you think Paulie Barnes has done all those things?"

"We know he has. That's what we've learned from the E-mails."

"Is he a computer genius, Erin?"

"I wouldn't jump to that conclusion. It doesn't take a nerd to do any of this stuff, it just takes a few minutes on the Web to find these services and then a little while longer to follow some instructions. I could do it, you could do it, anybody could do it."

"But hackers get found, Erin!"

"Fewer than you think, and only by international cooperation and high-level string pulling, and that really does take computer geniuses and a whole lot of time and patience, which we don't have."

"So we have to give up finding him that way?"

"I would, yes."

Suddenly I have a bright idea. "Hey, but what about the E-mails he exchanged with Deborah? Or the one he sent to the condominium manager at Key Largo? Do you know about those?"

"We can't get him that way, either, Marie. He went through layers of remailers to get to the condo manager. When he e-mailed Deborah, he didn't go to all that trouble, he just used a fake name through a free server, but he did it at a public library."

"Which means?"

"I found the library, but they get hundreds of people on their computers. Whoever he is, he didn't give them any reason to remember him, and they don't videotape their patrons."

"What library?"

"The one closest to you, Marie. He was right there. He only went under deep cover when he had to, and that's when he started getting in direct contact with you."

"Dammit, Erin!"

"Hey, don't let anybody tell you it's a brave new world, Marie. When it comes to these guys, it's a cowardly one. What do you want me to do next? Besides baby-sit, I mean."

"I can't think of anything else," I say, feeling frustrated and angry. "The cops and Franklin are handling it from the evidence angle. I don't know what else to do now, Erin."

"Take care, that's one thing."

"Yeah. And you take care of Deb for me."

"I will. She's a nice girl. Want to talk to her now?"

But I don't want to. I don't want Deborah to hear the discouragement I can't keep out of my voice right now. "No, I've got to go. Just tell her I'm fine and not to worry about me."

"Yeah, right," my private investigator says with a dry laugh, just before she hangs up. "Just like you won't worry about her."

While I talked to Erin, I kept an eye out for Hubert Templeton to come back around into the front yard again. I won't push myself on him if he doesn't want to talk to me, but I'd like a chance to say hello to him if he'll allow it, maybe even show him the supposed account of what happened to my parents and see what he might say about it. Midway through my phone conversation, however, I heard a slur of tires on gravel and turned just in time to see him drive away in a battered old black pickup truck. He glanced in our direction, nodded once, then kept on going.

Steve and I walk back into the inn slowly enough for me to tell him what I've just learned. Once inside, we find that Mo Goodwin is still waiting for us behind her reception desk.

"I'm so sorry to keep you waiting," I tell

her. "We're ready to check in now. Do I understand correctly that all of your rooms are suites? So there are two rooms?"

"Yes, ma'am. I hope that'll be all right for you?"

"Does that mean there will be a bed or a sofa for my friend here?"

She glances up at Steve, blushes again, and looks confused. "Well, but — well, I could probably give you a rollaway, if that would be okay?"

"That would be fine," I say, looking at Steve, who nods to confirm it.

The woman still looks flustered and confused, but she goes on to say, "If you'll follow me, I'll take you on upstairs now."

"Don't you need to see my credit card?"

"Oh, no, that can wait until you're ready to leave. I'm not worried about that. Everything's included in the one price." Her worry lines dissolve in a quick, warm smile. "And anyway, you're in Sebastion now."

Apparently that means they trust strangers here.

I'm certainly not in Florida anymore.

With Steve carrying our bags, we climb the wide, carpeted steps, following her up to the second floor. Once there, she leads us down a carpeted corridor — wide enough for Steve and me to walk abreast behind her — to a double door at the end. For no apparent reason, she knocks at it. Getting no response — but then, whom did she expect, the previous tenants, ghosts? — she applies her key to the door and opens it. Then she hands that same key to me, steps aside, and leaves us there, after promising to deliver the rollaway. "If you decide you'd rather have an extra room," she says, in her hesitant way, "I could turn one of our empty suites into a single bedroom."

"I'm sure this will be fine," I assure her.

She seems to believe that Steve and I are going to stumble all over each other if we share this suite, and maybe we will, but it would be pretty pointless to put my bodyguard in another room altogether.

I enter first, and find myself in the main bedroom of a lovely sunny corner suite. There are three inside doors, all of them closed like the doors to prizes on an old game show. Straight ahead of me there's a cushioned bay window where the sun is pouring in past the branches of one of the huge oak trees. The cheerful room is so large that a full-size couch, a card table and four chairs, an armoire, and a four-poster bed don't even crowd it. The quilt on top of the bed looks handmade, and there are reading lamps on either side of it. This feels like a writer's heaven to me, the sort of retreat where I could work undisturbed on finishing a book while somebody else does all the cooking and cleaning for a month.

"One of those doors leads to another room," I suggest to Steve.

Although he hasn't said so, I'm positive he has never been in a bed-and-breakfast lodging, any more than he had previously flown in an airplane. It's possible this is his first hotel room of any sort. If so he's starting high up the line; these are luxury accommodations complete with white eyelet pillow shams, white terry cloth robes hanging outside the armoire, and bottled water at bedside, the kind of inn that most women adore, but where burly men like Steve feel ill at ease. As I watch him move carefully around the room, opening doors, he does look rather like an ox in a linen closet.

It may be beautiful, but it's old, and everything creaks — the wide wood planks beneath the area rugs, the stairs we climbed, the doors he's jerking open — not because the hinges need oil, but simply from the age of the wood. (I recall the ash-tray tucked under the ledge of the reception desk and hope that our landlady doesn't smoke in bed.) The furniture probably creaks, too. I envision the delicate chairs collapsing under his bulk every time he sits in one.

The first door Steve creaks open reveals a small closet, the second one opens onto a huge bathroom, all porcelain and tile.

He pulls open the final door.

My cousin opens it from the other side.

25

Marie

"Nathan?"

I don't know which of the three of us looks more startled — me, to find my cousin is here, Steve to confront a stranger in my suite — one so good-looking, tanned, and stylish he could pass for a movie star, no less — or Nathan, who has run smack up against the scary bulk of my bodyguard.

"Nathan! What are you doing here?"

"Who are *you?*" Steve demands of him, looking ready to kill.

"Are you kidding?" My cousin looks from me to Steve, then back again. "What do you mean, who am I? What do you mean, what am I doing here? I'm her cousin, asshole."

"Steve, it's okay. This is my cousin Nathan from L.A." And to Nate I repeat, "What the hell are you doing here?"

"Very funny," he says, moving cautiously

away from Steve and closer to me. Behind him I see a second bedroom, smaller than the one we're in, but just as pretty. "You send me an E-mail and tell me to get my ass to Sebastion, and I drop everything and pay full price to get here today and then Rocky Graziano here scares the shit out of me, and you want to know what I'm doing here? Which one of us has lost our mind, that's what I'd like to know."

He's close enough to reach for me, and with a grin, he does.

I hug him fiercely, and we exchange cousinly smooches, but then I push myself back from him.

"I didn't tell you to come, Nate."

"Yeah, you did. You told me to come here and to get one suite for both of us."

"No, I swear I didn't, but I think I can guess who did." Glancing over at Steve, who is still glowering at the entrance to the second bedroom, I say, "Come on. Let's sit down, and I'll tell you about it." I lead him over to the bay window and make him sit there with me. Steve comes only as close as the four-poster bed and takes a seat on the edge of it, as if he's leery of getting any closer to us. But he leans forward with his elbows on his knees, to watch and listen to us.

"Uh, Nathan, this is Steve Orbach. Steve, this is my cousin, Nathan Montgomery."

"We've met," says my cousin, wryly.

My cousin Nathan has a heart of gold; truly, he's the kind of guy for whom other people would celebrate his good luck if only he had any, apart from being born looking like F. Scott Fitzgerald. But here's this beautiful, sweet-natured man who is unlucky in his parents, his love life, and most of all, his career. Because of that, I know there is a certain conversation we have to get out of the way before we can go any further.

"How's your karma?" My lifetime of experience with Nathan has taught me that it's always a good thing to find out as soon as possible what tragedy has recently befallen him. That's so I don't feel like a self-centered jerk after I've chattered on for an hour while he listens kindly, only to find out when I do give him a chance to speak that his cat died yesterday and he was just washing out the litter box when I called. Thursday, when I phoned him from my car, was an exception, an emergency, and so we have some catching up to do.

"Sucks as bad as ever," he says, sounding casual, like somebody who's used to misfortune.

"Oh, dear. Well, tell me the worst of it."

"Now? The whole sad litany?"

Nate knows this routine, too, and he'll play his part until we run through it. This is our script, in which the facts change, but the general tenor, unfortunately, does not.

"Every sad morsel," I assure him. I glance over at the man sitting on the bed. If Steve's face weren't so naturally impassive, I'm sure it would be reflecting disbelief right about now. How can we talk about anything else, he must be thinking, when lives are at stake? He doesn't know Nate, that's all I can say.

"You still dating that actress person?"

"No."

"Why not?"

"She left me for another actress person."

"Oh, Nathan. Are you sad? Should I pretend I'm sorry?"

"You never did like her," he accuses. "It's okay, I've had distractions."

"Oh, dear, that sounds bad."

"It is. Marie, my agent died!"

I grab for one of his hands. "No! Not again! I mean —"

"Yeah, different agent. Same fate."

I have to laugh, as people who love him always do. He's so damned funny about being cursed. "You're not joking, right?"

"This is the problem with writing comedy.

People can't tell when to take me seriously."

"Oh, stop it. But that's terrible, Nate! I'm so sorry."

He writes screenplay after screenplay and they get "optioned," which is Hollywood-speak for "going nowhere," and he earns thousands of dollars from them. But in the ten years he's been trying to get a film produced, not a single script of his has made it to the big or the little screen. I don't know how he keeps going, but he does. Sometimes I worry that my success must stare him in the face like an evil queen in a mirror, though he has never once made me feel that way.

And now his agent's dead. Poor Nate.

It always seems so ironic to me that Nathan looks the very picture of success, much more than I do, but then he claims that's what you have to do in Hollywood. In the New York publishing world that I inhabit, they're accustomed to writers looking like ordinary people, or like tweedy college professors, or even slobs. In this as in many things, it's different in L.A.

Today, my cousin is elegant in soft summer slacks and a short-sleeved silk shirt, both a gorgeous pale gray, with soft gray loafers that look as if they had to have been made by a little Italian shoemaker in a small shop on the Ponte Vecchio. By comparison, I'm rumpled and gritty in travel slacks and shirt. I've often thought that Nathan missed his calling in Hollywood by about fifteen years, because he might have made a beautiful child star. Instead, he's a ne'er-do-well, grown-up screenwriter. It's funny, I'm the one with the Hollywood screenwriter grandparents, but it's Nathan who followed in their footsteps, though he's no blood relation to them, but only to me and my mother. When I look at him, I wonder if I'm seeing a bit of her. But then, I wonder that, too, whenever I look at myself in mirrors.

Knowing better, I still hope for the best in this latest bad situation of his. "Did she leave you with one of her associates?"

"Well, she probably would have, but it was that associate who killed her."

"You're making this up!"

"Okay." He grins. "That part I made up. But my agent really did die. And no, the sucky answer is no, she didn't leave me with an associate, because it was a one-agent shop — who else could I get in L.A.? No big agency will have me. I think her poodle inherited me. I've finally done it, I've officially got a dog of an agent."

"Oh, God." I have to laugh, though I want to cry for him.

"But, hey, it's a really smart poodle. Hell, it can't be any less successful with my stuff than she was."

"And so, anything happening with your scripts?"

"Yeah, well, like a farmer who is land rich, cash poor, I am option rich, movie poor. I'm all hat and no pony. All scepter and no crown. All crust and no filling. All —"

"All talent and no audience." I refuse to laugh at his schtick when it degrades his own ability. "No audience *yet*, that is. Yet."

"No sightings of the Loch Ness monster. Yet."

"What did she die of, Nate?"

"Old age. Sitting by telephones waiting for producers to call. It'll kill you."

"I believe it. Listen, Nathan," I say, taking his other hand, too.

"Excuse me," Steve interrupts from the bed. "I'm going outside."

Apparently, he's had all he can take of this brother-sister act. We watch until the door closes behind him.

"Who's Bruto?" Nathan immediately demands. "Where's Franklin?"

"Franklin's fine, he's back home in

Bahia, taking care of business and his family. Steve is my bodyguard."

When he sees that my mouth quivers on that word, he turns my hands over so that now he's the one who's doing the holding. As long as Nate's on this earth, I can never ever claim that nobody loves me and that I might as well go eat worms.

"So it's true," he says, looking worried, "and it's bad."

I can only nod while I try to keep from crying. "It got worse last night, Nathan. This Paulie Barnes sent me an account of what he claims is the murder of my mom and dad."

My cousin's mouth drops open, closes, opens again.

"You look so flummoxed," I tell him, half-smiling, half-laughing, "it's almost funny."

"What does he say, for God's sake? Who does he say did it? Do you believe him, Marie?"

"I'll let you read it, and you tell me what you think."

"Bad things aren't supposed to happen to you, Marie, they're only supposed to happen to me. I thought I had the exclusive contract on disasters. When you lost your parents, that was supposed to use up your entire quota of calamity for one life-time."

I find a smile for him again. "I forgot to read the fine print."

"I'll say. Wait a minute! Did you say Orbach? Wasn't that the name of the guy in your last book, the one you saved from the death penalty?"

"I wasn't the only one who helped him —"

"It's *him?* Let me get this straight, Marie. You protect yourself from one psycho by inviting another one to live with you? Are you *crazy?* Have you lost your fucking *mind?*"

"He's not a psycho, Nate."

"He murdered his *mother.*"

"Yeah, well, she had it coming."

Nathan laughs a little wildly. "Well, aren't *we* getting relativistic in our old age?"

"Nate, he's okay, trust me, okay?"

He shakes his head, looking disgusted with me. "Look," I argue, "I can understand why somebody who doesn't know Steve might hesitate, but he's tough and he understands the criminal mind and he'd do anything for me." A niggling thought sneaks into my brain: actually nobody really does know Steven Orbach all that well.

Suddenly Nate is pulling me over into

another warm, hard hug.

"God, this stinks, Marie. This is awful, even worse than dead agents."

"Don't be silly." I laugh a little against his shoulder. "Nothing's worse than a dead agent."

Nate laughs, too. "Well, that's true. But this is pretty bad."

I pull back from him. "But none of this explains why you're here, too."

"You sent me an E-mail, or I thought you did."

"What did I say in it?"

"You said, Dear Nate, I need your help. Please meet me at the Southern Inn in Sebastion tomorrow."

"You sweetie! You dropped everything to come."

"Of course, wouldn't you?"

"Yes. Why didn't you call me and ask me about it?"

"I wasn't supposed to, remember? We were trying to hide the connection between us, to protect poor little Deborah. Who is a sweetie, by the way."

"I thought you'd like her. What do you think of Erin?"

His expression turns wry. "*Sweet* is not a word I'd use to describe that woman. Interesting, sexy —"

"*No,* Nathan," I say, alarmed. "You don't want to mess with her."

He grins at me. "You have no idea what I want to mess with, Cousin."

I make a face at him. "Well, don't even tell me."

"So I guess we think your Paulie Barnes sent me the E-mail?"

"I guess we do. Do you remember the address on it?"

"No, sorry, although I do remember thinking it wasn't your usual one. I thought maybe you'd switched servers, or something. So we think he sent it, but we don't know why?"

"We haven't a clue."

"There's one thing to be said for it."

"There is? What?"

"We haven't been in Sebastion together since we were kids," Nate comments. "And now we're back."

"Is that supposed to be the good news?"

He laughs. "I don't remember this town at all."

"You were too little."

"You weren't exactly large, yourself. What do you remember?"

"Practically nothing." I stare out at the branches of the nearest oak tree. "I just *think* I remember things, because of what other people have told me."

"Like what, Marie?"

"Like about my mother and my father. I have some notes I took from a conversation I had with a woman named Eulalie Fisher." I turn and look at him. "Do you want to read them?"

BETRAYAL

By Marie Lightfoot

━━►◦◄━━

CHAPTER SEVEN

She lifted a slim silver case from the antique table beside her, and opened it. The first time I ever met Eulalie Fisher was the first time I saw her smoke. I tried to hide my surprise at the sight of the pristine white cigarettes lined up in a single row within it. "I allow myself one a day," she told me, "never with a drink, and I never allow myself more than one drink on any occasion. If I drank more than one, I would probably smoke. If I smoked more than one, I might drink. I don't suppose you smoke at all?"

"No, thank you."

"Thought so." She plucked one out with her fingernails, clicked the case shut, and put that down, and then picked up a little silver lighter, and lit up. She took a delicate drag, then gazed at me curiously through the bit of white smoke that hung between us now. "Did you ever?"

"Cigarettes, no. Drink, yes."

"Um. Your mama smoked like a chimney, course your daddy did, too, course who didn't back then? In many ways it does seem to me that life was a lot more fun back then, at least for the rich white folks like us. Nowadays there are so many belts to strap us in and bags to suffocate us, and helmets to keep the wind from blowing in anybody's hair. So many dreadsome deaths to fear. Not that people didn't go on ahead and die back then, and often dreadfully, but it was easier not to have to worry so dang much about it all of the time."

"It's not much fun anymore? Even for rich, white folks?"

She smiled a bit. "Not so much, but at least now there are more rich black folks to share the misery. I suppose we have to call that progress." She took another delicate drag, closed one eye against the smoke. "Has anybody ever — I mean really ever described your mama to you?"

"Well, I — I don't know, if you put it like that."

"You've seen pictures."

"Sure."

"What did you think?"

"Of her? I guess, pretty and she looks like fun."

"You don't know the half of *that*," she tells me, arching her eyebrows in emphasis. "Sit down and I'll explain your mama to you. No picture can ever capture any of us and certainly not Lyda Montgomery Folletino. What I can tell you is that most of the boys and men in Sebastion were in love with her. She was a natural-born flirt, not so serious as you are, and of course, males respond to that. Most of the time, Lyda didn't mean nothin' by it, but I do believe she paid a high price for it in the end."

"How so?"

"Well, because it encouraged her to believe she was invincible. I would bet you any amount of money that up to her dying day Lyda believed to her toes that no man alive would ever, could ever possibly hurt her."

I thought that over, trying to relate. "Did it make her — daring?"

"Daring! I should say! A thing like that, a conviction that you are safe in the company of men, will make a girl take risks she oughtn't. It'll fool her into thinking every man's a bit of a fool in general and a fool for her in particular. I don't believe it will give her a high opinion of women, either."

"Why's that?"

"Because she'll observe that other women aren't so daring, she'll draw the conclusion that they're timid little mice by comparison with herself, and she might begin to preen a bit."

"You say she didn't think any man would hurt her."

"I believe that's so, yes."

"Do you think that she hurt any of them?"

"Darling, of course she did, how could she not, a girl like that?"

"Eulalie —" She had invited me to call her that instead of Mrs. Fisher. "You're not intimating, are you, that my mother had affairs?"

"Before or after she was married, do you mean?"

"Yes."

She smiled slightly through the smoke. "Yes is your answer, yes is mine. Would you mind very much?"

"How could I? I didn't even — I don't even — know her."

Her gaze was a bit skeptical. "Well, I wouldn't actually know anything for sure about what she did in that regard after she married your father, or what she didn't. Perhaps we'll give her the benefit of the doubt, even though it *was* the sixties and that kind of thing was going around like the flu."

Even though she was talking about my own mother, I had to laugh.

"Maybe she behaved herself. She did love him. Your father, I mean. And besides, whether or not she had an affair doesn't have a thing to do with the price of peas."

I laughed again. "Eulalie, if I had lived here all of my life, would I sound like you?"

"Well, darlin', we can't all be sweet magnolias. At least a few of our daughters have got to grow up to be prickly pears, or we won't never make no progress at'all."

"Do you think I'm prickly?"

"My dear, I think you're northern."

Nothun, she pronounced it. I risked teasing her. "If I said 'ma'am,' would that help?"

She looked amused. "It might, some."

She stubbed out her cigarette and then leaned back and asked me a question that gave me a little jolt. "And what would you most like to know about your daddy?"

"Oh. Do I get only one question?" When

she smiled at that but didn't answer, I said, "All right. I want to know, did he love my mother? Did he love me?"

"That was two. Maybe I'll give you three. Don't you want to know if your mama loved you?"

"I guess I took that for granted."

"Yes, that's right, that's a verity. You may take your daddy's affection for both of you for granted, too."

"Affection?"

"He was a distant kind of man, my dear. Passionate, but perhaps not for people. More for causes, if you know what I mean. Always thinking big thoughts, which I suspect he had to do just to keep up with your mama. She was a pistol! No, that's not quite right, she was a live wire, but of two different natures, such as you find on a car battery, do you know what I mean by that? One wire is red and the other is blue, I believe, and if you attach the wrong one to the wrong post, you get dangerous sparks and maybe even an explosion. That was your mama. Smooth and happy as a Rolls-Royce engine most of the time, but cross wires with her and you'd better stand back. I suppose you know where they met?"

"No! Do you?"

"I do, and it's a funny story. Supposedly, they met right in front of a movie theater in Hollywood. It was the premiere of one of those films your grandparents wrote. Your daddy was all dressed up in a tux, escorting his parents, whom I believe he could hardly stand, but toward whom he felt a certain filial loyalty one can only admire. Your mother was picketing the film."

I laughed.

Eulalie was pleased at my reaction. "I thought you'd like that. It was some union question, perhaps, or it may even have been a question of employing women and minorities in the film. At any rate, they met straight out of a movie script, you might say. Your mama waved a picket in your father's face and yelled something unpleasant at him, and he looked down and saw this darling girl who obviously agreed with everything he held to be important in life, so he asked her if she would go out with him and try to convince him of her views."

I laughed again, delighted with this story.

Eulalie's eyes twinkled, too. "I don't know how long it took your mama to catch on that he didn't need very much convincing."

"Wait a minute," I ask her. "Are you saying that they were liberals to start with, but that they changed their minds?"

"I don't know what they were, darlin'. I'm merely passing on to you the stories they told on themselves."

"Why did they move here?"

"To get away from there, I expect. And of course, your mama's people had been here since the sands of time began to run. They were family, such as it was. A viper's nest of segregationists is what they were, in my opinion, and about the only good thing that could be said of any of them was that they had never betrayed any of their friends to a Senate committee as your other grandparents had. Although knowing the Montgomerys, that was probably only for lack of opportunity."

"But if my parents started out as liberals, they must have hated it here."

"No, I don't believe they did, child. No more than mercenary soldiers in a field of war. No more than spiders in a web."

"Affection," I said, without realizing I'd spoken out loud.

Her face took on a sympathetic but sardonic look. "They loved bigger things, dear. Truth. Justice. The American Way. We just never suspected the manner in which they defined that Way. Of course, it meant you came in second. But then, I suspect you understand that, don't you? If you don't mind my asking, 'cause I'm a nosy old woman, what comes first in your life, before your work?"

"Nothing," I admitted.

"Hm. You are their child, it's sure."

"Would I like them?"

"Probably. Your mother could charm the honey out of hives and your father had a sweetness about him that none of his high-mindedness could ever quite disguise. On the other hand, they made enemies, and maybe you'd have become one of them, as they were enemies toward their own families."

She looked suddenly old and very tired.

I said quickly, "I should go."

She merely nodded her head and waved a hand at me, seeming to have been overtaken by weariness, or possibly by hard memories. The movement of her hand had such a grandeur and grace that I found it impossible to take offense at her easy dismissal of me.

26

Marie

"It isn't much to go on," I admit to Nate, after he finishes reading it. "But it's the closest I've ever come to getting a sense of what they were like."

"Your mom sounds hot."

"Please! That's my mother you're talking about!"

He smiles, and I know he's only teasing me to make sure I don't get maudlin on him. "You ever do therapy, Marie?"

"You know I have, Nathan. Isn't it required for every American born after, oh, 1940?"

Nate laughs again and lays a hand on the scene he just read. "So, what'd your therapist think about all this?"

"She wanted to talk about my abandonment issues."

"And?"

"I told her, I don't got no steenking

abandonment issues."

My cousin appears ready to argue with that, but fortunately for me, just as he opens his mouth, there's a knock on the door of our suite.

I call out, "Come on in, Steve! It's your room, too!"

But when the door opens, it isn't Steve Orbach who's standing there, but Maureen — Mo — Goodwin, with a hesitant expression on her face.

"I'm sorry to bother y'all."

"That's all right, please come in."

She does, but just barely, and doesn't close the door behind her. "I have been asked to extend an invitation to you from Miss Eulalie —"

"Mrs. Fisher?" I glance quickly at Nate, whose face registers the sheer coincidence of this. "How in the world does she know I'm here?"

An embarrassed look crosses Mo Goodwin's plain face. "Probably because of me. I hope y'all don't mind. I told my mother I had new guests and she asked me who, and I told her, and she told my dad and he mentioned it to Mr. Clayton and he told Miss Eulalie, and then she called me." She shrugs apologetically, as if to say, What can you expect in a small town like this?

"No, that's fine, I don't mind at all, I just wondered."

It's odd to consider the strange connection between Mo Goodwin and me, of how our parents once were friends together in a dangerous enterprise. Her own parents' sense of betrayal by my parents could well explain how awkward and uncomfortable she seems to be around me. Now she says, as if reading from a formal invitation, "Miss Eulalie and Mister Clayton kindly request the pleasure of your company at a light supper at their home tonight. She says she'll be havin' a few folks over to meet you. My parents. The Wiegans. The Reeses."

The white members of Hostel, I realize with a start.

"Miss Eulalie asked me to beg your forgiveness for her not callin' you personally, but she doesn't believe in telephones anymore."

I have to smile. It sounds so like the woman I met.

"Anymore?" I inquire. "What happened?"

Lackley Goodwin's middle-aged daughter shrugs again. "It was those telephone solicitors, you know, callin' at supper time. Miss Eulalie finally got as how she just couldn't stand them anymore, so she had the telephone company come and rip out her telephone lines."

"But what did Mr. Clayton think of that?"

For the first time, Mo Goodwin can't seem to help but loosen up and grin a bit. "Mr. Clayton got himself a cell phone that he likes just fine."

"A little more in tune with this century than she is?"

"Oh, my, yes! I used to be his secretary at the bank —"

"You did?"

"Yes, ma'am, before my parents invested in this place and I got a chance to run it. At the bank, Mr. Clayton took to fax machines right off, and you'd have thought that computers were invented just for him. I taught him myself how to surf the Web. Mr. Clayton just loves new gizmos. I'll swear, he takes to 'em like ham on beans."

I can sense my cousin's inner amusement at the sound of that.

"Since she doesn't have a phone, will you pass on to them that we'd love to come?"

"Am I included?" Nathan asks, sounding surprised.

"Oh, yes, they mean to invite you, too," Mo says politely to my cousin. "Miss

Eulalie specifically said so, and when I told her — I hope you don't mind — that y'all have another friend with you, she said, the more the merrier."

"That's very kind of her." I get a mental image of fierce-looking Steve mixing at a southern soiree. "What time?"

"They eat early. Six o'clock."

"Will you be there?"

"I'm invited," she says ambiguously, and then leaves, quietly closing the door behind her.

Nate looks thoughtful. "I guess we didn't exactly sneak into town, did we?" Gently, he then asks, "Will you let me read the other thing now, Marie? The one that's supposed to be about your parents' deaths?"

"Murders," I correct him, and hand it to him.

A few minutes later, he looks up and says, "I don't know. Do you?"

"It sounds pretty real," I tell him. "It feels real."

"Yeah," he agrees, sounding sad for me. "It does."

"Look on the bright side, Nathan."

"There is one?"

"Sure. If this is true, at least I'll know for sure they're dead."

He just shakes his head, having no smart retort for that.

Next, I let him have the other chapters I wrote before there was ever a Paulie Barnes to force me to do it. When he's finished with all of that, we don't even stop to talk about it. It's as if it's too much for him to absorb all at once, and I'm suddenly feeling far too restless to sit still. We go looking for Steve, and when we find him outside, the three of us get into my rental car and drive around the area to sightsee.

On our way out of the inn, I see Mo Goodwin and pause to ask her a question. "Where could we go to get some copies made?"

"How many do you need, Ms. Folletino?"

"I wish you'd call me Marie." I smile at her, but in her shyness she isn't looking right at me, and so she doesn't see it. "I need eight copies of three pages."

"We have a copy machine. I'll do it for you."

I hesitate, thinking of what it is I want copied, but I realize that it might not be a bad thing if she were to read it. Maybe she knows something I should know, and maybe she'll even decide to tell me so.

"That's very kind of you. I'll pay for them, of course."

"What's that all about?" Nate asks me, on our way out.

"You'll see," I tell him. "It's a surprise, for later."

I'd tell him what it is — I'd tell Steve, too — but I don't want anybody talking me out of doing what I want to do.

On our Magical Memory Tour, we make a stop in front of my parents' old home, an impressive pile of architecture that's vacant now and gone to seed. The "famous" parson's chamber is not visible from the street, nor is the magnolia tree that the young black man saw from the windows of it. There's a circle drive where Hubert Templeton would have kept the car running while my father ran in to get my mother. It's easy to imagine the front door flung open and three dark people standing in the shadows of the hallway, watching. I'll have to settle for imagination. I have no actual memory of this house or of the events that happened in it, just a recurring dream of myself as an infant riding in the backseat of a car, at night, with my daddy.

After that stop along memory lane, the three of us park briefly in front of the house where Nate and I lived with his parents.

"Want to ring the bell and ask for a tour?" I ask him.

But he shakes his head vehemently. "No. Let's go."

We drive the streets down which the white Hostel members of Sebastion were paraded on the evening of June 12, 1963, and I tell Steve about it.

"You think Julia and Joe were in that crowd?" Nate asks me, referring to his own parents, my mother's brother and his wife. "Throwing stones?"

"I kind of doubt it, Nate. That would be too undignified for your mother, and your father wouldn't want to stick his neck out. Anyway, don't you think they'd leave that to the rednecks?"

"As if they aren't rednecks, themselves," he says, with a derisive snort. "Just better dressed, with a few more years in school, not that it improved them any."

But these are old complaints, and we tire of them quickly.

We circle the town, taking a look at all the roads that enter and exit from it, wondering which of them leads to a crossroads where two people might have been shot and killed on the night of the parade.

It's a small city/town, and our tour doesn't take much time, at least not by the clock. In terms of our personal histories, however, it covers an awful lot of forgotten ground.

When we return to the inn to change for dinner, we argue about whether or not to stay crowded into a single suite or to ask Mo for another one. It quickly becomes clear to me that neither man wants to leave me alone with the other one. To avoid nastiness, I capitulate: we'll manage with just this one set of rooms. We divvy up the suite, with me assigned to the smaller back bedroom and the two men taking the front one. Steve insists that my cousin have the bed, and he takes the rollaway that somebody has placed in our suite in our absence. Although there's only the one bathroom it has doors opening into each of the bedrooms, so we ought to be able to manage okay, though I wish they weren't so stubborn.

As per my request, I find a neat pile of stapled copies stacked on the desk in the front bedroom. Before Steve or Nathan can see them, I take them into my room and stash them in my suitcase. Then I grab my laptop and head out the door.

"You guys can have the bathroom first. I'm going downstairs to work."

"By yourself?" Steve asks sharply. "I'll go with you."

"No, I'm fine, remember what you said? I'm still safe until I finish his book."

Neither of them looks particularly happy at the idea of being left alone with the other, but they're just going to have to get along. Nathan could get a private suite if he wanted, but he hasn't shown any more inclination to leave my side than Steve has. I'm beginning to wonder if each one thinks he's protecting me from the other.

It's a thought that has me grinning to myself as I close the door on them.

On the wide staircase I meet a surprise: Rachel Templeton.

"Mrs. Templeton!"

Her head jerks up, and she frowns at me. I've startled her, and she looks angry about it, as if she had been deep in her own thoughts and now I've interrupted them.

"I didn't mean to scare you. Do you remember me? I'm Marie Lightfoot? Marie Folletino? I was here in Sebastion five years ago, and we talked about my parents?"

On that trip, I stayed in Birmingham and commuted here. Looking back at that choice now, it doesn't make much sense. I can only surmise that I didn't want to get any closer than I had to, didn't want to spend any more time here than I needed in order to interview a few people.

"I remember," she says, without warmth.

This black woman who once worked for my parents is in her sixties now. From the looks of the vacuum cleaner she's lugging up the steps, she is still working as a housecleaner, only this time for the Old Southern Inn. It makes my heart hurt to realize that although many things have changed since those days, for a black woman with little education, some hard things never changed. Here is Rachel, still sweeping up the dirt from under the feet of white folks. Or, maybe I should say, wealthier folks, since surely some of the tourists who stay here now are black. She's wearing blue jeans, with a man's shirt hanging over them, and her head is wrapped in a white turban. I get a glimpse of the beautiful girl she once was, but the years have lined her face and deepened the shadows and circles under her eyes.

"What're you back here for?" she asks me, blunt as a hammer.

She was a little friendlier than this the last time I saw her, but not much.

"I'm just trying to find out a little more about them."

She shakes her head, as if she thinks I'm foolish to pursue it.

"You're working late," I comment, kind of desperately, as if I think that if we stand here on the steps long enough she'll warm up to me.

"I work another job first."

Stricken at the idea of this sixtyish woman working two jobs — or more? — to make ends meet, I'm at a loss for any other words except, "How is your husband?"

"Hubert's doin' okay."

"Where's he working these days?"

"Little of this, little of that. Yard work. Got himself a truck, pickin' up some towing business out on the highway. Never run out of that kind of business."

Into the awkward pause that follows, I say, "Please give him my best regards."

She nods, unsmiling. "I'll do that." Without another word, she starts to move on around me. I turn and watch her labor on up the stairs. I ache to ask if I may carry the heavy appliance for her, but she'd find that absurd. She has been carrying such loads most of her life. How can this possibly be fair or right, that these two courageous black Americans could still be piecing their

414

income together from such laborious tasks as cleaning houses and towing wrecks? Where's the justice in that?

And then it's my turn to be startled.

At the top of the stairs, as if aware of my eyes focused on her back, she suddenly turns to glare down at me. "If I had a mama and a papa like you had I'd never ask a single question about them. You oughtn't to be prying. You ought to just let it go. Hubert and I, we put up with you and all your questions one time, 'cause we felt sorry for you. It wasn't your fault, what your parents did, but now here you are back again. You ought to just be ashamed of them and be done with it, instead of carrying on about writing a book about them, like they was something to be proud about. You ought to take yourself on home is what you ought to do, and forget about us, and don't never come back to Sebastion."

Stung, I shoot back, "Maybe it wasn't their fault."

Her expression is bitterly scornful. "And maybe the sun don't rise."

"Maybe they were murdered."

But that only deepens her contempt. "You think everybody's an innocent victim? You got a lot to learn, girl, but if you're smart, you won't try to learn it here."

She picks up her vacuum again and turns her back on me.

Feeling shaken, I turn and continue on down the stairs.

Hardly aware of where I'm walking, I end up in the parlor.

There's no one else around, but there could be a whole convention of people in here and I wouldn't feel any less alone. There was something so alienating about what she said to me, the way she said it, the cold, determined way she froze me out when she walked off. I feel as if I'm my mother, rejected by her friend whom she once loved and trusted. There are all kinds of betrayals in the world and one of the worst is to think the worst of people who have never previously given you any reason to doubt them. If I were my mother, I'd feel terribly betrayed right now, which is really ironic, considering that Rachel and Hubert think they're the ones who have the right to feel that way.

For reasons I can't fully explain or understand, that brief encounter has left me feeling as if I want to cry, more than almost anything else in the past few awful days has done.

I need a balm, some kind of connection with other people.

Bless E-mail. When all else fails and I'm a long way from home, E-mail can still provide the illusion of connection. I find a comfortable armchair, sink into it, and then use the battery-operated modem capabilities of my laptop computer to access the Internet.

There's nothing from Paulie Barnes.

I don't know whether to feel relieved or worried by that.

Dr. Aileen Rasmussen has checked in to say she has been thinking it over and is now convinced that Paulie Barnes's real issue is control and that any loss of that control could likely trigger the underlying anger, which could be directed against me. "Watch out," she says in her E-mail. "Be careful."

Gee, thanks, Aileen, that wouldn't have occurred to me.

"I've studied the MacDonald novel closely," she adds, in a rare complete declarative sentence in an E-mail. "Attack on someone close to you? Attempt on life of child? Those happened in book. Still looking for indicators."

Me, too, Aileen. Busy looking for indicators here.

There's also a message from Franklin. An outraged message that makes him

417

sound so much like a Jewish mother that I end up smiling and feeling a little better, instead of feeling guilty. He has written:

You leave without talking to me? I get a message on a machine? You don't tell me where you've gone, or why you left in such a hurry? Where the hell are you? Are you all right? Why did you leave? This was a lousy thing for you to do, Marie, I don't care how worried you are about my children. Do you think I don't care what happens to you as well as to them? I thought I was already pretty clear about that. Do you think I don't have a right to know where you go and how you are during a time like this? What do you think I'm made of, iron? Do you think it's easy for me to go to work and do my job when every second I'm thinking about you, and where you might be, and whether you're even alive?

Jesus Christ, Marie. All right, I'll tell you what, let's work on the assumption that you're alive and reading this, shall we? That being the case — I hope — here is some information you may want to have about the items you saved for fingerprints.

There aren't any. All clean except for one set on the FedEx envelope, two sets on the letter and book that came in it, and one set on the cassette tape. This accords with the number of prints that should be on those items based on the fact that only you, or Deb, or both of you touched them. No other prints. Of course we will need to make it official by getting your prints and hers to check them against, but I'm not expecting any useful surprises there.

The FedEx envelope was mailed from one of their freestanding mailboxes, so there was no attendant to witness who dropped it off. But here's the surprise about that package: the credit card number? It's one of yours, Marie. It's your own credit card. How did he get hold of it?

I am stunned by this revelation. He used my own credit card?

He must have fished one of my receipts or credit card company bills out of my trash, or maybe he got hold of a bill I charged at a restaurant or store. That sort of thing is supposed to be all too easy to do.

Franklin's E-mail continues:

As for the tape, Ernie doesn't know how it got there. He says his men aren't allowed to run the radio/CD/tape players in his customers' cars. He says that would be like a housecleaner who uses a client's entertainment center when they're gone. He says now and then his customers wander around and people sometimes wander in off the street just to look at the cool cars. He tries to keep them from touching anything. Ernie is so upset about this that you'd think somebody had stolen your car instead of just leaving a tape in it — and I didn't even tell him what this was all about. He says to tell you he's sorry and the next time you come in he'll only charge you an arm instead of an arm and a leg.

Good ol' Ernie. He's such a perfectionist himself, he may not even find it strange that we're obsessing over a cassette tape.
Franklin then says,

I never heard back from Paulie Barnes after I sent him that E-mail. Either — like you — he doesn't want to bother with me, or — like you — he thinks he doesn't have to, or he's smart enough to know he'd better not try.

He closes with:

For God's sake, tell me you're all right. We're fine.

There's a postscript that would be funny if it weren't for the circumstances.

Dog's fine, too. I can tell you what I found out about that, but you'll have to respond to this if you want that information.

My return E-mail to Aileen says only, "Thanks."

I take more time over the one to Franklin, finally settling on, "I'm really sorry. I didn't have time to reach you. I want to tell you where I am and why I'm here, but I think it's better that I don't." I don't want him flying out here, in a fit of male protectiveness. "But please, will you tell me about the dog anyway?"

And then I close my computer and go back upstairs.

When I open the door I find two handsome men waiting for me, both dressed in suits, although one suit looks about three times more expensive and stylish than the other one. They're also both seated in chairs, and both staring at a television that is turned onto a sports show, and neither of them is talking to the other.

"You guys look great," I tell them.

Nate looks over and smiles at me. "Your turn. I'm pretty sure we left you a dry towel, didn't we, Steve?"

The big man just nods, looking stiff and uncomfortable.

"I'll hurry," I promise, mostly for his sake.

As I scurry into my bedroom and close the door behind me, I realize I may not have been very sensitive here. If Steve's gay, I've put him in a bedroom with one of the best-looking men he'll ever see, and there isn't a chance in hell that he will benefit from that. The irony is that Steve looks like a man's man — which I guess he is, in a manner of speaking — while my cousin looks just a little too pretty. But when it comes to sexual orientation, looks can be deceiving. If heterosexuality were a disease, Nathan would have all the symptoms of a chronic condition. In fact, I frequently tell him that seeing all those women is going to kill him someday. To which his standard reply is, "Yeah, but what a way to go."

After a quick shower, I open the closet where I have hung my little black dress that travels almost everywhere with me. I wish Franklin were here to go with it.

A light supper with company?

Sounds like black strappy heels and my mother's little pearl necklace, which can also go anywhere, with anything, and which I carry in a soft pouch in my purse when I travel. As I affix it around my neck I think of her backing up to my father, asking him to fasten it for her. I imagine his fingers brushing the nape of her neck while she holds her hair up out of his way. The latch clicks. He bends to softly kiss the back of her neck. She turns around, releases her hair, lifts her chin toward him, and smiles. He bends to kiss her again.

"Ready?" he asks her.

"Ready," I whisper to myself.

27

Marie

It's a picnic in the Fishers' backyard, and it takes me a while to realize that it is in many ways nearly a duplicate of that other picnic almost forty years ago. The same people have been invited, with the addition of Nathan, Steve, and me. The only difference in the guest list is that there are no "neutrals," as Eulalie called them; nor is she expecting any diehard racists to knock on her front door tonight, as far as I know.

But everything else looks eerily the same.

Clayton Fisher is serving mint juleps again, and in a strength sufficient to get any number of women drunk tonight, just as before. Eulalie has laid out a spread of dishes that matches almost exactly what she told me she served that night, from fried chicken to jambalaya.

"I can't believe it," I whisper to Nathan and Steve.

"What?" my cousin asks.

"This party . . . it's just like the one they held here the night my parents disappeared."

Both men stare at me.

"That's weird," Steve says, for all of us.

"How do you know?" Nate demands.

I give him a look. "I'm a writer. I know these things."

He laughs a little and looks around us, taking it all in, just like the writer he is, too. Slowly, over the course of this long day of wandering down memory lane, the two of them have reached a kind of rapprochement, wary with each other, but polite. Nathan apparently still suspects that Steve will murder me in my bed, while Steve seems to suspect everybody who gets near me, just on general principles.

Eulalie Fisher and the other women guests have worn light summer frocks tonight. "You look like a black orchid among the daisies," Nate whispers to me. He is his usual stylish self in an L.A. summer suit that makes the other men here look like high school principals. More than one person has commented that I am the "spittin' image of your mama," but nobody tells Nate he resembles his portly, conservative father. As for Steve, questions of style don't even enter into it. He has on clean pants, an ironed shirt, shined shoes, and there's nobody who's going to remark upon it one way or another. The guests slide around him; even Clayton Fisher's hospitality meets its match in Steve's sober, watchful presence.

By the time I have my epiphany about the party, I have already drunk one of Clayton's famous mint juleps. Feeling no pain, much less inhibitions, I walk over to my hostess and ask her directly about my theory.

"Eulalie, did you do this on purpose?"

"Do what, darlin'?" she asks me, all southern female innocence.

While Steve seems content to hold down a corner of the yard, arms folded against his chest, alone, and while Nate charms the socks off of everybody else, I refine my question for my hostess.

"Did you purposely duplicate the June twelfth, 1963, picnic?"

Her blue eyes widen — even at eighty, she is still the most beautiful woman here — in what looks like shocked surprise. Slowly, Eulalie turns around, carefully taking in the view of her own party.

"My Lord, you're right as rain. It is."

When she turns back to me, I see what

looks like pain in this elegant woman's eyes. "Child, I never meant to. I hope you'll forgive me. This was purely unconscious on my part. I don't know where I dredged this up from my memory, but now I do so wish I hadn't."

I briefly touch her arm, wondering if her claim is true. Surely nobody's subconscious can be this accurate without a little outside assistance. In fact, the only reason I have recognized the uncanny similarity between the two parties is that I possess a description of the original one in my notes, which were augmented by Eulalie's diaries, bits and pieces of which she shared with me. Plus, she's one of those incredible hostesses who keeps a written record of all of her dinner parties, of who attended, and what she served them and how they liked it, of how she decorated her tables and what she wore, of who said what memorable thing to whom, or who stole a kiss, got drunk, or otherwise made stars or donkeys of themselves. Without such written records as Eulalie's, I'd have a much harder time as a true crime writer in recapitulating past events.

"It's all right," I assure her, even if a part of me persists in suspecting that she did this for some reason of her own. "I just wondered."

"I don't suppose anybody else will notice," she says, probably accurately.

Now, standing near me, she claps her hands, as if punctuating the end of this topic. If she planned the party to match in this way, did she intend for me to notice, or did she intend to set some kind of mood, establish an evocative atmosphere for reasons I can't fathom? Or is this truly the coincidence she says it is?

"People! Clayton has something to say!"

Her voice has weakened with age, her hair has bleached to silver, her bones have shrunk, but she still wields the power in her marriage to cause her husband to turn instantly and smile over at her.

With his white hair, and wearing an old-fashioned baby blue and white seersucker summer suit with a white shirt and red tie — other flashbacks to that earlier picnic — Clayton looks so dapper that it's hard to imagine how he might have looked even handsomer on that June evening so many years ago. Now, as then, he gazes at his bossy wife with an amused, mock-surprised expression on his face.

I know more or less what he's going to say before he says it.

"I do?" he calls out as several people begin to chuckle.

"Tell them to fill their plates!" she calls back.

Clayton Fisher gazes benignly around at the couples he has known for so many decades. "Fill your plates, people!"

They all laugh and start moving toward the feast.

They've heard all this before, and so have I.

I feel as if I've entered a time warp.

At first, it was terribly awkward when the party started.

"Have you met Anne and Marty Wiegan? And this is Michael and Lyda's girl, Marie, can you believe it? And this handsome young fella is Joe and Julia's boy, Nathan. And, I beg your pardon, I'm terribly sorry, I've forgotten your name again — ?"

"Steven Orbach."

"Yes, of course, Steven is a friend of theirs."

The dark oily strands of hair no longer drape across Marty Wiegan's scalp, which now is bald and as shiny as kitchen tile. They're all in their sixties and seventies now — except for the older Fishers —

these former radicals, these daring couples who risked their lives and lost their reputations. Austin Reese has changed from eyeglasses to contact lenses, so he actually looks a little younger than he did when I interviewed him several years ago. Lackley Goodwin, formerly so rotund, is now so gaunt that I wonder if he joined the fitness generation; if diet and exercise don't account for it, he might have cancer or some other wasting disease. Austin's trying his hand at a novel, I learn, now that he's retired from running the math department at the college. Lackley is playing "too much golf." The Wiegans have retired to their little place outside of town, where Marty raises roses and tomatoes. Of the men, only Clayton — the eldest by far — still goes into his former job a few days a week, but then they'd have me believe that "bankers never die, they just lose interest."

It's obvious that Hostel was the high point of their lives.

"I'll tell you the truth, Marie," Marty Wiegan confides over his own mint julep. "It was thrilling. We were spies, we were saboteurs of the status quo, we were soldiers of fortune, but it was all for love and not for money. We felt like heroes. This group" — his fond glance includes Austin

and Lackley, who are chatting with us —
"is like a band of soldiers who've fought a
war together. I feel like a vet, don't y'all?"

Austin's face is wreathed in a smile of
reminiscence.

"Got a few war wounds, too," Lackley
says, wryly, no doubt recalling the night of
their public "humiliation." In retrospect, it
must feel as if it was a parade of pride,
their shining moment in life, never to be
equaled again.

"Too bad we don't give Purple Hearts to
civilians," I say.

The men look gratified by my comment,
and I'm glad of that.

I have met the wives of these men previously, on my earlier forays into Sebastion,
but only in passing. They are Anne
Wiegan, Melinda Reese, Delilah Goodwin, all of whom added a detail or two to
my gathering of information about that
original picnic and those days, but none
of whom I talked to in any depth. The
women's stories hadn't seemed so en-
twined with the story of my parents
during that final twenty-four hours or so,
and so I hadn't bothered overly much
with them. Now I find them to be ordinary small-town southern grandmothers,
but ones who grow richly animated when

talking of those former, heroic times.

"I remember your parents," they say, with great tact, to Nathan.

"I'll bet they do," he murmurs under his breath to me.

"How have you been all these years, my dear?" they ask me kindly, in one way or another. "Such a tragedy that befell you. You were so young. But I understand you've managed to make quite a success for yourself with your writing. That's just grand. We're all so happy for you."

Both of us, Nathan and I, stumble over ourselves at first, trying to make it clear that we are on their side and not aligned with our parents' views of the world. It's almost embarrassing how hard we work to prove we're on the side of the angels until finally it's clear that nobody here this evening expects us to be clones of our parents.

Once we know that, I begin to relax enough to drink too much.

"Easy on the booze," Steve warns me, looking censorious.

"I think it's too late," I tell him, with false cheer, and then I even tease him a little, which I would never have done two drinks ago. "You're the bodyguard. *You* stay sober." I'm glad to be a little drunk. I feel as if I'm going to need some false courage to accomplish what I have to do tonight. Then Nathan fusses over me, saying, "What's going on, Marie? You don't usually drink this much. Don't tell me you care what these people think of you."

"What's going *on?*" I snap at him. "What do you *think* is going on? Everything that's happening — it's all knocking down my inner fences too fast. I wasn't ready for any of this. I don't want to be here. I don't want to be in this town, at this party, with these people. I'm not ready for this."

Paulie Barnes is forcing my hand, forcing my history, forcing me.

"May I ask all of you something?"

Eight faces, plus Steve and Nathan, turn toward me as we sit around the Fishers' circular table. Candlelight flickers on them, turning aging faces soft and young again, until I can almost imagine I am seeing them as my parents did. The empty plates have been removed, the remnants of the feast cleared away, and now we sit facing one another with coffee, brandy, or some other libation. They've all been so nice to me — and the mint juleps have been so potent — that I'm flying high.

Surely they won't mind if I ask them

what I'm dying to know.

Anne Wiegan says, "It sounds so funny to hear 'you all' pronounced as two separate words. Marie, honey," she teases, "if you're going to be spendin' any time here, we're gonna have to teach you how to talk right. But you go ahead and ask us what you want to, anyway. We'll try to understand what you say."

Everybody laughs, including me.

"I've brought something with me," I tell them, feeling nervous in spite of the liquor. "Something I'd like you to read. I have copies for everybody."

Nate's head jerks up, and he looks intensely curious.

What are you up to now? his expression says to me.

For an instant my brain clears and I comprehend more fully the nature of just what I'm about to ask them to do. This is no joke. No party game. "I hope this won't upset or offend you, at least not too much. I realize it's a lot to ask of you. It's just that, I have to know. . . ."

A shift in mood washes across the table.

With Steve's help, I pass out the copies that Mo made.

"What is this?" Clayton Fisher asks, leafing through it.

"Oh, my God," Delilah Goodwin says, within two paragraphs of reading it.

Eulalie looks at me with a raised eyebrow and merely says, "Marie?"

"I apologize," I tell them. "I have to beg your tolerance of this and of me. What you are holding in your hands is a purported account of how my parents died. I can't tell you where I got it, because I don't know. It was sent to me anonymously. I'm asking you all to read it. I want to know what you think of it."

"I can't read in this light," Austin Reeves says, fretfully.

Clayton moves a candle closer to him.

Nathan, who wasn't in on this plan, looks pale and upset across the table from me. Steve looks no more or less stoic than usual.

"Oh, my God," Delilah breathes again and again as she reads. "Oh, my God, my God . . ."

Finally, they finish, all of them, and look up at me.

I ask them bluntly, "Could this be true?"

Nobody answers that, no one seems to want to break the silence, so I ask another question.

"Do you recognize anyone from the descriptions in that account?"

I see Austin and Clayton exchange worried glances.

"Yes," Austin says. "All right, yes, I do. You do, too, don't you, Clayton?"

Our host nods reluctantly but doesn't say anything.

"Who?" Marty demands. "Who do you know in this?"

Austin looks at him and says, "Think who had relatives in Oregon, Marty. There's only one person here in Sebastion who had relatives like that in Oregon. You know who I mean, don't you?"

"Oh, Jesus, yes."

"Tell me," I beg.

"What about the crossroads?" Marty asks, ignoring me and turning toward his wife. "Who's got property by the crossroads?"

She shakes her head, and even in the candlelight her face looks pale. "I know who you're thinking of, and so am I. He's the only person I know who had a farm out by the crossroads, and who also always drove pickup trucks, and who also belonged to the KKK."

A gasp comes out of me, but nobody seems to notice.

"The pickup trucks," Melinda says then.

"Yes," Clayton says. "They all drove pickup trucks."

"Who?" I ask them, practically beg them. "Who?"

"And the land with the caves on it —" Austin says.

For the first time, Eulalie speaks, sounding infinitely weary. "We all know who you mean, Austin." She turns her beautiful face toward me. "We all know who these people are," she says, tapping the papers with her fingers. And to the others, she says, "Let's face it. It couldn't be more clear if their very names were spelled out for us."

My heart is beating so fast.

"I'll swear I would never have thought they were smart enough," Eulalie says with a sigh.

"It didn't take many brains or much courage, either, for that matter," her husband remarks with a wry twist to his mouth, "to round up a dangerous bunch like the eight of us, and then to ambush two unarmed people on a deserted highway in the dark."

Across the table, Marty Wiegan's face darkens with anger.

"Then you think this could all be true?" I ask them.

Around the table, they nod their heads, they murmur affirmatively.

"You could take this to the sheriff?" I ask them. "Or the FBI? They could issue warrants on these people you're talking about, and arrest and charge them with the murder of my parents?"

Marty throws down his napkin onto the tabletop and I hear him curse under his breath. Anne, his wife, who is seated to my right, reaches for my hand to hold. "Marie, I think that I can safely speak for all of us when I say that we all believe that this account may well be true. And we all know exactly to whom it refers. But it won't do you any good to go looking for any of them. We can give you the names, but you won't have ever heard of them. They were all ignorant, crude men, KKK members, and you won't even recognize their names."

"That's all right, that won't stop the police from —"

"They're all dead, Marie," her husband tells me, angrily.

"Dead? What?" I am confused by this. "How can they all be dead? Were they killed, or something?"

"No," Clayton says, speaking coolly enough to nearly sober me. "Nothing like that. These were older men at the time, my dear. They did their bad deeds, they lived their squalid lives, and they died in the usual kinds of ways. Disease, heart attacks, what have you, nothing out of the ordinary. They're just dead and gone, that's all."

I'm stunned. My parents' murderers. Dead, themselves.

"Where's the justice?" Anne Wiegan asks of no one in particular.

"But . . . ," I say, then stop, trying to figure out what my own last question is. "But . . . if you think this story is true . . . and you believe you know who these people, these killers, were . . . and if they were KKK members . . ."

There is a charged, expectant silence around the table now.

It is Clayton Fisher who breaks in to state the appalling question for me, to his friends. "Why would the Klan have killed Michael and Lyda if they were all on the same side? And if Michael and Lyda weren't allied with the Klan, then were they still on our side? And if that's so, and they weren't the ones who gave our names away and betrayed us that night, then . . . who did?"

The couples, old friends, former revolutionaries in their quiet ways, look around the table at one another until finally Austin Reese asks, "Who were the only people who didn't get either marched downtown or arrested that night?"

His wife moans and puts her face in her hands.

"Hubert," somebody else whispers. "And Rachel."

"No," I hear another person cry. "No!"

"Why would they? Of all people?" Eulalie demands. "Why *would* they?"

"There may have been some private grudge that we don't know about," her husband suggests. "Or maybe for money."

"I don't know about the grudge part," she argues back at him, "but I certainly don't believe it could have been for money. Because if it was, where did it go? As far as I can tell, Hubert and Rachel have never been anything but poor."

"I didn't say it had to be a lot of money," he gently points out. "Jesus himself was betrayed for a mere thirty pieces of silver."

"What shall we do?" Marty asks them suddenly.

"I'll see the sheriff in the morning," Clayton says. He pats the copy of the story I forced them to read. "I'll take this with me."

"Not so fast, Clayton," Lackley Goodwin says. "You can't just go charging in there accusing people of murder, not even dead men, not even *those* dead men. We've got to think about this some more. If we go accusing people, we've got to do it coherently, we've got to have all the answers to all the questions that are going to get raised."

"Like what?" Austin asks him.

"Well, for one thing, why would they only embarrass us, but then kill Marie's parents? I mean, we didn't even get arrested! Did they hate Michael and Lyda more for some reason? Were Michael and Lyda a bigger threat to segregation than we were?"

"It was Michael who started Hostel, remember," Clayton reminds them in his most authoritative banker's manner, and nobody contradicts the frank and painful things he says next. "He sniffed out the liberals among us and recruited every one of us. I think we all have to admit that Michael was our guiding light. Would we ever have started such a thing without him? There's a simple answer to that, whether it flatters us or not, and that answer is a no. Would we have reestablished it without him? We did not, did we? Time has already told the truth of that. When they removed Michael they removed our brain, and when they killed Lyda, they took the heart clean out of us. Lyda was our passionate one, wasn't she? She was a burr under the saddles of the bigots from the time she was a little thing."

"How could my father stand to teach there?" I blurt, wanting to know what I've always wanted to know. "How could any of you?"

Lackley Goodwin nods, as if he understands my total incomprehension. "When you live in the water, Marie, you've got to swim. We would have been working in racist environments *any*where we went, not just at Jim Forrest. But since we were there, it was superb cover —"

"I *knew* it," I whisper.

"We thought that no one," he continues, "would ever suspect two teachers and a couple of administrators from Jim Forrest —"

"And one banker from town," Clayton interjects.

"Hubert says that my father got a phone call that night," I tell them. "It sounds as if it was a warning, but who would have known to call them?" I look over at Eulalie. "I think that's why they didn't go to your party that night, Eulalie. I think they were planning to be here, but then my dad got that phone call."

"Maybe it wasn't a warning call," Austin

Reese says, slowly, as if he's thinking out loud.

"What do you mean, Austin?" Delilah asks him.

"I mean, maybe it was intended to get Michael and Lyda scared and running, so that then they could be ambushed outside of town."

Theirs is a sudden appalled silence, into which I toss the question, "Why didn't they take me with them?"

"I'm sure they meant to come back for you, child," Eulalie says.

"Well, then, if they couldn't do that, why not just leave me in the house with the people who worked there, or send me home with Rachel? Why leave me in a run-down motel where anything could happen to me?"

"If they were running from the Klan," Lackley Goodwin tells me, "they'd have likely been scared their house might be torched that night, and they wouldn't have wanted to get any of their black employees into trouble, either. They couldn't very well have sent you home with Rachel or with Hubert, because they were Hostel members, too."

Delilah adds, gently, "I'm a mother, Marie, although my children are grown.

But if I thought that somebody was going to come looking for Lackley and me to kill us, the last thing I'd want is to have our children with us. And if on top of it, I didn't have much time to plan what to do with them, why then I just don't know what I'd do."

"Why not leave me with Julia and Joe?" I persist.

"Because —" Anne Wiegan suddenly glances at my cousin, who has sat through this without saying a word. When Nate catches her glance, he saves her from having to answer.

"Because," he says, "my parents might not have helped them."

We all sit for a moment with that awful realization.

"Was the motel Hubert's idea?" somebody asks then.

None of them seems to know. I interviewed Hubert, but that was a question I didn't think to ask him. They suspect it doesn't matter who had that idea, however, and I agree with them.

"I'll bet it was Hubert," Anne Wiegan says, and then sounding infinitely sad, she adds, "at least he thought to spare the baby." She looks directly at me, and I see in the candlelight that tears are running down her face. "I loved your parents dearly, Marie. I grew up with your mother, she was always one of my best friends, but she always seemed special somehow. She thought bigger than the rest of us, she did bigger things, she was braver and bolder than I could have ever hoped to be. When she brought your father home with her, I thought he was the perfect man for her. At first, I thought he was unfriendly, as if he thought he was too smart and sophisticated for the likes of us, but when you got to know him he was the kindest, most honest man, he really was. That's why it was so shocking when it seemed they had betrayed us. I didn't think I'd ever get over the hurt of that. And now it pains me more than I can say to find out that we were the ones who betrayed them, all along, by not believing in them. We should have *known*," she cries to the others. "We should have known that Michael and Lyda simply couldn't do that."

"But the FBI said it was them!" Delilah says. "Clayton, isn't that what that FBI friend of yours told you?"

Across the table from her, he nods, looking grim.

"The Feebs always have their own agendas," Marty says, darkly.

"What should we do now?" somebody asks, for all of them.

"I want everyone to read and reread this carefully," Clayton directs, taking unquestioned charge now. "Make notes. Write down anything that supports what we believe to be true. We'll meet tomorrow night to decide exactly what we're going to say and to whom we're going to present it."

"Where?" Austin asks him. "Do you want us here again?"

"At the inn," Marty suggests. "I'll tell Mo to put on some coffee and save us the parlor."

"We owe it to Marie," his wife says, looking directly at me.

"No," I tell them, my voice quavering for the first time. They aren't the only ones who are feeling guilty, but at least I have the excuse that I never knew my parents, or only knew them through the memories of people like these. "Nobody owes me anything. We owe it to my parents."

At the door, when the "party" finally breaks up, Eulalie folds me in her arms and whispers, "Oh, my God in heaven, can you ever forgive us?"

28

Marie

"There's at least one thing wrong with their theory," Steve tells Nate and me as we all walk back to the inn following the party. His unemotional tone has an astringent quality that sharply cuts into the wallow of emotions that the booze and the amazing evening have left me in. "It's fine to identify the men who killed your parents. That's one thing. But if they're all dead, then who sent that story to you?"

"Who is Paulie Barnes, in other words," I say, slowly.

"Yeah," Steve says. "And what's his connection to all this?"

"And why," my cousin adds, "did he bring you here . . . why did he bring *me* here?"

"To reveal the names of the killers?" I guess.

"But why does he think he needs me, for

447

that?" Nate asks. "And why did he pick such a cruel way to do this to you?"

I sag against him, and he quickly puts an arm around me to prop me up. "It isn't over, is it, Nathan?"

"Not on your life," Steve says.

"I call *that* an unfortunate choice of words!" I mumble, making my cousin laugh. "But speaking of my life, do you two realize we're only two blocks from where it started?"

"You want a plaque on the door?" Nathan jokes.

"No, I want to go over there."

"Now?"

"Sure. Why not? It's a beautiful night, we have the streets to ourselves, we don't have anything else to do, and I want to walk over there. Will you guys come with me?"

Steve doesn't really have a choice, not if he wants to guard my body, but even Nathan agrees to come along. I offer each of them an elbow as we walk along, but only he hooks his arm through mine.

The old homestead appears even larger by night than it did by day. There are three stories, counting the large attic, and by modern-day standards, it's nearly a mansion. My mother came from a bit of money herself, and my father's traitorous parents made a lot of money writing screenplays during the years when better writers couldn't get hired because of their alleged Communist affiliations. It all came down to me, what my aunt and uncle didn't spend on my education and vacations for all of us, but this house didn't. They sold it when they moved Nathan and me to Florida, and they used the proceeds to buy their next house. (My father had made the mistake of making his brother-in-law my trustee.) "Marie's parents would want her to have a nice place to live" was their rationale at the time for spending my money on a vast place on the water, and when they sold that, they made another bundle and claimed it all belonged to them, since "Marie's parents would want her to have a nice place to come home to anytime she wants." I long ago decided that it isn't worth fighting about, although if my life had turned out differently, if I hadn't made so much money of my own, I might have another attitude about it.

The last owner of this house was out of luck, apparently.

Though the white paint is dingy gray

and peeling now, there's still enough of it to make the house gleam white under the quarter moon. We amble up one side of the circle drive, not even trying to be quiet, since the houses on either side appear to be vacant, too. Once this was a gorgeous block of southern-style homes, all grace and charm, but now it has an empty, haunted atmosphere.

"Too bad," Nate says, and I know what he means.

Too bad this beautiful house is falling down, too bad the town is deteriorating, too bad for so many reasons, too damn bad.

"I want to go inside," I announce.

"It isn't safe," Steve warns.

"And it's all boarded up," Nate observes, pointing out the plywood that is nailed over one of the downstairs windows.

"Well, I know one room that will still be open," I tell them. "Follow me."

I take off toward where I see that the gravel drive branches into the west side yard and I follow that weedy path until it brings us around to the rear.

"Oh, my God," I breathe, and stop in my tracks.

"What?" Nate asks, sounding alarmed.

"It's the magnolia tree! The one that

James told me he could see from the window of the parson's chamber."

"Don't scare me like that. I thought you saw a ghost."

The old tree has grown to monstrous size, which magnolias can do here in the South. Its branches push against the house now and offer even more privacy and darkness than they did when my parents were hiding runaways here.

"Come on!"

The past, as it's been told to me, is rushing in on me now. Maybe it's the mint juleps I drank, maybe it's the accumulation of all that's happened in the last few days, maybe it's only that I'm living on an emotional edge, but I feel as if I'm walking back into that night when my parents disappeared. There's the door at the back of the house, the one that was always left open in the old days so that visiting preachers might come in and stay the night. I touch my hand to it, and it gives, and as it gives way into a dark and empty room, I feel as if I can sense them on the other side of the wall. I hear Rachel talking to the other black woman my mother sometimes hired. I hear my parents talking in their room upstairs as they dress for the Fishers' picnic. I hear a telephone ring, hear my father walk to answer it, hear the muffled distress in his voice. I hear a baby cry and my mother hurry to comfort it.

"It's creepy," Nathan says, behind me.

Steve hasn't come in. When I look back and see him framed in the doorway, he looks as if he doesn't want to join this game.

"The bed probably was there," I tell Nathan, pointing to where I mean. "Look, here's the bathroom! Not much left of the fixtures. James said this was the first time in his life he ever used indoor plumbing." I walk back out of the bathroom and into the bedroom again. "And over there, that would be a natural place to put a table."

"There's something on the floor," Nathan says, his voice sounding hollow in this echoing room. "Somebody left something here. You want a souvenir, Marie?"

"What is it?"

He's standing nearer to it, so he bends and picks it up.

"Just an ashtray. Some homeless person must have spent the night in here. He left his cigar."

The hair stands up on my head, on my arms, on my neck.

"His what?"

"Cigar."

Max Cady smoked cigars. In MacDonald's

452

book The Executioners, *Max Cady smoked cigars.*

Somehow, I manage to get out the words to tell them.

"Jesus, Marie! You're scaring the crap out of me," Nate exclaims, once he's heard it. Quickly, he sets the ashtray back down on the floor. "You think this Paulie Barnes was here?"

I hurry over to crouch down and take a look.

Just as in the book, this is a "well-chewed" cigar.

"Yes," I say, feeling like a deer being watched by somebody in a hidden blind. "Let's get out of here."

"You can't say that soon enough to please me," my cousin says and helps me to my feet so fast he nearly knocks me over. "Let's get the *hell* out of here. But how did he know we'd do this?"

Thinking of the incident with the hawks in the Keys, I say, "He didn't. He just likes to plant his little traps in case I fall into them."

As we hurry back down the gravel drive, I'm thinking, *He's been here, he's been in Sebastion.* Or, worse, he's in Sebastion now.

I'm shaken by finding the cigar, and so I disappear quickly into my bedroom, leaving the men to talk about it if they want to, or watch TV, or read, or sleep. I just want to be by myself. No, that's not true. I want to be with Franklin.

Since the closest I can get to doing that is with my computer, I turn it on and check my E-mail. When I see his familiar e-address in my mailbox, I nearly feel like crying from gratitude.

"All right, I'll tell you about the damned dog," he starts in, and even with all that has happened tonight, even after being scared out of my wits by a well-chewed cigar, I can't help but grin at my computer screen. He sounds so pissed. Just like Franklin.

The damned dog's name is Mabel. We're keeping her, because there's no way to take a dog away from little kids. I should say *I'm* keeping her. Truly refuses to have her stay there until Mabel is house-trained, so I've got the job of crate-training her. Don't get me started on this. This isn't what you need to know anyway.

We tried to track Mabel through humane societies, dog pounds, and pet shops, but no luck. What we've finally decided is that she's a stolen dog. Yes, I'm doing everything I can to find her owners — that's the only possible way of getting rid of her that the kids could understand — but I'm not hopeful. I think we've got us a dog.

Oh, all right. She's a nice dog. Poops a lot.

In the bedroom in Sebastion, I suddenly have a fit of the silent giggles. Out of an act of meanness, something rather adorable has come. The kids must be thrilled, even if their parents aren't.

Franklin's E-mail continues:

As for the ribbon with the card that had your name on it, it's just a generic ribbon and card with your name typed on it. Probably impossible to trace, but that doesn't mean we won't try. I've talked to Detectives Anschutz and Flanck, by the way, and the three of us are coordinating everything we're doing.

Okay, I told you about the dog. Tell me about you.

And that's all. No "Love, Franklin," no endearments, no nothin'.

But it's way more than enough. It speaks of continued care and concern, and that's all I need to feel right now, that's almost comfort enough. And suddenly I realize it would be stupid to withhold from him the information about what has happened tonight. I've got to tell him. He can share it with the detectives. I need their expertise, all of it. And so I spend the next hour writing everything I can think to tell him, and I send it off into the ether.

My mailbox chirps. A new E-mail has arrived from Paulie Barnes.

My dear Marie,

Do you give any thought to life after death?

If there is such a thing, will you come back to haunt me? How will I know that it's you, my dear? Will you slam doors, make the lights flicker, pour salt into sugar bowls as poltergeists do? I can't quite picture you making whoo noises in the night, or floating down corridors in a filmy white dress —

Reading that, I remember my dream and am frightened and appalled that he could latch on to an image so close to the reality of something in my own head.

They say that when dead people hover around the living, it is because they are stuck at the place where they died. They can't move on. I hope for your sake that doesn't happen to you, Marie, because I don't think you'll want to linger in the place where I will kill you. Believe me, you won't like it there. You won't want to be conscious there even one more minute than you have to. But then, you don't have to worry about that, because I'll be helping you to hurry on to investigate the afterlife.

When you've severed the thread of life, once you've shuffled off this mortal coil, I suggest that you speed away. Unless, of course, you wish to stick around to see how our book is doing?

I tell you what, Marie. I promise that I'll drop back by the place where you died to give you a sales report. I'll read the reviews to you and any fan mail we receive through my E-mail that cannot — as you have no doubt learned by now — be traced by any law enforcement agencies.

And now for your final assignment, your last chapter.

You've written how we "met," which is to say how I first contacted you. You've written as much as you know about your own background. And you've done a nice job of describing for me your terror at what awaits you. Now I want you to write down your feelings about what it is like to know that you're going to die very, very soon, and that you don't know where, or why, or how, or by whom. Submit that to me by morning, Marie. If you don't, I'll be checking in with your cousin Nathan to see what he can tell me about you, and I won't ask him gently.

It is signed as always, "Yours truly, Paulie Barnes."

And at the top is the now-familiar return address in the body of the E-mail: executioners@capefear.com.

Without even stopping to wonder if I'm doing the right thing, I forward it instantly to Franklin. Somehow, just knowing he'll know makes me feel a little better. He hasn't said he misses me — though why should he, all recent things considered? He hasn't said he loves me, nor have I said it to him, he hasn't even said whether his ex-wife is going to "allow" me into her children's lives again. But he's still there. Still hanging in here with me, through everything. Through thick and thin, some people might call it, which is on a moral par, I'd think, with those other well-known clichés such as "rich and poor, in sickness and in health."

I think I can get to sleep on the strength of that, alone.

It's only as I'm falling asleep that something else strikes me.

Our shy innkeeper, Mo Goodwin, is so quiet and unprepossessing that I didn't even notice her absence tonight. I did note that only white former members of Hostel were there, but I hadn't missed Maureen. She said she'd been invited, too, but she never showed up, and nobody mentioned her. Somehow I have a feeling that's the story of Maureen Goodwin's life, that she never shows up and nobody misses her.

29

Marie

It's no fun to wake up to a hangover and a ringing telephone.

"Marie, it's Robyn Anschutz," announces the obscenely energetic voice in my ear. I may have to kill her for calling so early, only since she's a homicide detective, she'd probably find out I did it.

"Robyn."

"Paul is hollering at me to tell you it's him, too. You okay?"

"Yeah. Need caffeine. Or a blood transfusion."

"Wild night, huh? Listen, the reason I'm calling. All *right*, Paul! I hear you! The reason we're calling is that we've been going down that list of murderers in your books, and we think maybe we've got something. A. Z. Roner? The doctor who killed nurses, the one that Franklin put away and you wrote about?"

"Yeah." I'm picturing the skinny, fresh-faced, homicidal, rapist former high school valedictorian in my bloodshot mind's eye. "He's still on death row, right?"

"Yes, but are you aware that his older brother moved to Florida to be close to him?"

"No! Where in Florida?"

"Well, near Starke, so he's not all that close to Bahia, but close enough. And do you remember anything about Roner's younger sister?"

That was several books ago, and I have to scrape the dregs of my memory to get there. "Oh, my God, Robyn, she lives here in Alabama! I can't remember —"

"Mobile. Quite a little coincidence, wouldn't you say?"

"Well, it may only *be* coincidence, Robyn, but I've got to tell you that was just about the most uncooperative family I ever interviewed. They stuck by him to the bitter end. I used to think that Franklin could have shown them video-tapes of A.Z. doing the crimes and they'd still have claimed that somebody framed him."

"What did they think of you, Marie?"

"They thought I was going to make him look good."

"Oops. Think they could be real, real pissed at you?"

"I know they are. They wrote to me after the book came out. But they were up front about it, Robyn. There wasn't anything sneaky or anonymous about it, they just came right out and told me I suck."

She laughs. "I'm glad I don't get fan mail. But listen, Paul and I think we're on to something here. We're going to find out if by some chance the brother loves computers and the sister is a frustrated writer. You met them when you interviewed them, right? You remember what they both look like? We think you ought to keep an eye out for them, Marie."

"I will. And thank you so much, both of you."

"Do you have anything new for us?"

"Yes, I'll send it to you today."

"Hey, listen, does it ever rain where you are?"

"Yeah, it's incredibly green here."

"I wish I was there," Robyn Anschutz says. "Maybe they'd let me wash my car."

Over breakfast downstairs served by a quiet Mo Goodwin, Nate asks, "Who the hell was that who called so early?"

"My police friends in Bahia."

"Yeah?"

"They think that Paulie Barnes could actually be a brother and sister of that homicidal doctor I wrote about a few years ago, remember him? A. Z. Roner? Killed nurses?"

"That creep? Hey, this is great that they know who it is."

"They don't know for sure," I caution him.

Mo has brought us platters of scrambled eggs, cheese grits, country ham and redeye gravy, bacon, sausage, toast, various juices, and coffee, a combination that I wouldn't have thought I could face this morning. But now I find that I am surprisingly hungry. Maybe it's optimism.

"If it's good enough for the cops, it's good enough for me," Nathan insists. "I'm going home."

"You're leaving?" I stare at him.

"Look," he says, leaning toward me, trying to cut Steve out of this conversation, "I've been thinking about it. You don't need me here, Marie. I don't even know why I am here. You've got to admit, nothing really bad has happened — nobody's died, nobody's been injured, nobody's been kidnapped, for God's sake —

and it looks like nothing bad is ever going to happen. I don't mean to be selfish, but I haven't got time for these stupid games the Roners are trying to play with us." His intensity takes on a wry look. "I've got scripts to write that will never sell, Marie. I'm a busy guy. It takes a lot of time and energy to fail as often as I do. And I hate this town. It gives me the creeps. I don't want to be here, not even for you. I want to go home."

I feel devastated that he would leave me like this.

Scraps of childhood memories come, unwelcome, reminding me that my beloved cousin has a long history of leaving me in the lurch. I use the term advisedly, because the first time, or at least the first one I can remember, was literal. I had "lurched" onto a tree limb, propelled from the step he made from the interlocked fingers of his small hands. I flew upward, landing hard enough on my midsection to knock the wind out of me. It hurt, it scared me, I thought I was going to die because I couldn't breathe. When some air found its way back into my empty lungs, I started to wail that I wanted down. Nate ran off to get his mom, I thought. But nobody came to my rescue. When I got my wind back I began to bellow. I was so little, up so high, and I was so scared and in pain and pissed off by then that I must have sounded like an enraged baby rhino bawling for its mother.

Julia came running, but not out of any concern for my plight. "Hush, Marie! You'll wake the dead! What will the neighbors think! What have you done this time? How did you ever get up there?" If clichés came in streams, my Aunt Julia would be Niagara Falls.

Nate trailed behind her, avoiding my eyes.

Seems he'd gone running in to get her, but got distracted by lunch. Or at least he claimed he ran to get her; even at the time, I suspected he panicked and ran away. He didn't take any of the blame for it, either, just stood there silently while she berated me.

Julia got me down by wrapping her strong arms around my legs and pulling. I cried like a banshee at the vicious scraping I was getting on the tree bark.

Nate did nothing to help her, said nothing to help me.

But I didn't rat on him. I didn't say, "It was his idea, too! He pushed me up there and left me!" I let him get away with all of it, because I knew the worst that I would get was the scolding, but that she'd whip him if he got in trouble. They had odd ways of showing their love, my aunt and uncle. "We're only doing this because we love you," they'd tell Nathan as they applied the belt, the hand, the back of the metal spatula to bare skin, and they meant it, too. In their home, it was a much better fate to be neglected. That's why I always let him get away with it, with everything. I loved him, I felt horribly sorry for him, he was my little brother who needed my protection. And he loved me, too, or at least, most of the time he did. Even as a little girl I understood there were times when he could only love himself — although I couldn't have phrased it like that — and so I let him do it.

"You understand?" he asks me now, looking for my usual sympathy.

I can only nod, with narrowed eyes and clenched jaw. *Oh, yeah, I understand all too well. Spoiled brat! And I helped make you this way, not that I'm going to take the blame for your childhood, or for mine, either.*

"I can get myself to the airport," he tells us magnanimously.

"That's good," is my hurt, childish retort, "because neither of us will take you."

"Oh, come on, Marie, don't be like that."

But it's thirty-five years too late for me not to "be like that." I stand up from my half-eaten breakfast and throw down my napkin like a petulant toddler. It's all I can do to stick out my lower lip and accuse him, "You always leave me hanging! You forget about me, you don't help me, you don't love me!"

Maybe I'll go eat worms after all.

When my cousin/brother drives away from the inn almost an hour later, we haven't made up. At all. Haven't spoken. Haven't crossed paths in the same room. Have carefully avoided each other's "space." He, getting into his own rental car, moves like he can't wait to get out of here, doesn't even look back to see if I'm coming to say good-bye. And I, hiding in the shade of a pin oak tree at the side of the inn, miserably watch him leave. Who is this cousin I thought I knew? Ah, but that's just the problem. He is *exactly* the cousin I know so well. The better question might be, Who is this incredibly childish version of the *me* that I thought I knew so well?

Maybe it's being here, in Sebastion. It got to both of us.

We're reverting, Nathan and I, to the

ages of about three and six. If we keep going backward, by tomorrow I'll be dead. Oops. Not a good line of thought, all things considered.

As I turn to go back inside, I think of the lyric from the old rock and roll song, *I've got to get out of this place, if it's the last thing I ever do.*

I can only hope it isn't.

Not that Nathan would care!

Once he's gone, I walk slowly back up to the suite. I'm already feeling horribly guilty about letting him go without a forgiving hug. These aren't the times when you want to let somebody you love get away from you without making amends first, if there ever was such a time. But I feel so betrayed! Trust is a big, big thing with me. I guess when you've grown up thinking your own parents dumped you, trust does tend to become a bit of an issue, as they say in the psychotherapy trade. It appears that martyrdom may be a bit of an issue, too, judging from my turned-down mouth and my slumping shoulders. But jeeze, I've always been there for my cousin when he needed me; it *floors* me that he wouldn't stay for any other better reason than that I wanted him to, I needed him to.

I was so glad to see him. I would have stayed for *him*. I would have done anything for him.

Except let him go? Except let him grow up, Marie?

"Oh, shut up," I tell my Inner Therapist.

Immediately upon opening the suite door, the first thing I see is Steve Orbach standing by the bay window, and the next thing I see is a wallet lying on the floor at the edge of the bed facing me. I walk over, pick it up, and hold it up so he can see.

"Yours?"

He shakes his head.

"Oh, that idiot!" I exclaim, suddenly furious all over again. "Nate must have taken his wallet out for some reason while he was packing, and he probably set it down on the bed and it fell off and . . . I can't believe he did this. . . . Oh, never mind, yes I can. This is so like him. This is just like him!" Steve is looking at me, expressionless. God only knows what he thinks of the sibling tantrums he's witnessed today. "Steve, he can't get on the plane without his driver's license. We're going to have to run up to the airport and get this to him."

I get the impression that my bodyguard was standing beside the window watching over me as I stood hiding under the tree.

Now he asks, "Has he got a cell phone with him?"

"If he does, I don't know the number."

"Then let him find out the hard way."

"He really wants to go home."

Steve shrugs heartlessly, as I should probably do, too.

"A little inconvenience won't kill him," he says, no doubt accurately.

"I know, but —"

I just can't do it, not when it comes to Nathan, not even now.

But when I walk over to the dresser to grab my purse where I left it earlier, Steve says, "You stay here. I'll go."

"I was thinking we'd both go."

"No. I'll drive faster without you."

"You're leaving me, too?" I hear the whining, self-pitying note in my voice, and then I feel my face flush. This is embarrassing. I've got to get myself together here. Surely I can survive for a couple of hours without him or Nate, not that Nathan would have been much protection anyway. "Okay," I say, forcing a calmer tone. But then I spoil it by adding a postscript that makes me sound like Dr. Aileen Rasmussen stating the obvious. "Don't get a speeding ticket."

He smiles slightly and I get the feeling

that he's just barely keeping himself from saying, Yes, Mother. What he says, instead, is, "I'm not planning to. I'm also not going to leave you alone."

"What do you mean? You can't be in two places at once."

"No, but this might be a good time for you to talk to the cops."

"About what? Last night, they decided —"

"Yeah, they decided, but that doesn't mean you have to do what they think, does it?"

"I guess not, but —" Suddenly, I collapse onto the side of the bed. "My God, Steve, I've got to snap out of this. Do you know what's happening to me? I'm turning into a kid, I'm acting as if all the adults know best and I have to do what they say. But I don't, do I? You're right. I need to start making some independent decisions here."

"What if you showed the cops that story about your parents and let them tell you what *they* think of it?"

I think that over, finally saying, "I don't know about that, but there are plenty of other things I could ask them, instead, if I decide not to do that. And maybe I can hang around the police station until you get back."

"That's what I was thinking." He steps toward me a couple of paces. "Ms. Lightfoot, no disrespect to your cousin, but he's so full of shit it's a wonder his eyes aren't brown. He shouldn't have left like that. I promise you that I won't take any chances with you."

It's good to hear him say that. An automatic defense of Nathan rises to my lips, but for once I bite it back.

In no time at all, Steve takes off with the wallet and the Lexus, after dropping me off at the edge of downtown Sebastion.

30

Marie

Even though Sebastion's fortunes and population have dramatically eroded in the past few decades, it's still the county seat, and home to the county sheriff's office, instead of a police station. There's not much to the headquarters, I discover, just a plain, square, cement block building with a handful of jails and open office space. When I walk in, there's a uniformed officer doubling as receptionist/secretary, and the deputy sheriff's on the premises, but apart from two sheriff's cars parked in a lot to the east, that's about it for law enforcement in Sebastion today.

When I see that the "receptionist" is a white man and the deputy is a black woman, I find myself awed at how much the world can change when it has a chance to. I'm in the heart of Alabama, for God's sake, and I'm just about to take my case to a black female cop.

My parents would be so pleased, and I'm so pleased to be able to think that of them.

It's at that moment that the underlying message of last night's party really hits me for the first time, and the impact is so strong that I nearly turn around and go back outside to find a bench to sit down on. My parents were not killed by the KKK. My parents were not traitors to their Hostel friends. They were, themselves, betrayed. They were what I longed for them to be and never believed could come true — decent people doing the right thing for the right reasons.

I'm tired and hungover and stressed-out.

It's all I can do not to burst into grateful tears right there in the lobby.

"Can I help you, ma'am?"

Self-control is a wonderful thing sometimes. "Yes, sir." I smile, trying to draw forth my southern heritage. "I'd like to see the sheriff, if I may."

"He's not here. Deputy do?"

"Deputy'll do," I say.

She's angry before I open my mouth.

"If you're here to accuse Hubert and Rachel Templeton of having anything to do with the disappearance of your parents almost forty years ago, you'd better have some damned good evidence before you go slandering those good people's names to me."

For a moment, I'm so startled, I can't think.

"Clayton Fisher was here?" I thought he wasn't going to come in to report this until at least after the meeting at the inn tonight. Why did he do this prematurely? I'm caught off balance here, unsure what to say or where to head with this. "You know who I am?"

"Yes, he was, and yes, I know." She nods, a quick, furious jerk of her head up and down. I needn't worry about where this is going; it looks as if she's going to take charge of that, and most vehemently. "You listen to me. I don't care who the hell these white people think they used to be in this town." She leans toward me, shaking a finger at me. "That doesn't give them a right to go accusing Mr. Hubert and Miss Rachel of *any*thing, much less anything like you're talking about —"

"I'm not —"

"Well, somebody is. And what I hear is that you gave them some information made them jump to this ignorant conclusion. You ever met Mr. Hubert and Miss Rachel?"

"Yes."

"They strike you like people could ever do such a thing?"

I shake my head and tell the truth. "No."

"Me, neither. And I've known them all my life. You got some proof you didn't make this whole story up?"

"No, but I didn't make it up."

"Who you get it from then?"

That's the part, the whole truth, that I didn't tell the couples at the party last night. I just told them I received it anonymously. But now I tell this resentful cop the rest of it. "I've been receiving threatening E-mails. That information was included in one of them."

"Who's threatening you?" She looks highly skeptical.

"I don't know."

"What's the threat?"

"To kill me, to hurt my friends if I don't do what he tells me."

"What's he say you have to do."

"Write a book about my own murder."

She blinks. "I thought I'd heard everything."

"Me, too," I confess. "Listen, can we just talk? Without accusing anybody of anything? Can we just talk?"

After staring at me while I hold her gaze,

she finally, with every show of reluctance, says, "I guess."

"Just because they didn't get arrested that night," she says, after she has heard it all, "that don't mean nothin'."

Her name, I have finally found out, is Florence Sachem, but that's all the personal information she gives out, except for the earlier comment, when she said she's known the Templetons all her life. From that, I take it she's a local girl, and she knows these locals — at least the black ones — well, or thinks she does. She and I are not any better friends at the end of my recital than we were at the start of it, but at least she's listening and thinking about what she's hearing from me.

"But why wouldn't they?" I ask her. "All the other —"

"Yeah. Every damn one of the other black members of Hostel paid dear for it, and they even threw in a few nonmembers just because they could. But I'll tell you why Hubert and Rachel probably didn't, and maybe you'd have to be more southern than you are to understand this. Even then, they were well respected around here. Hell, between them, they worked for practically every big white family in town, Hubert doing errands and yards, Rachel working in their houses, taking care of their children."

"But she was so young —"

Florence gives me a disgusted look. "Think. I'm going to give you the benefit of the doubt and suppose in my mind that you know a little black history. Black girls went to work in people's homes when they were practically babies. Seven, eight years old, they could sweep a broom. Rachel, she must have been no more than twenty when this all happened, but that would have meant she'd been working for twelve, fifteen years already. She came from a good family, everybody knew that. Hubert, he didn't, but he had a way about him — you've met him, you know this — that people liked, no matter what their color was. I think the truth is, not even the crackers had the stomach for putting Hubert and Rachel in prison. I mean, hell, their wives would of give them hell for doin' that. It would have meant losing the best yard boy" — she says it with a bitter twist to her mouth — "in town, and the best lady's maid, too. You see what I'm sayin'?"

"Yes, but it doesn't prove anything."

"Just like you don't prove anything," she snaps right back at me.

There's a crackle of static from their police radio behind us, and she holds up a hand to listen. All I hear is a jumble of numbers. As long as I've been hanging around cops, I never have memorized their codes, so I don't know what this message says that makes her suddenly stand up and look dismissively at me.

"Accident out on 65 south."

"Highway 65, to Birmingham?"

"Yeah, I gotta go, but you listen up. I am not, repeat not, goin' to tolerate this kind of slander on the names of those fine people, so you can just forget —"

A sense of foreboding makes me interrupt her.

"Do you know what kind of vehicles were involved?"

"Didn't you hear it?" She's disdainful of me as she adjusts the gun belt at her hips and grabs a notebook off her desk. "One car wreck. Nice new Lexus. Totaled. Driver thrown from the car, got a life flight called from Birmingham."

I stand up, feeling my face drain of blood.

"Where will they take him?"

"Him?" She stops for an instant, looks at me curiously. "You think you know these people?"

"It's just one person. The driver. A friend who came down with me."

She frowns and almost looks sympathetic. "I'm sorry to hear it." And then she relents. "You can come with me, if you want to."

With my heart in my throat, making speech impossible, I can't even thank her for that small favor.

I ride with the deputy, forty-five miles south of town. This is a beautiful stretch of road. Ahead of us, an overpass connects the hills. Thick forest lines the road on either side. Trees arch overhead and thick bushes fill the spaces in between. From both directions, the highway curves toward the overpass, which is situated right where you might not be able to see it until you were directly on it. Driving here, we passed two signs warning of this curve, this danger. But if you were coming too fast, if you were reaching down for a dropped cigarette, if you had only turned your head to tell the kids in the backseat to settle down, you might miss the warnings, speed into the curve, and trying to correct too late, skid off into the cement pilings.

Even from here, I can see the wreck is a terrible one.

There are brake marks — thick black slashes — but they're not long ones.

Judging from those, he didn't have much time to react. And the truth is, he hadn't been driving all that long, certainly not compared to other men his age. When they were getting their first driver's licenses and their first cars, when they were surviving the usual fender benders that some teenage boys collect like other kids collect stamps, Steve was in prison. In the space between one prison sentence and the next, he did learn to drive. But then it was years later — and not very long ago — that he actually got to do it like a normal citizen. Maybe he knew how to come out of a skid, and maybe he didn't. Or maybe there wasn't time, even if he had known.

He drove the Lexus into the concrete post supporting the underpass.

It must have happened fast; it looks as if it did.

If anything saved him — and I don't know for sure yet that it did — it will be that he went in crooked, grazing the cement with only the passenger side of the vehicle. That entire side of the car is caved in, very nearly sliced off. The driver's side is as intact as if it had just come off the showroom floor, although the driver's side door is wide open, as if it's waiting for somebody to step in to give it a test drive. Even though that side doesn't have a scratch, the impact must still have thrown the driver about like a rag doll, even if he was wearing a seat belt. I've been in a car a few times with Steve by now and I don't remember that he ever belted himself in. If he was thrown out of the Lexus, as Florence told me he was, it's hard to imagine how he even survived.

She lets me walk up to the wreck with her, and when we reach it, she looks at me squarely. "Was he suicidal?"

"I don't think so."

Even considering his miserable life — and without even knowing if it has improved all that much — I'm pretty sure Steve didn't want to kill himself. At least, not today. He was just in a hurry to catch my criminally scatterbrained cousin whom disaster follows as night the day. Agents die, girlfriends leave him, bodyguards get wrecked.

Florence touches my arm, with a modicum of sympathy. "If you'll wait, I'll drive you to the hospital if you want to."

31

Marie

Hours later, after nightfall, I am back at the inn, wearily climbing the stairs to my suite. There's nobody around to greet me, and I'm glad of that. If the Hostel members had their meeting, I missed it, and I'm glad. They can do what they want to, I don't care. I don't want to see anybody, I don't want to have to talk to anybody.

I just want to get onto my computer and flame-throw a scorching E-mail at Paulie Barnes. Maybe he's a brother and sister, or maybe he's not, but I still think of him as one man, one evil entity. It's the only way I can picture him in my mind, and right now I know how I want to see him look when he reads what I have to say. I want his eyebrows to singe when he reads it. I want his fingers to blister when he touches his keyboard to open it. I want his eyes to fry in his head when he sees what I say to him.

And if what I have to say doesn't set him on fire, I want spontaneous combustion.

If he weren't playing his games, if he hadn't forced me to hire Steve, if he hadn't brought me here, if he hadn't lured Nathan here, if the whole thing hadn't unnerved Nate to the point that he fled, then Steve Orbach wouldn't be lying in intensive care in Birmingham, Alabama, right now.

"Damn you" is too mild a curse.

Maybe the police won't be able to find him. But I'll go after him, to the end of my days, if I have to. I may have chickened out long ago when it came to pursuing the truth about my parents, but I won't give up on this one.

Steve is alive, but with grievous internal injuries, broken bones, and a head injury for which the standing procedure is to induce a coma until and if the swelling in his brain recedes. He has never regained consciousness.

I open the door to my suite and nearly faint to find a man in it.

"Surprise!" says my cousin, who is sprawled on the couch with his feet up on the coffee table. He grins at me, as if nothing has ever been wrong between us. "I lost my damned wallet, can you believe that, and they wouldn't let me on the airplane. I was so pissed, I wanted to tell them to take their empty seat and shove it. I'll get home some other way. What's the matter with you? You look like you lost your best friend."

I just stare at him. I can't even tell him. My mouth won't work.

"Oh, hell. What? You still mad at me for leaving?"

Without a single word, I walk past him and go into the other bedroom and slam and lock the door to it. From the other room, I hear my cousin calling in a plaintive, annoyed voice, "Marie!"

I know I have to tell him. I just can't do it until I am sure that I won't direct that flamethrower at him.

I open my E-mail, ready to do battle with Paulie Barnes.

But he has beat me to the scene of carnage.

What I see, what I read, fills me with horror.

Dear Marie,
    Did you think I didn't mean it?
    You misjudged me, didn't you? You decided that because I hadn't really

hurt anyone up until now that I never would do anything like that. It's too bad — for your "bodyguard" — that you didn't believe me. His injuries are entirely your fault. You must blame yourself, you and your foolish cousin. I don't recall granting him permission to leave. Perhaps now both of you will take me more seriously?

So that large young man was your protection, was he?

How safe do you feel now, my dear?

Yours truly,
Paulie Barnes

I jump out of the chair as if the E-mail were a snake.

Steve warned me of this. He told me so. When I first hired him, he predicted that eventually Paulie Barnes would try to separate me from everyone, including him, and that's when he would strike at me. He has done it. He has managed to separate me from Franklin, from my hometown cops who know me and would take a personal interest in my welfare, from the professionals who normally assist me, and now from my bodyguard. And if Nathan hadn't come back, I'd even be separated from —

I run across the room and fling open the

door to the other bedroom.

"Nathan, what's the real reason you wanted to leave today?"

He's reading in the bay window, and now he glances up, looking like he used to look when I would catch him doing something he wasn't supposed to do, like eating my Popsicle.

"What do you mean? I just wanted to go home."

"You don't look like it now. You look perfectly happy to sit there reading forever. How come you just had to go home this morning, but you don't just have to go home tonight?"

Unless I'm mistaken, the "caught" look on his face is turning to serious fear.

I hurry over to him, kneel down beside him, take his hands and beg.

"Please. Please tell me. It's really important to tell me the truth."

Nathan looks around, almost as if he thinks somebody else might be in the room with us. He lowers his mouth to my left ear and he whispers into it, "I got an E-mail last night, Marie. From him. He said I had to leave you this morning, or he'd hurt you. He said I had to pretend to go back to L.A. and he said that I couldn't tell you why. He even told me to drop the wallet, to give me an excuse not to get on the airplane. He said it was okay for me to come back here tonight."

"Why did you do it?"

"So he wouldn't hurt you!"

"But what did you think he was up to?"

He shrugs, looking unhappy. "I just thought it was some kind of crazy test, you know? Like he was testing to see if he had me under control the way he has you. And I don't think I'm smart enough to mess with that. I didn't dare tell anybody. I would have told Bruto, but how do I know that he's not Paulie Barnes himself, just jerking you around for his own pleasure? I didn't know what to do except to do just what he said. That's what *you've* been doing. If even you follow his instructions, I figured that's what I'd better do, too."

Now it's his turn to plead with me.

"What's going on, Marie?"

Before I answer him, I get to my feet and walk over to the side of the drapes and pull the cords to close them. Then I ease down onto the bay window cushions with him.

"He's not Paulie Barnes," I tell him gently. He's going to feel terrible about this, and I can't prevent it. "Steve took the Lexus. He was going to try to catch up with you at the airport and give you your wallet. On the way, he had a terrible accident. He hit an overpass. He had to be lifeflighted into Birmingham, and he's in a hospital now in critical condition."

I watch his tan fade, as if I had pulled a plug that drained him of color.

"I thought it was an accident, Nathan," I continue. "A cop even asked me if it could have been a suicide attempt. But I just now read a new E-mail from Paulie Barnes. He's taking credit — if you want to call it that — for causing Steve's accident."

As I expected, he looks completely stricken, horrified.

The first words that come out of his mouth are the right ones.

"Is Steve going to be okay?"

He didn't think of himself first, he thought of someone else.

"I don't know, sweetie."

And then he says the next best thing he could say.

"What can I do?"

This is more like the Nathan I love.

"You can go with me to the local sheriff's department and help me tell them that we believe that Steve was either forced off the road, or was a hit-and-run." I take hold of one of his hands again. "I was a jerk this morning. I'm really sorry."

But he only smiles sadly, and this time it is Nate who gets to forgive me.

"What were you supposed to think? I did it on purpose so you wouldn't ask many questions. I knew it would piss you off." He grins just a tiny bit, though it disappears quickly. "I'm sorry I left you thinking that I had deserted you. But I hope you know I wouldn't really do that?"

"Not even if I was up a tree?"

"What?"

He was too young, he doesn't even remember.

"Nothing. Thank you. If I wasn't sure of it before, I am now. Come on, let's go."

"This is my fault. What happened to Steve is my fault."

"No! If there was ever anything in this lifetime that was not your fault, Nathan Montgomery, this is it. It's Paulie Barnes's fault. You were trying to help. He was trying to kill."

Deputy Sachem is off duty, but within twenty minutes she comes in to hear this story of ours. In civilian clothes, she still looks like a cop, just like Robyn does when she puts on a pair of blue jeans and a Florida Marlins T-shirt over bare feet. I've had Robyn and Paul out in my little boat and I'll swear they looked like detectives even in their swimsuits.

When we're finished talking, Florence looks at me strangely.

"What?" I ask her.

"How could this Paulie Barnes know your friend would be alone in the car?"

I blink, unable to answer that. It hadn't occurred to me.

"Common sense," she continues, "would say that you'd be there, too, wouldn't it? Would you have been driving?"

"No, I'd have been in the passenger's —"

I don't even finish the phrase. Nathan hasn't seen the car. Florence and I have. We stare at each other now in the shared knowledge of exactly what happened to the passenger's side of the Lexus. *The good news,* I think at that moment, *is that if he was trying to kill me, that must mean he's finished with me.*

But the bad news, from his point of view, is that I'm not dead yet.

"Who was the tow truck driver?" I ask her.

That pisses her off. "It was Hubert Templeton. So what? It's Hubert at least one-fifth of the time we get calls, because he owns one-fifth of the tow trucks in Sebastion. This happened to be his time up. What? You think Hubert made himself a little business? Got there early and forced your friend off the road so he could tow the car?"

"We wouldn't know his motive," Nate says, coolly.

"Well, I *would* know his motive for just about everything," the deputy snaps back at us. "It's goodness, that's what it is."

"If you say so," Nate says.

She picks up a pen from her desk and rams its point into a pad of paper at her elbow. "I do damn well say so." But at the back of her eyes, do I see the beginnings of doubt? Is she wondering about the coincidence of the only black man who didn't get arrested, who didn't pay any penalty for his Hostel membership, just happening to show up at the scene of a near-fatal accident that could easily have included me in its body count?

Is Hubert Templeton "Paulie Barnes"?

"I don't understand," I say, talking out loud, "why a black man would betray Hostel and then turn my parents over to be murdered by the Klan."

"You can't understand it," the deputy says, more calmly now. Calmly enough to sound convincing. "Because it didn't happen. Couldn't happen. Would never happen in a million years, or even for a million dollars. Trust me on this."

Nate and I glance at each other. I can tell what he's thinking: *If you say so.*

32

Marie

Nate wants us to drive into Birmingham tonight to sit by Steve's bedside, but speaking of motives, I know guilt when I hear it, and so I plead complete exhaustion. I figure that only by piling on another kind of guilt can I hope to dissuade him; merely telling him that we can't do anything for Steve won't work. I agree with him, though. I wish we were there. I wish somebody could sit by his bedside.

"Does he have any family?" Nate asks me on the way back to the inn. "Do you have to call his mother — oh."

When we enter the inn, we smell cigarettes.

There's a light coming out from under the door of a room I think might be Mo Goodwin's bedroom.

"I sure hope she's awake," I whisper to my cousin, "if she's smoking in there."

Nate purposely stumbles against a table leg, making a small racket.

"That ought to do it," he says, with a small grin for me.

And sure enough, as we're going up the stairs we hear the television change channels in her room. If Maureen wasn't awake before we got home, she is now.

I take my shower first, and then turn it over to Nate.

By the time he's finished and calling good night to me from the front bedroom, I'm deep into some reading. " 'Night," I offer, absently. It's my goal to carefully re-read and rethink everything I have about my parents and their friends. As I do so, I can detect my own skepticism about them, my own bitterness that I felt when I originally wrote some of this stuff. I never believed that my father felt so desperately sad when he left me. My account of what my mother and father are alleged to have said that night reads like sarcasm.

I want a chance to rewrite it.

Now I do want to write a book about them, about the modern-day Underground Railroad they started here in Sebastion, and about their courageous friends of both races.

Now, at least, I've got a real story to tell, and it's my story, too.

There are only a few things missing now.

Maybe I'll dream of the solutions while I'm sleeping tonight.

I lay the papers down on the floor by the bed, turn out the lamp, lie back on the pillow, and close my eyes. But not to sleep. Scenarios and unanswered questions float through my mind, a couple of which I haven't had time to think about any earlier today. *Why did Clayton Fisher take the account of my parents' murders to the sheriff's office this morning instead of waiting, as I thought he had promised, for the agreement of the other members of Hostel? What was their reaction when he told them he did that?* Did *he tell them? Why did he jump the gun like that, rushing to accuse Hubert and Rachel Templeton? A couple of other, apparently unrelated things pop into my mind, seeking connection and explanation. Why didn't Mo Goodwin join her parents and their friends — and my little group — at the Fishers' party? She told us she was invited to it. When we got home from it, she was here. So why didn't she go? Is she just too much of an introvert to face that much socializing? She's surely known these people all of her life; she even worked for Clayton for a time at the bank, she said. You'd think there could hardly be a more comfortable social occasion than that, among old friends of her family, one of them her former employer and his wife. I suppose, however, that for a truly shy person, there's really no such thing as a comfortable social event. I wouldn't know from shy, myself, but I think it must be a horribly crippling condition. I'm a recluse, myself, at times, but that's just the result of being a full-time writer. I can't say that I "enjoy" it, exactly; it's just how the job gets done. Nobody remarked upon Mo Goodwin's absence, at least not in my hearing, not even her parents. Wouldn't you think, I ask myself as I lie there not sleeping, that somebody would have thought to ask, "Where's Mo?" But as far as that's concerned, why was she the only one of the next generation who was invited? Probably only because she used to work for Clayton, I decide, and because she knows us a little bit from being our innkeeper here.*

Suddenly, I just have to know the answer to something.

"How late is it?" I mutter, and look over at the bedside clock.

Eleven. Too late to call Florence Sachem at her home? In my mind's ear, I can hear Robyn Anschutz chiding me, "Marie. It's never too late to call a detective with an important question or observation about a

497

case." When Sachem gave me her card today I weaseled out of her a home phone number and wrote it on the back of the card. I fling myself out of bed and rummage through my purse until I locate it, and then carry it over to the telephone on the desk.

That's odd. I'd swear I left my laptop on the right side of this desk and not on the left where it is now. Maybe Nathan moved it? Or, more likely, Mo was up here cleaning, although after dinner seems rather late to be doing that. Then I recall seeing Rachel Templeton on the stairway. She was working late. That must be it.

Only then, as I'm sitting down there, do I notice two small, pale pink notes that have been left on the desk for me. The top one says, "Ms. Lightfoot. Please call the intensive care unit at Birmingham Medical Center and ask for Jean." It's signed, "Mo," and she has written down a number for me. I drop the deputy's card. Without even pausing to read the second note underneath, I make the call. "This is Marie Lightfoot," I tell the female voice who answers. "I got a message to call Jean?"

"This is Jean," she says, and her voice goes so soft and kind that I could scream. "I'm so sorry, Ms. Lightfoot. I'm afraid I have to tell you that Steven Orbach passed away three hours ago."

I must be saying words, because she answers me.

"Yes, tomorrow is fine," I hear her say, apparently in reply to something I've told her. "We'll wait for your instructions. Since you're not his immediate family, is there anyone else you'd like me to call for him?"

"No," I tell her. "There's no one else."

Gently, I set the phone down.

I look toward Nate's bedroom door, but there's no light coming out from beneath it. I can't bear to wake him to tell him this terrible news. I can't bear even to *be* awake to know it.

Oh, Steve, you had so little time to be a free man.

He had such a sad, violent and limited life, and it didn't seem likely to get much better, not at the heart of it, at the heart of him, not even with a massive infusion of money from his lawsuits. (Oh, I can't bear to tell Tammi Golding, either — his lawyer, my friend.) Did anybody ever love him? Would anybody ever have? There's no chance for that now.

During our trip here, he gave me one

glimpse inside of his current life when I asked him, "How is it for you, being free?" He was blunt. "It's not a friendly world for people like me."

I get up from the desk, walk over to the bed, lie down again, bury my face in a pillow, and whisper into it, "I'm sorry, Steve, I'm sorry your whole life sucked." I sob until I almost fall asleep, but just before that happens I am jolted awake by the realization that the sheriff's department may not know that their "accident" report is now a homicide.

I sit at the desk again, calling from the darkened bedroom.

As I wait through several rings for the deputy sheriff to answer, I watch the movement of shadows on the thin white curtains I have pulled across a window. It's the branches of the oak trees, dancing in a wind that has kicked up, a precursor to rain. I remember rain. We used to have some of that back home in Florida. Carrying the phone with me, I walk over and pull the curtains back. Then I tuck the phone receiver under my chin so I can raise one of the window panes to see if the air smells like rain and —

"Hello?"

"Florence, this is Marie Lightfoot." I

don't even bother to apologize. "Do you know that Steve died at the hospital tonight?"

"No," she says, sharply. "Nobody told me."

"So it's a homicide investigation now."

"Maybe. I'm sorry about your friend."

"Maybe? I have something to ask you. The other Hostel members who were at that picnic the other night specifically asked Clayton Fisher not to talk to the police until they'd had a chance to be sure of their theories. They didn't want to accuse the Templetons, any more than you want to, not until and unless they felt really sure of their facts. So I was awfully surprised that you already knew, and that Clayton had already been in to see you. Why do you think he did that?"

There's a long silence, long enough for me to ask, "Are you there?"

"Yeah, I'm here. I can't tell you that." But then she can't resist adding, sarcastically, "Maybe it's because he thinks as highly of the Templetons as I do, you ever think of that? Maybe he just wanted to give me a chance to see what's coming up against them."

"That's not exactly an objective point of view, Deputy."

"Yeah, well, you'd think it was if you really knew them."

And you can lump it, if you don't like it, is the meaning I infer from her tone. Someone less prejudiced in their favor might think that Clayton jumped the gun because he was convinced of their guilt. Someone might think that he didn't want to take the chance that his white friends would chicken out of accusing their black civil rights compatriots. As smooth and forceful as that old banker is, he'd have known how to plant suspicion without appearing to personally accuse them.

As she's talking, I notice the second message, the one I ignored in the aftermath of learning of Steve's death. Ordinarily, my heart might beat faster at the sight of what it says, as if what she's saying in my ear isn't enough to do that already. This message is also from Mo, judging by the look of the similar handwriting, and it says, "Can I talk to you? I'm the one who called you."

She called me? For a moment, I don't get it. When did she call — ?

Oh, my God. So she's the one!

Three times in the past, I've had mysterious phone calls from some woman who never seemed to catch me when I was answering the telephone. It was always a brief, scared-sounding message hinting that my anonymous caller had something important to tell me about my parents.

Recalling that voice, I think, yeah, could have been Mo.

Soft voice. Shy, scared, deerlike quality. A southern accent that was perceptible even in the few words that were left in her messages to me. Yes, I can believe it was she.

"Florence," I interrupt. "I have something else to tell you . . ."

Somehow, afterward, I finally sleep.

Something wakes me again. A smell of smoke? I look at the clock: 1 a.m. A very strong smell of smoke, and getting thicker, worse. I cough, then cough again.

Move, Marie!

I struggle out of bed, calling, "Nate! Nate!" When I reach the door that separates our room, I feel it with the palms of my hands to see if there's fire on the other side, but it is as cool as air-conditioning. I fling it open and call, "Nate, there's smoke, wake up!"

When he doesn't get up from the bed in that room, I hurry over to shake him awake, only to find that he's not even there. For a wild moment I fear that he has changed his mind and fled back to L.A. after all. No, that can't be. I know now that he wouldn't do that. I run back into my bedroom, throw on slacks over the underpants and long cotton shirt I wore to sleep, slip into sandals, grab my purse and my laptop computer, and head for the door to the suite.

It is slightly warm but doesn't have the heat of fire.

I open it and look out into the hallway.

There's a thin layer of smoke floating up from downstairs. I hear a noise, a crackle, like flames.

"Fire! Fire! Wake up!" I scream, and go pounding on doors to wake people. "Fire! Get up!" As the other guests start to come out, looking frightened and half-asleep, I head for the stairway. Halfway down I meet my cousin coming up. Even in the midst of greater shocks, I'm surprised to see that he's fully dressed in the clothes he wore earlier this evening.

"Nathan, is there a fire downstairs?"

"It's in Mo's bedroom," he says, looking frantic.

"Oh, my God! Why were you down there?"

He takes my hand, and as he's running

past me, pulls me with him back upstairs. "I was looking for a cigarette," he says over his shoulder.

"But you don't smoke!"

"After this day? Are you kidding? Anybody would start smoking again! I wanted a drink and a drag. I thought she'd have one." When I look back down, he violently tugs at me, almost pulling me off balance. "Don't go down there, Marie! We've got to get people to a fire escape, did you notice if there is one? There has to be one, doesn't there?" He glances back at me again, looking anguished. "There were flames in her doorway, Marie! I couldn't get in. I couldn't get in to save her! We've got to get out. Everybody does. We've got to get everybody out!"

"Nine-one-one?" I shout out at him in the increasing noise and chaos.

"I called them! Get out now!"

He pushes me toward a door that another of the guests has opened onto a fire escape at one side of the big house. I run toward it, thinking that Nate is right behind me. But when I step onto the wrought iron of the fire escape and turn back to check on him, he's no longer there. "Nathan! Nathan!"

"Go, go! Move! Let us out!"

505

Other guests are crowding in behind me. I'm blocking their escape. There's nothing I can do but start down.

"Nathan!" I scream, looking back as I descend.

We reach the bottom of the fire escape and now I see flames through the windows of the first door. My God, it's already out of control. Where is that rain I thought I smelled a little while ago? *Nathan! Nathan!* While other guests run away from the side of the building, I start to run around it, desperately looking for a way I can get back in. The flames haven't reached the second floor yet; there's time . . . plenty of time . . . I know it, I know it . . . for him still to get out. What's he doing in there? Why did he go back? Was there some other guest he was trying to save?

"Nathan!" I scream, and I realize I'm sobbing it.

I run around the other side of the house, nearest Mo's bedroom, where the heat is greatest, where the shadows are thickest from the trees that shelter the house. In the near distance I hear a siren. *Hurry, hurry!* I can't get in this way! I can't find a way in anywhere! The heat is intense, the smoke is becoming blinding. If I don't leave this area, I could lose my orientation and actually run toward the fire by mistake. While I still can see where I'm going, I turn toward the deeper shadows and stumble into them.

When something grabs me, at first I think it's tree branches.

Only when the grasp tightens painfully do I realize it's human arms.

"Nathan," I sigh, in relief. "Thank God you —"

A hand comes over my mouth. I feel myself lifted, then carried, and more swiftly than I would have imagined possible — so quickly I can only think of killers I have written about and how fast they moved when they caught their victims, too fast for most people to have time to think, to react, to resist — I feel myself flung into a vehicle, a backseat. Hands grab mine, hands grab my feet. I am bound before I can kick, before I can claw. Tape is slapped onto my mouth and over my eyes. I feel my tied wrists lifted and something attached to them. The same thing happens to my ankles. When I tug, I feel myself trapped at both ends of my body, unable to do more than squirm and make grunting noises. That movement results in a horrible blow to my shoulder. The message, though not spoken, is excruciatingly clear: *Shut up and stop moving.* Fuck you, I think, and keep grunting my animal noises through the tape, through the awful pain in my shoulder, my limbs. I keep squirming, moving. Maybe there's something I will hit with my movements, something that will make a noise, alert other people, get me help —

The next blow is terrible and repeated three times.

I would scream with pain, but I can't.

If I cry, I may not be able to breathe. I cannot cry at this pain.

He's getting his wish, whoever he is. I subside. I lie still.

I feel something thrown over me that covers me from head to foot, a blanket or something even heavier, a tarp.

33

Marie

For what seems an endless time, I hear chaos.

Then there are sirens, shouting, more sirens. From the sounds of it, a fire is being desperately fought.

I am left alone in this vehicle.

When I recover enough from the shock and agony of the blows, I try to move, to make enough noise to be heard, but it's useless. There's too much noise outside, no one will hear me.

I give up and lie there, concentrating on getting air through my nose.

After a few minutes to recover, I try to escape again. And then again. I keep trying until I finally have to admit to myself that I am captured, and there's not one damn thing I can do about it.

Paulie Barnes, I think, as I lie there.

I guess I am going to meet you, at last.

★ ★ ★

There's time to think, if only I can get my fear-soaked mind to calm down a little bit. There's time to go back over everything that has happened since only last week, to remember the E-mails, the surprises, the threats, the coercion, the fear. But out of all of that jumble of remembering, only one new thought emerges: logically, there are only a few reasons I can think of why the deputy sheriff "couldn't tell" me why Clayton Fisher previewed for her that material about my parents' deaths. If he was there only to make sure the Templetons got accused, as I first suspected, I don't really think she would have been fooled by his suave attitude. She's so protective of them that surely even Clayton would have gotten her defenses up. So what did that leave as possible reasons for his surprising visit? It occurs to me now that he could have told her something incriminating that she couldn't reveal because it wasn't proven yet, or he could have told her something she couldn't reveal without exposing him as the source of the information. What was that wily old banker doing? Was it just a small power play, jumping the gun to show he still held the reins in town? Or is there something he knows that he didn't want his friends to hear? And then it hits me: as the main banker and loan granter in town, Clayton would always have known who owned pickup trucks, and who owned land with woody areas, and who owned property with caves on it.

There was a pickup truck in his own driveway last night, an old one that looked as if he kept it around only because he had some affection for it. I'd be surprised if he actually drove it anymore; he and Eulalie surely prefer the new black Cadillac that was parked next to it.

Half the men — and some of the women — in this town no doubt have always owned pickup trucks and not just the rednecks, either. But not all of them would own land outside of town.

I'm sweating under the heavy plastic tarp. I'm worried about Nathan and whether or not he got safely out of the fire. It's almost more than I can do to try to think my way out of this, but if I can't move, I don't see how I can fight my way out of it. If my captor ever lets me loose, my limbs will be stiff, the blood will have run out of them, my throat will be raw from all the smoke I'm breathing in through my nose. I'll be lucky if I can walk, much less run or kick or scream. *Think, Marie.* It's the only defense I have right now. But at least if I die, I'd like to know who killed me, and why.

I remember something that Steve said back in Florida around the time that all of this began, hundreds of years ago. He said I was probably going to be safe, for a while, because there was still the book to write. But he warned me that eventually Paulie Barnes would attempt to separate me from everyone who might be able to help me.

And that is just what he has done.

"He's very efficient," Steve warned us.

Right again.

When my captor comes back for me, I cannot see him.

I can only listen as a door in this vehicle opens, as he gets in and arranges himself on the seat, which I take to be the driver's. I hear him starting the engine.

I hear and feel us driving off.

He says nothing, whoever is at the wheel.

It seems we drive forever. At moments, that's all I want to do, just keep driving so that I never have to find out what awaits me at the end of this long ride.

But finally, as things must, I sense the end coming.

We have traveled over paved roads, and then over a rough road.

He stops the vehicle. I still don't know for sure what it is. Car? Truck? I think it's a truck, partly because of the sound the doors make when they close. And also because there's a faint smell of diesel fuel, although that could be a diesel Mercedes, but there's also a feeling of greater size than a car. As he drove, I heard a constant rattling of metal, as if something was rolling around in a flatbed, and there seemed to be a louder, more hollow noise under the tires on the road.

I hear him open his door. Get out. I don't hear it slam shut.

He's leaving his door open. Why? So he can leave fast?

It's a shock to hear the door closest to my head open, such a shock that my whole body retracts from it. I pull back instinctively against my bonds, as if I might be able to withdraw from what comes next.

His touch on my body.

He pulls at me, yanking my whole body across the rough floor, hurting me with every movement, until he can grab me well enough to pull me out entirely into cool air and soft rain. He stands me up and then abruptly lets go of me. My limbs numb and paralyzed by my bindings, I fall hard to the ground, screaming inside my taped mouth at this new, shocking pain.

Down on the ground, he rips the tape from my mouth.

My eyes are still covered so I cannot yet see who he is.

Rough hands grab me under my arms and pull me up again, and I fight to keep my balance. I smell sour breath. I smell cigar smoke. I'm standing now, but dizzy, in pain, afraid of falling hard again. And then I do fall, crying out.

"Christ, unleash her," a man's voice says.

Oh, God, I know that voice!

Then in what seems like one blinding movement, the tape is torn from my eyes. I feel a touch of metal against my ankles, and then suddenly my legs are free. I feel another press of metal against the inside of my right arm, and then my hands spring loose.

"Get up," the same voice commands.

I stand blinking in darkness.

I am in a field bordered by thick woods.

And I see that Paulie Barnes is not one man but three.

Marty Wiegan, Austin Reese, and Lackley Goodwin.

They are the reason why Clayton Fisher went alone to see the deputy.

It was Franklin who said maybe it's more than one man.

Now I finally get it, the importance of the John D. MacDonald book, the "clue" in the book that Aileen Rasmussen kept harping at me to figure out.

It was all in the title, I didn't even need to know anything else.

These are The Executioners of my parents.

Lackley Goodwin, looking gaunt as a cancer victim in the final stages, asks me, "Do you know where you are?"

I look around me, try to answer, but start coughing and cannot speak at first. Finally, I say, "How am I supposed to know that?"

One of them steps up and turns me roughly around, 180 degrees, and then gives me a little push in the middle of my back. Just as I lose my balance and scream out, a hand grabs my arm, pulling me back to an upright position. I had felt as if I was about to fall into space, and now I see why: he has pushed me up to the very brink of a hole in the ground, a dark drop-off.

"Now do you know where you are?" Goodwin asks me.

But I don't, I'm confused, I don't get it. "No," I tell them.

"Don't you know a cave when you see one?" he asks, in an insinuating tone that sends cold shivers through me. Behind me, two of them snicker. *My God, they've brought me to the cave where they buried my parents' bodies.* Now that I know that the dark hole — maybe ten feet across at ground level — is a cave, I begin to hear something from its depths: running water, a sound of a waterfall deep within.

"This is where you dumped my parents."

"Very good. It's too bad that you'll never see it by daylight, because this is one of the prettiest caves in all of Alabama, if I do say so myself."

Carefully, very carefully because I'm afraid of losing my balance, I turn around so that I can see them all. It scares the hell out of me to have my back to the cave, to that terrible drop into nothing, but I have to see them.

Even in the darkness I can see that they're smiling at me. They have shotguns, each of them.

"I don't understand," I admit to them. "How could you do something like that to my parents — or to me — and still be the kind of people who would help civil rights workers escape to freedom?"

Marty is the one who fits the last horrifying piece to the puzzle.

"What makes you think," he says, with a sly grin, "that they escaped from us?"

BETRAYAL

By Marie Lightfoot

CHAPTER EIGHT

From the time they were boys growing up together in Sebastion, they adored plots and plans, sneaky tricks, practical jokes, subterfuge, and sabotage. If they had been born in a later generation, a game such as Dungeons and Dragons might have satisfied their lust for adventure and subversive action. Perhaps they could have satisfied that urge with something innocuous like "paint ball," where they could chase one another in the woods, carrying fake guns loaded with paint to shoot harmlessly at their "prey." Or maybe when they were young men they should have joined the CIA or the FBI and openly claimed what they were born to be by their very natures: spies and double agents.

But they weren't born into an age of fantasy and fun and games; they were born in more serious times. The guns they learned to use in their boyhoods were real. The issues that galvanized them were as real as ammunition. And so their boyhood desires had all the opportunity in the world to develop into the real thing. They came by their motives honestly, too; those motives were bred into them as naturally as they, themselves, were born into their own secretive natures, for they were all three born into the comfortable status quo of the white South. In common with most of their peers, they liked it just fine and would do almost anything to keep it that way. In their case, they did do "anything."

"Lyda's brought herself home a Yankee husband," one of the three informed the other two, early on. "I hear he's a real strong integrationist. How about we have a little fun with Lyda and her new husband? He's got himself a job at the college; we'll be working with him, we may as well have some fun with it. Let's just sidle up to them and see what the enemy is up to, how about it? We'll have us a good time."

That's all it was at first, nothing more than a parlor game, really, putting one over on that silly Lyda Montgomery with her silly views on race relations. A side benefit to their game was that it pleased their wives, who had grown up with Lyda and been influenced by her liberal views. For Melinda, Anne, and Delilah, it came as a relief when their husbands seemed at first to be charmed by that handsome, smart new husband of Lyda's, and then even to admire him. It was fun to form a little social group with the Folletinos, whom the other wives admired, and who had such interesting and brave ideas about just about everything.

The men played up to Michael, agreeing with him when he ventured radical views, but doing it quietly, so he'd think they didn't want to get themselves or him in any kind of trouble. They pretended great respect for him. All the while they saw him as one of those deadly earnest sorts, like annoying Lyda, an intellectual who took himself and his damned causes seriously enough to be amusing to them but dangerous to the white society they cherished.

"You've got to blend in around here," they advised him.

Watch how we do it, they told him.

They showed him how to act like everybody else, so nobody knew what you really thought, how deeply — deeply! — you wanted freedom and justice for all those poor suffering black folks. Voting rights! Free and equal accommodations! Equal job opportunities!

"Absolutely, Michael, we couldn't agree with you more, and if there's ever anything that we can do to help. . . ."

They were natural recruits for Hostel when he formed it.

"Lyda doesn't quite trust us," one of them observed to the others.

"We'll have to prove ourselves to her," another one said, with a crocodile smile, and so at the first opportunity, he said to the other members of Hostel, "the next time you get a name of some poor black kid who needs help, give it to us and we'll pick him up."

They were kind as butter on a burn to every refugee they picked up and delivered to a first-level safe house. They didn't want any of the escapees to complain about them. By the time there were reasons for complaint, it would be too late for anybody to hear about it. But all of that changed when they got the opportunity to move a man along to a second or third safe house. That's when they got to take off their masks of tolerance. That's what they lived for, those were the moments of their glory.

"You're getting out here."

"But there ain't no house, here, where am I s'posed to go —"

"Just follow the way my gun is pointing, son. That's where you're supposed to go."

It was a service they were performing to humanity, to their own families, to their precious way of life that had existed for a hundred years, and to the South as they knew and loved it best. Get rid of the troublemakers. Eliminate the bad seeds. And no one would ever know, because if an unknown black man didn't get on a bus going north, if he didn't make it all the way to Chicago or New York City, there was no one but themselves to know.

"We heard from his auntie in Philadelphia. He got there fine."

"Michael suspects something," one of them said one day.

"What? What could he suspect?"

"I think maybe he got word that the last one we drove never made it to the North. He asked me about it, he said was I sure

that was the boy's mother who called me."

"What'd you say?"

"What do you think I said? I said I was positive."

"Did he believe you?"

"Of course, but that won't be the end of it."

"Then let's us make an end of it."

"How?"

"That cave is big enough to hold two more people in it."

"What two?"

"Michael and Lyda."

"If we do that, it'll be the end of Hostel, too."

"Good, I'm tired of this game. If we're going to end it, let's do it up right and let's do it in a way that nobody will ever suspect we had anything to do with any of this."

"How?"

"We know something about Michael that most people here in town don't know, don't we? His own parents are Communists. There's an FBI program, COINTELPRO, that's still on the lookout for Reds. All we have to do is tell them that Michael has Communist connections and they'll break up Hostel as a potentially subversive organization."

"You sure about that?"

"I'm positive. They use it all the time like that." He laughed. "You ever hear of ol' Ben Turner?"

"No."

"Benjamin Turner was his name. He was the first Negro ever to be elected to the U.S. House of Representatives from Selma, Alabama. This was during the Reconstruction, in the 1870s, you know. Well, sir, Turner was so furious about how Selma got treated during the war that he, himself, introduced the bill in Congress that gave back to the Confederate soldiers their rights to vote and to hold office." He smiled a bit. Michael is a bit like that, isn't he? You might say that he belongs to the great foolish tradition of Benjamin Turner. By meaning well, he has let the snakes back into his very own garden where they will proceed to bite his friends to death."

"What's going to happen to us if Hostel gets opened up to public view?"

"We get embarrassed, I guess. But isn't that better than getting charged with a bunch of murders, even if they were only of Negroes?"

"Maybe we shouldn't have gotten involved with any of this."

"Are you kidding? We're soldiers. We have served history."

"You're right. We should be proud. When do you want to do this?"

"There's a party at the Fishers on the night of June twelfth. All the white Hostel members will surely be there. I think that's the night to do it."

"Well, if we're going out, let's do it in a big damned way."

The planning was simple but precise: deliver the facts about Hostel to the FBI on the condition of their own anonymity as double agents. Urge the FBI to plan a breakup of Hostel on the night of June 12. Suggest that they blame Michael Folletino for the arrests that night, telephone Michael and anonymously warn him that Klan members were coming to torch his house and kill him and Lyda. Warn him to get out of there as fast as possible. Then follow them and wait for the right place and opportunity to ambush them. The only tricky part was timing. If they got held downtown at the police station too long, they'd miss their best chance to kill the Folletinos. But the FBI got them out quickly. All they had to tell their wives then was that they were going out in their trucks to check up on the black members of Hostel. Then they were free for the rest of the night to do whatever they wanted to do.

They couldn't know that the president would help them out by giving a speech that inflamed their fellow bigots, drawing them to the streets to watch the parade of Hostel members, drawing down even harsher fates onto the black members, and creating such chaos all over the South — what with the speech and the Medgar Evers assassination — that nobody cared when a couple of wrongheaded white people went missing.

It didn't even take them long to get forgiven by their friends.

"We never meant it," they told the society into which they'd been born. "We were only playing along to see what the rest of them were up to." And to their own wives and to Eulalie and Clayton, they said, "We're telling people that we were only playing along with Hostel, so maybe we can find out what they're up to. If that's what we have to do to serve integration, why, we'll gladly humble ourselves to do it."

But it wasn't much of a game, not compared to the excitement of what they'd already experienced, and over the years, it paled. They craved another game, a bigger one with stakes as big as what they used to know.

When the Folletinos' famous grown-up writer-daughter first appeared in Sebastion, asking questions, they took it as a warning shot.

"If she ever really tries, she could find out something."

But she didn't really try, she eased off, let it go.

And then one day Lackley Goodwin happened to glance at a *People* magazine that his daughter Mo had brought home with her from the supermarket. And there was an article about little Marie Folletino and her black boyfriend, just like her parents would have wanted her to have.

"Read this," he told his two friends.

Their amusement turned to dismay and fury when they read:

Lightfoot's own past is shrouded in tragedy due to the mysterious disappearance of her parents from their home in Sebastion, Alabama, when she was only a few months old. The author acknowledges she has attempted to apply the same investigative techniques she uses in her books to solving that personal mystery, too.

"I haven't gotten very far with it," she says.

But now and then she gets strange phone calls that lure her on to finding out more.

"Somebody leaves me messages," she tells *People*, "in which they claim to have knowledge about my parents, but they never tell me what it is. They sound sincere and scared, that's all I can say. I wish whoever it is would contact me again."

The three men looked at one another.

Apparently, they had a traitor somewhere near them.

Lackley never suspected it was his own daughter, not until the night of the meeting with the Fishers at the inn when they were going to discuss the "guilt" of Rachel and Hubert, a handy pair of scapegoats. That's when he sneaked upstairs to search the Folletino daughter's room and found the note that Mo had written her: *"Can I talk to you? I'm the one who called you."*

"How are we going to find out who it is?" they asked one another at the start, long before they knew the traitor was one of their own offspring, and the least likely one, at that. Long before they knew they were going to have to set a fire to destroy all — all — of the traitors who threatened them.

"By forcing things," Austin said. "By playing a little game with the daughter, just like we did with her parents, and with the very same conclusion for her that there was for them."

Until the very end, when Lackley suffered qualms about his daughter, it was all great fun, serious and deadly fun, a recapturing of the finest hours of their valiant youth. They were soldiers again, outsmarting all enemies, banding together in a tight brotherhood of thrilling espionage. They devised a scheme to plant a story in a tabloid that would serve as a first notice to her. They would invent a stalker, an anonymous killer who threatened her and forced her to do what they wanted her to do. He would tell her he had a harebrained scheme to write a book with her about her own death, so that she would be forced to tell them everything she was doing, every step of her way, and so that they could get her to give them all of the information she had already gathered about her parents and their disappearance.

Quickly, step by step, they would lure her here.

Austin would plant himself near her in Florida so that he could spontaneously act as needed, move as she moved, furnish details the three of them needed to convince her that the man they invented, "Paulie Barnes," was genuine.

The other two would stay behind in Sebastion, seeing to airline tickets, a room at the inn, planting the idea for a copycat picnic at Eulalie's house with their wives.

"You know, it could be her aunt and uncle."

"What could be?"

"Our traitor, maybe it's Julia Montgomery who's placing those calls to her."

"Julia doesn't know anything."

"Maybe, maybe not, but she and Joe might have suspected something."

"So what? If there were ever people opposed to integration —"

"Then maybe it's their son, that Hollywood liberal. He's more like the Folletinos than he is like the Montgomerys. Maybe he heard them talk about us sometime, maybe he put something together —"

"But then why wouldn't he just tell his cousin that?"

"I don't know. But let's bring him here and find out."

Their skills were rusty from long disuse, but they sharpened them.

Once upon a time they were able to move at a moment's notice, make contingency plans at the drop of a hat, strike with cunning and subterfuge, kill without warning, which they would get a chance to demonstrate when they ran Marie's bodyguard off the highway.

They could do it again, one more time, they knew they could.

This was going to be fun.

34

Marie

I am so horrified and nauseated at what my executioners have implied that I can barely stand up on my own.

"You *killed* them? You *killed* those men?"

"Not all of them, just as many as we could get away with doing."

I can't tell who said that. I don't care. They're all the same to me.

"Is there anything else you want to know?" one of them asks me.

"How did you do it? Why did you kill my parents? Why have you done this to me?"

"Shall we tell her?" That's Austin's thin voice, I think.

And so they do tell me, giving me the information I will need to close the book on my parents' deaths. Their tone and their words mock me, my parents, and the good cause of the real civil rights. It's all I can do to stand there hearing it, without breaking down, but I let them spin it out, let them brag on themselves, because every minute they talk is a minute more that I get to live and to try to think of a way out of this.

But at the end, I have thought of no way out.

When they're finished, when I finally know that I am going to lose everything anyway, I hurl their contempt back at them with everything I've got in the last few minutes of my life.

"Oh, you really changed history, didn't you?" My own voice drips a sarcasm that could shorten my life by a few seconds, but I can't help myself now. "You sure made a big difference in the history of the world, didn't you? Hell, you must have slowed down the march of civil rights by, what, a few hours? People all around the country and the world were so horrified by what people like you were doing to black people down here that civil rights legislation suddenly looked like the right thing to do, didn't it? Because of that week! Because of murderers like you! Aren't you proud? Just think what you accomplished! And, hey, just look around you! The proof of how much difference you made is everywhere now, isn't it? I can see it when black people check into any hotel they want to, and go into the finest restaurants. I can see it in public swimming pools . . . in television commercials . . . on the Supreme Court . . . in presidential cabinets. I see it in mixed marriages and on baseball fields. Wow, you guys sure stemmed the tide of history, didn't you? And just look what you did to your own hometown — it now has half the population it used to have, most of the businesses are closed, the whole town's in complete decline. And you can take the credit for all that!"

"Shut up!" Austin snaps at me. "We'd be heroes if people only knew."

"Oh, right," I shoot back at him. "You want heroes? I'll give you heroes. How about the black sharecroppers who walked miles on their bare feet, hungry and terrified, in order to line up in front of courthouse doors to try to register to vote when they knew even before they ever left home that it wasn't going to happen for them that day and maybe on no other day in their whole life? And then when they went home, they knew they could get turned off their land, fired from their jobs, beaten or burned out, just for having made the trip. You want people to pick their heroes? Okay, then! We'll pick them from the poor and the frightened black sharecroppers who knew fear — every single day — like you have never known it. We'll choose our heroes from the ordinary people who stood all day in the sun, day after day, to try to register to vote. The ones who were bitten by dogs and beaten by cops. The ones who were cursed at and spat at and raped and murdered and thrown into jails for wanting to be treated like full human beings. They were scared to death almost all of the time, every day of their lives for themselves and for their children, but they walked for freedom anyway. Don't you *dare* try to claim the title of hero for yourselves." I can't help it. Saliva pours into my mouth like a physical symptom of the contempt and loathing I feel for them, and I spit, aiming it at them.

The blow from one of their hands comes at me so fast I have no defense against it. I don't even know which one of them hit me. It knocks me sideways, instead of backward, leaving me prone and teetering at the edge of the abyss. I'm breathless from the pain of it, trying to hang on to my wits. When I look up again, when my vision clears, I see what awaits me next.

They raise their shotguns to their shoulders and aim them at me. They aren't even going to put a bag over my head, like they did with my parents, to spare themselves the sight of my head exploding. At any moment they're going to pull their triggers. I can't get up and run or they'll shoot me. I am faced with certain death from them in front of me and almost-certain death from the fall behind me.

I won't let them have the satisfaction.

In the instant before the blast comes, I roll over the edge. My feet drop heavily into nothing, my fingers cling to the top. I was hoping against hope for the miracle of a ledge below the surface, or a tree root to cling to, or rocks on which to plant my feet. There is nothing, only emptiness and the knowledge that I can't hang on for more than a few seconds. By that time they will be here. They will point their weapons down onto my head, my dangling body, and they will do what I have only ineffectually delayed. Or they will do what I've seen a million times in movies — one of them will raise his foot and bring the sole of his shoe down on my hands.

In my anguish a cry rises from my heart and screams inside my head, shocking me in my last moments: *Daddy! Mommy!*

My killers are above me now. I feel their shadows.

I will drop, I will release my grip, I will die on my own.

But when the blasts come, they aren't aimed at me.

The body that tumbles into the cave is not my own, though it nearly knocks me down with it. And the strong hand that reaches down and grasps one of my forearms to hold me up belongs to Deputy Sheriff Florence Sachem. "I can't hold on," I whisper to her.

"You don't have to," she tells me. "I'll hold on to you."

She and her men have shot my would-be executioners.

The one who fell past me into the cave was Austin Reese. Lackley Goodwin and Marty Wiegan lie wounded on the ground above. As for me, I am weeping as I am pulled from the cave where my parents lie below. There was a part of me that almost wanted to go, a part of me that almost believed that if I let go and fell I could finally see them, finally be with them. Now I'm glad to be alive as I lie gasping on the ground, recovering my breath and strength. But there will always be a part of me that longs for them.

"Have you seen my cousin?" I ask her as she escorts me away.

She nods, smiling slightly at me. "He got himself a little singed getting Mo Goodwin out of there, but he's going to be fine."

Nathan rescued Mo! I'm so glad, so proud. This will change him.

She helps me into the backseat of her sheriff's car, gently because my shoulder may be dislocated and I hurt all over.

"Why did Clayton come to see you?" I ask her again.

"He wasn't accusing them," she says and smiles reassuringly at me. "He was protecting them. He felt the Reeses, the Goodwins, and the Wiegans were rushing to judgment, and he wanted to warn me. Mister Clayton thinks the world of Hubert and Rachel. He didn't want to see them hurt. And while he was there, he said he could think of other people who owned pickup trucks, who had fields outside of town, who owned property with caves on them. People named Reese, Goodwin, and Wiegan."

"I knew it," I murmur to myself.

In the car, driving away from that killing field, she says to me, "Then there was the fire, and your cousin was frantic because he couldn't find you. And when I looked around about the only other people I couldn't see after that fire got put out were those three good citizens. They were gone. Their trucks were gone. You were gone."

The deputy smiles, grimly, sadly.

"I just followed history to find you," she says.

We gathered two nights later for a picnic in the Fishers' yard. Florence Sachem was there, looking like a cop in a dress. She arrived with the good news that the prosecution was already gearing up for the two surviving killers. Clayton and Eulalie were there, of course, though they looked like wraiths, so heartsick were they by the knowledge of the murderous heart of Hostel. Mo Goodwin was there, looking freer without the burden of the awful lonely knowledge of what her father and his friends had done, and Hubert Templeton came alone. "Rachel, she's too bitter," he confided in us. "Too bitter. I think one day it will kill her, this bitterness, and there is nothing I can do to cure her." Nathan and I sat close together, and he insisted on holding my hand until Franklin arrived, a surprise visitor from another planet, to take his place and put a strong arm around me.

Clayton seems older now, less suave and sure of himself.

"I think Sebastion died that night," he told us. "I always wondered what went wrong with this town, where we went wrong to make it slide downhill so fast, but I never knew the horror at the heart of it. I thought it was something as banal as the economy, I didn't know it was . . ."

The old man trails off, leaving his wife to sigh and whisper, "Our fault. We didn't see the truth of them. Why not? I'll never know why not. I'll never forgive us."

"Cut that out, Eulalie," Hubert chides her. "We did some good."

"On balance?" she replies. "Was it worth it, Hubert? To save a few at the cost of killing others?"

"We had to try," he says. "We were part of something bigger and that bigger thing, *that* was worth it. It was a war. We won, Eulalie. We took some bad hits. But we're still winning."

Mo sits near me, and I reach for her hand. "You called me those times. What did you know? What were you going to tell me?"

"From the time I was a little girl," she says, "nobody ever knew when I was around. I could listen in. I could overhear things. Terrible things. I had to tell somebody, but I was afraid of my father, afraid of what he and his friends would do to me if they found out what I knew."

Her mother hasn't come. None of the other wives have.

It's a terrible thing to believe something about your family and then to discover many years later that you believed a lie. I know all about that, because for most of my life I believed lies about my parents. Or half-believed them. I didn't want them to be true, and it is the greatest gift imaginable to know that all of us were wrong. Their bodies will be brought up from the bottom of the cave, if we can manage it, along with those other bodies of men who were young and angry, scared and brave beyond measure. Families will be sought and notified. As for my family, my parents will be buried, not here in Sebastion, but in Florida, where I am, where I can visit them and get to know them in a different way, as the people they really were, a mother and father I can love.

A memorial will be built, not to my parents or to Hostel, but to those other men who died on the dangerous road to freedom.

Franklin kisses the side of my face to let me know he cares.

"I wish I could have known them," he says to us.

Eulalie glances at me and I hold her gaze as I say, "I wish I could have known them, too."

35

Marie

The Miami Book Fair is a monster, one of the largest in the world, with authors and publishers, editors and agents, and thousands of readers flocking in to buy books, get autographs, hear speeches, and sit in on panels. They've put me on a panel with some of my favorite Florida writers: T. J. MacGregor and Rob MacGregor, Elaine Viets, and Martha Powers. I wish John D. MacDonald could be here. I'd ask him to sign a copy of *The Executioners* for me.

I don't think this panel is going to make it through to the end, though.

There's a storm coming up over Miami Beach; we can see huge black thunderclouds from where we sit in an open tent, each with a microphone in front of us. We're seated at a long table on a dais that has been set up in front of a big crowd of readers, bless their hearts for coming.

I think we're all about to get drenched.

We're so excited at the idea of it that none of us can keep our minds or our mouths on our topic. The audience members keep nudging one another and looking east. T. J. MacGregor is signaling to her beautiful daughter, Megan, to ask if she's got their umbrella. In the third row, I see my assistant, Deborah, bend over and bring hers out from under her chair. I would ask Franklin DeWeese if he thought to bring an umbrella, since I neglected to — but he's off at the children's section with Diana and Arthur. I didn't recommend that he bring them to hear me and these other writers talk about murder and mayhem. I wouldn't get to share an umbrella with them, anyway, even if they were here listening to my panel, because I've been declared off limits by their mother. She can't stop her ex-husband from continuing to see me, though. I can't believe — can't bring myself to accept the possibility — that this situation with the children will last. I miss them. It makes my heart ache even to consider the awful possibility of never hugging Arthur again. I'm glad to be distracted by a question from the audience.

"Ms. Lightfoot?"

"Yes?"

"I hope you don't mind if I ask this, but are you ever going to write a book about what happened to your parents?"

"Yes, I probably will. In fact, a lot of it's already written."

Beside me, Martha Powers exclaims in her throaty voice, "Rain! I felt a drop!"

There's a stir of excitement in the crowd and on the panel.

We're going to have to clear out of here at any minute if the lightning gets any closer. We smile with delight at one another, wondering what to do next. I literally don't know what the next few moments of my future hold. Maybe I'll be answering another question from the audience, maybe I'll be fleeing the storm.

But there's one thing I do know.

I may not be able to predict my future, but I finally know my past.